It wa...r

DISF...

Desires

Be swept off your feet and into the past
with award-winning authors Julia Justiss
and Joanne Rock, and their brand-new
stories of forbidden love...

Seductive Stranger

BY JULIA JUSTISS

&

The Wedding Knight

BY JOANNE ROCK

After publishing poetry in college, **Julia Justiss** served stints as a business journalist for an insurance company and editor of the American Embassy newsletters in Tunis, Tunisia. She followed her naval officer husband through seven moves in twelve years, finally settling in the piney woods of East Texas, where she teaches French. The 1997 winner of the Romance Writers of America's Golden Heart for Regency, Julia lives in a Georgian manor with her husband, three children, and two dogs. Visit her online at www.juliajustiss.com

Joanne Rock is a former teacher, public relations coordinator and copy writer, and decided to follow her dream of penning romance novels when she became a stay-at-home mum. A Golden Heart winner and two-time Golden Heart finalist, Joanne won several writing awards prior to the release of her steamy romances. Now the mother of three boys, Joanne finds that writing provides a delightful counterpoint to hectic family life.

DISHONOURABLE

Desires

JULIA JUSTISS JOANNE ROCK

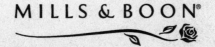

MILLS & BOON®

MILLS & BOON and MILLS & BOON with the Rose Device are registered trademarks of the publisher.

First published in Great Britain 2005
Harlequin Mills & Boon Limited,
Eton House, 18-24 Paradise Road, Richmond, Surrey, TW9 1SR

DISHONOURABLE DESIRES
© Harlequin Enterprises II B.V., 2005

Seductive Stranger © Janet Justiss 2003
The Wedding Knight © Joanne Rock 2004

ISBN 0 263 84567 2

108-0805

Printed and bound in Spain
by Litografia Rosés S.A., Barcelona

CONTENTS

Seductive Stranger

BY JULIA JUSTISS

To Catherine
My sweet, lovely, and talented daughter.
Strive always to be the best
And accept nothing less.

PROLOGUE

Sudley Court
Spring, 1808

APOLLO WAS RIDING down her drive.

Or so it seemed to Caragh Sudley, hand over her eyes and breath seizing in her chest as she squinted into the morning sun at the solitary horseman trotting down the graveled carriageway toward Sudley Court.

She was returning to the manor after her early-morning ride when the sound of hoofbeats carrying on the still morning air drew her toward the front entrance. At first merely curious about the identity of the unexpected visitor, as the man grew closer she was stunned motionless by the sheer beauty of horse and rider.

The pale sunshine threw a golden nimbus about the gentleman's hatless head, making his blond hair gleam as if the sun king himself were arriving in regal pomp, his chariot exchanged for the gilded beauty of a palomino. The brightness behind them cast the rider's face in shadow and silhouetted in sharp relief the broad line of shoulders and arms that were now pulling the stallion to a halt.

She shook her head, but that dazzling first impression refused to subside into normalcy. The tall, powerfully built beast tossing his head in spirited response to his rider's command, creamy coat rippling, was magnificent, the man now swinging down from the saddle no less so.

A dark-green riding jacket stretched across his shoulders and fawn breeches molded over saddle-muscled thighs, while up closer she could see his blond locks had tints of strawberry mingled with the gold. His eyes, no longer in shadow once he'd dismounted in her direction, were a shade of turquoise blue so arresting and unusual she once again caught her breath.

The chiseled features of his face—purposeful chin, high cheekbones, firm lips, sculpted nose whose slight crookedness added an intriguing hint of character to a countenance that might otherwise have seemed merely chill perfection—only confirmed her initial perception.

'Twas Apollo, Roman robes cast aside to don the guise of an English country gentleman.

Should she behold him, her sister Ailis would surely be calling for her palette and paints.

Caragh smiled slightly at the thought of her imperious sister ordering the man this way and that until she'd posed him to her satisfaction. And then realized this paragon of Olympian perfection was approaching her—plain Caragh Sudley who stood, jaw still dropped in awe, her face framed by limp wisps of hair blown out of the chignon into which she'd carelessly twisted it, the skirts of her old, shabby riding habit liberally mud-spattered.

She snapped her mouth shut, feeling the hot color rising in her cheeks, but as the visitor had already seen her, she would only make herself look more ridiculous by fleeing. How unfortunate, the whimsical thought occurred as she tried to surreptitiously brush off the largest clumps of mud and summon a welcoming smile, that unlike Daphne, she could not conveniently turn herself into a tree.

"Good morning, miss," the visitor said, bowing.

"Good morning to you, too, sir," she replied, amazed to find her voice still functioned.

"Would you have the goodness to confirm that I have reached Sudley Court? I need to call upon the baron."

"That would be my father, sir. You will find him in the library. Pringle, our butler, will show you in."

He smiled, displaying just a hint of dimples. "Thank you for your kindness, Miss Sudley. I hope to have—"

Before he could complete his sentence, her sister emerged from the shrubbery of the garden behind them, a lad laden with an easel and paintbox trailing in her wake. "Caragh! Did that package from London arrive for me yet?"

Caragh waited a moment, but her sister paid no attention to the newcomer. "Well, has it?"

Caragh's delight faded in a spurt of resentment she struggled, and failed, to suppress. With the arrival of Ailis, her all-too-short exchange with the Olympian would surely come to a premature halt.

Wishing her sister could have intruded a moment earlier or five minutes later, she replied, "If it has, Thomas will bring it when he returns from the village." She steeled herself to glance at the stranger.

Who was not, as she expected, staring in open-mouthed amazement at her stunningly beautiful sister, but rather observing them both, his expression polite. For a moment Caragh wondered about the acuity of his eyesight.

"Blast!" her sister replied, still ignoring the newcomer. "I only hope I have enough of the cerulean blue to last out the morning."

Blushing a little for her sister's lack of manners, Caragh motioned her head toward the visitor. "Ailis!" she said in an urgent undertone.

Her sister cast her an impatient glance. "You show him in, Caragh, whoever he is. I cannot miss the light. Come along, Jack." She motioned to the young lad carrying her supplies and walked off without even a goodbye.

Caragh's blush deepened. "M-my younger sister, sir. As you may have guessed, she's an artist—quite a good one! But very—preoccupied with her work. She's presently engaged upon an outdoor study requiring morning light."

"Who are we mere mortals to interrupt the inspiration of the muse?" he asked, his comment reassuring her that he'd not been offended by her sister's scapegrace behavior. "But I mustn't intrude upon your time any longer. Thank you very much, Miss Sudley. I trust we shall meet again."

Before she could guess his intent, the visitor took her hand and brought it to his lips. After that salute he bowed, then led the stallion off toward the entry.

For a moment Caragh stood motionless, gazing with wonder at the hand he'd kissed. Her fingers still tingled from the slight, glancing pressure of his mouth.

When she jerked her gaze back up, she noted the visitor had nearly reached the entry steps, down which one of the footmen was hastening to relieve him of his horse. Quickly she pivoted and paced off toward the kitchen wing. She'd not want the stranger to glance back and find her still staring at him.

Once out of sight, her footsteps slowed. The handsome visitor had bowed, kissed her hand and treated her as if she were a grand lady instead of a gawky girl still a year from her come-out.

Best of all, he had not been struck dumb when Ailis appeared. He had actually managed to continue conversing intelligently after her sister left them. Nor had his gaze followed Ailis as she walked away, but reverted back to Caragh's much plainer face.

The few remaining pieces of her susceptible heart that had not already surrendered to warmth of the stranger's smile and the bedazzlement of his blue-eyed gaze, succumbed.

But of course, in the London from which he must have come, he probably met beautiful ladies every day, all of them elegantly dressed in the latest fashion, and so had schooled himself to maintain a polite conversation, no matter how distracting the circumstances.

Briskly she dismissed that lowering reflection. The thoroughness of his training did not diminish the excellence of his behavior. Indeed, he was a *Vrai* and *Gentil Chevalier, beau et courtois,* straight from the pages of an Arthurian legend, she concluded, freely mixing her literary metaphors.

But who was he? Suddenly compelled to find out, she headed into the house.

Creeping past the library, where a murmur of voices informed her the visitor must still be closeted with Papa, she slipped into the deserted front parlor, hoping to catch one more glimpse of the stranger before he departed.

Perhaps when I make my come-out in London next year, I shall meet you again. Only then, I shall be gowned in the most elegant design out of the pages of La Belle Assemblée, *my hair a coronet of curls, my conversation dazzling, and you will be as swept away by me as I was by you today…*

She was chuckling a bit at that absurd if harmless fantasy when the closing of the library door alerted her. She flattened herself against the wall until footsteps passed her hiding place, then peeped into the hall.

Once again, sunlight cast a halo around the stranger's golden head as he stood pulling on the riding gloves the butler had just returned to him. Caragh sighed, her eyes slowly tracing the handsome contours of the visitor's face as she committed every splendid feature to memory.

After retrieving his riding crop, he nodded to acknowledge the butler's bow and walked out.

Resisting a strong desire to scurry after him and take one last peek through the fanlight windows flanking the entry, Caragh made herself wait until the tramp of his boots descending the flagstone steps faded. Then she ran to the library, knocked once, and hurried in.

"Papa," she called to the thin, balding man who sat behind the massive desk, scribbling in one of the large volumes strewn haphazardly about his desk.

Making a small moue of annoyance at the interruption, her father looked up. "Caragh? What is it, child? I must get back to this translation before the cadence escapes me."

"Yes, Papa. Please, sir, who was your visitor?"

"Visitor?" her father echoed, seeming to have difficulty remembering the individual who had quit the room barely five minutes previous. "Ah, that tall young man. Just bought Thornwhistle, he told me. Wanted to pay his respects and inquire about some matter of pasturage. I suppose you shall have to consult with Withers about it before he returns. I simply can't spare the time now to bother with agricultural matters, not with this translation going so slowly."

Apollo would be calling again. Delight and anticipation buoyed Caragh's spirits.

"Very well, Papa. If I will be meeting with him, however, perhaps you had better tell me his name."

"His name? Dash it, of what importance is that? I expect he'll announce it again when he returns. Now, be a good girl and take this breakfast tray back to the kitchen. It's blocking my dictionary."

Inured to her father's total disinterest in anything not connected to his translation projects, Caragh suppressed a sigh. "Of course, Papa." Disappointed, she gathered up the tray and prepared to leave.

"Goodbye," she called from the threshold. Already immersed in his work, her father did not even glance up.

Then a better idea occurred, and her mood brightened. Depositing the tray on a hall table to be dealt with later, she hurried in search of the butler, finally running him to ground in the dining room where he was directing a footman in polishing the silver epergne.

"Pringle! Do you recall the name of the gentleman who just called? He is to be our new neighbor, I understand."

"Lord Branson, he said, Miss Caragh," the butler replied.

"And his family name?"

"Don't believe he mentioned it. But he left a card."

"Thank you, Pringle!" Caragh hurried back into the hallway. There, sitting in pristine whiteness against the polished silver tray, was a bit of pasteboard bearing the engraving "Quentin Burke, Lord Branson."

Smiling, Caragh slipped the card into her pocket. Her own Olympic hero come to earth now had a name. *Quentin.*

CHAPTER ONE

Sudley Court
Early Spring, 1814

GIVEN WHAT a Herculean endeavor getting them to London was turning out to be, 'twas small wonder it had taken her more than five years to manage, Caragh thought, gazing into her sister's stormy face. Indeed, loving animals as Caragh did, she would probably have preferred mucking out the Augean stables.

"Ailis," she said, trying to keep the aggravation out of her voice, "you know you promised me last week that we would surely be able to leave this Friday. The boxes have been packed for days, Aunt Kitty is expecting us, and quite probably has set up appointments for us in London which it would be very rude to break with so little notice."

"Oh, bother appointments," Ailis responded, with a disdainful wave of one paint-spattered hand. "What difference does it make when we leave? The shops will still be there, as will the endless round of dull parties hosted by acid-tongued old beldames interested solely in dissecting the gowns, jewels, lineage and marriage prospects of their guests. Besides, you know I agreed to leave only after I complete the painting."

Stifling her first angry response, Caragh took a deep breath.

After reminding herself that at least one of them must remain reasonable, she said in a calm voice, "We had a bargain, Ailis! I will allow you to visit the galleries, continue your own work, and even take lessons—but you must do your part, and conduct yourself with the modesty and propriety expected of a young lady embarking on her first Season. Behavior which would not include embarrassing our aunt by compelling her to cancel obligations at the last minute—or issuing blanket condemnations of individuals you've not yet even met."

"Who will, I daresay, turn out to be exactly as I've described them," Ailis retorted. "Were I not so anxious to have the benefit of Maximilian Frank's tutelage, I would never have agreed to go at all. 'Twill be a waste of time and blunt, as I've warned you times out of mind. I've no desire whatsoever to marry."

The anxiety always dormant at the back of Caragh's mind returned in a rush. "Ailis, Papa won't live forever. How do you intend to exist if you don't marry?"

"Since you seem so enamored of the estate, why don't you marry? I could come live with you, and everything could continue as it's always been."

Which might have been a perfectly acceptable alternative, except that the only man Caragh could envision marrying still saw her only as his good neighbor and friend. "Believe me, you would find it much more comfortable to be mistress of your own establishment." *Where you can order people about with full authority,* Caragh added silently.

Even so, she had to compress her lips to keep a smile from escaping at the thought of the havoc her temperamental sister would wreak in the household of some hapless brother-in-law, should she ever become a permanent guest in his home.

No, 'twas still best to try to find Ailis a complacent husband of her own.

"You know when Cousin Archibald inherits, he'll move his family here," she reminded Ailis. "Though he would, of course, offer to let us stay, I am sure he would prefer not to have two female dependents hanging about. There's little chance of going elsewhere, since Aunt Kitty hasn't the room to house us permanently, and with our inheritance tied up in dowry, we'd not have the funds to set up a household of our own. Surely you don't see yourself hiring out as a governess or companion! 'Tis unfortunate, but if you wish to continue living in the style you do—and keep on with your work—you shall have to marry. At least London will offer a broader choice of potential husbands."

Although Caragh had delivered more or less the same speech on several occasions over the last few weeks, for once her volatile sister's eyes hadn't glazed over. Indeed, Caragh noted with a spark of hope, Ailis actually seemed to be paying attention this time.

"I suppose you are correct," Ailis replied, her expression thoughtful. "I shall hardly be able to work in peace here at Sudley with Cousin Archibald's five little demons roaming about."

Caragh exhaled an exasperated sigh. "That is just the sort of comment you must cease voicing aloud, if you do not wish to spoil all your prospects! Beauty is well enough, but a gentleman of breeding will want his bride to display courtesy toward others and moderation in her speech. And besides, Cousin Archibald's children are quite charming."

Ailis shrugged. "If you like loud, sticky-fingered, impertinent nuisances. The last time they visited, the eldest drove me to distraction, following me like a ghost everywhere I went, while the younger ones burst in whenever they chose, and the squinty-eyed smallest swiped my best detail brush to sweep her doll's house. She's lucky I didn't break her arm when I found she'd stolen it."

Before Caragh could remonstrate once more, Ailis disarmed her by breaking into a grin. "Come now, Caragh, you know you were as happy as I was when the grubby brats finally departed! And I concede that you have a point. I shall have to give some thought to my future. *After,*" she said, rising from her chair, "I finish this painting. I must get back to it before the light shifts. I just wanted to let you know I would not be ready by Friday."

"And if you might grant me the boon of revealing such confidential information, when do you expect to finish it?"

Oblivious to Caragh's sarcasm, Ailis paused in her march to the door. "Perhaps by the middle of next week. I shall let you know."

Closing her eyes, Caragh uttered a silent prayer for patience. She would have to dispatch an immediate note to Aunt Kitty delaying yet again their arrival in London. She only hoped their aunt hadn't already arranged the tea with the patronesses of Almacks she'd mention in her last letter. Cavalierly missing such a meeting would doubtless strike a serious blow to her sister's chances of a successful Season.

As she had so often as her sister grew to adulthood, Caragh wished she might consult their long-dead mother. Reputed to have been a headstrong beauty, she might have known better how to successfully handle the equally beautiful and tempestuous offspring who so closely resembled her. At least, Caragh thought the two strikingly similar, based on the miniature she'd tucked away in her desk, the sole image she retained of the mother who had died when Caragh was seven. Her grief-stricken father, unable to bear gazing on the portrait of a lady he'd lost so tragically young, had had the full-length portrait of his wife that once hung in his library removed to the attics.

"Never mind, Pringle, I'll show myself in."

As the voice emanating from the hallway beyond the salon penetrated her thoughts, Caragh's eyes popped open and her heart leapt in her chest.

Over the last six years, her own London Season had been put off for one reason after another—Papa's episode of ill-health, a disastrous fire in the stable wing, the necessity to take over managing all the estate business when their manager Withers died unexpectedly, and most recently, Ailis's reluctance to leave Sudley Court. The shy, awkward girl who'd nervously discussed pasturage agreements had become an assured young woman whose competent hand kept the household and estates of Sudley Court running smoothly.

In that time she'd learned, with no great surprise, that Quentin Burke was not an Olympian, but a flawed and mortal man like any other. She'd even, over the course of managing their horse-breeding operation, encountered among the aristocratic clients who came to Sudley Court, men as handsome as Lord Branson.

But one thing remained constant. The gentleman who had captured her sixteen-year-old heart one fair spring day still held it in as firm a grip as when she'd first lost it to the stranger riding down her drive. And he was just as unaware of possessing it as he'd been that long-ago morning.

She felt her lips lifting of their own volition into a smile. A swell of gladness filled her chest as the man whose face was dearer to her than sunshine, whose friendship had come to be as essential to her existence as air and water, strolled into the room.

"Oh, famous, Quent!" her sister said, meeting him at the door and offering her fingers for the obligatory salute. "You can natter on to Caragh about London while I get some work done."

"Lovely to see you, too, Ailis," he replied as she drew her hands back and skipped out. He turned to Caragh, a twinkle in those arresting turquoise eyes that, despite the passage of years, could still make her dizzy.

"A lovely surprise to see you, Quentin," she said. "I had no notion you'd be stopping at Thornwhistle this soon after your last trip. When did you arrive?"

She caught her breath as he kissed her fingers, even that slight touch setting her whole body humming. She struggled to resist the impulse to close her eyes and savor the sensation.

"My estate business finished up early," he replied, dropping into the wing chair beside her. "So I thought I'd spend a few days at my favorite property—and stop by to see if my favorite neighbor would actually manage to coerce her beauteous baggage of a sister into London this Season. No, I shan't stay for tea—" he waved her off as she headed to the bell pull "—but I should not refuse a bit of conversation."

Sighing, Caragh reseated herself. "I believe we shall eventually make it there. Though I had to resort to bribery, and only succeeded because Maximilian Frank fortuitously returned from Italy to set up a studio in London. Ailis is mad about his paintings, which are…not in the usual style." She paused to take a deep breath before continuing, "I-I've agreed to let her have private lessons with him. And I trust you'll not bandy that fact about!"

"Lessons!" he echoed, clearly astounded. "A gently-born

maiden taking drawing lessons from the illegitimate son of an East India merchant? Da— Merciful heavens, Caragh!" He shook his head. "With the chit cozening you into permitting behavior as questionable as that, do you really think you'll manage to marry her off?"

Although Quentin's query only echoed what she often asked herself, nonetheless Caragh felt herself bristle. "You can't deny her stunning beauty, and her dowry is quite handsome as well. In addition to that—"

"She's reached the age of twenty still lacking even the most rudimentary of domestic skills and her manners are... uncertain at best. Now, now," he said, waving off her sputtering attempts to remonstrate. "You know I'm fond of her, and freely admit she is amazingly talented. But even her doting sister must acknowledge she's certainly not the sort of meek, biddable, conventional miss most society gentleman seek in a wife."

Caragh sighed again. "No," she admitted. "I just hope to find for her a gentleman whom she can like and who will treasure her for what she is—not what she isn't."

"If you can bring her to notice one. Is she still spurning all her would-be suitors as imperiously as ever?"

Caragh had to grin. "Oh, yes. The squire's son brings her flowers once a week, which she can't be bothered to accept, and crossed and recrossed sheets of Darlington's turgid poetry arrive in nearly every post, which she tosses in the fire unread. Even the Duke of Arundel's youngest son, having apparently heard tales of her storied beauty from his Oxford classmates, found a pretext to stop by and see Papa on some spurious mission from his classics professor. Ailis either ignores them completely or treats them with a contemptuous disdain that seems to inflame them to further protestations of ardor. Perhaps they think of her as a challenge, as the suitors of Ithaca did Penelope."

"Only she paints instead of weaves?" Quentin asked with a grin. "Speaking of classical scholars, how does your father? Should I call on him now, or is he currently so lost in versifying he will resent any intrusion?"

"I believe he is revising today, so you may enter the library with impunity. It must be going well, for he actually joined us for breakfast and conversed with Ailis for almost half an hour."

Apparently Caragh was less successful than she'd thought at keeping the bitterness out of her tone, for the look Quentin fixed on her was sympathetic. "Caragh, you know that in the depths of his heart, your papa values all you do to keep Sudley functioning. Even if he seldom expresses his appreciation."

"A gratifying if entirely fictional notion, though I thank you for it," she replied drily, having long since given up hoping her father would notice her or anything she did. Nor did she feel guilty any longer for the stab of resentment that pierced her at witnessing his sporadic demonstrations of affection for the one living mortal he occasionally did pay attention to— her beautiful sister, who could scarcely be bothered to converse with him and had never lifted a finger to assist him.

Caragh shook herself free of those ignoble thoughts. "I trust you found everything at Thornwhistle in order?"

"In excellent order, as you well know. Let me once again commend your stewardship! Manning told me you'd taken care of having the north meadows reseeded after the heavy rain earlier this month. With you already so encumbered with the burden of managing Sudley and arranging a removal to London, I certainly appreciate your taking time to oversee my paltry affairs!"

A flush of pleasure warmed her cheeks at his approval. "'Twas nothing. I promised I would keep an eye on things, so I did. Friends assist friends, after all."

"So they do indeed," he confirmed, reaching over to press her hands…and setting her tingling once again. "What should I do without my good neighbor? In fact, I think 'tis about time I did something for you."

An electrifying vision flashed into her mind—Quentin hauling her into his arms and kissing her senseless. Her cheeks firing warmer still, she beat back the image, mumbling something disjointed about there being no obligation.

"I don't feel 'obligated,' I *want* to help. That is, I expect your father is not accompanying you to London?"

She barely refrained from a snort. "No."

"Given the shambles the estate was in when I inherited, I've not previously felt I could afford to be away for any length of time. But now that everything is finally in good order, I believe I can safely allow myself a respite."

"An excellent notion," Caragh said. "These last few years, we've scarce been able to persuade you to pause long enough to celebrate the Yule season with us."

"Quite wonderful celebrations, and I cannot thank you enough for including me. I even concede," he added with a hint of a smile, "that from time to time I've longed for a break. But the hard work has been worth it, Caragh. It's taken eight long years, but I'm proud to say I've just returned from our bankers in London, having redeemed the last of Papa's debts. Branson Park is unencumbered at last!"

"Quentin, that's wonderful!" Caragh exclaimed. "How proud you must be!"

"I knew you, more than any other, would understand what that means to me. And so, though I had no real need to visit Thornwhistle, I simply had to come and share the news with you."

Those breath-arresting blue eyes paralyzed her again while his handsome face creased in an intimate smile that made her long to throw herself into his arms. She dug her fingers into the armrest of her chair, fighting to squelch the desire and remain sensible. *A friend,* she reminded herself urgently. *He sees me as just his good friend.*

"I'm so pleased that you did," she managed to reply at last. "But I can't imagine you lapsing into idle dissipation. What task shall you take on next?"

"I've just completed the other major task dear to my heart—the refurbishing of Branson Hall. A project for which you have been a major inspiration, by the way."

"Indeed? How so?"

"I don't suppose I ever told you what a profound impression Sudley Court made on me during my first visit—the beauty of its design enhanced by loving and meticulous care. I vowed that very morning that one day, I would restore Branson Park to a similar level of perfection."

He shook his head and laughed. "If you could have seen my home as it was then, you would know how truly audacious a dream that was! Oaken floors dirt-dulled, carpets threadbare, window hangings in tatters, half the rooms missing furniture or swaddled in Holland covers!"

Caragh shook her head dismissively. "Whatever its state when you began, having seen the improvements you've installed at Thornwhistle, I have no doubt the house is now magnificent!"

"It is," he acknowledged in a matter-of-fact tone that held not a trace of boastfulness. "I should love to show it off to

you—but first, you've a Season to manage. And since I've decided I deserve a reward for finally completing two such
major projects—and have just purchased a property outside
London which will doubtless require a period of close super-
vision—I've decided to go to Town for the Season myself.
Now, what do you say to that?"

He would be in London, where she might see him and ride
with him and chat with him, not just for the few weeks of his
periodic visits to Thornwhistle, but for an entire Season?
"That would be wonderful!" she exclaimed.

He smiled, apparently pleased by her enthusiastic response.
"So I thought as well. I can be on hand to squire you about
when you have need of an escort, and perhaps help you cor-
ral Ailis, should she fall into one of her…distempered starts.
Besides, with Branson now restored to its former glory, I suppose it's time for me to complete my duty to the family and
look about for a wife."

Alarm—and anticipation shocked through her. Before she
could dredge up a reply, he patted her hand. "You, my good
friend, could advise me on the business. Since females know
things about other females no mere male could ever fathom,
you could be of excellent help in guiding me to make the right
choice."

She could guide him. In choosing a wife. As his good
friend. Her half-formed fantasy dissolving, Caragh sucked in
a breath and somehow managed to force a congenial smile to
her lips. "O-of course. I should be happy to."

His smile deepening, he squeezed her hands. "I knew I
could count on you! Now, if you think it safe, I'll go pay my
respects to your papa. When do you expect to depart for the
metropolis? Must you supervise the rest of the planting?"

Thrusting her agitated feelings aside to be dealt with later, she forced herself to concentrate on the immediate question. "No, Harris can handle that and the repairs on the tenants' cottages. 'Tis Ailis I'm waiting on. She refuses to depart until this current painting is complete, which should, God willing, allow us to depart by the end of next week." Caragh couldn't help another exasperated sigh. "If she doesn't redo the blasted thing yet again."

"Excellent," Quentin replied. "Since, given your skillful care, I'm sure I will find nothing of importance requiring my attention at Thornwhistle, I should be ready by then as well. Perhaps we can travel to the metropolis together. Only think how diverting it shall be! Two workhorses like you and me, pulled from our traces and forced to concentrate on nothing more compelling than what garments we shall wear or which entertainment we shall attend! I declare, after a period of such frivolity, we shall scarcely recognize ourselves!"

After bringing her hands up for a salute, he released them. "Shall we ride tomorrow morning? Good, I shall see you then." Sketching her a bow, he walked out.

Caragh watched him go, her lacerated heart still twisting in her breast.

If having his company here were not already delightful torment enough, she was now to suffer through a Season watching him search for a wife? No, even worse—advising him on that choice!

A mélange of misery, outrage and hurt swirled within her at the thought. Sternly she repressed it.

Enough bemoaning, she reproved herself. She would do what she must, as always.

But even as she girded herself to endure the unendurable,

from deep within her came unbidden the girlish fantasy she'd thought to have long ago outgrown. The image of a beautifully gowned, impeccably coifed Caragh Sudley whose elegant appearance and sparkling wit shocked Quentin Burke into finally realizing that his neighbor was no longer just an engaging and capable girl, but an alluring woman.

A woman he wanted.

'Twas not so impossible a fantasy, she thought, a renewed sense of purpose filling her. *Mayhap London will hold more surprises than you imagine, Quentin Burke.*

HALF AN HOUR later, after listening politely to a monologue about the latest progress of his host's magnum opus, Quentin escaped into the hall. Ascertaining from Pringle that Caragh was closeted with the housekeeper, he resigned himself to waiting until tomorrow's ride to speak further with her and headed down the entry steps to collect his bay gelding from the waiting groom.

Fresh and eager for a gallop, the horse danced and fought him for the bridle, so he'd proceeded some distance down the carriageway before Quentin got the beast settled down. He turned in the saddle then to look back one last time at the graceful Palladian facade of Sudley Court.

In the bright noon sun, the weathered stone walls glowed a soft gold beside the dazzling white of the columned portico, whose pristine classical lines always stirred his soul. The scythed lawn, the clipped shrubs and neatly tended flower beds complemented the well-maintained appearance of the structure itself, conveying an impression of timeless order and serenity. As did the rest of the estate, from the stables that housed the famous Sudley horses to the sturdy stone out-buildings to the recently rethatched tenants' cottages.

His own Branson Park was now its equal, he thought with a surge of deep satisfaction. His only regret was that his dear mama had not lived to see it. Still in all, he had much to celebrate, and as he'd told Caragh, good reason to indulge himself with a few months' dissipation.

Especially since doing so would enable him to repay in part the loyal friendship Caragh Sudley had extended him since he bought Thornwhistle, the first of his investment properties, nearly six years ago. Though a Season in London might allow her a welcome break from her myriad duties at Sudley, Quentin thought it unlikely that anyone who'd charged herself with trying to steer the Beautiful Baggage through the social shoals of a Season was likely to have much time to relax. He could help her shoulder that burden, and see she took some time for herself.

What an intriguing assembly of unusual talents his good friend possessed! One of the most skilled estate managers he'd encountered, she could converse knowledgeably about agricultural matters in one breath and in the next, offer an allusion from the classics so beloved by her papa. An absolute genius at handling any beast with four hooves, she was a better rider and as fine a shot as he and could speak about the bloodlines of a horse or a hound with authority. From the first, he'd found her altogether as easygoing and companionable as any of his male friends.

Indeed, around her he could relax and almost forget she *was* a female. She never bored him prattling on of gowns and gossip and would rather challenge him to a game of whist or billiards than sit over her embroidery or tinkle the keys of a pianoforte. Best of all, she alone of the unmarried females of his acquaintance employed not a particle of the annoying flirtatiousness to which most gently-bred maidens, particularly since the radical improvements in his fortune, were wont to subject him.

He chuckled, remembering how she'd appeared the first day he'd ridden down this drive to call on her father. While still at a distance, he'd taken the small lass in the shabby gown for a maidservant. Once he drew nearer, he'd amended that impression, deciding with her slender figure, her pale face haloed with wisps of golden-brown hair and her great hazel eyes raised up to stare at him, she more resembled a wood sprite.

That whimsical first impression changed to irritation when he returned two days later to consult with her father—and was received by her instead, declaring *she* would discuss with him the leasing of the Thornwhistle pastures. Believing it a novel but no less blatant ploy to gain his notice by a chit barely out of the schoolroom, he'd uttered a repressive setdown. Only to be handed his head on a platter when she flashed back that since she, and not the baron, handled the disposition of agricultural matters at Sudley Court, he could work with her, or leave.

He stayed. He quickly came to admire her competence, and over the intervening years always consulted her about estate business during his frequent visits to Thornwhistle. From the first she'd offered to oversee the solution of any small problems that occurred between his periodic inspection trips, and occasionally he'd taken her up on that offer, with excellent results.

He smiled again at Sudley Court's stately facade, knowing well how many hours of Caragh's toil were represented in its timeless beauty. For years, she had shown herself a shrewd manager and a staunch friend. He would indeed, he thought as he urged his horse back in motion, prize her opinion on the necessary but uninspiring business of acquiring a wife.

He only hoped he could be of equal assistance in her quest to find a suitable husband for her sister. Despite Ailis's dazzling beauty, he was certain the hunt would not be easy, and keeping the baggage from committing some irretrievable social faux pas until they'd accomplished the matter harder still. Caragh might well have need of his steadfast support.

It was likely to be the only support she received. Lady Catherine Mansfield, the aunt with whom the sisters would be residing, he knew to be silly and rather feather-witted, unlikely to offer much resistance if the strong-willed Ailis set her mind to something, no matter how ill-judged. And despite his conciliatory words to Caragh, Quentin privately thought Baron Sudley shockingly remiss in his duty to his family—not unlike, he thought with a bitter twist of his lips, his own sire.

Though Caragh handled the mulitiplicity of duties it entailed magnificently, still the baron should never have pushed the heavy burden of running the estate off on his daughter's slender shoulders. Neither had Sudley ever, as far as Quentin could tell, attempted to exert a father's steadying influence over his headstrong younger daughter.

Reaching the end of the lane, Quentin turned his mount back toward Thornwhistle and kicked him to a gallop. He could not in good conscience be too severe with the baron for neglecting his duties, however, when he himself had for several years been putting off one of his own.

With his debts paid and Branson Park refurbished, he had no further excuse to delay finding a wife who could maintain the splendor he'd so painstakingly restored and breed the next generation of Bransons to carry on the name.

Which was why, despite any problems Ailis might cause, knowing his dear friend would also be in London made him view the upcoming Season with much greater enthusiasm. With Caragh nearby to visit and ride and confer with, to brighten even the most insipid of ton parties with her dry wit and stimulating conversation, perhaps the dull business of finding a wife might not be so tedious after all.

CARAGH PEERED OUT the fanlight windows flanking the front entry to find Quentin riding away. She'd hoped to catch him before he departed and invite him to remain for nuncheon, and perhaps discuss further what appeared would be their joint venture in London.

He was already beyond hailing distance, however. Just as well she'd missed him, she told herself, sighing. She must take these papers in for Papa's signature and get a letter written to Aunt Kitty so James might ride it into town to be posted this afternoon.

After lingering until Quentin disappeared around the corner of the carriage drive, Caragh headed off to face her father. Best to catch him straightaway, before he became reabsorbed in his work, and thus annoyed by her visit.

She knocked once and waited, then knocked again. When a third rapping on the heavy oak panel still had not produced a response, with a resigned shake of her head, she pushed the door open and walked in.

"I'm sorry to disturb you, Papa, but there are some documents you must sign."

Her father started, then looked over, his expression distracted. "Caragh?" He glanced out the window at the sunny afternoon garden before turning back to her. "As 'tis still light out, it cannot be time for dinner. So what is the matter now, child?" He drew his brows together, frowning. "You know I detest interruptions when I am nearly at the end of a chapter!"

"I regret the intrusion, Papa, but I must mail back immediately the authorization the lawyers sent you to allow them to set up an account for us in London." When he continued frowning, she added, "You do remember Ailis and I are to leave next week?"

His frown faded, leaving him thoughtful. "Yes, I recall your mentioning it. You've arranged to have matters here at Sudley taken care of in your absence, I trust?"

Suppressing her aggravation, she took a deep breath and began to repeat once again the information she'd conveyed to him at least three times already. "Naturally, Papa. The spring planting is nearly complete and the colts from this year's foaling are already bespoken. Pringle and Hastings have instructions for managing the household, and Harris will inform me of anything requiring attention on the farms, so," she concluded, her tone turning a touch acerbic, "you need not fear some domestic disturbance will disrupt your work."

He nodded, apparently satisfied, and bent to sign the papers she extended. But after he'd affixed his seal, as she reached to pick them back up, he caught her hand. "I suppose, much as I despise London and all the memories it holds, I…really ought to be accompanying you there."

She looked up, startled. His eyes, usually bright with fervor for a distant time and people long dead, had misted over.

Caragh knew the tragic tale—the Quorn country hunt at which the handsome young baron and London's reigning belle had fallen in love, marrying as soon as the banns could be called and then retiring to the country. Her mama's triumphant return to the metropolis six years later, where, despite her long absence and the presence of younger beauties, she soon reclaimed her mantle as Queen of the Ton. Her untimely death from a fever a bare two months afterwards, upon which her father quit the metropolis, vowing never to set foot in the city again.

Tenderness rose up to penetrate her resentment. "It's all right, Papa. Aunt Kitty will take good care of us, and you should almost certainly find the busyness of a Season tedious. Nothing but dressmakers and social calls and parties, and the city so noisy that working would be difficult. You wouldn't wish your progress to be slowed now, not when you're so close to finally finishing the first draft."

Her father straightened, the sorrow leaving his eyes. "You are right, of course. Did I mention I'd received a letter yesterday from Briggs at Oxford? He thinks the university might be interested in publishing my translation, and asked that I send him a copy once it's complete! Though it's not nearly ready for that—I've scarcely finished the draft, and there's much, much work remaining. Still, his interest was very heartening."

"'Twill be a magnificent achievement. We're so proud of your scholarship, papa."

"Thank you, my dear. You will…watch over Ailis? There are so many dangers and temptations in the city, and unlike you, she's not very…practical. She doesn't always realize what is best for her."

Ever Ailis. Once again suppressing that lingering sense of hurt, she replied, "You may trust Aunt Kitty and I to keep her from harm."

"I expect I can. And—keep yourself safe, too. You've been a good daughter to me, Caragh. Better than I deserve, probably."

A lump formed in her throat, preventing reply, and ridiculous tears gathered at the corners of her eyes. He might not be the most considerate of papas, but Caragh still loved him, and his rare praise touched her deeply.

"Here, then," he said, handing over the documents. "Enjoy the idle gaiety of the metropolis. And with this, I trust you will not have to interrupt me again? Having just read them over, I'm not entirely sure I've caught the rhythm of the last cantos correctly, and I cannot quit now until I've rewritten them. I shall not manage it before midnight if I'm compelled to stop every hour to attend to some trivial household matter."

Their tender moment of tenuous connection was obviously at an end, Caragh thought, suppressing a wry grin. "I shall endeavor to see there are no further interruptions."

"Good. Have Cook send my dinner in on a tray, won't you? Between Quentin's visit and all these perturbations, I've lost so much time already today, I shall have to work straight through the evening."

After his jovial and unusually attentive presence at breakfast, Caragh had assumed her father, who on most days barely noticed the dishes placed before him, would for once appreciate a well-prepared dinner. To the Cook's delight, she'd instructed her this morning to prepare a meal more elaborate than their usual simple fare.

The kitchen would already have begun upon the menu she'd chosen, a fine roast with several removes and Ailis's favorite cherry tarts for dessert. Upon learning her efforts for her master were to be reduced to a covered plate upon a tray, Cook was likely to suffer palpitations.

"If you insist, Papa. What time should you like it?"

But her father, having evidently expended the full measure of time his self-absorption would permit for something not directly connected to his work, had already returned his gaze to his manuscript. Knowing any attempt to wrest his attention away would likely be greeted with a sharp rebuke and a recommendation that she do what she thought best, Caragh made no attempt to repeat her inquiry. Silently she gathered up the papers and left the library.

Though the task awaiting her in the city might be no less thankless than the duties she was leaving behind at Sudley, as Caragh looked down at the document that would fund their visit, she felt her spirits lift.

In London there would be bookshops, theatres, exhibitions, entertainments the likes of which she had never before experienced. She'd have a whole Season's worth of time to enjoy, as Quentin described it, an existence devoted mostly to frivolous dissipation.

And one last chance to dazzle open the eyes of Quentin Burke.

CHAPTER THREE

ON A FOGGY morning three weeks later, Quentin pulled up his lathered mount at the far reaches of Hyde Park and turned to Caragh, who was reining in her equally spent mare beside him. "That was marvelous!" she cried.

A profusion of gold-brown tendrils peeping out from beneath her riding hat, her cheeks becomingly flushed from the wind, she favored him with a smile so brilliant he was doubly glad he'd hit upon the happy notion of stealing her away while the fashionable world—including her sister and aunt—were still asleep. "It was indeed," he agreed.

"Thank you so much for insisting we come! I've been so busy since arriving, I've scarcely had a moment to myself, and have dearly missed a daily gallop."

"Then you must resolve to take one with me every morning, no matter how busy you are. I hope your campaign to launch Ailis is going well, for you've been quite neglecting me the last two weeks. Whatever happened to our plan to spend the Season in frivolous dissipation?"

"And here I've tried to be courteous and not place demands upon your time!" she replied indignantly, nudging the mare to a walk. "Besides, I *have* been frivolous. Ailis and I have indulged in a positive orgy of shopping, expending funds whose total I refuse even to estimate, though I am quite certain the sum could fund seed and repairs for Sudley for the whole of next year. We've visited Hatchard's, been to Gunter's for ices and had a splendid evening viewing the feats of equestrian daring at Astley's. Anyway, with Tattersall's and Gentleman Jackson's and your clubs to visit, I take leave to doubt you've felt neglected."

Signaling his gelding to keep pace beside the mare, he grinned at her, pleased to have roused her fighting spirit. Yes, these morning rides were a good first step, but he'd have to think of other ways to detach her from Ailis and ensure she didn't waste her entire Season in London playing duenna to the beauty. "You must take care that your impractical sister doesn't tow you down River Tick before the Season even begins."

"Oh, 'tis not Ailis who likes shopping—it's our aunt. Although it seems we've purchased enough clothing to outfit seven women, Aunt Kitty assures me we've acquired only the barest essentials. Ailis considers an excursion to the dressmaker more curse than enjoyment, and told me yesterday she refuses to stir another step from the house if our destination requires her being measured, pinned or basted."

"How go the plans for her presentation?"

"Well enough, I suppose. These first two weeks we've been laying the groundwork, Aunt Kitty says, having suitable gowns made up to allow us to pay calls on the most important hostesses." A mischievous sparkle glinted in her eye. "Indeed, 'tis a good thing my aunt sleeps until noon, for she would have apoplexy were she to know I'd gone riding in this old habit! And I must admit, we have spent a good deal of time visiting galleries, meeting with Mr. Frank and setting up Ailis's lessons."

Quentin frowned. Nothing that tied Ailis to the middle-class world of working artists was likely to advance her marital prospects among the ton. "You were not able to dissuade her from that?"

Caragh threw him an exasperated look. "You sound like Aunt Kitty. No, I couldn't dissuade her. Considering her main reason for agreeing to come to London was to further her artistic education, I thought to have a better chance of winning her cooperation on social matters if I first allowed her to begin lessons. I've made it quite clear that if she doesn't honor her part of our bargain and participate in the ton activities Aunt Kitty considers necessary, I am prepared to cancel the sessions and return with her to Sudley."

Quentin chuckled. "Ah, blackmail! And how did she receive that bit of news?"

Caragh grinned back at him. "Without throwing a tantrum, if that's what you're implying. I think I've finally managed to bring her to realize that with Cousin Archibald in line to inherit, she simply must make plans to secure her future. Since, for a woman, marriage to an agreeable partner is the only practical way to achieve that, 'tis best to act now, while she is still young and lovely enough to have a real choice. In any event, my genteel threat seems to be working. Aunt Kitty had the Almack patronesses to tea, and Ailis was on her best behavior, at once demure and charming. Lady Jersey and Countess Lieven both pronounced her a handsome, pretty-behaved girl and promised vouchers."

"Ailis, demure? Now *that* I'd like to behold!"

"Give her some credit, Quentin," Caragh protested. "She can behave when she wishes to."

"Ah, but how long will she wish to?"

As soon as the teasing words left his lips, Quentin regretted uttering them, for the sparkle faded from Caragh's eyes. The thought that her sister might not choose to contain her high-spirited and rather unconventional nature until she was safely affianced would have to be his friend's chief worry.

Before he could think of some light comment to bring the smile back to her face, Caragh shrugged, as if shaking off whatever unpleasant thoughts his remark had aroused. "The first of the new evening gowns is to be finished by tomorrow, so Aunt Kitty intends to present us to a select circle of friends at dinner before going on to the Duchess of Avon's ball. And so, if you will not be too *busy*—" she stressed the word, giving him a darkling look, "may I count on you to attend?"

"Of course. And I'd be happy to escort you to the Duchess's ball as well."

She made him a little bow. "Thank you, my gallant knight. There shall also be the small matter of Ailis's presentation ball the end of next month. Aunt Kitty is already awash in fabric samples, trying to decide whether to deck out the ballroom in white netting and baby's breath or pink satin and roses."

"Now that's a charming image: Ailis in white satin and ostrich plumes, or pink silk and rosebuds, launching off to snare a mate." Quentin tried to picture Caragh, currently wearing a shabby, outmoded riding habit all too typical of her wardrobe, dressed to the nines and gliding into a ballroom. He couldn't. "Which of the two garments shall you choose?" he asked, suppressing a chuckle.

She swiped at him with her whip. "Neither, as well you know! Ailis shall be in pearls and white satin, and would doubtless darken your daylights if she heard you describe her as intending to 'snare a mate.' Why should she bother, when suitors flock to her quite willingly? I'll wear something in green, probably, as befits the elder sister. It is to be my presentation as well, you know."

Although after his father's death Quentin had been too preoccupied tending to the business of restoring his estates to visit London, he'd assumed that Caragh must have had the obligatory Season at eighteen and returned to Sudley by choice. "You were never presented?" he echoed, incredulous. Though the baron was an indifferent parent at best, Quentin could hardly believe he would have neglected so important a responsibility.

"No. With one thing or the other, there was never time." She glanced away from him, faint color flushing her cheeks. "Are you going to say *I* am off to 'snare a mate?'"

Quentin felt an unpleasant jolt, such as he sometimes experienced when picking up an iron poker after walking across the thick Axminster carpet in the library to tend the fire. "Certainly not!" he blurted without thinking, distracted by the intensity of the disagreeable sensation.

When Caragh looked over sharply, eyebrow raised, he hastily continued, "Not that you wouldn't be perfectly capable of attracting a desirable offer, but—well, surely you cannot focus on anything else until you get Ailis riveted, which should take the Season at least. Nor can I imagine your father wishing you to stir far from Sudley."

"Perhaps not. But at some point, I shall be forced to 'stir' from Sudley, unless I'm willing to be reduced to the status of superfluous dependent in the household over which I was formerly mistress."

She was right, he realized suddenly. This Season she really ought to concentrate on finding a husband not just for Ailis, but for herself as well.

Unsettled by the dismaying consequences that possibility

engendered, he protested, "But your father is in excellent health. There's no reason to believe your cousin will inherit anytime soon."

"Lord willing, Papa will be baron for a good many years. But that makes it no less important for me to settle my future now, for the same reasons I've argued to Ailis," she pointed out.

"I suppose so." But even as he agreed, Quentin was conscious of a strange sinking sensation. Although he realized Caragh was no longer the shyly charming young girl next door but a woman grown, somehow he'd vaguely assumed she would stay on at Sudley for the indefinite future. That their friendship would continue unchanged, as warm and vital a presence in his life as it had been these last few years. Surely she wished for that, too!

"Make what plans you must," he said at last, giving her his most charming smile, "but I absolutely forbid your taking any steps that might endanger our friendship!"

She smiled sweetly. "Perhaps my eventual husband will be a friend of yours. Then we could all be friends together."

Somehow that solution didn't seem particularly appealing. Unwilling at the moment to examine any more closely the reasons behind the sour feeling that had settled in his gut at the prospect, he was glad to seize upon a diversion.

"I thought you said Ailis always slept late. Isn't that her, riding toward us now?"

Caragh swiveled in the saddle. "Why, yes, it is!" Her initial expression of surprise turned grimmer when a tall young man on a flashy black stallion rounded the corner of the bridle path in her sister's wake.

The man caught up with Ailis, who slowed her horse and turned to him. Though they were too far away for their conversation to be intelligible, Quentin read in the flirtatious arch of the girl's neck, the sinuous bend of her body as she leaned toward the man—and the arrogant confidence with which the newcomer inclined toward her—that the two were more than chance-met acquaintances. He squinted into the sun, trying to identify the vaguely familiar male figure.

"Who is the gentleman?" he asked, giving up the task.

Caragh's lips had thinned and her expression was eloquent of disapproval. "Viscount Freemont. He's something of a patron of the arts, I understand. He was at Maximilian Frank's studio the first day we visited, so of course, the artist introduced us. Since then, he's 'happened' to drop by several times just as Ailis was finishing her lesson, escorting us home on the first occasion and insisting we accompany him to Gunter's for ices on the second. Although she received him, Aunt Kitty confided that his reputation is rather—fast. You know him?"

"Not personally, although he's a member of White's. Family is impeccable, but the talk in the clubs holds him to be wild indeed. Certainly not the best sort of companion for an innocent maid entering upon her first Season. Particularly," he added as they approached, "a young lady riding at dawn with nary a groom in attendance."

Caragh gasped in consternation, but as they urged their horses nearer, Quentin's guess was soon confirmed. Freemont and her sister walked their mounts side by side, their heads as close together as Ailis's position in the sidesaddle would permit. Her groom, unlike the man who trailed Quentin and Caragh at a discreet distance, was conspicuously absent.

They made a striking pair, Quentin had to admit. Ailis, her dazzling blond beauty displayed in a form-filling habit of pale-blue velvet, mounted sidesaddle on her gray, and

Freemont with his Adonis-handsome face and blue-black hair, his tall, broad-shouldered figure all in black on his midnight-hued stallion.

Caragh exhibited no appreciation whatsoever of the picturesque tableau. "I shall have to have a chat with Ailis," she muttered, her jaw set.

When they reached the couple, Ailis hailed them cheerfully, no hint of guilt or embarrassment in her manner as she presented the viscount to Quentin. However, Freemont's quirk of the lip and raised eyebrow as he returned the acknowledgement showed clearly, Quentin thought, anger stirring, that the gentleman was quite conscious of the impropriety of his actions.

"Do ride along with us," Caragh invited. Picking up on the urgent look his friend threw him, Quentin sidled his mount up to Freemont's, while Caragh cut her mare in between the viscount's stallion and her sister's horse.

The viscount grinned at the maneuver, but signaled his horse to drop back. "The dragon protectress?" he drawled.

Quentin gave him a stone-faced look. "As the *lady* is a particular friend, I'd advise you to mind your language."

"No offense intended. I suppose so luscious a damsel has need of protecting."

Quentin found any desire to engage in socially innocuous conversation deserting him. "From you, perhaps?" he retorted.

"Most definitely," the viscount agreed with a laugh. He eyed Quentin up and down with a mockingly assessing look. "You're an ally of the protectress, then. Should I expect a challenge?"

Restraining the desire to pull the viscount from his saddle and plant a fist in the middle of that arrogant face, Quentin replied, keeping his voice carefully even, "Not if you remember the maiden in question is a young lady of quality and treat her accordingly."

"Ah, but a damsel not at all in the common way, you must admit. An amazingly good artist, for one. Such drive! Such fire! It quite compels a man to wonder where one might *lead* such a passionate creature."

Curbing his temper, Quentin forced himself to ignore the man's baiting. "If you wish to wonder about it while enjoying the young lady's company, I'd advise you to curtail any… inappropriate conduct that might *lead* her family to cut the acquaintance."

Freemont laughed out loud. "You think she would be governed by the dragon, should her inclinations run otherwise?"

Quentin glanced at Caragh, who was leaning toward her sister, speaking in tones too low for them to hear.

"I wouldn't underestimate her influence."

Freemont followed his glance and raised an eyebrow. "Perhaps you are correct. Although certain gentlemen might consider that just adds spice to the challenge."

Quentin clenched his teeth, wishing furiously he had the authority to ban Freemont from calling on Ailis then and there. "Certain *gentleman?*" he grated out, his voice dripping scorn. "I wonder, Freemont, do you box?"

"Occasionally," the viscount replied, turning back to him with that irritating smirk Quentin longed to smack off his face.

"We should have a go at Jackson's some day. You look to be almost up to my weight."

"Perhaps. Although in general I prefer to protect my pretty face. Makes it easier to entice the ladies, you know. Branson," the viscount nodded a dismissal and spurred his mount to a trot.

Ailis had broken away, riding ahead of her sister, and once

again the viscount brought his mount beside Ailis's sidesaddle. "Shall I escort you home, my angel?"

"You need not put yourself to the trouble," Caragh called out quickly. "Lord Branson and I will take her. We couldn't invite you in for refreshments in any event, for we shall have to depart again almost immediately."

"I'm sure Holden would not consider it a trouble," Ailis said, giving the gentleman in question a provocative glance from under her long lashes.

The viscount seized Ailis's hand and brought it to his lips. "No service I could render you would ever be a trouble, Miss Ailis."

"There, you see?" Ailis nodded toward Caragh, then turned back to the viscount. "Let's have one last good run. Race you to the chestnut copse!"

Before Caragh could protest, both riders spurred their horses and galloped off.

Doubtless realizing that tearing after the pair, like a nursemaid chasing her recalcitrant charge, would only make her appear ridiculous, Caragh did not, as Quentin had feared, go in pursuit. Instead, she reined in, letting him draw up beside her.

"I worry about her," she said quietly.

As well you should, Quentin thought. "Would you like me to make further inquiries into the viscount's character?"

Her face cleared and she looked up at him, her eyes shining with gratitude. "Would you? Yes, I should very much appreciate it! Naturally, of all the admirers she's had fall at her feet, she has to notice the only one whose behavior I fear may not match the level of his breeding. And she's such an innocent, she has no notion how easily an unprincipled blackguard could ruin her reputation and her prospects."

By the time they'd cantered to the far side of the park, there was no sign of her sister or Freemont. Caragh sighed. "I shall have to speak to her again, more forcefully, once we're back at the house. And then drag her off for one last fitting, which means she's likely to be in a tearing ill-humor the rest of the day."

Quentin curbed his first, bitter retort. Blast the baggage! Could Caragh not have even one morning's respite from dealing with her troublesome sister?

"Let's get you back, then," he said, keeping his tone light. "And when you go for those fittings, I hope you'll be getting yourself something pretty, too." He reached over and squeezed her hand.

And felt another small shock—but this time, a pleasant one. Startled, he released her hand. "Shall we be off?"

FOR A BRIEF MOMENT, Caragh left motionless the hand Quentin had squeezed. Faint tremors reminiscent of the first, strong jolt that had pulsed through her at his touch still throbbed through her fingers. Surely he had felt it too, that…force that surged between them?

But Quentin was already riding off, seemingly oblivious. Well, perhaps not. With a small sigh of disappointment, Caragh wrapped the reins back around the hand and kicked the mare to a canter.

During their short ride together, she'd refrained from taking Ailis to task about her conduct in coming unchaperoned to the park, not wanting to trigger her volatile sister's temper or spur her to an ill-judged and probably public reaction. But once they arrived home, the jobation Ailis urgently needed to hear could not be put off.

Bless Quentin, who apparently did intend to support her in dealing with Ailis, just as he'd promised. Although, if he turned up anything truly salacious when he investigated the worrisome viscount, she wasn't sure how she was going to induce Ailis to give Freemont up.

Well, no point worrying over that now. At the moment, she had the more pressing, if no less disagreeable task of delivering a lecture to her probably unreceptive sister.

As expected, she found Ailis in the sitting room they shared between their two chambers. She entered upon her knock to find her sister gathering her painting supplies in preparation for the afternoon's lesson.

"Oh, hullo, Caragh. Be a dear, and buy me another package of this yellow pigment while I work with Max today, won't you? I'm sure I won't have enough to complete the sunset study he's helping me with."

Her thoughts concentrated on marshalling her arguments in a way most likely to make an impression on her sister, Caragh absently accepted the packet Ailis extended. "Did you enjoy your ride?"

"Yes, 'twas very pleasant. Put this thinner in my box, won't you?"

Caragh stowed the tin Ailis handed her. "I was surprised to see you, though. I didn't realize you'd planned on riding this morning."

"I hadn't planned on it, until Holden came by this morning and invited me. He is a handsome devil, isn't he? Such a countenance! I told him I should like to do his likeness." She sidled a glance at Caragh. "Bare-chested, in Greek draperies."

"Ailis, you didn't tell him that!" Caragh gasped.

Her sister merely grinned. "I shall have to talk to Max about arranging it."

"Perhaps you should concentrate on finishing the sunset study first," Caragh countered quickly. "Indeed, you must take care not to let Lord Freemont act the devil he looks. This isn't the country, Ailis, and the more…casual manners we practice there will not do in London. You really shouldn't address him as Holden on such slim acquaintance."

Ailis shrugged. "'Tis what Max calls him. I should feel rather foolish 'my-lording' him in the studio."

"Perhaps such familiarity might be permitted there, but certainly not among the polite world. And if you ride with him, you must bring a groom along."

Ailis stopped in her packing and looked up. "A groom?" She tossed her blond head back and laughed. "Is he supposed to rob me of my virtue in broad daylight within the confines of Hyde Park? Or beside some merchant's cart on some busy London street? Such a feat of equestrian skill would be worthy of Astley's!"

"I agree, the likelihood of him compromising you on horseback is slim. Still, as nonsensical as the rules of behavior seem to you, Ailis, to flout them brings discredit not only upon you, but also upon Aunt Kitty—and me." Caragh smiled, trying to soften the reprimand. "And although I certainly would never bother with it in the country, in town I take a groom even when I ride with so good and longtime a friend as Quentin."

"Which is both ridiculous and unnecessary, since Quent would hardly try to compromise you, even had he a perfect opportunity," her sister retorted.

Caragh bit her lip against the pain of her sister's tactless words. "True enough," she allowed. "Still, we've only just met

Lord Freemont, and know little of him. Surely you'll agree that the character of the gentleman with whom you might spend the rest of your life is vitally important."

"Who said I have any intention of marrying him? It's just that he alone, of all the so-called gentlemen I've met thus far, does not bore me senseless reciting bad verses in praise of my eyebrows, or turn cow-eyed and speechless when I enter a room. He admires my *work,* Caragh—and he's quite knowledgeable about painting, as well being a major patron of Max and several other artists. He talks to me of things that matter, treats me like a *woman*—not some celestial being upon a pedestal to be gazed upon with awe."

Caragh could well understand the appeal of a gentleman treating one like a woman. "I can see how refreshing that would be. But we've hardly arrived. Once we begin attending parties, I imagine you will meet any number of handsome and well-spoken men who will admire both your beauty and your intelligence."

"Society gentlemen?" Ailis sniffed. "Not if they are like the coxcombs whose portraits Max has done."

"Since Mr. Frank meets them as employers, his relations with them would naturally be…different than that of a lady they wished to court, or marry."

"Indeed?" Ailis raised her eyebrows. "I should think their treatment of an employee—although to treat someone of Max's genius as a mere servant is preposterous!—would be much more illuminating of their character than their behavior as suitors."

As Maximilian Frank made no secret of his often contemptuous opinion of the aristocracy, Caragh wasn't surprised to hear that the man's impressions of some of his employers were less than complimentary.

"I suppose you are correct. Still, Mr. Frank is known as something of a radical. I'd be a bit cautious about accepting without question his rather Jacobean views on the equality of man and the abolition of the monarchy."

Ailis grinned. "I shall not go that far…yet."

Caragh gave her a severe look. "There are certainly men of true character among the nobility—is not Quentin Burke an example of that? I just ask that you be open to meeting them. And that you be a bit more…circumspect in your dealings with Lord Freemont. Here in London, the code of behavior for unmarried ladies is very strict, and with your presentation—"

"Bother my presentation!" Ailis exclaimed, tossing down the paint case and rounding to face Caragh. "I've told you all along that it matters little to me whether I'm a success with the ton or not, as long as I achieve *my* goals in London. I like Holden and I intend to continue seeing him, so you might as well accustom yourself to it."

Caragh struggled to keep her anger in check. "And you, dear sister, had better 'accustom' yourself to the fact that if you wish to *remain* in London, you will honor our agreement and not do anything to embarrass Aunt Kitty."

Caragh braced herself for an explosion, but to her relief, Ailis held up both hands. "Come, let's cease quarrelling over trivialities. I'll agree to try to remember the rules of dull propriety, if you will cease preachifying on the virtues of virtue."

Although Caragh wasn't sure she ought to concede the point while Ailis still referred to the serious matters under discussion as "trivialities," her sister was offering to compromise—a rather unusual occurrence. At any rate, 'twas probably the best she was likely to wangle from Ailis at the moment. "Agreed. Now, at the risk of immediately breaking our truce, I must remind you that we have one last fitting this morning on the gowns for Friday's rout."

"Not today!" Ailis groaned. "I must finish the sketches for the sunset study by this afternoon!"

Once Ailis immersed herself in her art, she was as hard as papa—and even less congenial—to pry loose. "Do the fitting immediately," Caragh cajoled, "and I promise I'll occupy Aunt Kitty so you may have the rest of the day to work on sketches."

Ailis gave her a reluctant smile. "Blackmailer."

"Revolutionary." Caragh linked her arm with her sister's. "Let's be off to battle tape measures and straight pins."

And so Caragh was able to bear her sister off to the mantua-maker. While Ailis, a long-suffering expression on her face as they stood being pinned and prodded, doubtless used her time to contemplate her sketches, Caragh found herself wondering if Quentin was merely being kind in recommending that she buy herself something pretty.

Well, she thought, taking a nervous breath as she regarded her image in the glass, if this gown didn't inspire him to see her in a new light, nothing ever would.

CHAPTER FOUR

As IT turned out, Quentin did not join Caragh for dinner at Lady Mansfield's townhouse, nor did he escort them to the Duchess of Avon's ball. What he'd expected to be a short visit to his new property outside London turned into a day-long marathon of dealing with disgruntled tenants and trying to assess how best to remedy the damages wrought by years of mismanagement on the part of the estate agent, whom he dismissed upon the spot.

Knowing by midmorning he would not be able to get away, he dispatched a servant with his regrets and a note promising Caragh he would seek her out upon his return and lend her his support for whatever remained of the evening.

Night had long since fallen when he galloped back to his lodgings. After downing a platter of cold meat and a tankard of ale while his valet helped him into his evening clothes, he hurried off again, arriving in time to be presented to the duchess along with the last of the guests waiting in what must have been an endless receiving line. That duty completed, he went off in search of Caragh, his progress slowed by a number of hopeful mamas determined to add his name to their blushing daughters' dance cards.

Recalling with sardonic amusement the scant attention such ladies had paid him eight years ago, when all he possessed was a modest title, a heap of debts and a crumbling estate, Quentin noted at the corner of the ballroom a large gathering of gentlemen. As he struggled closer through the crush, he saw Ailis at the center of a milling group of admiring swains.

Who had, he noted in fairness, a great deal to admire. In a pure-white gown of simple cut that emphasized the classical perfection of her profile, her blond curls threaded through with pearls, matching pearls at her ears and throat, she looked the portrait of innocent maidenhood. Though he might privately deplore her rag manners and the cavalier manner in which she took advantage of her sister, he could not deny Ailis possessed beauty enough to dazzle even the most jaded palate.

The throng vying for her attention included not just younger and more impressionable men, but a number of older, cultured gentlemen as well. Also among the group, he noted, were those of the dandy set who, although they themselves had no intentions of becoming leg-shackled, always wished to be seen among the court of the latest Incomparable. An indication that Ailis was well on her way to becoming the diamond of the Season.

He devoutly hoped Caragh could harness that attention to lure her sister and some unsuspecting victim into matrimony before the ton discovered how drastically the lady's character varied from the appearance of docile, well-bred loveliness she currently presented.

Nearby, its wearer obscured by the press of gentlemen, he saw a tall nodding ostrich plume in cherry red, which must denote the presence of Lady Catherine. He did not as yet see Caragh.

Having elbowed and pushed his way through the crowd,

he maneuvered past the current contender for Ailis's attention to present his compliments. The slight raise of her brows as she rose out of her demure curtsy told him that, for the moment anyway, she was finding the role of Innocent Virgin highly entertaining. For Caragh's sake, Quentin prayed that amusement lasted long enough to get the chit safely riveted.

Reassured that the unpredictable Ailis seemed to be on her best behavior, Quentin relinquished his place to the next eager gentleman and backed out of the crowd, still searching for Caragh. As he scanned the vicinity, a flash of light from the corner snagged his attention.

The crowd shifted and once again the glitter of what must be candlelight reflected by golden fabric caught his eye. A moment later, a dark-coated man moved aside, revealing first the gilded silk of a lady's skirt, then the lady herself. As Quentin's appreciative gaze moved upward, he felt his lips curve into a smile.

The fluid gown gave an alluring hint of its wearer's hips and molded closely over a very fine bosom, its décolletage low enough to entice, but high enough to thwart all but an arousing glimpse of what lay beneath. Aroused in truth, Quentin's eyes wandered slowly over shoulders showcased in a teasing puff of gold-dipped fabric, up a graceful neck where curly tendrils of honey-gold hair escaped from a loose top-knot of Grecian curls. And finally came to rest on lips curved in a half smile in a heart-shaped face that was…Caragh's?

Shock made his jaw drop and halted him in mid-step. Suddenly dizzy, he closed his eyes and shook his head. But when he opened them again, the vision hadn't changed. The alluring woman in the enticing gown truly was his neighbor and friend, little Caragh Sudley.

He'd never again be able to consider her "little." The thought sputtered through his head before he jerked his gaze from that slither of gown and tried to reassemble his scattered wits.

Before he managed that feat, she spotted him. In a flutter of gilded skirts, she approached. "Lord Branson, I had about despaired of you!" she said, extending him her hands.

For a long moment he stood staring at her, oblivious to her outstretched hands as another bolt of entirely unplatonic appreciation sizzled through him. He couldn't seem to tear his gaze from the soft, never-before-viewed skin of her neck and shoulders and collarbones, that shadowed cleavage that positively dared a man to tug the silk bodice lower and feast his eyes and lips on the treasures just teasingly out of view....

Desperately he tried to channel his errant thoughts back to properly fraternal channels and summon some intelligent reply. "C-Caragh, how…how lovely you look tonight. L-like a glimmer of candlelight!"

Tantalizing. Seductive. He clamped his lips shut before he could add the words, while Caragh raised her eyebrows, no doubt surprised by his stammering enthusiasm.

Feeling himself flush, he stumbled on, "A very…stylish gown indeed." *And how intriguing the view!* "If this is an example of the new wardrobe you've been accumulating, I heartily sanction the expense."

A soft blush tinted her cheeks and her clear eyes sparkled. "It is, and thank you. Aunt Kitty will be quite thrilled to know it meets with your approval. Though you needn't empty the butter boat over me—or do you mean to practice your wife-wooing wiles?"

"Are they working?" he asked as he belatedly bent over her fingers she still offered.

She uttered that throaty gurgle of a laugh that always brightened his spirits, made him want to chuckle in return. *Relax,* he told himself, trying to calm his still-agitated mind. *Despite the gown, it's just Caragh.*

"As I expect the mamas of the young ladies you decide to court will soon be drenching you in quite enough flattery, I shall not answer that," she replied.

He did laugh then, before brushing his lips against her knuckles. A faint, heady scent of honeysuckle enveloped him and a low hum seemed to resonate between their joined fingers. He straightened slowly, finding himself strangely reluctant to let her go.

Don't be a clutch, he rebuked himself. *This is* Caragh, *not some demi-mondaine.*

While he struggled to order his disturbing and unprecedented reactions, Caragh stood quietly, her face tilted up to his, an expression of puzzlement—and something else he couldn't quite place—in her eyes.

Finally, her blush deepening, Caragh gently detached the fingers he'd forgotten he still held and placed them on his arm.

HE CERTAINLY SEEMED dazzled, Caragh thought hopefully. And surely…surely he must have felt it too, that little shock when he kissed her hand. That sort of quivering that still vibrated between them, her gloved fingertips resting where she could almost feel the pulse beat in his wrist. Surely such a reaction could not be all one-sided?

Or was he just confused at seeing her out of her drab outmoded garb and in this form-revealing ball gown? *Find out,* a little voice whispered.

"Is the gown the height of fashion?" she asked. "The mantua-maker swore 'twas so, but we are so newly arrived, I have nothing to base my judgment on. You've visited London often enough. Would you say the décolletage is right—neither too daring nor too matronly?"

His gaze drifted down to her chest and lingered there. He opened his mouth, closed it. The intensity of his stare made her skin heat. Then, cheeks reddening, he abruptly raised his glance back to her face. "It is…attractive. But you might wish to have the bodice cut a trifle higher in future. You don't wish men to gape at you."

"Would they gape?"

"They will if you show them much more," he muttered.

He *had* noticed! Caragh exulted. Having been achingly aware of *him* from the moment he first rode down her drive, excitement buoyed her spirits at this confirmation that, for the first time, it appeared Quentin was finally seeing her not as his helpful little neighbor, but as a woman.

Just what did he mean to do about the realization? Heart pounding with recklessness and hope, Caragh vowed to find out.

"Did your business prosper today? I hope the problem was resolved."

He was still staring at her as if he didn't quite recognize the woman addressing him. But given the din in the ballroom, perhaps he hadn't heard the question.

She leaned closer, close enough to see the shades of blue shimmer in his turquoise eyes, to denote each separate golden lash that framed them. From inches away, he exuded the heady fragrance of shaving soap and virile male. Her glance lowered to his firm lips, and for a moment she couldn't remember what she was supposed to be asking.

Now or never, she thought, and took a deep breath, trying

to slow the trip-hammer beat of her pulse. "Ailis is dancing this set, which should keep her out of mischief for the moment. It's too noisy and crowded here for conversation. Come out on the balcony with me and get some air." She tugged at his arm.

To her alarm and delight, he nodded and led her out of the ballroom.

The breeze on the balcony was chilly. After closing the doors behind them, Quentin turned back to Caragh and noticed her shiver.

"You don't have your shawl! Perhaps we should go back in. I don't wish you to catch a chill."

With him standing this close, her blood was more apt to boil, she thought. "No, the cold is…refreshing."

"Stand here in front of me, then. I'll block the wind." He maneuvered her a step closer into his warmth.

Lift her head, and she could feel the breath from his lips… "How did you find matters on the new estate?" she managed to ask.

"In a muddle, I'm afraid. I have, by the way, set some further inquiries abroad about the matter of Lord Freemont. I hope to have a full report for you soon."

"I'm relieved that he hasn't appeared this evening. Perhaps he views such ton entertainments as the duchess's ball too tame."

"Quite possibly."

"In any event, I can only be glad for his absence. It frees me of worrying that he might tempt Ailis into doing something improper."

As she was tempted, she thought, her glance once again lingering on Quentin's lips. If she were to brace a hand on his shoulder and raise up on tiptoe, she could brush her mouth against his….

He was staring down at her, gaze focused on *her* lips. Did his blood pound like hers to the pulse of her nearness? Was a voice shrieking in his head, as it was in hers, for him to lean through the small distance that separated them…and kiss her?

Past the lump the size of a crumpet that had somehow lodged itself in her throat, Caragh managed to whisper, "Though sometimes, being improper is…quite tempting."

Time seemed suspended, breathing ceased, and with every nerve braced in anticipation she thrilled to his mouth's gradual descent. Her eyes fluttered shut.

The first brush of his lips was sweet and so intoxicating she immediately hungered for more. Her hands rose of their own volition to grasp his lapels and she leaned into Quentin, deepening the kiss.

He clutched her shoulders and opened his mouth, gave her the ardent wash of his tongue against her lips. Her pulse leapt, something heated and urgent tightened within her, demanding release.

But before she could think to seek his tongue with her own, he stepped back suddenly and pushed her away. Already nearly boneless, she would have fallen had his strong grip at her shoulders not kept her upright.

"Your…your aunt will be missing you," he said, his voice uneven. He steadied her on her feet and then, with an insistent hand to the small of her back, propelled her back into the ballroom.

In his haste he half pushed her across the floor until they located her aunt, whereupon he quickly removed his hand. "I think I need a glass of the duchess's excellent champagne," he said, avoiding her glance. "May I bring each of you ladies one?"

Nearly weeping with disappointment, Caragh clamped her lips, still fired by his touch, tightly together to keep them from trembling and nodded.

He set off immediately. Around her, bejeweled dancers whirled like colorful tops through a waltz, Aunt Kitty's high-pitched voice babbled a falsetto note over the chorus of a hundred conversations. Caragh saw them, heard them, but comprehended nothing.

Well, she thought despairingly, the daring ball gown had done its work. Quentin Burke now realized that Caragh Sudley was a woman, with a woman's desires. And, she noted, watching him struggle with obvious impatience through the crowd, the knowledge thrilled him so much he couldn't wait to get away from her.

QUENTIN DOWNED a glass of champagne in one gulp, his hand trembling, then seized another.

What had come over him? Kissing Caragh Sudley on the balcony as if she were some…lightskirt out of the Green Room!

He was lucky he'd come to his senses before she fainted or struggled free and slapped his insolent face. True, she'd looked so impossibly lovely, so—seductively female, 'twas little wonder that shock had made him overreact. She shouldn't have surprised him so!

Of course, he realized she was now a woman grown. Still, he didn't appreciate having the fact brought home as blatantly as it had been by that demirep's excuse of a gown! Any man seeing her in it would instantly conceive thoughts just like his, which meant he'd better snap up the champagne and get back. And here he'd expected his escort tonight would protect *Ailis* from importunate suitors!

He paused to take a long, slow sip. He'd have to make it clear to Caragh that she must never wander out onto deserted balconies with gentlemen. Some other man with more muscle than morals might have taken advantage of her innocence, imprisoned that slender body against his chest and tasted much more than that tempting mouth.

Though it would have been the last thing the bounder tasted for a fortnight, once Quentin's fists got done with his lecherous lips.

Still, Caragh's suddenly changed appearance was…troubling. Not that he grudged her the frivolous, flirty gown, but he certainly preferred seeing in her familiar, sensible, Caragh-type garb.

Did he indeed? his still-simmering body instantly riposted. Could not passion add a spicy zest to what was already a deeply enjoyable friendship?

Not before a tolling of wedding bells, his mind answered. The implications of that conclusion shocked him anew. Though he'd never before conceived of marrying Caragh— any more than he'd considered marrying Alden or any of his male friends—the idea, now that he did consider it, wasn't without appeal. He might keep his good friend permanently close…and indulge in every fantasy that golden gown had evoked.

The idea fizzled for a moment, but then like champagne left too long in a glass, went flat. For one, he had no idea if Caragh would be interested in proceeding in such a direction. More important, though he'd never made the attempt before, he knew instinctively that though they might be able to travel the road from friends to lovers, there would be no coming back.

Growing up with all male cousins, he'd not had any female

playmates. Caragh was the first and only woman with whom he had ever developed a true friendship, except for his mother. He certainly didn't see Caragh in that guise, however deep had been the affection he bore for that sainted lady. As for his other relationships with females…

There'd been the blond charmer right after he left Oxford, with whom he fancied himself violently in love until she informed him that, as he stood to inherit only a debt-ridden barony, she must not let him dangle after her any longer. Stung by that dismissal, he'd willingly let his Oxford mates introduce him to females of another class, who were pleased to settle for well-paid pleasure of the moment and no promises for a future.

But even such uncomplicated relationships had the potential to become disruptive. He recalled with a grimace a well-endowed opera singer whose coloratura shriek and unerring aim with a wine bottle had rendered the ending of their affair singularly unpleasant. And three years ago, there'd been Alden's younger sister, with whom he thought he'd established a teasing, older-brother rapport. Until his friend, in some embarrassment, asked him to stop visiting him at home for the present, as his sister was fancying herself in love with the still-ineligible Quentin.

When he examined the matter, he had to conclude that every dealing he'd had with women since coming of age had been complicated—except for his friendship with Caragh. In that bond alone had he managed to combine the easy camaraderie he shared with his male friends, the exhilaration of discussing matters of importance he found at gatherings of estate managers, and the stimulation of intellect he found when debating his scholarly acquaintances. It was, in sum, a relationship like no other. A relationship he valued like no other.

A relationship he would go to great lengths to preserve and had no wish to risk losing by trying to overlay it with the tantalizing but dangerous and unpredictable elixir of passion.

No, far better to rein in his overactive imagination and overeager body, lest he stumble into a situation that led not to marriage and happy-ever-after, but to heartache and the permanent loss of one of his dearest friends.

His troubled mind settled by that sage decision, he drained the last of the second glass and motioned the waiter to hand him two fresh flutes. Straightening his shoulders, he paced purposefully back to the ballroom, ready to banish all thoughts evoked by provocative golden gowns and keep Caragh Sudley firmly where she belonged—as a dear *platonic* friend.

CHAPTER FIVE

SEVERAL MORNINGS later, Quentin awaited Caragh in her Aunt Kitty's parlor. Too concerned and restless to take a seat in the chair to which the butler conducted him, he stood by the hearth, gazing into the fire.

The facts he'd just confirmed about the character of Ailis's favorite admirer, Viscount Freemont, were disturbing enough that he'd felt compelled to bring a report of them to Caragh without delay. The urgency of his mission had succeeded, at least for the moment, in relegating into the background the discomfort he still harbored after that incident with Caragh on the balcony at the Duchess of Avon's ball. Feelings that, he admitted, had led him to avoid her for the past several days.

Resolving to keep his relationship with Caragh platonic was certainly wise. However, acknowledging a decision as wise and managing to carry it through were two entirely separate matters, a fact he'd been forced to admit as soon as he'd walked back into her golden proximity that night and handed her the champagne. Neither his imagination nor his body proved easy to restrain, leading to an awkwardness that had marred the rest of the evening.

He must do something to alleviate that subtle tension, restore them to the easy relationship they'd always enjoyed…though as yet he had no idea what. However, years of focusing on only the first step in solving what might otherwise seem nearly insurmountable problems had allowed him to bring his estate back from the brink of disaster. Perhaps he should use that technique here, put aside for the moment these disturbing new impulses and concentrate instead on the most pressing concern—the matter of Ailis and Viscount Freemont.

The news he must impart was sure to distress Caragh, confirming as it did that the viscount was most definitely not a fit suitor to a maiden of her sister's tender years. Especially one as volatile and heedless of convention as Ailis.

Caragh's appearance at the parlor door a moment later distracted him from his musings. And disturbed him, he admitted with exasperation and an almost wistful annoyance, far more than it ought.

Her fashionable muslin morning gown, in a soft green that complemented her gold-burnished curls and hazel eyes, was neither low-cut nor especially form-fitting. Yet once again Quentin found himself instantly, intensely aware of the swell of her breasts beneath the modest round neck, the curve of shoulder that seemed to emphasize the graceful lines of her throat, the lips, now curving into a welcoming smile, that had yielded so bewitchingly under his own…. He jerked his gaze upward.

Damn and blast! he swore silently, his neckcloth now choking his suddenly overheated neck. Subconsciously he must have been hoping, he realized, that time and the prosaic light of day would dissipate the disturbing alchemy that had surrounded them that night at the ball.

Obviously it had not. Working to stifle his body's instinctive reaction, he watched her approach and wondered whether the tantalizing physical appeal that now struck him so forcibly had bonded itself inseparably onto the strong fraternal attraction he'd always felt for his easygoing, intelligent neighbor. After that scene on the balcony, would there be no way to separate them again?

"What a nice surprise, Quentin," she said, extending her hands.

"Hullo, Caragh." Cautiously he took them, steeling himself for the zing of response that raced through his nerves when he touched her.

She jerked her hands free and turned aside, as if she, too, had been scorched by that brief contact.

"I'll have Evers get us some tea," Caragh said, breaking the uneasy silence. "Is this a social call, or does some business bring you here? Whatever it is, I hope 'tis nothing that requires my going out. With Ailis's come-out ball in just a week, the household is in an uproar, Aunt Kitty is all flutters, and I've a thousand details still to attend before we go to Lady Cavendish's rout tonight." She looked up at him inquiringly.

Dropping his gaze from her too-compelling eyes, Quentin gathered his disjointed thoughts.

"I'll be brief, then, and we can dispense with tea. But I felt you ought to hear this as soon as possible."

"What is it?"

"I'm afraid I have some rather disturbing information to impart concerning Lord Freemont. Perhaps you'd better sit down."

"Oh, dear. Should I call for brandy?" she asked wryly as she seated herself on the sofa and motioned him to a place beside her.

"Perhaps. And ready a gag and some restraints for Ailis."

Caragh sighed. "I was afraid it would be bad. So, tell me the wretched whole."

Despite her unprecedented behavior on the balcony, for which he must surely be somehow responsible, Caragh had always been a calm and rational individual, so best to just tell her directly, he decided. Without further preamble, Quentin began, "To his credit, I can report Freemont is indeed a knowledgeable patron of the arts and a generous supporter, particularly of talented newcomers. The rest is not so positive. I regret to confirm that the rumors of his taking under his protection a number of the highest flyers are quite accurate. Worse, however, it appears he has also made mistresses of females outside the demi-monde, all of whom have borne him illegitimate offspring. One of them was even gently born, though whether or not he seduced her into ruination with false promises of marriage I could not ascertain. His club mates report he is quite proud of his prowess among the ladies and frequently boasts that no female, be she duchess or drudge, will ever leg-shackle him into marriage."

With a soft exclamation of distress, Caragh closed her eyes. For an instant, Quentin worried she was about to faint. After all, stalwart she might be, but she was still a lady bred, and his news must have shocked her.

"Damn him!" she exclaimed, relieving him of concern for her maidenly sensibilities. "Why, of all her suitors, did Freemont have to be the one to entice Ailis? I shall have no choice now but to forbid him the house."

She shook her head and sighed. "As his rogue's reputation is more likely to enhance his appeal to Ailis than lessen it, keeping them apart is going to be the very devil. Especially as I've no doubt the wretch will attempt to see her during her lessons with Max, once I refuse to receive him here."

"I suppose there's no chance of suspending those…?"

She jumped to her feet and paced to the window, her speaking glance rendering a verbal response to that question unnecessary. "She's already contemptuous of the rules that govern proper behavior, unconcerned about the judgments of society and since she evinces no desire to marry anyway, certain to be furious at my banning her from seeing Freemont. I wouldn't dream of trying to ban her lessons as well."

"If she has so little inclination to marry, are you sure you're right to more or less force her into it?"

"How else is she to survive if she doesn't marry?" Caragh demanded. "Make her living as an artist? Oh, I don't expect you to understand! Even when your estates were crumbling, you had the freedom to choose your course of action! You might have sold off some land, sought employment in the church or the army, or even abandoned everything and emigrated to the Americas. But we have no funds not tied up in dowry and no authority to manage even those! There is no choice, no chance, for a woman outside marriage. It's Ailis's whole future at stake here, and I can't stand by and let her ruin it, even if I must push her to it against her will."

She looked so fierce, he wanted to applaud her—and so desperate, he wanted to take her in his arms.

But, remembering what had happened the last time he'd done that, he'd better restrict himself to verbal support.

"You know I'll help in any way I can. Would you like me to break the news to her? I'm the one who confirmed the truth of Lord Freemont's behavior, after all. Perhaps she would take it better were the information to come from an impartial outsider."

Her fierceness faded, leaving her looking weary and discouraged. Once again, Quentin resented the thankless effort Caragh expended on her sister's behalf.

"I appreciate the offer, but no. She'll doubtless rail and complain and weep. I won't subject you to that."

Having observed a few such scenes with Ailis, Quentin shuddered. Unable to force himself to face that daunting prospect again, he said instead, "Then how can I help?"

"If you could escort us tonight? Perhaps you could amuse and distract her on the journey, occupy her until her other admirers bear her away—and keep Lord Freemont at bay, should he happen to be present. That is…" she colored and looked away, "if my…behavior the other night didn't give you a disgust of me."

She knows I've been avoiding her, he thought with a hot flush of guilt. "No, of course not! I…expect 'twas much more my fault than yours. It was just…a surprise."

"An unpleasant one, apparently," she said dryly, her cheeks still rosy as she reached over to adjust the perfectly straight pleats in the window curtains.

"No! That is, not…exactly." As uncomfortable as this abrupt shift in conversation made him, perhaps 'twas best to address the problem head-on. Oh, that they might resolve it now, banish the lingering awkwardness that had grated at him these last few days and recapture the pleasant relationship he so prized!

Doggedly he made himself continue. "But…I've never thought of you in…those terms. We've been friends, good friends, for years, in a relationship that has been straightforward, congenial, and as enjoyable for you, I hope, as it has been for me. Proceeding down the road we dallied near that night would…complicate it."

With a gusty sigh, he ran a hand through his hair. "Usually, everything about dealing with women is difficult! That's why I found you so different, so delightful. What we've shared over the years is unique in my experience. I…I just don't want to do anything that might ruin that."

"I see," she said softly, toying now with the curtain tie-backs. "But…isn't it possible that taking that…road might lead to a relationship even more enjoyable? And if so, would that not be worth the risk?"

"I don't know, Caragh," he said, determined to be as honest as possible. "This whole matter is beyond the realm of my experience. I do know your friendship is very special to me. And I know that if we try to make it…more, things between us will have to change. If…what happened then wasn't pleasing to us both, I fear we'd not be able to turn back and recapture what we have now." He shrugged his shoulders, helpless to explain it any more clearly. "And what we have now is too precious for me to chance losing."

For a long time she said nothing. Quentin sat motionless, terrified he might have already said too much and offended her beyond repair, furious at himself for not having avoided the conversation.

Finally, when he thought he would have to either babble something else or bolt from the room, Caragh eased his anxiety with a smile. "You could never do anything that would destroy what we have." She took a long, unsteady breath. "I shall be your friend 'til my last breath."

Everything would return to the way it had been before the ball. His spirits soaring on a burst of euphoria, he sprang up and strode to the window. "As I will be yours," he promised, seizing her hand and bringing it to his lips.

A charged awareness sizzled through the hand that held hers, burned in his lips as they brushed her fingers. Startled, he released her.

Yes, everything would return to the way it had been…as long as he could ignore this disconcerting, and annoyingly automatic physical response to her.

HER PRECIOUS DREAMS turning to cinders, Caragh watched Quentin's troubled brow clear, unmistakable relief lighting his eyes. Sternly repressing a missish desire to burst into tears, she finished the prosaic business of setting a meeting time and place, then walked Quentin to the door and bade him goodbye. Her chest felt hollow, her heartbeat echoing within its hope-deprived space like Quentin's retreating footsteps in the empty hallway as she listened to him depart.

She'd tried to reassure herself when, instead of calling on her the day after the ball, Quentin had sent a note. Tried to buoy her sagging spirits as one by one the days slipped past with no further word from him, telling herself that her radically changed appearance had surprised Quentin—she had wanted to shock him, hadn't she? Of course he would require some time to adjust to the new and startling fact of their mutual attraction. Once he did, he would want to at least cautiously explore this new development.

But she knew now her instincts on the night of ball had been right. The speech he'd just delivered proved beyond doubt that attracted to her Quentin might be—but he wasn't happy about it. He had no desire whatsoever to attempt to take their relationship to another level. Indeed, he'd practically begged her to allow them to go back to the way they'd always been.

She stifled a bitter laugh. She supposed her female vanity should be gratified that he wasn't repulsed by her physical charms, though, as the end result was the same, it made little difference.

No, Quentin Burke was not willing to admit the physical connection that whispered between them. All he wanted was for them to remain platonic friends.

Friends.

Could she bear that now, knowing he had responded to her touch? When she hungered for so much more?

It appeared that, unless she were prepared to do without him entirely, she would have to endure it. He was not prepared to offer her anything more—and she'd just given him her word she'd accept that decision.

Until this moment, she hadn't realized how much her heart had counted on persuading Quentin Burke to follow a very different path. The stark truth that he would not hurt more than she could have believed possible.

Blinking back the tears that stung at her eyelashes, for a few minutes she allowed herself to grieve, to acknowledge the devastating depth of that sweet and painful longing. Then she took a long, ragged breath and forced herself to walk from the room.

Like other unpleasant facts about her life she couldn't do anything to change, she would think no further on it now. Besides, she had a pressing duty to perform that was just as unpleasant.

Telling Ailis she must give up Holden Freemont.

SINCE Lord Freemont sometimes stopped by to escort them to Ailis's art lesson, Caragh first summoned Evans to inform him that the viscount would no longer be received by their household. Then she mounted the stairs to her sister's chamber.

Her head throbbed with an ache almost as sharp as the one piercing her heart. But, despite her personal anguish, she must somehow summon words convincing enough to persuade her volatile sister to end her friendship with Lord Freemont. She

could only hope that desperation would make her eloquent—
and pray that for once, Ailis would prove reasonable.

She stood for a moment before the door, girding herself for
the combat to come. Then, putting her own unhappiness aside,
she knocked on the door and entered.

Ailis looked over in surprise. "Caragh—I was just about
to summon you! I wish to go to the studio early today. Max
said it would not disturb him to have me there while he works
and I need to complete underpainting the background before
today's lesson."

"I've no objections. But first, I need your agreement on a
matter of much graver importance."

Occupied in packing her art supplies, Ailis didn't even
look up. "I can't imagine anything more important than getting the background right. But if you will allow me to go to
the studio early all *week,* I'll agree without discussion to participate in whatever tiresome social ritual about which you're
preparing to harangue me. Only please, no more teas with that
pack of old harridans that govern Almack's."

"Really, Ailis, that description is as unflattering as it is in-
accurate, and is just the sort of imprudent comment I would
have you refrain from voicing, even to me! Lady Jersey—
who, I must point out, is barely older than I am—is known
for her wit and charm. Countess Lieven and Princess Ester-
hazy both combine a lively intelligence with a vast—"

"'Silence' Jersey would rather skewer with her wit than
charm, and the others do not enjoy discussing anything outside their narrow little aristocratic experiences. But come, let
us not pull caps. What do you wish from me now?"

For an instant Caragh wavered, tempted to let herself continue lecturing Ailis on a breach of propriety much less con-

tentious than the one she'd come here to discuss. But she knew she'd best harness the limited span of attention her sister spared to anything not directly connected to her art for addressing the problem of Lord Freemont.

Letting the easier topic go, she took a deep breath. "I'm afraid what I must ask will be difficult, and you may not understand or agree with the necessity of it. Nonetheless, it is crucial that you obey me in this. Ailis, you must cut your acquaintance with Lord Freemont."

A tin of mineral spirits suspended in one hand, Ailis looked up, her eyes wide with surprise. "Cut *Holden's* acquaintance? But he's the only man of our class in London who understands art and is not crushingly, boringly conventional. Why should I avoid him?"

Briefly Caragh recounted to her sister the litany of transgressions the viscount had committed. However, as she'd feared, Ailis appeared unimpressed.

"A penny-press tale of rumor and innuendo," Ailis said with a wave of her hand as she returned to packing up her brushes and paints.

"So I had hoped. But concerned about your deepening friendship with him, I asked Quentin to investigate the allegations. He did—and what I've just related is fact, not rumor. I'm sorry, Ailis, but surely you see you cannot continue to associate with a man who has shown himself to possess so reprehensible a character."

Ailis shrugged. "So he keeps opera dancers and actresses. If that offense renders a gentleman unacceptable, I should have to give the cut direct to half the men of the ton."

"He did more than that, Ailis. Making mistresses of women of a certain class is regrettably all too common, but there is a code of behavior to which even such gentlemen adhere. 'Twas offense enough that Lord Freemont dallied with servant and shop girls, but when he trifled with a girl of his own station, he transgressed beyond redemption. To seduce such a girl and not marry her—to make her an outcast among her own class and a disgrace to her family, is just not done, Ailis!"

"How do you know *she* did not pursue *him?* I, for one, have no trouble imagining a girl finding him fascinating enough to willingly forfeit her family's good opinion and her place in society. And how many 'gentlemen' would refuse a comely woman if she threw herself at his head?"

"Even if it transpired as you describe—though I take leave to doubt that any gently-born girl, no matter how lovestruck, could be heedless enough to actively seek her own ruination—a true gentleman *would* have refused her. And quietly returned her to family. Besides, there's the matter of the…illegitimate children he's sired."

"Once again, a natural and certainly not uncommon occurrence among gentleman who take mistresses. As long as he provides for the brats, I cannot see what all the fuss is about."

Exasperated and alarmed, Caragh stared at her sister, trying to understand the girl's seeming acceptance of actions she herself found unforgivable. Was Ailis dismissing Caragh's arguments simply because she resented being ordered to give up her friend? Or could she honestly excuse Freemont's profligate and irresponsible behavior?

Shrinking from that disturbing conclusion, she persisted, "Even if it is as you say, do you really see no harm in the viscount's having allowed a girl to ruin herself and her child, subjecting the innocent babe—his *own* innocent babe—to the lifelong shame of illegitimacy?"

Ailis shrugged again and resumed packing her supplies. "The girl was most likely content. And if she did regret it later—though I can't imagine why anyone would regret being excluded from a society as vain, boring and hypocritical as ever I predicted before coming to London—'twas her own fault for not knowing what she wanted."

At least at this moment, Ailis was not going to be brought to admit Freemont's guilt, Caragh realized. Submerging her distress over what that might say about her *sister's* character, she shifted her focus to the more pressing task—getting Ailis to shun the viscount.

"If you cannot see his culpability, I am sorry. But society considers his character flawed, and so do I. Holding that view, I cannot allow you to associate with such a man and put at risk your own reputation and your chances to make a good marriage."

Caragh paused, bracing for the reaction, but intent upon packing her supplies, Ailis did not even glance up.

"I've instructed Evers," she continued after a moment, "that we will no longer receive Lord Freemont. I expect you to respect that decision. I further expect you to refrain from seeing Lord Freemont, or speaking to him should we chance to encounter him—even at the studio."

With that, she had the dubious pleasure of knowing she had once again captured her sister's full attention.

Ailis set down a vial of paint and turned to face Caragh, her eyes narrowed. "*Society* may do as it likes, and so may you. But Holden has been a friend to me—a friend who understands and shares the things *I* consider important! How dare you forbid me to see him? Is not attending these endless social functions punishment enough? Do you wish to make me totally miserable?"

"What I wish," Caragh replied, trying to hold on to her temper, "is to secure you a future that allows you to continue doing what you want. You know the only way you'll be able to pursue your artistic ambitions is to marry a congenial man who will approve of that goal! Destroy your reputation by associating with Holden Freemont and you'll destroy any chance of achieving that."

"Smile sweetly, say nothing of substance, and marry, marry, marry! Faith, how *sick* I am of that refrain!" Ailis retorted as she flung her last brush onto the case and then flounced to the window.

Her own temper dangerously near a boil, Caragh stalked after her. "Then perhaps you'd better remember that if you don't marry, marry, marry, after father's death your dowry will become a part of the estate—to be dispensed, along with all funds, at Cousin Archibald's discretion. Papa has always indulged your passion for painting—but how willing do you think our dear cousin will be to spend money on canvas, paint or lessons? Be sensible, Ailis!"

Though her sister's rigid jaw, flashing eyes and rapid breathing spoke of a fury that might already have galloped far beyond the reach of reason, Caragh grabbed her sister's arm and forced her to turn around. "You *will* listen to me! Papa's lawyer already agreed to make your having sufficient funds to continue your painting a part of the settlements when you marry. I hope and trust you will find a gentleman with whom you *wish* to spend your life. But even should you not, surely you can see it would be easier to cajole some starry-eyed contender for your hand to agree to those terms than to try to persuade Cousin Archibald to do so! Is giving up Lord Freemont so much compared to safeguarding your artistic future?"

"Cousin Archibald," Ailis hissed through gritted teeth, "can go to devil!" Jerking her arm free from Caragh's grasp, she once again stormed away.

At this last evidence of intransigence, Caragh's reserves of patience finally ran out. "Very well," she said to her sister's retreating back, masking her anger and irritation behind a veneer of calm. "But heed this, and heed it well. We made a bargain before we left Sudley that you could pursue your painting while I found you a husband—which, if you continue to associate with Lord Freemont, will become impossible. If you refuse to give him up, there is no point in our remaining here. Defy me in this, and we will return to Sudley at once."

Ailis stopped in mid-stride, then slowly turned to face Caragh. "You would stop my lessons and drag me back to Sudley?"

"I don't wish to do so. But if I must, I will."

Her face contorting in rage, Ailis grabbed the nearest object—a small vase from the bedside table—and hurled it at Caragh, who, with years of experience in dealing with her sister's wrath, ducked out of the way.

As the vase shattered against the far wall, Ailis shouted, "I hate you! And I hate this shallow, useless society you keep pushing me to move in! I won't give up Holden, I won't give up lessons and you cannot make me!" Tears beginning to spill from her vivid blue eyes, she crossed her arms and glared at Caragh.

Shaken and near tears herself, Caragh glared back. "No, I cannot make you behave. But I can restrict your actions until you've calmed down and had time to think. I'm sending word to Mr. Frank that you are indisposed and cannot come to your lesson today. Perhaps you can use the time to envision what your life will become if you refuse to comply—and end up losing your lessons forever."

"You wouldn't!" Ailis gasped.

Caragh strode to the bell pull. "I'll have Mary take him a message at once."

Tears flowing freely now, Ailis stared at Caragh. "Get out!" she cried at last. "Get out and stay out! Oh, how I h-hate—" her words ended in a sob.

"I know," Caragh said softly as her sister flung herself on her bed, weeping, "how you hate me."

Heartsick and weary, knowing she could accomplish nothing else until Ailis calmed, Caragh left. The pain in her throbbing head now so intense she feared she might be sick, Caragh stumbled back to her room by blind reckoning, jerked on the bell pull and sought her bed.

Numbly she waited for the maid to bring her cold compresses and headache powder. She could only hope after the storm of fury had passed, Ailis would recognize the truth of her arguments and honor their bargain—so that Caragh would not have to carry out her threat.

CHAPTER SIX

LADY CATHERINE'S townhouse seemed uncommonly quiet when Quentin arrived that night to escort the ladies to Lady Cavendish's rout, a circumstance soon explained when the butler conveyed to him that neither his mistress nor Miss Ailis intended to go out. Only Miss Caragh awaited him in the salon, the butler explained.

Surprised and a bit concerned, he followed the servant down the hall, curious to hear Caragh's explanation for her missing relations.

His concern intensified the moment he walked into the salon. So pale and drawn was Caragh that alarm overpowered that punch-to-the-gut physical awareness that hit him now whenever she came near.

"What is it, Caragh? Are you ill?" he asked as soon as Evers withdrew.

"I must look wretched indeed for you to greet me thus," she answered wryly, motioning him to a seat. "I've a bit of the headache still, but otherwise I'm quite well, thank you."

"Evers told me your aunt and sister would not be down. Is the malady contagious? Or," he guessed, reading the tension lingering in her eyes, "did Ailis treat you to a scene that left both her and Lady Catherine prostrate?"

For a moment the pain in her eyes intensified and she

sighed. "I suppose there's no reason to mask the truth—not from you. Yes, I'm afraid it was rather wretched. Just hearing about it second-hand was enough for Aunt Kitty to take to her bed."

Anger at Caragh's supremely self-absorbed sister shook Quentin again. "You told her she must no longer receive Freemont…and she took it badly?"

"About as badly as you could imagine. Not only does she refuse to admit his unsuitability, she vows she will not give him up. To which I threatened to remove her from London and her precious art lessons. To demonstrate how seriously I meant that, I cancelled her lesson today and compelled her to remain at home. Whereupon she locked herself in her room and now refuses to admit anyone."

Once again Quentin felt that deep compulsion to take her in his arms. He settled for grasping her hand and squeezing it. "I'm so sorry, Caragh. It must have been awful for you."

To his horror, her chin trembled and tears welled up in her eyes. Before he could think of some comment to avert the impending flood, she pulled her fingers free of his and swiped at her eyes.

"It…it was, but you needn't worry that I'm about to turn into a watering-pot. Between Ailis and Aunt Kitty, I've had enough of scenes and sobbing! Still…I—I only wish Ailis realized I'm trying to do what is truly best for her."

"She blames you."

Pressing her lips together again, she nodded.

Once again, Quentin yearned to gather her against his chest, offer the comfort of a sympathetic shoulder. But he dared not, any more than he could give voice to his furious opinion that Ailis should remain in her room on bread and water until it finally penetrated her single-mindedly selfish skull that Caragh not only had her best interests at heart, but for years had submerged her own needs and wishes to care for her supremely unappreciative sibling.

Caragh took a shuddering breath, pulling him from his mental recriminations. "Maybe you were right," she said softly. "Perhaps it is wrong of me to try to force her to marry when she has so little inclination. But neither can I give her free rein to ruin herself and bring scandal down on poor Aunt Kitty's head! Perhaps I should just pack us up and head back to Sudley—even if I have to drug Ailis and lash her to the carriage to get her there."

"I'll bring the laudanum and the rope."

Her unexpected gurgle of a laugh surprised him—and warmed him to his toes.

"Oh, Quent, I'm so glad you stopped by! But I mean to release you from escorting me tonight. As Ailis will not be in attendance, I won't need reinforcements to head off potential disaster. And since I myself shall be doing nothing more dangerous than attempting to explain Ailis's absence to her hordes of disappointed suitors, I believe I can manage on my own."

"Perhaps you ought to stay home and rest as well," he replied, giving her tired face another inspection.

"Here?" She gave an eloquent shudder. "After Ailis's tantrums and Aunt Kitty's swooning, even the vestiges of a headache aren't enough to keep me in this abode of lamentation! No, a few hours of ordinary conversation with individuals not in the process of railing or fainting sounds quite appealing! However, since I imagine you consider such entertainment rather tame, I acquit you of the duty to come with me."

Though Quentin had been tempted at first to accept

Caragh's offer and hie himself off to the more congenial surroundings of his club, he decided upon the spot to squire
Caragh—and make sure she enjoyed herself.

For one evening at least, he vowed, still furious with Ailis
on her behalf, someone would make *Caragh's* happiness a
priority. Unfortunately, he had a hard time keeping his mind
from contemplating ways of distracting her from her familial troubles that had little to do with ballrooms or society
banter.

Firmly squelching such thoughts, he replied, "On the contrary! I'd been looking forward to it."

At her raised eyebrow, he grinned. "Looking forward to
spending time with you, then," he amended. "And supporting
you, as you have so often supported me. That's what friends
do for each other, after all."

Her eyes lifted to his, then roved his face before stopping
to linger on his lips. "Yes…friends do," she said, almost in a
whisper.

The intensity of her glance was as potent as a touch.
Quentin's lips burned from it, and suddenly from deep within
him boiled up a fierce need to pull her into his arms, to feel
her lips, rather than her gaze, upon his own.

Before he could decide whether or not to commit such insanity, Caragh turned away and called for her wrap. Shaken,
Quentin wasn't sure whether to be relieved or regretful.

AMUSING CARAGH turned out to be much easier than Quentin
had expected, given the tumultuous day she'd suffered.

By the time they climbed into her coach, she'd masked her
troubles behind her habitual calm. With a few well-informed
questions about the problems he had encountered at the new

property, she soon launched a conversation about pasturage and tenants that outlasted the wait in their hostess's receiving line.

After that, he stood aside while she greeted and consoled a crowd of gentlemen disappointed at the absence of her sister. Still, Quentin noted that several discriminating men in the group lingered after the others wandered off, evidently as interested in Caragh as they were in her more striking sister.

Garbed in another new gown of pale green that brought out the hazel of her eyes—and whose simple, unadorned style once again emphasized the ample curves of her body—she was lovely enough to engage any gentleman's interest. Concern over her distress had at first muted his awareness of her as a woman, but by the end of their carriage ride, he was once again uncomfortably conscious of her strong physical allure.

The orchestra struck up a tune, and one of the gentlemen led Caragh off. A number of other couples left for the dance floor, thinning the company around him until he was rather too visible to matchmaking mamas for comfort. Not wishing to fend off any who might approach, Quentin strolled after Caragh into the ballroom.

She was dancing with Lord Sefton, an affable baron a few years Quentin's senior. And though that gentleman appeared to be making proper conversation, Quentin noted his eyes frequently dropped to the attractive décolletage beneath his nose.

He would be tempted, he thought, eyeing the man with distaste, to stalk over, pull Sefton aside, and demand that he stop ogling Caragh as if she were some Covent Garden ballerina. Except that he suffered from a similar fascination himself.

Nor was he the only gentleman watching her. Sir Desmond Waters, one of the group that had surrounded her after they left the receiving line, had also drifted into the ballroom and stood near the dance floor, his attention fixed on the graceful lady in the pale-green gown.

Unsettling as it was to see her the object of masculine attention, Quentin knew it was nonsensical to allow that to irritate him. After all, as she'd pointed out back at Sudley, no less than Ailis did Caragh need to marry, and nowhere else would she find a larger selection of potential husbands. Though Quentin would prefer that they go on as they always had, at least in his head he understood how prudence demanded that Caragh take advantage of her time in London by fixing some worthy gentleman's interest—a development, he reflected gloomily, that would inevitably bring about changes in their relationship.

Unless…he could insure their friendship changed as little as possible by promoting a match between Caragh and one of his friends!

His spirits rebounded as he considered the advantages of such a plan. If Caragh chose a friend of his as husband, since the man would already be assured of Quentin's honorable character, he was unlikely to be jealous or mistrust Quentin's long-standing relationship with his bride. Quentin, in turn, could be assured that Caragh wed a man worthy of her. Melding the two separate friendships into a single, comfortable whole would be much more feasible were he already on intimate terms with both parties.

In addition, knowing she was his *friend's* wife would reinforce his efforts to ignore her physical appeal.

Yes, he decided, promoting such a marriage for Caragh offered his best chance to see her suitably settled while preserving their relationship with as few alterations as possible.

To devote full concentration to this delicate matter, he'd

have to put off his own search for a spouse. But since he'd prefer to have Caragh's assistance in that, and she would be unable to focus on his affairs until her troublesome sister was safely riveted, he'd most likely have to wait on that anyway.

Besides, he was in no hurry to get leg-shackled. Unlike a maiden who needed to marry in her tender years, he was just coming into his prime. And as long as his refurbished fortunes, if not his looks, remained intact, he thought sardonically, there would be no shortage of eager aspirants to the honor of becoming his wife.

After subjecting his catalog of unmarried friends to a rapid mental review, he set off through the ballroom to hunt down the most likely contenders. To his satisfaction, he spied the man at the head of his list, Lord Alden Russell, in conversation with their hostess.

Waiting until Russell extricated himself from that garrulous lady, he waved his friend over.

"Quentin, well-met!" Alden said as he approached. "Have a glass of champagne with me in honor of my escaping Lady Cavendish without promising her a dance!"

"Since it's that lady's champagne, it hardly seems fitting," he said, grinning. "Besides, I'm about to entreat you about something myself."

"Please, no accompanying you to inspect some weed-infested acreage in the wilds of the country!"

"It was just outside York and the inn where we stayed had, as I remember, a very superior claret," Quentin countered. "But this request should be a pleasure. Are you acquainted with Miss Sudley?"

Alden groaned. "Please don't tell me you need me to dance with some squinty-eyed ape-leader dear to the heart of your sainted mother! Perhaps I should throw myself on our hostess's tender mercies after all."

"She's hardly an ape-leader," he assured Alden, accepting the glass his friend snagged for him from a passing servant. "Miss Sudley is the lady in green—dancing over there."

Alden lifted his quizzing glass in the direction Quentin indicated. After subjecting Caragh to a head-to-toe inspection, he let his gaze linger, as Sefton's had, upon her bosom.

"My apologies for maligning you," he said, turning back to Quentin with a grin. "I'd be happy to dance *that* little lady into a dark corner."

Although Quentin had often traded such assessing remarks with his friends, with Caragh the female being assessed, he found Alden's comment unexpectedly irritating. "That *little lady*," he replied rather stiffly, his enthusiasm for Alden as a potential suitor dimming, "is a good friend of mine."

Alden's grin widened. "Wouldn't mind making her a good friend of *mine*—that is, if you've not already put your bid in?"

"My 'bid'? This ain't the Cyprian's Ball," Quentin replied, his irritation increasing. "Miss Sudley is a lady, you'll remember."

"And a particular friend, you said? Meant no disrespect, as you should know." He cocked an eyebrow and studied Quentin. "Sure you haven't an interest there yourself?"

"Only in seeing that, as she is newly come to London, she meets gentlemen of the better sort. Though I begin to doubt my wisdom in including you in that number," he added.

"Quentin, you wound me!" Alden protested, clapping a hand to his heart. "I'm the soul of gentility."

"See that you demonstrate it. Miss Sudley, you might remember, is my neighbor at Thornwhistle. I imagine you've heard me speak admiringly of her on any number of occasions. An intelligent and charming girl."

"Then I should be delighted to do the pretty. You'll introduce me?" He placed a hand on Quentin's elbow and urged him forward.

By now Quentin was beginning to regret he'd approached Russell, but having come this far, he couldn't fob the man off without truly offending him. Reluctantly he allowed himself to be led onward. "I suppose so. But I must warn you to treat her…gently. She's had a rather agitating day, and for once does not have to chaperone her younger sister. I want her to enjoy the evening."

Alden snapped his fingers. "Now I recall the name! *She's* the elder sister of the new blond Incomparable?" He halted and subjected Caragh to another long look. "Lovely enough, though she can't hold a candle to the chit, which is why I didn't recognize her, I suppose. The duenna's night to play the belle, is it? Well, we shall just have to see that she does."

Alden picked up his pace, angling for the edge of the ballroom floor where Caragh had just made her final curtsey. Quentin had no choice but to trot in his wake, already questioning the wisdom of what he'd just set in motion.

"Thank you, my lord, for a delightful dance," they heard her say to her partner as they approached.

Lord Sefton patted her hand. "'Tis me who should thank you, m'dear, for having the courage to allow such a heavyweight to guide you about the floor."

Caragh laughed. "Nonsense! I've seen you in the field, my lord, and there's not a better rider to the hounds at any weight. I'd not otherwise have allowed you to buy one of Sudley's best colts last spring." As she gazed up into her partner's face, she spied Quentin approaching, and a smile leapt to her lips.

"Coming to claim a dance, I hope, Lord Branson?"

A shaft of delighted gratification warmed him as he bowed to her. "Miss Sudley, Lord Sefton. I believe you know my friend, Sefton, but allow me to present him to the lady. Lord Alden Russell, Miss Sudley."

Caragh murmured a polite greeting and curtseyed. While Russell's salute of her fingertips was entirely proper, Quentin felt he retained her hand a tad longer than necessary. And need he stand quite so close?

"I've been eager to meet you, Miss Sudley," Russell said. "Branson tells me you are a most accomplished lady—a fair Athena, able to train any horse to bridle."

Sefton shook his head approvingly. "Indeed. The Sudley stables breed the best hunters in England!"

"Hardly the 'gray-eyed Athena,'" she said, looking at Alden with heightened interest. "You are a student of the classics, Lord Russell?"

He shook his head, an engaging smile on his lips. "Not a scholar of your father's caliber, I fear."

"Fair Athena" indeed, Quentin thought, throwing Russell a disgusted look. "Miss Sudley inherited her grandfather's eye for horseflesh," he said, determined to fix the conversation in more prosaic channels. "In the course of stocking my properties, I've inspected the best animals on the market, from Devon to Yorkshire to Coke's at Norfolk, and I've seldom seen a farm produce such consistently superior beasts."

"The colt I purchased has certainly proved superior, m'dear. I hunt with three mounts now—switch from one to another to keep 'em from tiring, carrying my twenty stone over a good long chase! Though that horse of yours has such heart and speed, I swear he'd go the distance and none the worse for it—not that I mean to let him, of course. Dash it, I'll offer you a thousand guineas if you'll promise to sell me another come spring."

"A generous offer, my lord, but I'm afraid all the foals for this spring are already bespoken."

"You must promise me one next year, then. Truly, you should persuade your papa to expand your operation. You've a steady customer in me, and I daresay I know a dozen more who'd leap at the chance to purchase Sudley stock."

Caragh shook her head regretfully. "Though I've often dreamed of doing so, I fear we haven't sufficient pasturage at Sudley to expand."

"Perhaps Sudley should buy more acreage, ma'am," Russell said. "It so happens that I have a farm that might be suitable—prime fields, but rather at a distance from my other holdings. Since the tenant chose to emigrate to the Americas when the lease ran out, I've decided to sell it rather than seek a new occupant. I should be happy to offer it to your father—and gain myself such a delightful new neighbor."

To Quentin's irritation, Russell accompanied that speech with a beguiling smile that caused Caragh, innocent of dalliance as she was, to blush. "Thank you, my lord. I shall certainly keep the possibility in mind."

As the orchestra tuned up, couples filtered past them to the floor. "If I might have the honor of the next dance, Miss Sudley?" Russell asked.

Did Quentin only imagine her directing a brief, longing glance toward *him?* After that short pause, she replied, "I'd be delighted, sir."

As Russell walked past him to claim her, Quentin stayed him with a hand. "She's an innocent, remember," he murmured in Alden's ear. "Rein in the flirtation."

"I'll be artless as an altar boy," Russell promised, a gleam in his eye as he pulled free and offered Caragh his hand.

Damn, it would turn out to be a waltz Alden had purloined. Disgruntled more than he wished to admit, Quentin could do little but remain at the edge of the floor making desultory conversation with Lord Sefton, who soon sought out a more encouraging audience.

Watching Caragh dance with Russell, Quentin found himself noticing small details he'd never particularly noted before. Such as how a man was permitted to clasp his partner so closely, 'twas virtually an embrace. That when danced energetically—and Russell was certainly energetic—the waltz's spiral patterns allowed a man to spin his lady in circles dizzying enough that she cried out in mingled alarm and exhilaration, while her breasts, temptingly displayed by the low décolletage of her gown, rose and fell rapidly with exertion.

Gritting his teeth, he looked away from the sight. Russell couldn't seduce her in a single dance, after all. Quentin would do better to stop watching their progress around the floor like a hound held back from the hunt and concentrate on conjuring up other, more suitable prospects for Caragh.

Though he tried to keep his mind on that important matter, his glance strayed with lamentable frequency back to the floor. Alden's gaze seemed to be focused where it should be, on Caragh's *face*. Still—wasn't he clasping her rather *too* closely, even for the waltz? And continually inclining his lips to her ear, as if murmuring some intimacy?

Two actions in which Quentin could not permit himself to indulge, he thought with some indignation.

He took a deep breath and tried to soothe away his annoyance. Just because he must restrain himself around her, surely he wasn't…jealous of Alden's ability to act freely.

He had about succeeded in calming himself when the dance ended. However, rather than escorting Caragh back to where he stood waiting, Alden took her elbow and began to walk her away from Quentin.

Puzzled, Quentin stared for a moment at their retreating figures before an explanation occurred. That blackguard better not be attempting to take her out into the garden! With a flash of indignation, he sprinted after them.

Instead of guiding Caragh to the tall glass doors leading onto the balcony, though, Alden turned aside and disappeared with her into the hallway.

A deserted anteroom would be just as bad as the shadowy garden, Quentin thought grimly, as he dodged through the crowd after them. Before his temper heated any further, though, he burst into the hall—and saw they were still strolling down the passageway.

As he quickly narrowed the distance between them, Alden glanced over his shoulder. The amused twitch of his friend's lips told Quentin he wasn't at all surprised to find him in rapid pursuit.

"You seem in a bit of a hurry, Quent," he drawled. "Hunting someone?"

"We were about to partake of some refreshment," Caragh said. "Would you join us?"

"I'm sure he would," Alden said. "Branson does like to remain close to his *friends*."

"My pleasure, Miss Sudley," Quentin replied, throwing Alden an annoyed glance over Caragh's head.

After tussling over who would procure Caragh champagne and a plate of fine slivered ham, the threesome moved to a small table. "Miss Sudley, you must tell me more about the horses you raise—before I claim my second waltz," Russell said.

"Unfair," Quentin found himself objecting. "I've not yet had the pleasure of even one waltz with Miss Sudley."

Caragh looked up at him, her eyes widening with surprise and her cheeks turning pink. "I should be happy to waltz with you, Lord Branson."

Then he remembered the implications: Caragh in his arms, her soft brown ringlets teasing his chin, her rounded curves almost but not quite touching him. The mere idea of holding her that close tightened his body and made his senses swim. Which was exactly why, he belatedly recalled, he'd meant to avoid waltzing with her!

But he couldn't fob her off now, leaving the field to Russell…or disappoint the eager anticipation he read in those great hazel eyes.

Take her home, he decided. If he could persuade her to leave now, he could avoid both the danger of waltzing with her himself and the threat inherent in allowing Russell to do so.

"But how thoughtless of me!" he exclaimed. "I should rather have asked if you were feeling up to it. Though you've done an excellent job of masking it, with the heat and candle smoke so thick in here, your head must be paining you more than ever. Allow me to escort you home instead. I know you must be anxious to check on your aunt and your sister." Quentin turned to Alden. "Miss Sudley's relations were a trifle…indisposed this evening."

Even as imperative as it was to part her from Alden, Quentin felt guilty for the worry that immediately shadowed her eyes.

"Perhaps you are right," she conceded. "I do still have the headache a little, and I should like to check on…my relations."

"Allow me to escort you," Alden interposed quickly. "You could console me for the loss of that second waltz by giving us an opportunity to become better acquainted. I'm entirely trustworthy, as Branson will attest! You can rely on me to get you home safely."

Over Caragh's head, Russell gave him a disingenuous smile. Quentin felt a sudden urge to slap it off his erstwhile friend's lips.

"I'm sure I can," Caragh was replying, "but I'm afraid Ailis would not be able to receive you tonight. Tomorrow, however, if you wish to call, I trust she will—"

"Miss Sudley, when I call, it won't be to meet your sister," Russell interrupted softly.

Lips still parted, Caragh stared at Alden, confusion on her face until the import of Russell's words finally registered. Once again her face colored and she lowered her eyes, stuttering some inarticulate reply.

Quentin had to grudgingly concede his friend some credit for making Caragh, accustomed to being relegated into the background by her sister's dazzling beauty, realize that a man might find her desirable, not just as a conduit to her sister, but in her own right.

Credit he might give, but not to the point that he'd allow Alden the prize of escorting her home. "Kind of you, Russell, but there's no need for you to go out of your way. I'm concerned myself about Lady Catherine, who is a dear friend. As

I'd planned to stop in to check on her in any event, I will escort Miss Sudley."

Once again, Alden's sardonic grin told him his friend didn't believe a syllable of his excuse for dispensing with Alden's presence. "Based on your greater acquaintance with the ladies, Branson, I will relinquish my claim—this time. Miss Sudley, I look forward to becoming as great an intimate of…your *family* as my Lord Branson."

With a flourish, he caught Caragh's hand and brought it to his lips. "You may count on me to call tomorrow, ma'am. Quent—many thanks for your diligent efforts on my behalf." He executed a cocky bow and walked away.

"Ass," Quentin muttered. "Ask," he repeated hastily as Caragh looked over. "Must ask the butler for your cloak. Shall we go?"

Her gaze lingered on him a moment as if she, too, found his behavior odd, but he was thankful that she did not take him to task for it.

"Very well," she murmured. "I must admit, I am rather weary. I shall be very happy to fall into my bed."

Oh, that I might fall there with her. The thought escaped before he could quell it. Perspiration breaking out on his brow, Quentin seized Caragh's elbow and hurried her down the hall to the entrance, where he hailed the butler and requested their wraps.

It was more than past time to see his "good friend" safely home.

CHAPTER SEVEN

BUT ONCE they'd entered the carriage for the ride back to Lady Catherine's, the anxiety he saw in her eyes once again held his physical impulses in check.

"You fear Ailis will still be angry?"

Caragh sighed. "Yes. I've never seen her in such a temper. She's grown ever more…independent-minded since we've arrived in London. I increasingly worry that at some point, she will cease to pay even a modicum of attention to my advice and do something truly rash. And if she should, with the interested gaze of the ton fixed on her, there will be no hiding it or explaining it away, as I might to our friends and neighbors back at Sudley."

"Very likely she shall do nothing more rash than indulge herself in a good cry," Quentin said, trying to set Caragh's mind at ease and hoping his words proved true. "In any event, should you need me to contain any potential damage, I hope you know you have only to ask."

She gave him a tremulous smile. "Truly, Quent, I don't know what I should do without you!" Gazing up at him with tear-sheened eyes, she squeezed his hand.

An instant of her touch reheated all his simmering desire. Neither did he know how he could do without her—without the soft, trembling lips that, with just a slight downward bend of his head, he might claim. Without caressing the curves he knew lay concealed beneath her cloak, without turning the troubled shudder of her sigh into agitation of quite another sort.

Surely she must be as aware as he of currents flashing between them! As if responding to his thought, her eyelids fluttered shut and she leaned those seductive, barely parted lips closer.

Even as his rational mind screamed at him to tear himself out of the magnetic pull she exerted, he inclined toward her, until he could feel the warmth of her breath on his own lips—

With a jolt, the vehicle stopped, jerking him away from her. The rush of cold air admitted as the carriage door was opened swept him back to sanity.

With more force than he'd intended, he pushed Caragh toward the open door. After a shocked second of immobility, during which he couldn't seem to summon a word of explanation or apology, she scrambled off the seat, leaving him gazing into frigid night air.

Damn and blast! he swore silently, his hands shaking as he gathered his hat and cane to follow her. If he couldn't manage to maintain better control over himself than this, he *was* going to ruin everything.

Furious with himself, he remained a few prudent paces behind her as they mounted the entry stairs. Better bid her good night immediately, before midnight and moonlight led him into doing something even more foolish.

When Evers met them at the threshold, he waved away the butler's offer to relieve him of his coat and hat. And for the first time since the…he couldn't come up with a word to adequately describe the madness that had seized him back in the carriage, Caragh looked at him.

Her face seemed as serene as ever, though the light from the hallway sconces was too dim for him to be certain.

"Will you not stay while I see about Ailis and Aunt Kitty?" she asked, her voice calm and unrevealing.

"No. Upon reflection, both ladies are probably already asleep. Don't disturb them on my account."

He should apologize, and he would—later. In his still-muddled state of mind, he couldn't think how to do so without opening the way for a discussion of the whole incident, something he was too fog-brained to handle now.

"Very well," she replied after a slight pause. "I'll bid you good night, then."

"I must go out of town again tomorrow, but expect to be back by nightfall, so if you have need of…anything, send me a note. I will call as soon as I return." He swept her a bow. "Good night, Caragh."

She stared at him another long moment, her expression unreadable, and then dipped a curtsey. "My lord. Thank you for your escort, and may you have a safe journey."

HAVING TURNED DOWN the footman's offer to find him a hackney, Quentin paced off into the chilly night. A brisk walk would steady his nerves and help him sort out how to end, once and for all, this irrational behavior.

If he had been able to practice the years of self-discipline necessary to restore his fortunes, surely he could manage the far simpler task of controlling his physical appetites!

Except that thus far, it had not proved all that simple. Since he knew he possessed willpower in abundance, it appeared he must be consistently underestimating the strength of Caragh's allure.

That troubling conclusion stopped him in mid-stride.

If his response to her was proving impossible to prevent and very difficult to control, perhaps remaining platonic friends was not so wise a policy after all.

A flare of excitement flashed up from deep within him at the prospect of allowing his frustrated impulses free rein. Ah—to be able to touch her, taste her, follow this fascination as far as it took them!

But she was not a Cyprian with whom he could amicably part once the initial excitement of an affair faded, he reminded himself. Touching Caragh meant springing the trap of wedlock.

Which might be a joyous bond, if passion cooled from its first, fast boil to a permanent simmer while leaving every other facet of their relationship unchanged. But if, after the initial fever of lust chilled, they were confronted with the wreckage of a friendship, wedlock would become a prison of life-long regret.

Was the gamble worth the risk? For a moment Quentin teetered on the edge, enchanted by the prospect of what might be, daunted by the threat of what might be destroyed were he to act on his desires.

In the end, once again he could not quite persuade himself to chance losing the precious and familiar by taking that bold, irreversible leap.

Better instead, he decided, to first give one more go to finding a suitable suitor for Caragh—someone, he thought, recalling with resentment Alden's subtle digs, less insinuating than Russell about Quentin's interest in Caragh and more cognizant of the privilege Quentin was offering in allowing him to court her.

Someone, too, that he could stomach seeing dance with and woo and touch Caragh as he himself could not.

Quentin couldn't at this moment envision such a man.

But enough reflection for one night. Tomorrow, while on the road to and from his property, with his mind and body freed from the witchery Caragh's presence seemed to work on him, he would think further about the matter.

Feeling suddenly weary, he summoned a link boy to find him a hackney. Yes, tomorrow he'd be able to make sensible, responsible decisions that would keep the treasure of their friendship undamaged. But just for tonight, as he drifted to sleep, he would allow himself to remember again the thrill of her lips almost touching his while her sweet honeysuckle scent filled his head.

HER EMOTIONS and impulses still in turmoil, Caragh silently watched Quentin walk out. After dismissing Evans and the footmen, she went into the salon, poured herself a glass of port and took it up to her chamber.

Dispensing with her maid as soon as the girl had assisted her into her night rail, Caragh dropped wearily into the wing chair before the fireplace. A few sips of the fortified wine warmed her throat but could not banish the chill in her heart. Telling herself sternly that she would not weep, she rested her head in her hands.

For a while she'd almost let herself hope. There'd been between them the same simmering urgency she always felt, but tonight Quentin seemed acutely aware of it as well. For all that he'd introduced her to Lord Russell, he'd loitered close by, watching them, and she was certain, had whisked her away from the party to avoid letting his friend waltz with her. And then in the hackney—just when she was certain Quentin would kiss her at last, he'd brusquely pushed her away.

As if revolted by her behavior and, most likely, his own.

She might as well face the fact squarely. Quentin Burke would not be drawn against his will into acting on his attraction to her. And he had a stronger will than any man she knew.

Are you sure? a little voice asked. Could she force the matter, exploit the heat flaring between them to push him beyond control?

Seductive as the idea was, after brief consideration she dismissed it. Given his behavior tonight—and she had no reason to believe his reactions were likely to change—should she succeed in seducing him, he wouldn't thank her for it. No, he'd likely be even more revolted than he'd seemed tonight—and angry with her besides, for breaking her word and tricking him into something he didn't want. Rather than gain a lover, she might very well destroy what remained of their friendship.

Friendship. With what she really wanted just out of reach, the word had a bitter, almost taunting resonance. Did Quentin's friendship mean enough that she was willing to endure being with him, longing for so much more than he was willing to offer?

She took another sip of the wine, considering. But the ache of wanting him and the ache of losing him were so intertwined, she gave up trying to decide which would be worse. She was too weary and disheartened, and besides, she had other problems to face.

She should tiptoe in and check on Ailis. Aunt Kitty must be asleep already, else she would have left word for Caragh to come up when she returned and relate every detail of the party she'd missed. Although her sister might be sleeping also, Caragh could at least gauge her current mood by seeing if her door was still locked.

She finished the last warming sip of port and fetched her wrapper. Quietly she slipped from her chamber and walked down the hall to her sister's door.

The latch, when she tried it, was still locked fast. She hesitated, but as she could see no light emanating from beneath the heavy oak panel, she decided not to call out her sister's name.

Ailis had evidently gone to sleep still nursing her anger, so there was no point rousing her now. Perhaps, Caragh thought without much conviction as she returned to her own chamber, by tomorrow morning, after a refreshing night's sleep, her sister might be more reasonable.

She herself slept poorly, disturbed alternately by dreams of an angry Ailis pelting her with paint jars and an aloof Quentin avoiding her. Soon after dawn she gave up the attempt and summoned a startled maid to help her dress.

Annie, the girl her aunt had assigned to serve both sisters, confided as she helped Caragh into her morning gown that Miss Ailis had remained in her room all evening, refusing to grant admittance to anyone, even the kitchen maid who brought up her supper tray.

Caragh descended to the breakfast parlor where, owing to the early hour, she was able to dawdle over tea and buttered toast in blessed solitude. Her head still hurt, her heart still ached, and she really would prefer not to have to deal with another of Ailis's tantrums.

But delaying the confrontation would only wind her nerves tighter. After lingering in the library until the hour was sufficiently advanced, contemplating possible ways to reason or bribe or charm Ailis out of her temper, she squared her shoulders and purposefully mounted the stairs to her sister's room.

The latch, when she tried it, was still locked tight.

Irritation stirred. 'Twas more than time for her sister to stop acting like a selfish, spoiled child who considered only her own wishes and needs. Ailis must start recognizing the realities of the society in which they lived and realize that her conduct affected not only her own position, but Caragh's and Aunt Kitty's as well.

She rapped sharply on the door. "Ailis, it's Caragh. Open the door, please! I'll ring for your chocolate and we can talk."

She waited, but neither a reply, nor the soft pad of approaching footsteps answered her demand.

She knocked again, harder. "Ailis, wake up! If you wish to be ready for your lesson, you must rise now. Be quick about it and we might even be able to arrive early. While you prepare, we can discuss that…other matter like calm and rational beings."

Still no response. Anger rising, she pounded on the oaken panel until she felt certain even a heavily-sleeping Ailis could not possibly ignore the ruckus. "Ailis, open the door now!"

But when the echo of her rapping died away moments later, she was left with nothing more than raw knuckles and a swiftly rising sense of grievance. "Very well, Ailis," she said to the stubbornly closed portal. "I'm going to fetch the housekeeper's keys. Whether you wish it or no, talk we must, and we will do so *now.*"

Caragh stomped away. By the time she'd tracked down the housekeeper and borrowed her keys—an easy task, as that lady was more than happy to be spared the risky job of disturbing the tempestuous beauty—her anger was tempered with a niggle of worry.

Surely Ailis hadn't become so incensed that she'd done herself a mischief? No, 'twas nonsensical, Caragh reassured herself, damping down a sudden spiral of fear. More likely she'd open the door to find nothing more alarming than a roomful of splintered crockery.

Despite that soothing thought, her fingers trembled as she turned the heavy key in the lock. "Ailis, I regret having to invade your privacy," she called out as she walked across the threshold, "but you've left me no…"

As Caragh glanced around the chamber, her heart leapt in her chest and the rest of her words were washed from her lips, as if by water spilled over newly-inked parchment.

The heavy window curtains were still drawn, leaving the chamber dimly lit. But even in the shadowy half light, Caragh could see the room was neat as a nun's cell, the assortment of painting supplies that normally cluttered the dressers and tabletops vanished. The bed linens were drawn up and tucked in, appearing already made up for the day…or never slept in the previous night.

Propped against the pristine pillows reposed a note in her sister's scrawling hand, addressed to Caragh.

CHAPTER EIGHT

HER HEART POUNDING in cadence with her throbbing head, Caragh tore open the folded piece of vellum and scanned it.

The message was predictably brief.

Caragh, I am off to do what I must. I shall be taken care of, so don't worry.
A

Her first shock giving way to a sick numbness, Caragh drew open the drapes and methodically surveyed the room.

Ailis must have left sometime the previous evening. Never concerned about tidying up after herself, Ailis would not have smoothed the bed linens had she rested even briefly.

As Caragh expected, the wooden chest in which her sister transported her art supplies was gone, along with all the brushes, paints, oils, and varnishes that filled it. Were she embarking on a journey of any length, Ailis would sooner leave naked than without her paints.

Next Caragh threw open the clothes press. Missing were the old gowns her sister had brought with her from Sudley, as well as her new day and afternoon gowns and her riding habit. Missing also were her warmest pelisse, an assortment of kid half-boots and her sturdy walking shoes.

Nearly all the dinner and evening garments still hung in isolated splendor to one side of the half-empty wardrobe, the crystal beading on the gown nearest her winking in the dim light like a mocking eye.

Caragh closed the door on it and walked over to the bureau. A few spangled scarves and some mismatched gloves lay scattered like driftwood at ebb tide on the bleached wood of the empty drawers that had previously been stuffed with her sister's garments.

Her last hope that her sister's flight might have been an impulsive, short-lived exercise in pique expired. Ailis had taken all the belongings she needed to live a life outside society—permanently.

As that dismaying conclusion shocked through her, on legs gone suddenly rubbery, Caragh sank into the chair beside the untouched bed. Choking down the nauseating panic rising in her throat, she seized her sister's note and read it again.

Going to do what I must... Which would mean painting without restrictions, of course. *I will be taken care of...*

Smoldering anger revived to displace the panic. Caragh knew of only one person likely to "take care of" her sister while allowing her artistic bent free rein. That notable rake and patron of the arts, Holden Freemont.

Caragh leapt up, her momentary weakness banished in a swell of grim determination. Her most urgent task was to trace her sister and drag her back home quickly, before word of her disappearance leaked out. Whether or not to press Ailis to continue with their original plan of finding the girl a husband was a decision that could wait until her sister was recovered, though Caragh's first inclination was to give up what increasingly seemed to be a nearly impossi-

ble, and certainly thankless, endeavor and take the girl back
to Sudley.

But first, she owed it to Aunt Kitty to find Ailis before her
sister's typically heedless and self-absorbed action not only
ruined the girl's reputation, but humiliated her innocent aunt
as well.

That Ailis had obviously thought nothing of repaying all
Caragh's efforts on her behalf with the worst sort of scandal
cut deeply, but she damped down the hurt to be dealt with
later. Squelched too were the guilty recriminations already
whispering at her that somehow she should have foreseen
this…that she had obviously been too indulgent and should,
over the years Ailis had been in her charge, have worked
harder to mold her sister's headstrong nature to conform to
their society's standards.

Briskly she exited the room and relocked it. She'd likely
have a lifetime to regret the path that had brought her to this
moment. She must focus now on finding Ailis before anyone
in the household discovered she'd fled.

Setting her mind to work on that problem, she paced back
to her chamber, sending a passing footman to summon Annie
and carry a message to the stables.

A pity Quentin was out of town, she thought as she pulled
her riding habit from the wardrobe. His discretion was un-
questioned and his assistance would certainly have proved
useful. But with every moment carrying her sister farther
from London and closer to a scandal that could ruin them all,
Caragh didn't dare await his return.

By the time the maid knocked at her door, she'd concocted
a plausible, and partially truthful, story. "Annie, help me into
this habit, please."

"Of course, miss." The maid hurried over to attack a row of tiny buttons. "Beggin' your pardon! If'n I'd a knowed you was to ride, I woulda had the habit ready."

"'Tis my fault. I, ah, neglected to mention earlier that Lord Branson requested my assistance at his new estate outside London." Quentin *had* said he'd appreciate her advice on the choice of a new manager there—sometime.

"Don't worry," Caragh added hastily to quell the look of distress coming over the girl's face, "I know carriage travel makes you queasy, and in any event, 'tis so slow that I prefer to ride there." Also true—though his new estate was not her destination today. "I'll take a groom, so you may remain comfortably here in London."

"Why, that be right kind of ye, miss! Are ye sure ye'll not be needin' me?"

The fewer who observed this little errand, the better, Caragh thought. "No, I shall be perfectly fine. Rob will watch out for me."

The buttons accomplished, Annie went to fetch the riding hat while Caragh pulled on her boots and gloves. "I'm not sure how long I shall be away," she continued. "Please explain to Lady Catherine when she wakes that since I'll have Rob's escort, and probably Lord Branson's as well for the return journey, she needn't worry if I'm late."

"Yes, miss, I'll tell her when she rises."

"And Annie, I've had…communication with Miss Ailis this morning." Which she had, in a manner of speaking. "She's not…recovered from her agitation, so I've relocked her door and ask you to insure that the household leaves the room undisturbed until my return."

"But what of meals, miss? She had no dinner last night."

"When my sister takes a notion in her head, eating loses all importance."

Annie looked dubious, but nodded her compliance. "Very well, miss. I'll have Evers inform the household."

Nodding a dismissal, Caragh gathered up her crop and strode from the chamber. Though she was nearly certain Holden Freemont was a party to her sister's flight, she should first make sure. So, although propriety dictated that a single lady never called upon a gentleman, as she ran lightly down the stairs, she decided to go first to Lord Freemont's townhouse. If he had indeed run off with Ailis, she thought acerbically, the small detail of Caragh's paying him a call unchaperoned would be more than lost in the furor over that much larger scandal.

As she exited the house, she found her mare and Rob the groom awaiting her at the foot of the entry stairs. Bidding the man to follow her, she set off immediately.

As she rode that short distance, her mind flitted though a tangled undergrowth of possibilities like a mouse pursued by a hawk. If Freemont *had* gone off with her sister, were they headed to Gretna Green? Surely even a rake of Lord Freemont's ilk wasn't so lost to decency as to aid a gently-born maiden to flee her home without intending to marry her.

He'd not flinched from such a thing before, she recalled. But that girl was a member of a rather obscure family. Though the ton accorded its privileged males much more leeway than the females, surely if Freemont were to compromise one of Society's newest Diamonds and then not marry her, he would find himself as ostracized by the ton as her sister.

The scandal would be bad enough even if they wed over the anvil. However, much as she loathed the idea of calling such a scoundrel "brother," the consequences to the whole family if the two did not wed were so dire that for the present, Caragh didn't wish to even contemplate them.

Moments later, they arrived before Lord Freemont's house on Mount Street. Now to bluster her way in. Taking a deep breath, Caragh dismounted and handed the reins to her groom, who went wooden-faced once he realized at whose dwelling they'd stopped—and what his mistress meant to do.

She turned and walked purposefully up the entry steps, the disapproving stare of her groom burning into her back. No matter how this turned out, she thought with a sigh, he'd have quite a tale tonight with which to regale the residents below stairs.

Having been mistress of a large estate for ten years, Caragh soon overcame the initial reticence of Freemont's butler to part with any information concerning his master. A few moments later she walked back out on shaking knees, having confirmed that Holden Freemont had indeed left London in his traveling chaise the evening previous. Bound not for Scotland, or so he'd told the servant, but for his estate in the country.

Which meant ruination for them all, if Ailis had in fact left for *Berkshire* in Freemont's company. Once remounted, Caragh sat with the reins slack, dread a cold lump in her gut as she fought down a paralyzing sense of helplessness and forced herself to concentrate on determining what she should do next.

Would Ailis have journeyed with the viscount, even after determining he had no intention of marrying her?

For several moments Caragh sat pondering the question, eventually concluding with chagrin that, tempted by the freedom to paint without restrictions and a strong infatuation for the handsome aristocrat, her sister would probably not be overly upset to discover that Freemont's destination was not Gretna. Ailis had ever protested she had no interest in marrying.

Still, the viscount, though wild, was older and more knowledgeable than her heedless sister. Upon further reflection, Caragh simply could not believe that Freemont would throw away his own standing in the ton to run off with her sister without intending marriage.

Perhaps, she tried to rally herself, Ailis had warned Freemont that her family was going to forbid her to see him, prompting the viscount to suggest they elope. Wishing to delay any pursuers who might seek to stop them before the couple could reach Gretna and be safely wed, he might have deliberately given his butler erroneous information.

Caragh could only hope 'twas so. Armed with that hope and the detailed description of Lord Freemont's carriage she'd bullied out of a footman, she decided to ride out of London and check for news of the fugitives at the first few posting stops along the Great North Road.

A crested, red-lacquered coach with its wheels picked out in yellow should be notable enough that some tollgate keeper or posting-inn groom would remember it.

"Miss, which direction do ye wish to ride? The horses be gettin' restless."

"North, Rob," she replied, wheeling her mount around. "We ride north."

Her goal was Islington, first stop on the road toward Gretna. The nature of her quest making it impractical to withhold the information any longer, during the ride there Caragh confided to the groom the barest outline of what she suspected. The shock and censure she'd steeled herself to see did indeed flash through his eyes. But Rob made a quick recovery, generously offering to do anything he could to help her recover her missing sister.

Taking him up on that pledge, as they neared the town, Caragh sent Rob to canvass the establishments on the left while she stopped at those on the right. Between them, they questioned landlords and stable boys at every inn and hostelry along the main road. But even with a small coin as a prod to the memory, no one recalled seeing a coach matching the description they gave.

Thanking heaven that they had set out early, with the stoic groom in her wake, she pressed on toward Barnet, stopping now at each of the villages along the way. By the time they reached this second major junction, Freemont should certainly have needed to change horses.

Whatever hope she still cherished of catching up with a sister bent on a runaway marriage slowly died as, one by one, they interviewed the landlords and stable masters of all the posting inns around Barnet. Not a single one recalled servicing such a vehicle or speaking with its commanding, aristocratic ebony-haired owner.

Freemont might have avoided stopping at a public inn by changing horses at the home of some friend along the route, but such a possibility was slim, and she knew it.

In any event, Caragh did not have sufficient funds, baggage or retinue to continue pursuing the fugitives up the Great North Road. If she wished to check the main road to Berkshire and still return to London before nightfall, she would have to turn back south now.

HOURS LATER, a weary, heartsick Caragh rode back into London. Her exploration along the road to Berkshire had been as fruitless as her trek north. It seemed that her sister and Freemont, if she indeed had left the city in his company, had taken neither route.

Fear, worry and anger roiled queasily in her empty stomach. Though she'd urged Rob to fortify himself with meat pies and ale at several of their stops, she herself had been able to stomach only some strong, hot tea. Especially since, with afternoon waning, she'd been forced to turn their horses once again back toward the city. Though she knew better than to commit the folly of continuing to search until nightfall caught them alone and unprotected along the London road, it went against every feeling and instinct for Caragh to return to Aunt Kitty's with her sister's whereabouts still unknown.

But as she jolted toward Mayfair on the last of the ill-gaited job horses they'd hired that day, a new inspiration revived her flagging spirits. Calling Rob to follow, with a last, desperate surge of hope she urged the placid beast to a trot and headed east toward the City.

Maximilian Frank's studio was located on the top floor of a building near Covent Garden. Keen as her sister was about her lessons, there was a chance that, even if Ailis had peremptorily decided to leave the city, she would have somehow contacted her mentor to let him know her plans. And if she had, Caragh prayed she might have informed the artist where she meant to go—and with whom.

Looking startled and a bit embarrassed, Frank's maid ushered Caragh to the small downstairs parlor. Her master was working and could not at the moment be disturbed, the girl said, resisting Caragh's demand that she be allowed to speak with the artist at once.

Not until Caragh threatened to bypass the girl and go up

unannounced did the maid finally concede to allow Caragh to follow her, muttering darkly that Mr. Frank was going to be that put out. Reaching the top-floor studio, she banged on the door, announcing in strident tones that Miss Sudley was without and insisted on speaking with him *immediately*.

After a long pause, during which the maid threw Caragh a resentful glance, the door finally opened. Pressing her last coin into the maid's hand, which brightened the girl's face considerably, Caragh walked past her into the studio.

Clad in a velvet dressing gown, his hair in disarray, the artist surveyed her with a glance that was half-irritated, half-amused. "Miss Sudley? To what do I owe the honor of this…unexpected visit?"

On a divan half-hidden behind a screen adjacent to the easel at the center of the studio lounged a very beautiful and nearly naked woman. Her cheeks heating, Caragh realized just what sort of work had been in progress.

Refusing to let embarrassment hinder her, she said, "Mr. Frank, I apologize for bursting in upon you in so unmannerly a fashion, but the matter is urgent. May…may I speak with you in private, sir?"

The maestro's thin lips quirked in a smile. "Since I've already been…interrupted, I suppose you may. Florrie, fetch more wine, won't you, love? This shall take but a moment."

In a languid uncurling of limbs, the girl rose, arranging about her a diaphanous wrap that did little to conceal charms the artist was still observing with obvious appreciation. Seeming fully conscious of the effect she was having on half her audience, the girl glided over to them, letting her body brush against Mr. Frank as she passed. She tossed a dismissive sniff in Caragh's direction before she exited, as if to imply she had no worries that this mud-spattered, hollow-eyed aristocrat would distract her paramour for long.

After the beauty's departure, the artist at last focused on Caragh. His bemused smile changed to a look of genuine concern.

"You seem upset, Miss Sudley. Please, take a chair. Can I offer you some refreshment?"

"No, thank you, I shall stay but a moment. I must question you on a matter of some delicacy, sir. I trust I can rely on your discretion?"

At his nod, she continued, "I…I am looking for my sister, Mr. Frank. She left my aunt's house sometime last evening and we have had no word of her since. I have reason to suspect she may have gone in the company of Lord Freemont. As you can imagine, it is imperative that I find her and bring her home as soon as possible."

"Did she leave you no indication of her intent?"

"There was a note, saying she was doing what she must and for me not to worry. As you can see, 'twas much too vague to be of any use in discovering her whereabouts. Would you happen to have any idea where she has gone?"

"As a matter of fact, I believe I do. That is, I was aware of your sister's ultimate plans, though I did not realize she intended to put them into effect this soon. Please cease worrying, ma'am! I'm sure your sister is quite well. Indeed, it was very bad of Ailis not to be more forthcoming, but if my suspicions are correct, you will find her not three streets from this very house. Where, you see, she has set up her own studio."

For a long moment, Caragh stood stunned. During this long day of searching and soul-searching, she had considered many possible explanations for her sister's disappearance—

but never this. She could not have been more astounded if the artist had told her Ailis had decided to tread the boards at the nearby Theatre Royal.

"Her own studio?" she echoed, finding her voice at last. "But—why? How? How could she have arranged such a thing?"

Maximilian Frank shrugged. "Your sister is a painter of great talent, Miss Sudley. She told me her chief ambition is to make her living as an artist. I, for one, believe she can do so. For particulars of the actual arrangements, you'll have to ask Ailis, but I believe Holden helped her find a flat and negotiated the terms."

Worse and worse! "Lord Freemont is k-keeping her?" Caragh asked, barely able to choke out the words.

The artist raised an eyebrow. "As to that, I couldn't say. Why don't you talk directly with Ailis? Unless I'm much mistaken, I believe you will find her at 21 Mercer Street, top floor."

At that moment, the dark-haired model opened the door. In the sudden silence engendered by her reappearance, she walked back through the room, hands cupping a crystal decanter of wine. As she bypassed Caragh, she allowed the belt of her robe to slip, gifting the artist with a full view of her naked torso. "Don't be long," she murmured.

Frank licked his parted lips, his gaze riveted on the girl's hip-swaying progression. After watching her rearrange herself on the divan, he finally recalled Caragh's presence.

"You now know everything I do," he said, motioning Caragh to the door. "Mercer Street, top-floor flat. Now, if you'll excuse me, Miss Sudley?"

"Of course. Thank you, Mr. Frank, and I apologize again for disturbing you."

"No trouble, Miss Sudley. I can understand a sister's concern." His glance sympathetic, he paused to pat her hand. "You mustn't be too angry with Ailis, my dear. When her head is full of a project, she forgets everything else, a common failing among artists, I fear."

After an exchange of goodbyes, Caragh walked out, the door closing behind her practically before she cleared the threshold. Numbly she descended the staircase.

And she'd thought that Ailis running off to the countryside was the worst thing that could happen! With a laugh that bordered on the hysterical, she almost wished her sister had left with Freemont. Better flight to the rural fastness of Berkshire than Ailis ensconced, probably with her lover at her side, right in the middle of London under the soon-to-be fascinated gaze of the ton.

Even worse than ruination in Society's censorious eyes would be Ailis's apparent intention to set herself up as an artist. Falling victim to a fatal passion could be understood, if still condemned. Betraying her birth and class by sinking to the level of a hired workman would be neither understood nor forgiven. If Mr. Frank's supposition were in fact true, Ailis would become an outcast shunned by all.

The social damage to the rest of her family would be almost as dire. Caragh uttered a groan. How was she to break the awful news to Aunt Kitty?

Though all she wished was to return to her chamber, lock the door, and pull the pillows over her aching head, she must first discover the truth of Mr. Frank's information. Mustering the last of her strength, she steeled herself to pay a call at Mercer Street.

CHAPTER NINE

TEN MINUTES LATER, Caragh stood before the door of a top-floor apartment, her stomach churning with a mixture of eagerness and dread. Feeling in her bones the ache of every mile she'd ridden this endless day, she knocked.

The door opened—to reveal a girl in the gray gown and mobcap of a maid. At least it wasn't Freemont, she thought, trying to quell a sudden lightheadedness as she released the breath she'd not realized she'd been holding. "Is…is your mistress Miss Ailis at home?"

"Who should I say is calling?"

So Ailis *was* here. Relief at finding her sister safe warred with the dread of realizing that the devastating scandal she had ridden all day in hopes of avoiding was now almost certain to overtake them. "Her s-sister," Caragh replied, her voice breathy as she struggled to get the word out. "But you needn't announce me. I'll show myself in."

Brushing past before the maid could protest, Caragh crossed the room, which contained a sofa and several armchairs buried under a quantity of boxes, to the door at the far side.

Hand on the latch, she paused briefly, squelching an hysterical bubble of laughter as she wondered what she could dredge up to say to the girl she'd nurtured and loved for years. The girl she'd discovered today she did not know at all.

Slowly she pushed open the door—to discover her missing sister within, arranging art supplies on shelves that lined one wall.

"Oh, Caragh, it's you," Ailis said, giving her a brief glance. "Now isn't a good time to visit. I must get these paints organized so I can resume work tomorrow. Do you recall whether the order I placed for brown ochre was delivered last week? I can't seem to find it."

Her sister's tone was light, conversational—as if they'd parted only a few hours ago after a cozy tea. As if Caragh had been fully cognizant of Ailis's plans and location. As if she had not spent the whole of a very long day galloping around greater London, half out of her mind with worry over her sister's safety, reputation and future.

Fatigue disappeared, incinerated by a blistering rage that flamed up out of every weary pore. For a moment she was too incensed to speak.

"Well, don't just stand there," Ailis said, looking her way again. "Since you're here, do something useful. There's another box of paints on the workbench—be a dear and start unpacking it for me."

"Ailis, I didn't come here to help you unpack!"

"No?" her sister replied, too intent upon her task to spare Caragh another glance. "Then why did you come?"

"Because I've been in the saddle since near dawn this morning, riding over the best part of two counties trying to find you!"

This time when Ailis looked up she met Caragh's gaze, eyebrows raised quizzically. "How could you possibly think I would leave London? My teacher, my work, are here."

"If you'd been a bit more specific in your note, I would have been spared an anxious and exhausting day!"

"Did I truly not mention where I was bound? Well, I was a bit rushed when I wrote. How did you find me, then?"

"I finally thought to pay a call on Mr. Frank, who directed me here…to your—*studio?*" With a sweeping hand motion, Caragh indicated the open room with its wide, north-facing widows, shelves filled with painting supplies, rolls of canvas stacked against the wall and to one side, a screened-off area containing a bed and dresser.

Ailis drew herself up proudly. "Yes. *My* studio."

"Ailis, do you really intend on…living here?"

"Of course. I hadn't thought to move in just yet, but then you enacted me a Cheltenham tragedy over Holden and I just couldn't tolerate any more. Fortunately, I already had the key for the flat, but it took all evening to pack my clothing and most of today to have the furnishings delivered."

"Was taking this studio *Lord Freemont's* idea?"

"He did suggest it, but I had planned on something of the sort from the very beginning."

It took a moment for the import of that statement to register. As comprehension dawned, Caragh said slowly, "You…decided to do this before we ever left Sudley?"

Her sister nodded. "Why else do you think I agreed to come to London?"

So Ailis had allowed Caragh to draw in Aunt Kitty and organize a Season in which her sister had intended all along to participate only until her true goal could be realized. As that incredible conclusion struck her, Caragh's saddle-weakened muscles seemed no longer adequate to support her.

She tottered to a chair. "Ailis, how could you deceive us so?"

Her sister shrugged. "Would you have arranged for me to come here had I confided my true intentions?"

That question being rhetorical, Caragh addressed another pressing concern. "But how shall you live? You cannot think Papa will frank you."

Her sister gave an airy wave of the hand. "Oh, I shall be quite all right. Before we left, Papa authorized me to draw on his bank for a considerable sum."

"Papa sanctioned *this*? I don't believe it!"

"Well, he didn't precisely sanction it," Ailis replied, a mischievous twinkle in her eye. "You know how he is, Caragh. I simply drew up the draft and presented it, telling him it was a matter of estate business. He signed it without looking up from his dictionary. I've already obtained one lucrative commission, with a promise of others. Holden has been a darling as well, helping me last night after I left the house and using his carriage to transport all my things. I don't know how I would have managed without him."

"Has he offered you carte blanche?" Caragh asked bluntly.

"He offered, but I declined." Ailis smiled—a satisfied, cream-pot, knowing smile. "He *is* my lover, though, a thoroughly delightful one! Though so indiscreet, the rogue, that I imagine soon everyone will know."

Ignoring Caragh's gasp, Ailis sighed and pronounced in theatrical tones, "I fear I am quite *ruined*—just as I intended. Now you will have to cease pestering me about a ton marriage and leave me alone to pursue my art."

Stung to the quick, Caragh retorted, "All I ever wanted was to secure your future so you might do as you wished!"

"Then you accomplished your aim, for I am doing so now."

Anger surged once again to the fore. "Ailis, did you even consider what doing—" she waved her hand to encompass the room "—this will mean to Aunt Kitty? To me?"

Ailis sniffed. "'Twill be a seven-day's wonder, no more. I expect Aunt Kitty can visit some friend or other until the gossip dies down. As for you, Caragh, I suggest you stop trying to live vicariously through the triumphant Season you've been pushing me toward since I was in short skirts and do something with your *own* life. And I don't mean tending Papa. Haven't you learned by now he will never notice or appreciate anything you do for him?"

Sentence by sentence, her sister's brutal, hurtful words piled like stones on her chest, making breathing difficult and response impossible, even had she been able to think of anything to say.

But Ailis didn't seem to expect a reply, for before Caragh could begin to dredge from her shattered emotions some sort of rebuttal, she continued, "It is rather late. If you aren't going to make yourself useful, you might as well go back to Aunt Kitty's and let me finish. I must begin work at first light."

Beyond words, almost beyond movement, Caragh stumbled to her feet and mutely walked to the door. Behind her, her sister had already resumed unpacking her boxes. "Higgins, put this tin of varnish on the shelf next to the oil. Careful, you clumsy girl! Don't drop it!"

A few moments later Caragh found herself back on the street with no memory of having descended the stairs. Rob met her at the door, his tired face lined with worry. "Did you find Miss Ailis? Is she all right?"

"Yes, Rob, she is here, and quite well. I'm afraid I dragged you about all day on a fool's errand."

Obviously not knowing how to respond to that, without comment Rob assisted her to remount. So drained was Caragh that she could barely support herself in the sidesaddle.

Yes, she'd been a fool, a pathetically blind, complacent fool! She would have laughed, had she not feared if she did, she would end by cackling uncontrollably—or dissolving into tears.

The stark fact was that Ailis was lost to Society—and her family—by her own choice. She'd made it clear she neither expected nor wanted anything further from them.

Somehow Caragh was going to have to break the news to their aunt—and figure out what to do with herself next.

After practically falling out of the saddle before Aunt Kitty's house, sustained by pride alone, Caragh steadied herself and walked up the stairs. Sore of heart and body after the day's ordeal, all she wished for was a long soak in a hot tub and the oblivion of sleep.

But she knew she must first speak to Aunt Kitty, slim as her reserves were for dealing with the hysterics her revelations were likely to produce in her excitable aunt. Having no idea where Ailis might have jouneyed today while in the process of moving her belongings, and therefore no idea who might have seen her in Holden's carriage, it was imperative that Caragh warn her aunt of the scandal about to descend upon them—*before* some saccharine-toned acquaintance delivered the news with sweetly false commiserations.

She half expected to find the house already in an uproar when she returned, but apparently her sister's mercurial disposition was well-enough respected by the staff that no one had ventured to interrupt her self-imposed isolation.

By now, Rob was certainly being grilled by the other servants on his day-long absence. Though she'd asked him to return noncommittal replies until she'd had time to acquaint her aunt with the facts, she knew the news couldn't be hidden much longer.

After passing her sister's still-locked door, Caragh found her aunt with her maid, completing her toilette for whatever entertainment she'd chosen to attend that evening.

"Caragh, dear, you're back!" Her opening smile faded as she took in her niece's bedraggled appearance. "My, you look…well-aired. If you hurry, you still can bathe and change in time for Lady Standish's rout."

"I'm rather tired, Aunt Kitty. I should prefer to stay home."

"I thought you might, after riding about all day. So energetic! Well, did you help Lord Branson accomplish his tasks?" Lady Catherine threw her an arch look. "Such a dear boy! I do hope he appreciates all you do for him."

Emotion clogged her throat when she considered Quentin's probable reaction to today's fiasco. She wasn't sure which would hurt more—his outrage at Ailis's actions, or the sympathy he was certain to offer her.

One heartache at a time, she told herself, fighting back the tears. Having reached the limits of her emotional endurance for today, she would *not* think about Quentin.

"Aunt, I must speak to you on a matter of grave importance."

A look of apprehension came over Lady Catherine's face. "Grendle, would you fetch my gold-spangled shawl? I left it in the library, I believe." As soon as the maid left the room, she turned to Caragh.

"It's Ailis, isn't it? I did knock at her door this afternoon, thinking certainly by now hunger would have overcome temper, but she refused to answer. She…she hasn't done herself an injury, has she?"

"Not exactly. You might rather say she's done *us* an injury." Caragh motioned her to a chair. "You'd better sit, Aunt Kitty."

"Dear me!" her aunt cried, sinking into an armchair. "I

knew I should have removed that Meissen vase from her room! Your uncle brought that back from India for me, and 'twas one of my favorites!"

"I'm afraid 'tis worse than broken pottery." Caragh sighed deeply. "There is no gentle way to phrase this, so I'll just say it directly. Ailis left your house in secret last night. I discovered her missing this morning. Fearing she might have eloped with Lord Freemont, I concealed her absence and spent all day riding about, trying to trace her."

"Lord have mercy!" Lady Catherine wailed. "Please, tell me you found her and brought her safely back!"

"She is safe," Caragh said, patting her aunt's hand. "But…but I could not convince her to come home. Aunt Kitty, I'm afraid she's rented a flat near Covent Garden and set herself up as an artist. She intends to support herself by painting."

For a long moment Lady Catherine stared at Caragh as if she were speaking in tongues. As the full import of the news slowly penetrated, the look on her aunt's face went from anxious to horrified. "Ailis intends to *w-work?*" she asked, her voice wobbling. "As an…artist? Here in *London?*"

Fortunately, Caragh had already located her aunt's vinaigrette, for, after uttering those awful words, her aunt's shocked face slackened and she fainted dead away.

Calling for the maid, Caragh caught the lady before she slid from her chair. Some ten minutes later, after a copious application of hartshorn and burnt feathers, with reinforcements from Lady Catherine's maid and two footman, Caragh managed to get her distraught relation to bed.

But the scene that unfolded before her aunt finally exhausted herself into sleep, filled with sobbing, lamentation, and calls upon a merciful Providence to send her to an early grave, was as awful as Caragh had imagined.

When at last Caragh was able to seek the solace of her own chamber, the tisane she'd ordered for her headache steaming at the bedside, she felt wretched enough for the grave herself. The soothing concoction dulled her headache from a hammer's pounding to a sharp ache, but though she was exhausted in body and desolate in spirit, her mind kept circling round and round the same path like a mouse trapped in a feed bin, making sleep impossible.

Ailis was correct about one thing. Regardless of what Caragh decided to do in future, there was no point in remaining in London for the present, to be talked about and pointed out by the curious every time she and Lady Catherine left the house. Aunt Kitty would probably suggest they retreat to the home of her good friend in Bath to weather the initial storm of gossip.

For a moment, a ghost of anger stirred. Lady Catherine loved her life among the London ton. For her aunt's sake, Caragh prayed that Ailis's iniquities would not be permanently laid at the door of the kindly relation who had had no hand in her upbringing and had sheltered her only briefly.

Her own situation was more problematic. The sister of Disgrace, she would never again be invited to the functions of the highest sticklers, lest she bring into some proper home the taint of Ailis's wrongdoing. It was quite probable she'd be shunned by most other hostesses as well, at least until they ascertained whether Society's leading ladies had decided Caragh might still be bid to their less-select assemblies.

If she wished to elbow her way back into Society, her best course would be to return to London before the end of the Season and face down the gossip. Her chances of making a good marriage—perhaps any marriage—had vanished with the departure of her sister from this house. But since the only man she wanted had no wish to marry her, the fact that she would no longer be considered worthy of wedding a member of the ton didn't trouble her overmuch.

And what of Quentin? He'd promised to call when he returned to London. Fortunately for Lady Catherine's peace of mind, he must have been delayed, for his paying her aunt a visit earlier today would have exposed Caragh's excuse for leaving this morning as the lie it was.

Which meant he'd most likely be by sometime tomorrow. Probably, if Lord Freemont were as indiscreet as Ailis indicated, directly after he'd visited his club and heard the appalling news.

Her heart ached at the very thought of his handsome brow creased in anger and concern. Though after the events of today every other soul she knew in London might give her the cut direct, she knew he would stand her friend.

Tears she made no attempt to stem began to slip down her cheeks. How her battered spirit yearned for the words of solace she knew he'd offer!

Seeing her distress, would he put aside cautious constraint and take her in his arms, let her lean against his strength and draw comfort from his steadfast affection?

But should he allow that, with her reserves of will and strength so low, could she trust herself not to trespass beyond the bounds of friendship? Could she feel his arms about her, and not seek the touch of his lips? What if her body ignored the commands of her weary mind…her fingers pulling him closer, her lips and tongue probing for entry? Would he shove her away in revulsion, as he had the night of the ball?

A wave of remembered pain and humiliation swept through her. No, she could not bear that again! Until she had recovered from the shock and hurt of today's events, sorted out her future and was certain she could once again greet him with the cool friendliness that was all he desired from her, she had better not meet Quentin Burke.

With that bleak realization, a sense of calm descended on her troubled spirit. Yes, she would leave London—but not in Aunt Kitty's company. Her aunt, along with delivering further lamentations Caragh had no wish to hear, would press her to do the socially sensible thing and return to London as soon as possible. Right now, Caragh wasn't sure what she wished to do.

She needed peace and solitude to determine what that might be. First thing in the morning, Caragh decided, she would begin packing, and as soon as Aunt Kitty awoke, inform her that she was returning home to Sudley.

CHAPTER TEN

IN THE LATE AFTERNOON two days later, the carriage transporting Caragh on the last stage of her journey from London pulled up before Sudley Court. Her sister's harsh words a goad driving her beyond sleep, she'd risen before dawn her last morning in the city to begin preparations for her departure. By the time a yawning servant tiptoed in to stir the coals on her hearth, she had her trunk already packed. Waiting only long enough to force down a Spartan breakfast and confer with her tearful aunt, before noon she'd collected her maid and departed on the mail coach.

Everything at Sudley Court looked soothingly familiar, she thought as the steps were let down. One of the footmen came to help her alight and immediately called out for Pringle, who was shocked to discover that the Young Person who'd just emerged from the hired carriage was in fact his mistress. Reassuring him as he escorted her into the hall that both her aunt and her sister were in perfect health, she promised to apprise him of the reasons behind her unexpected arrival as soon as she'd conferred with her father.

With his daughters no longer in residence, Pringle told her, the baron seldom left the sanctuary of his library. He'd even taken to having his meals there, instructing the staff not to disturb him except to deliver his tray. Which often re-

mained untouched on a side table, the butler said with a disapproving shake of his head, until its successor appeared
hours later.

After dismissing Pringle outside the library, Caragh eyed
the firmly closed portal with misgiving. She'd had a long
journey in which to ponder what to say to her father, her staff
and the neighbors. Knowing there was no easy way to tell the
tale, and anxious to get the painful matter over with, she'd decided to confront Lord Sudley immediately. Even if "immediately" were not, she thought with a flash of resentment as
she remembered her sister's words, a time her father might
deem convenient.

After rapping loudly enough, she hoped, to penetrate his
fog of scholarship, she entered the library.

Her father remained oblivious to her arrival, his eyes on the
manuscript in front of him, his lips silently mouthing the
translation he was doubtless in the process of formulating.
Caragh took a moment to observe the thin, intelligent face and
perpetually sad eyes of the man who had sired her.

A swell of affection rose out of the turmoil of grief, anxiety, resentment and fear to warm her briefly. She noted that
the finger tapping at his manuscript was ink-stained, and as
usual, his coat didn't match his waistcoat and the knot of his
cravat was slightly askew.

"Papa!" she said in a loud voice. "I must speak to you about
Ailis."

His brow knit briefly in annoyance, Lord Sudley glanced
up. "Caragh?" he asked, only mild surprise in his voice at discovering in his library a daughter who should have been still
in London. "Is it time for dinner already?"

Her absence had apparently been just another of daily life's mundane details, relegated by her father to the back of his consciousness, she realized with a pang. Quelling it, she continued, "Not quite, Papa. But I've just returned from London and I have urgent news. About Ailis."

"Ah, I recall. You took her to Kitty's for the Season. Urgent news, eh? She's received an offer from a worthy young man? Excellent!"

Anxiety over her father's reaction sharpening the dull headache that had plagued her for the last two days, Caragh slipped into the only armchair not stacked with books.

"N-not exactly, Papa. Ailis…decided to settle her future in another way entirely. You recall how passionate she is about her art? She…she has renounced wedlock and Society and intends to become a professional artist. I left her in London at her new studio."

Having decided these facts were upsetting enough without adding any reference to her sister's relationship with Lord Freemont, Caragh sat back to await her father's response. She had no idea, she thought with an odd sense of detachment, whether he would greet the news by weeping, tearing his hair, and accusing her of having been grossly remiss in her duty to her sister—or nodding politely in acknowledgement and returning to his work.

As understanding registered—of both the bare facts she'd recited and the implications she hadn't, Lord Sudley looked stricken, his dark eyes turning more mournful yet. Much as she'd tried to armor herself against it, at this evidence of her father's distress Caragh felt her initial guilt and anguish well up again. Desperately she blinked back tears.

After a long silence, her father swallowed hard. "She's lost to us, then?" he asked softly.

"I'm afraid so. I tried to reason with her, Papa, but she was adamant. Establishing a studio and living for her art are all she wants to do. All she intended to do in London from the first, apparently." She sighed. "The resulting scandal is going to be rather dreadful."

After that observation, silence stretched between them. Guilt stabbed Caragh again.

Angrily she pushed it away. She would not apologize to Papa for failing to instill in her sister an adequate appreciation for her position in life and the duty she owed her family. A failure that was also, after all, at least partly her father's.

But rather than calling her to account, her father continued to gaze mutely into the distance. "The ancients would say that we must each of us do what the gods within compel us," he said at last. "Regardless of the dictates of Society."

"Ailis is certainly doing so."

Her father nodded. "Is she happy?"

Startled, Caragh realized she'd not thought to ask herself that question. "Yes, Papa," she replied, recognizing the truth of the answer as she pronounced it. "I believe she is."

Her father lifted his hands in a helpless gesture, as if to indicate there was no more to be done. "Will you go back to London?"

"I-I'm not sure, Papa." Even knowing her father's detachment from everyday life, she was surprised to find him resigning himself to so irreversible a change in her sister's circumstances without further exclamation or argument. "I haven't yet had time to decide what I wish to do."

He nodded again and picked up his pen—a signal that their interview was at an end. "I suppose you'll inform me of your decision. Now, if you don't mind, I should like to finish this passage before dinner."

He will never notice or appreciate anything you do... Shaken by the force of the angry resentment seizing her, Caragh rose swiftly and fled from the room.

Having ascertained that his darling Ailis was settled and happy, her father had voiced not a single expression of concern over the scandal that a normal papa would have realized had blighted any matrimonial hopes his remaining daughter might have cherished. Nor had he offered a word of sympathy or understanding about how Ailis's unilateral decision had destroyed Caragh's sojourn in London and severely restricted *her* choices for the future.

Biting her lip to once again quell a drip of tears, Caragh went in search of Pringle.

First she'd brief the butler on the situation, that the staff might be prepared to offer appropriate but vague responses to the uproar of questions—and no doubt, criticisms—sure to erupt once the news of Ailis's disgrace reached the county. Finally, she would write a note explaining events to Lady Arden, the squire's wife and grande dame among county society.

She smiled a little bitterly. Would the neighbors among whom she'd grown up shun her or treat her with the same icy disdain she knew she'd be receiving in London?

Once she finished the note, she would at last be free, free from the responsibilities, the questions, the inquisitive eyes. She'd escape to the stables, saddle her favorite mare and ride.

Riding had always calmed her, quelled the headaches that built in her temples when the never-ending chores of running the estate and dealing with Ailis pressed too heavily upon her.

She'd ride now to ease the tension that had coiled tighter

and tighter since the brutal interview with her sister. In blessed solitude, she would at last have the leisure to examine the accusations that had fermented like a boil in her heart, lance them with the cold steel of reflection and determine which held truth, which reflected only her sister's self-absorbed view of the world.

And come back prepared to turn the conclusions she reached into a new direction for her life.

THE NEXT MORNING, Quentin rode back into London. The pesky matter of breaking in the new estate manager had taken far longer than the single day he'd predicted to Caragh. Feeling somewhat guilty for leaving her to cope alone with the ticklish task of cajoling her tempestuous sister, he wished to call on her as soon as possible to see how matters were progressing.

So, instead of heading for St. James Square, he directed his mount to Upper Brook Street. Pulling up his horse before the entry, still mentally rehearsing an amusing anecdote from his trip to cheer a possibly distressed Caragh, he was surprised to find a servant removing the knocker from the door.

Curious, he waited for a servant to take his mount. Although he supposed the butler might have felt that, with the quantity of callers visiting daily, the brass stood in need of polishing, he still felt a tremor of unease. Surely Ailis in her pique hadn't done anything so scandalous the family thought it necessary to make an abrupt departure!

His foreboding turned out to be justified, however, when a more than normally wooden-faced Evers replied to his request to see Caragh with the information that Miss Sudley was not at home. Quentin's concern deepened to alarm when the man added, after a significant pause, that none of the ladies were presently in residence.

"Good heavens, man, what has happened? And don't try to fob me off with whatever innocuous and uninformative reply your mistress directed you to offer! I'm well enough acquainted with the family to know the truth."

Ever's impassive facade creased into a worried look. "Aye, my lord, I expect you're that. 'Tis not my place to divulge, nor do I know for certain, all that occurred. I suggest you seek out Lady Catherine. Her dear friend in Bath, Miss Quimbly, has taken ill and requested Lady Catherine's assistance."

So the ladies had fled to Bath! Ailis must have done something truly awful, he thought grimly. After subjecting the butler to intense scrutiny, he concluded the man had indeed told him all he knew, or was permitted to impart.

"Very well. But should any of the ladies contact you, please convey to them my concern, and inform them I shall call on Lady Catherine as soon as possible."

"Very good, my lord. I expect as how my lady would welcome a visit."

Having unbent enough to offer that opinion, Evers resumed his impassive butler's demeanor and escorted Quentin out.

He'd lunch at his club, Quentin decided. Any action of Ailis's scandalous enough to require them to leave London just as the Season was reaching its height would likely still be the subject of conversation there.

Pausing in St. James Square only long enough to change into suitable clothes and down a tankard of ale, Quentin took a hackney to White's. The hour being rather early, the rooms were still thin of company. But among the octogenarians reading their newspapers, he hoped to find at least one acquaintance who could fill him in on the happenings in the city over the last three days.

He was thus relieved to see in his customary chair overlooking the bow window an older gentleman who'd been a friend of his father's—a fact Quentin had never held against the easygoing, genial old bachelor. Lord Andover was also an inveterate gossip, a trait Quentin had hitherto deplored, but which on this occasion should prove useful.

"Quentin, my boy, good to see you! Back from rubbishing about on your farms again, are you? Stap me, I cannot see how you abide all that rural rustication. Your papa would have expired from breathing a tenth of that country air."

"I'm sure he would, sir," Quentin replied, motioning a waiter to bring him a glass of wine and taking the seat adjacent to his lordship. "I trust you are well." He tapped the newspaper. "Events in town keeping you amused?"

"Indeed! There's just been the most interesting and unusual scandal! Concerns that beautiful Sudley chit that was making her bow this year. I say, don't you own some property in their county? Though from what I hear, you own property in nearly every county of England now. Going to become a regular Golden Ball of the Grasslands, aren't you, lad?" Lord Andover chuckled at his own turn of phrase.

"Not quite, my lord," Quentin replied, smiling gamely. "I do know the Sudleys, though. A scandal, you say?"

"Unlike anything I've ever experienced in my forty years in the ton!" Andover confirmed.

"What exactly transpired?" Quentin asked, curbing his impatience as he tried to lead the old man to the point.

But Lord Andover was not to be rushed. "I've seen a few faux pas in my day, slips of omission or commission that earned the lass who made them a trip home in disgrace. But ah, this!"

"Was the girl sent home in disgrace?"

Lord Andover grinned. "Indeed not. In fact, you being an intimate of the family and all, if you'd like the full story, I expect you could catch up with the little charmer over by Covent Garden. She's opened a studio there, I understand. Intends to paint portraits—a girl of gentle birth! Have you ever heard the like?"

"Miss Ailis Sudley has opened an artist's studio?" Quentin echoed, horrified to his bones. If this were true, such a breach of conduct and good breeding was more than serious—it was irreparable.

"So I hear. However, I also hear Freemont spends a lot of time there, so if you pay her a call, you'd better knock loudly, if you take my meaning." The baron wagged his eyebrows suggestively.

"Lord have mercy," Quentin murmured. No wonder poor Lady Catherine had rushed out of London.

The damage to the reputation of a widow well established among the ton was likely to be bad enough. But what of Caragh? His first shock gave way to a second as he pondered the impact Ailis's unforgivable behavior would have on her sister.

It took but an instant to realize that, for an unmarried country girl with neither great wealth nor the highest of rank to protect her, the results were likely to be catastrophic—and permanent.

Though after his morning ride, Quentin had looked forward to a snug lunch at White's, he found his appetite had vanished.

Caragh would have to be devastated. He must go to her at once.

Delaying for the moment his second-strongest desire—to seek out Ailis Sudley and strangle her on the spot—he finished his wine, listening with as good an appearance of interest as he could contrive while Andover went on to describe the lesser contretemps currently taking place among the ton. Then, excusing himself from lunch, he sent a footman to summon a hackney and gathered his things.

With luck and fast horses, he could be at Caragh's side by tomorrow.

The only bright note in this whole sorry situation, he thought with gallows humor as the hackney bore him back to St. James Square, was that for the foreseeable future, there would be no need to come up with a new list of potential suitors for the now-ineligible Caragh Sudley.

Within an hour he was back on the road, headed for Bath. Pushing on despite a steady rain, he managed to arrive, saddle-weary and mud-splattered, only a few hours past his original estimate. While thankfully availing himself of a bath, a hot meal, and the comfort of dry clothes at one of the city's best hostelries, Quentin sent a footman to ascertain Lady Catherine's location.

That task accomplished, he set out once again, sure Caragh would appreciate his diligence in speeding to her side, his anxiety to see her and ascertain her state of mind sharpened by three days of worry.

The butler who admitted him seemed doubtful of his reception. But after calling upon his most imperious manner to insist the man announce him anyway, then cooling his heels in the parlor for nearly half an hour, he was informed that Lady Catherine would in fact receive Lord Branson. Not until he'd supported that lady through a noisy spate of tears did he at last discover, to his extreme disappointment, that Caragh had not accompanied her aunt to Bath.

Nor, Aunt Kitty confided, still dabbing at her eyes with her saturated handkerchief, had her niece given her any word about when she meant to rejoin her, that they could begin repairing to the extent possible the damage Ailis had caused to the innocent Caragh's reputation. Which, Lady Catherine admitted, the conclusion bringing on another burst of weeping, was probably not going to be very much. Her poor Caragh was ruined almost as effectively as her scandalous sister!

Having ascertained that Caragh had chosen to flee to Sudley, Quentin exhausted the last of his limited reserves of patience, remaining for nearly another hour at Lady Catherine's side, inserting soothing murmurs during each pause in that lady's long lamentations about the situation. So eager was he to escape and ready himself to set off yet again, he did not even attempt to disabuse Lady Catherine of the erroneous conclusion she obviously drew about the nature of his affection for Caragh, after he let slip his intention to leave immediately for Sudley. At last, with Lady Catherine's arch blessing for being so *devoted* a supporter of her dear niece, he was finally able to break away.

Thoughtfully he considered the situation during his transit back to his lodgings. Knowing the ton's abhorrence for unconventionality, Ailis's behavior had likely dealt a death blow to any matrimonial hopes Caragh might have entertained. Sooner or later, he needed to take a wife—Society's opinion of whom did not particularly matter to him. Perhaps, he concluded as the chair men set him down at his destination, it wouldn't be such a bad idea to turn Lady Catherine's erroneous conclusion into reality.

By offering to marry his best friend, Caragh Sudley.

CHAPTER ELEVEN

TWO AFTERNOONS LATER, with a rising sense of ire, Caragh sat at the desk in the bookroom re-reading the missive the butler had just delivered to her from the squire's wife, Lady Arden.

My dearest Caragh,

I can only imagine how Distressed you must be at such Shocking Behavior by one of your Own Blood! So unfortunate That Girl's Infamy must needs cast a Shadow over your own hitherto Stainless Honor!

Rest assured, were I not at the moment Wholly Encumbered by my Duties here at the Hall, I should fly to your Side to support you in your Hour of Need.

However, there is still much to be done preparing for my Jenny's Come-Out next Season. Indeed, in view of that Important Event, and given the Tender and Impressionable Sensibilities of a Young Girl of her age, perhaps it would be best if you did not call here for the Present.

I have spoken to Mrs. Hamilton and we both feel that it would also be Advisable if you were to refrain for a Time from participating in the Parish Ladies' Benevolence Association. Naturally, as the Works of that Organization reflect back upon the Church, its

Members must be Exemplars of Unimpeachable Virtue.
We will of course notify you when, after a Suitable Interval, we feel it Proper for you to resume your Activities with us.

In the meantime, believe me your Most Sympathetic Neighbor and Friend!

Some friend, Caragh thought in disgust, tossing the letter onto the desk. Perhaps the note wasn't the cut direct she'd likely be receiving from her acquaintance were she still in London, but given that she'd just been politely banned from calling on her neighbors and participating in their association, it constituted her rural society's nearest thing to it.

Closing the ledger she'd been perusing, she stretched her tired shoulders. Lady Arden's reaction, though disappointing from one whom she'd previously believed to be truly a friend, was not unexpected. And if such was the response she was to receive even from people who had known her from the cradle, the tentative conclusions she'd drawn during her long ride two days ago were justified.

She had little desire to "earn" her way back into a Society that would ostracize one individual for the actions of another. Or for that matter, one that would condemn a lady simply for defying its conventions.

She'd also come to terms with her sister's accusations. Ailis had been right in asserting that Caragh had wanted social success for her, but not so she could revel in her sibling's reflected glory. She had only wished for Ailis to be sought after so that she might have the largest court of suitors from which to select her life's partner. Though Caragh had enjoyed the variety of entertainments London had to offer, with her main purpose for going to the city no longer achievable, she had little interest in remaining a part of the ton.

After much painful soul-searching, she had to concede there was, however, truth to her sister's allegation that for years, Caragh had assisted her father in the vain hope that he might someday notice and appreciate her. Worse, she recognized that she had acted in a similar fashion with Quentin—with similar results. Well, she would be Little Miss Do-Good-for-Everyone no longer.

Her sojourn in London, though short, had demonstrated that both the estate and her father could manage quite well without her. Quentin could hire an assistant for his manager at Thornwhistle, if the current agent proved unable to complete all his duties without her assistance.

Nor would she feel bereft at being excluded from the local benevolent association. Her main function at its meetings had been to keep the peace between Lady Arden, who considered herself the ranking female of the county, and Mrs. Hamilton, who boasted kinship with an earl and, as vicar's wife, thought her opinions should take precedence. Caragh had often returned from their meetings with a headache as severe as if she'd been dealing with one of Ailis's tantrums.

Papa had asked if Ailis's new life made her happy. Caragh had not previously had the luxury of embracing a task simply for the joy of it, but now, set free by circumstances from most of her former responsibilities, for the first time in her life she was considering what she truly wished to do.

Surely an upheaval in her life as dramatic as that caused by Ailis's disgrace meant the Divine Being must be impelling her to some new purpose. And, borrowing from the ancients, she recalled Aristotle's definition of happiness as the full use of one's powers along lines of excellence.

Frightening as it was to think of being cast adrift to make her way alone, still the notion of using her talents to build a new life caused a thrill of anticipation.

Since girlhood, only in one place at Sudley had she been truly relaxed and happy—with her horses. Some of her fondest childhood memories were of the long hours she'd spent with her grandfather in the barn he had built to house his broodmares. His good friend and hunting crony from Quorn country, Hugo Meynell, obsessed with producing a new generation of faster hounds capable of hunting foxes on the run, had urged the late Lord Sudley to experiment with breeding horses with the speed and stamina to pace his dogs. Her grandfather had devoted the last portion of his life to meeting that challenge.

Her parents, who had met on the hunting field, had actively assisted her grandfather's endeavors. Caragh remembered vividly the day when she, as a six-year-old, had proudly pointed out to a visitor the attributes of a Sudley colt. Her parents and grandfather had praised her lavishly afterward for her precocious expertise—one of the few instances when she could remember receiving her father's unqualified approval.

By the time her grandfather had died the following year, the Sudley stables had become known throughout the neighboring counties for producing quality mounts.

After Mama's death, however, her father withdrew from working with the horses his wife had loved so dearly, leaving the day-to-day running of the breeding operation to his agent and increasingly, to Caragh. She found it fascinating to evaluate the foals and decide which to retain for the program, which to sell. Exciting to see the young horses put through their paces. Exhilarating to experience the results of the careful mixing of bloodlines in the fleetness and strength of the horse carrying her across the field at a gallop.

So great had grown the demand for Sudley mounts that for the last several years, all the foals expected in the spring were bespoken even before their births. As she had told Lord Russell, for some time she'd longed to be able to expand their program, but that portion of the estate at Sudley that could be devoted to pastures and horse barns was already filled to capacity.

And so she would follow her talents and turn calamity into opportunity by purchasing another, larger property to devote solely to the breeding operation. She would establish her residence there—and leave behind the family and Society that neither needed nor valued her.

As she had already been exiled by the ton, taking the radical step of living alone and earning her own bread could do her no further harm. She was confident that the Sudley stock's superior reputation would bring clients flocking to her, regardless of her social standing.

She would seize this chance to make her life over in a fashion she, and she alone, chose.

She ran a fingertip down the ledger. Under her careful stewardship, Sudley was doing well. Having worked hard for ten years to generate it, she felt justified in allotting a portion of Sudley's income to fund her plans. Quentin's friend, Lord Russell, had already indicated he had a suitable property for sale. She would send her estate manager to inspect it, and if he approved the land, she would make an offer on it.

And Ailis had even shown her how to do it. Present Papa with legal documents—such as a bank draft and authorization to move the horses and equipment—and he would sign them without question, just as he had countless times over the years.

She would, of course, need one more thing to complete her happiness. But since making Quentin Burke love her was beyond her control, she'd also decided to limit her dealings with Lord Branson.

He was in London to find a wife, a task with which she had no desire whatever to assist him. As his marrying would inevitably put limits on their friendship and possibly lead to awkwardness between them, it was just as well that she intended to relocate away from Thornwhistle, where she would have few opportunities to torture herself with the thrilling, agonizing temptation of his presence.

For her own well-being, when she left her old life behind, she would leave behind also her friendship with Quentin Burke.

Dismissing the little voice that insisted turning her back on him would prove impossible, she focused once more on her accounts, intent on determining the largest sum for which she could responsibly write the draft. She had, she told the little voice firmly, cried all the tears she ever intended to cry over Quentin Burke. It was time to exchange girlish dreams for a woman's reality.

She turned a page, creating enough breeze to stir Lady Arden's letter and sent it drifting to the floor. Automatically Caragh bent to retrieve it, then stopped. *Coward,* she thought, *you hadn't even the courage to deliver your rebuff in person.*

Instead of picking the letter up, she trampled it under her foot.

Her first act of defiance, she thought with a giggle as she returned her attention once more to the ledger. Ah, how good it felt!

Just as Caragh finished adding the totals for the last entries, Pringle interrupted to announce she had a visitor.

Lord Branson awaited her in the parlor.

QUENTIN LOOKED UP to see a coolly self-possessed Caragh walking in. "Quentin, what a surprise!" she said, holding out her hands for him to salute. "How kind of you to stop by."

Relieved to find her much like her normal self, still, he had to applaud her sangfroid. Her greeting was as conventional and her tone as calm as if she had never undergone the catastrophe of taking Ailis to London.

Despite her brave front, though, she was too intelligent not to know just how dire her circumstances had become. Indeed, tucked beside his admiration for her fortitude lurked a touch of disappointment that she hadn't run, sobbing, into his arms.

"I didn't expect to see you here at the height of the Season," she continued as he brought her hands to his lips. "Was there some emergency at Thornwhistle?"

Surprised, he dropped her hands and stared at her. "Caragh, you must know I didn't come all the way here to inspect a farm! I want to help in any way I can. I'm so sorry I was away when…all this occurred. I came as soon as I learned what had transpired. Have you determined yet…what you mean to do?"

"Should you like tea?"

Carrying on in the face of disaster was one thing, but she was taking this business of maintaining appearances a bit far, he thought, exasperation nibbling at the edges of his concern. "If you wish. All I truly want is to tackle the problems Ailis has left you with."

"I do have a plan," she replied as she waved him to a chair and seated herself opposite. "In fact, your visit will save me writing to inform you of it. Since I intend shortly to remove from Sudley permanently, I shall no longer be able to watch over Thornwhistle. Its management is something for you to decide, of course, but I would recommend that you keep Manning on."

"Don't trouble yourself about Thornwhistle! Where do you mean to go? Joining Lady Catherine in Bath for a time would probably be best, so that she can assist you in planning your reentry into Lon—"

"Do not even speak of that!" her raised voice cut him off. Her face coloring, she lowered her tone. "I had only ever intended to remain in London long enough to see Ailis established. Since, in a manner of speaking, she now is, I have no desire to return."

"Surely you don't mean to live in permanent exile from Society? Come now, Caragh, I've never known you to run from difficulty! I admit, 'twill be rather uncomfortable at first, but once the scandal dies down, persons of breeding and sense will realize that you cannot be held accountable for your sister's actions. I grant you, vouchers to Almack's are probably out of the question, but I think that…" His voice trailed off as, smiling, she shook her head.

"Quentin, I'm not *afraid* to go back. I don't *want* to go back. There is no longer anything for me to accomplish in London."

So she did despair of marrying. She expressed that dismaying conclusion with such serenity that Quentin's chest tightened, tenderness at her bravery laced with anger at her sister's brutal theft of her hopes.

Before he could turn his muddled emotions into speech, she continued, "For a long time I've wanted to expand our breeding operation, but there simply wasn't sufficient space here at Sudley. So I've decided to purchase another property, move the breeding stock there and devote myself to running it. Alone."

"You intend to manage a horse breeding farm—by yourself?" he echoed, astounded. For a lone female to direct an enterprise whose primary clients were gentleman would be only slightly more respectable than opening an artist's studio. "You cannot be serious!"

She gave him a look of hauteur and raised an eyebrow. "I assure you I am. I thought you would appreciate my expertise enough to approve."

"I'm not questioning your competence—heavens, Caragh, I know better than anyone that it wasn't your Papa who solidified Sudley's reputation for producing superior horseflesh! But operating the farm with your father as ostensible manager, living under his roof, is a very different matter from running it openly while residing alone! You would doom yourself to being permanently ostracized by Society, with no hope of redemption should you later come to your senses!"

Her expression turned frostier and her eyes flashed. "I am in full possession of my faculties right now. I love working with horses, and as you yourself admit, I excel at it. What else would you have me do? Stay on at Sudley until Cousin Archibald inherits and wrests control from me? Live with Aunt Kitty on the fringes of Society, expected to be grateful for invitations to the larger parties and less exclusive routs? Dwindle into an old maid waiting for some gentleman, down enough on his luck to ignore scandal for the privilege of spending my dowry, to honor me with an offer of marriage?"

"Of course not," Quentin snapped, exasperated. "You can

marry me. It's certainly a better solution than running a horse farm!"

She grew very still, her eyes on his face. "I see," she said slowly. "You would sacrifice yourself to keep me from becoming a permanent exile from Society? How very…noble of you."

"Caragh, I didn't mean it like that!" Having shocked her—and himself—by rushing his fences, Quentin ran a hand through his hair, trying to redeem what even he recognized to be an ineptly-worded proposal. "I hadn't meant to blurt it out in so ramshackle a manner, but I have thought seriously about both our situations. I came here with the intention of making you an offer—and that was *before* I knew anything of your plans."

She studied him for a moment. "Why would you propose to me?"

He shrugged. "There's no point denying we both know your chances of making a match with any other gentleman of comparable birth and fortune are slim. And I, too, must marry sometime."

Watching her face, he could tell that un-lover-like speech was hardly convincing. Time to abandon caution and bring to bear the persuasive power of their attraction. He rose and came to her side.

"We've been friends for years, Caragh, the best of friends," he said, taking her hand. "I'd hate to see your bright mind and passionate spirit wasted in spinsterhood. I believe we could make a comfortable and congenial life together. Do you not think so as well?"

"I…I don't know. What has been between us as of late has not been…comfortable."

"Ah, *that*," he said, visions of Caragh in his arms—in his bed—sending a thrill through him. "It could be, I promise you, a delight." He bent to trace his lips across the top of her hand.

She jerked away as if scalded—and in truth, his lips sizzled from the heat of that contact as well. Jumping up, she paced to the window and stared out. "And what if you later met a lady who engaged your emotions—as more than a friend?"

"Since I have gone two-and-thirty years without finding such a lady, I have no expectation of doing so in future. Besides, I would never play you false, Caragh. Surely you have more faith in my honor than that."

She turned to smile at him, though her eyes remained pensive. "Yes," she said softly, "I have never doubted your honor."

Quentin felt an answering smile bloom on his face. He'd surprised her with his unexpected offer at a time when she was still upset and unsettled—and who could fault her, given the upheaval in her life? Once she'd had time to consider it, surely the affection between them would persuade her he was right.

Besides, Caragh was too sensible to refuse. He knew his value on the Marriage Mart, and for Miss Sudley to bring Lord Branson to the altar would have been accounted a triumph even before Ailis created her scandal.

And once she did accept him—ah, then he could sweep her into his arms and kiss her with all the passion he'd been restraining for what seemed an age.

She cleared her throat. He jerked his attention from that pleasing prospect back to her face.

"Honored as I am by your proposal, Lord Branson, I cannot permit you to make so great a sacrifice. I don't mean to be ungracious, but I have accounts to complete this morning."

She walked to the door and tugged on the bell pull. "Pringle will show you out. I hope you have a pleasant journey back to London."

Before Quentin divined what she intended, she curtseyed and slipped out the door.

For a few moments Quentin waited, before his brain sifted through the meaning of her words to arrive at the incredible conclusion that his good friend had just…walked out on him.

He'd been…dismissed! Dismissed as if he were some casual acquaintance paying a morning call, rather than a worried friend who'd spent three days tracking her down—and had just made her an offer of marriage. No, he thought, growing more incensed by the moment, dismissed as if he were a lackey interviewing for a position she had decided against offering him.

He had galloped all the way back to Thornwhistle before his first floodtide of anger—and hurt—receded. Reviewing their interview over a glass of wine and in the cooler light of reason, though, he had to wince. True, he'd never delivered a proposal before and the idea of her running a farm had shocked him into an unrehearsed and premature delivery of it, but he really should have done a better job of explaining his desire to wed her.

He was no expert on females, but he knew even one as sensible as Caragh probably wanted to be courted about so important a decision. Yet he'd included none of the sweet words of affection or tender vows of devotion a lady probably expected to accompany a proposal of marriage.

In fact, he'd botched the whole meeting rather badly. Coxcomb that he was, had he really expected Caragh to jump at his offer simply because he was Lord Branson of Branson

Park? Surely he should have known such a consideration would not weigh heavily with her. And, since he had broached his proposal as a means to salvage her reputation, she would, of course, return that gesture of nobility with one of her own, by refusing to accept his sacrifice.

By the time he'd finished off his dinner and a good bottle of claret, he'd decided he must return in the morning with a carefully written and well-rehearsed apology, followed by a much better worded proposal. One he felt confident that this time, she would accept.

He wouldn't mind letting her purchase a property and expand her breeding operation. No more than Caragh was he inclined to the idle life of the London ton, preferring the sense of accomplishment that came with hard work well done. As good as she was with horses, Caragh was sure to make a success of such an endeavor, and he would be proud to support her—as long as he was present to supervise when potential buyers came calling.

Just imagining the ribald jokes and suggestive innuendoes to which she would certainly be subject were she to pursue that absurd notion of running a farm alone made his temper rise and his hands clench into fists with the desire to pummel the yet-to-be-determined offenders.

Yes, he'd return tomorrow and be much more convincing—once he got her to hear him out. He frowned, a niggle of doubt shaking his certainty.

Caragh might be wary of receiving him, fearing an uncomfortable repetition of his arguments. Perhaps he should begin by ignoring the matter entirely, instead urging her to take him to the stables and explain her plans for expanding the Sudley operation. And then, while she was relaxed and in her element, once again the warm, witty, welcoming Caragh he knew so well rather than the wooden stranger who had occupied the Sudley parlor today, he would deliver his much-improved proposal.

Which, he devoutly hoped, *his* Caragh would promptly accept. For now that he truly considered the matter, to his surprise, he realized he'd grown entirely too fond of his dear friend's company to let her exile herself far from him in some remote rural village.

The following day, just before noon, Quentin set out for Sudley. By this hour, Caragh should have completed her morning duties and be amenable to a stroll to the barns. Then if his mission were successful, he could utilize her father's noon break to ask for Caragh's hand.

That formality completed, he could whisk Caragh back to the parlor to celebrate their new engagement with a glass of champagne and some even more intoxicating kisses.

Concentrating on that happy outcome quelled the unexpected nervousness that slowed his step and tightened his neckcloth as he handed over his horse and mounted the entry stairs. His attention distracted by mentally rehearsing his proposal, he only half heard the butler return his greeting.

Until the man startled him out of polishing his pretty phrases by saying that Miss Caragh was no longer at Sudley.

She had, Pringle regretted to inform him, departed this morning—for London.

CHAPTER TWELVE

IN THE AFTERNOON several days later, Caragh climbed the stairs to her room in Aunt Kitty's London townhouse. She'd sent word by messenger to Lady Catherine, begging leave to stay in the house during her sojourn in town.

To her surprise, rather than informing the servants of her arrival, her aunt journeyed from Bath to greet her personally. Though Lady Catherine did not judge that sufficient time had yet elapsed for them to attempt reentering London Society, still she wished, she tearfully assured Caragh, to lend her support through whatever trials had forced her poor maligned niece to return so soon to the metropolis.

Deciding there was no point in further upsetting her kind-hearted aunt by divulging her real reason for consulting with Sudley's lawyer, Caragh had allowed Lady Catherine to believe she had come merely on a matter of estate business for her papa. Before the end of this visit, though, she thought with a sigh as she entered her chamber, she would have to inform Aunt Kitty of her real plans—a confession likely to evoke an attack of hysteria only slightly less severe than the one brought on by the news that Ailis had set up her studio.

Poor Aunt Kitty, Caragh thought, her affection for her gentle aunt tinged by no small amount of guilt. What social millstones her nieces were proving to be!

Aside from that one regret, she judged the rest of her trip an unqualified success. Tossing aside her reticule, she smiled as she set down the folder of documents she'd brought back from the office of their lawyer. Mr. Smithers, having long known that Caragh and not her father directed estate business at Sudley, raised not an eyebrow at her request that he make an offer on a tract of land being offered for sale by Lord Russell. Though even the lawyer, she suspected, would be shocked at the notion of her being so unconventional as to move from beneath her father's roof to openly manage the enterprise.

She'd learned an hour ago that Mr. Smithers was now negotiating for the property and foresaw no difficulties in completing its purchase. As soon as the transaction was finalized, Caragh would return to Sudley to begin moving her livestock and equipment to the new property.

Which she hoped would be soon. She knew her brusque refusal of his suit and immediate departure must have wounded Quentin, but maintaining a cold distance—and escaping at the first possible instant—was the only way she survived their meeting. The urge had been far too strong to soothe her troubled spirit by throwing herself into his arms—where, for the first time, he seemed quite willing to receive her.

But only, she reminded herself bitterly, to use the power of their attraction to seduce her into accepting his…sympathy proposal. Oh, to have him change his mind about attempting to combine friendship and passion, not because he'd found her too enticing to resist—but out of *pity!* She still writhed at the thought. Her pride and self-respect would never forgive him that betrayal of their friendship.

Especially since, despite the lowering terms in which he had phrased it, she had been all too tempted to accept.

Her eyes stung and her heart twisted at the memory. His willingness to "sacrifice" himself for her might be noble, but she'd thought he knew—and appreciated—her capabilities better than to expect she would let Ailis's action reduce her to helpless dependence on Society's—or some well-meaning friend's—goodwill.

She'd thought she knew *him* well enough to expect his support and encouragement for her continued independence, rather than a mouthing of conventional proprieties.

If he were her Apollo, she'd better take care not to become Icarus, foolishly flying closer to the object of her fascination until he destroyed her.

Enough! she told herself, putting a hand to her forehead. She would think no more on that painful and humiliating interview.

But one thing she must not forget: Quentin Burke had not brought his fortunes back from the edge of ruin by being easily discouraged. If, after further reflection, he still believed her plans ill-advised, he would be back—with perhaps even more devious and seductive tricks to dissuade her.

She had better leave the City before he returned—or have her defenses primed to resist him.

The other decision she must make was less clear. Sighing, she picked up and reread the note Evers had brought her today—from Ailis.

Heard from Holden that you are in town.
Please come to see me.

For a moment, she stared at her sister's distinctive, boldly-formed letters as if they held the key to the puzzle that was Ailis.

Caragh's first impulse upon receiving the note had been to crumple it up and cast it into the fire. She'd been at the point of feeding it to the flames when a more considered reaction stopped her. Sighing, she returned to the desk and smoothed it out.

Ailis's cold dismissal of Caragh's loving care as mere self-interested manipulation had cut so deep, Caragh still had no words adequate to express the pain. Nor had she any desire to expose her lacerated spirit to more of her sister's barbed commentary.

And yet…they were sisters. The bonds of affection, on her side at least, were strongly forged—stronger, it appeared, than the hurt. Ailis might have wrenched responsibility for her future out of Caragh's hands, but despite the casual cruelty of her sister's methods, Caragh could not so easily turn off a lifetime's habit of watching out for her.

She ran a finger over the note once more. Ailis had added an atypical "please," which in her sister's cryptic way was tantamount to an apology. And Caragh did genuinely want to know how Ailis was doing, whether the promised commission had come through and whether she would, in fact, be able to support herself. The sum she had drawn from Papa's account, far less than her dowry, would not pay the rent or keep her in paints for long.

In her current state of social isolation, Caragh would likely receive neither hard news nor gossip about her sister's situation. Knowing that at this delicate juncture Aunt Kitty would not welcome a visit, even should her sister be moved to make one, if Caragh wished to know how Ailis was doing, she would have to go to Mercer Street.

She smiled ruefully, knowing her decision was already

made. And despite what *some* people seemed to think, she did not shrink from facing difficult, even painful tasks.

The early spring afternoon's light was already fading. Ailis would be finishing her day's painting, putting up her oils and cleaning her brushes. If she intended to visit, now would be a good time to call.

Still arranging your schedule based on Ailis's needs, Caragh thought, her smile turning bitter. How long-ingrained habits persist!

But Aunt Kitty would be resting in preparation for dinner. Caragh might slip out and back without having to explain where she'd gone.

That fact swaying the balance, she drew on her gloves, caught up her pelisse and strode from the room.

Some half-hour later, Caragh stood with her hand poised to ring her sister's bell, already regretting her impulse to visit and wondering if it were too late to recall the hackney that had conveyed her here.

Deciding that it was, and that she'd come too far to turn craven now, she gathered her courage and rang the bell. Still, nausea churned in her gut as she waited for the maid to answer. The wound was still too fresh, her tears too close to the surface.

Ailis herself pushed the door open with an elbow, her hands occupied in pulling off her painting smock. As she turned to see Caragh, her fingers froze on the ties.

Abandoning an attempt to smile, Caragh opened her lips to offer a greeting, but no sound emerged.

For a moment they stood staring at each other. Then Ailis tossed her apron aside and seized her sister in a rib-bruising hug. "Caragh! Oh, I'm so glad you came!"

In all the years they'd been growing up, her undemonstrative sister had rarely embraced her. As Caragh hugged her back, tears welled up and fell despite her best efforts to restrain them, catching in her sister's hair where they glistened like crystals set in a golden frame.

Finally Ailis pushed her away, her own eyes moist. "Here we stand like a pair of doltish watering-pots! Come in!" Tucking Caragh's hand in her arm, she pulled her into the room. "Higgins!" she called in the direction of what must be a small kitchen. "Bring us tea in the studio, you lazy girl!"

While Caragh removed her wrap, Ailis swept aside paint cloths and brushes to clear her a seat on the small divan, then dropped into the overstuffed chair beside it. She fastened her brilliant blue-eyed gaze on Caragh.

"You got my note, then?" At Caragh's nod, she continued, "I know I'm often oblivious to an individual's feelings, but I do know I hurt you. I'm sorry, Caragh. I didn't really mean what I said about…well, you know. When I'm angry, my tongue runs faster than my wits. But sooner or later I needed to make the break, and there was no easy way to do it. When the contretemps over Holden erupted, it seemed the perfect opportunity. I knew I must do something so…beyond the pale, that even someone as tenacious as you would have no hope of 'redeeming' me. And at least for a time, you would be too angry to try."

Caragh managed a watery smile. "You certainly succeeded."

Ailis grinned. "I don't mean to apologize for *everything*. It *is* time that you stop trying to smooth everyone else's life and get on with living your own."

"You'll be happy to know that I've come to agree with you. Not, however, without some painful reflection, so don't think to be absolved of all guilt."

"I quite refuse to accept any. Would you have ever ceased playing Wise Older Sister and Dutiful Daughter if I hadn't forced you to?"

"Once you were settled, I believe I should have reached that conclusion on my own."

"Perhaps. But you must concede my actions hastened the event. So, what is it you've decided to do?"

"Purchase more land and expand our breeding operations. You know I've had my eye on a new pair of Irish thorough-breds for the past year, but lacked the means—and space—to acquire them. With the addition of those bloodlines, within a few years Sudley foals should be the most sought-after hunting stock in England."

"So you don't intend to remain here and play the fatuous Society game? Famous! I must have Holden obtain some champagne so we may toast our new lives!"

Putting the fact that the viscount was apparently still involved with her sister aside to deal with later, Caragh said, "You've obtained the commission, then? You will be able to manage on your own?"

"Not just manage, but prosper." Her eyes taking on a spar-kle, Ailis gave her a mischievous look. "Of course, it's not quite the sort of commission you are probably envisioning."

"Is it not portrait work?"

"In a manner of speaking. 'Tis a series of life studies that will be bound in a folio. I excel at figure drawing, you know. Lord Wolverton commissioned one set, but Max tells me that quality work of this sort is so rare, he is certain that once Wolverton's friends see it, I can expect a number of other commissions to follow."

"Ailis, that's wonderful! I'm so proud for you." Caragh had

to admit to surprise, tinged with a bit of awe. She hadn't really believed that her sister would actually be able to earn a living at her art.

Ailis's smile widened. "While it isn't what I should like to do as a life's work, Max can sell the folios for so astronomical a sum that I shall have a tidy income to sustain me until I start winning commissions in oils. Besides, the drawings are rendered from life, so they are good practice, and doing them is quite…stimulating. Come, let me show you."

"I should love to see them." Rising, Caragh followed her sister to her work bench.

"This is the sketch that Lord Wolverton saw first—a study I'd done that Max liked well enough to hang in his studio. Originally I called it *Longing*."

Ailis held out to her a drawing of a young girl, her face tilted up and her misty eyes gazing into the distance with a mingling of sadness and desire. The girl's expression sounded so immediate a chord of recognition deep within her that, for a moment, Caragh ceased to breathe. "She looks as though she just lost her true love!"

"Perhaps. But Lord Wolverton thought she might have just found him." Ailis passed her a second sketch.

In this study the girl's expression had turned shy but focused, her eyes gazing out at the viewer as if mesmerized by someone beyond the picture's frame. She had loosened the wrapper she'd been wearing in the first sketch, leaving her bare shoulders exposed and telegraphing a seductive promise that caused a familiar tightening in the pit of Caragh's stomach. "Oh, my!" she said faintly.

Ailis passed her the next sketch. Only a trace of shyness remaining, the girl's eyes smoldered over her slightly parted lips while she held the robe together—just beneath her bare, taut-nippled breasts.

Caragh knew she should tell her sister to stop, but sound seemed to have dried in her throat. While she looked on mutely, Ailis presented the next.

Shy waif had disappeared, replaced by knowing Eve. The girl gazed out with confidence, wrapper sleeves at her forearms, the robe hanging open to display the whole front of her nude body, from full breasts down her rounded belly to the length of her slender legs. With her hip arched and one leg slightly bent, she held the fingers of one hand poised at the junction of her thighs, as if about to reveal the treasures within.

A flush of heat flooded Caragh's face, and she lifted a trembling hand to fan herself. "H-how many m-more?" she stuttered.

Ailis grinned. "Several. But perhaps you should sit down."

Caragh sank onto the stool Ailis pushed toward her. Which was fortunate, for her knees would probably have given way had she been standing to view the next sketch Ailis handed over. In this, the girl's unseen lover at last appeared, kneeling naked with his side to the viewer, his tongue reaching within the folds she had parted for him, his large member stiff and proudly erect.

Caragh's chest grew hot, her nipples tingled and a tight pressure coiled at the base of her thighs…at that point which the girl's lover was so assiduously stroking with his tongue.

Shocked, appalled and fascinated, she watched spellbound as Ailis displayed the rest of her sketches…the lover with his erection probing between the girl's thighs while he suckled her breast; the girl kneeling before her lover, filling her mouth with his penis; the two side by side, the lover's tongue buried in the girl's mound while she licked his taut member; and finally, the girl with her legs drawn up, her head lolling back and her hands clenched on her partner's shoulders while he thrust himself between her parted thighs.

"I now call the series *The Seduction,*" Ailis said as she reassembled the sketches.

For a long moment Caragh sat stunned. She had seen sketches of nude classical sculpture in her father's library and as a country girl, knew the rudiments of how animals coupled. But never before had she been made aware, in graphic terms, of the way in which a man and a woman could use their bodies to give each other pleasure.

When her stupefied brain finally resumed functioning, her first thought was to wonder how *Ailis* knew about it. "*Y-you* sketched these? But…but how could you?"

Ailis laughed. "Oh, Caragh, you're such an innocent!" Still chuckling, she walked over to pour a steaming cup of tea from a pot the maid must have brought while Caragh was sitting mesmerized. Handing it to her, she said, "Holden wasn't my first lover. Several years ago—"

"S-several *years?*" Caragh gasped.

"—when I became fascinated with figure study, I noticed a farm boy in the fields north of Sudley who possessed quite a magnificent physique. For a few pennies, I persuaded him to model for me. And, as I'm sure you can now understand, viewing his…attributes elicited a heated curiosity as to just how he might employ them. I now know he wasn't particularly skilled, but on the whole, the experience was both enjoyable and instructive."

"But the risks you took! What if you'd conceived a child?"

Ailis shrugged. "I didn't. At any rate, I know to take the proper precautions now."

Dizzy from trying to assimilate such a barrage of revelations, Caragh did not pursue that point. "But afterward? Were you not embarrassed to encounter the boy?"

"For a few more pennies, I had him promise not to approach Sudley land again." Ailis smiled. "He seemed rather dazed by the experience. Were he literate, I expect he would have claimed he was but a poor mortal seduced and abandoned by Aphrodite, disguised as an English gentlewoman."

"I can imagine," Caragh murmured, still astounded.

"One of the benefits of residing in London is the ease of obtaining models. As you can understand, it's better for the study of technique to work with a live model—"

"You sketched a model doing…that?" Caragh asked, her voice rising to a squeak.

"The girl was a prostitute, of course, so I expect she's performed acts more inventive than those. I haven't yet found a male model, so to compose some of the sketches, I posed myself and Holden before a mirror." Ailis chuckled again. "The darling boy was quite willing to participate."

Rendered once more bereft of speech, Caragh thought for the first time that it was perhaps beneficial that Ailis had left her family to set up her studio. If Aunt Kitty had ever discovered such sketches in Ailis's room, the poor lady would have expired in a fit of apoplexy.

Caragh wasn't entirely sure her own heart, still thumping wildly against her ribs, was strong enough.

"I can see you are quite overwhelmed, so I'll say no more for now. Besides, there's something else I wanted to ask. If you've decided to run your farm instead of clawing your way back to a place among the ton, you must have given up the idea of making a Society marriage. So what do you mean to do about Quentin?"

From lust to Quentin wasn't a far leap in Caragh's mind, but her still-overheated senses were making speech difficult. While she fumbled for words, Ailis waved a hand impatiently. "You needn't try to deny you're smitten by him. I may be absorbed in my work, but I'm neither blind nor dumb. Do you mean to marry him?"

That question effectively doused Caragh's ardor. "After your disgrace, he made me an offer. A noble sacrifice to save me becoming a spinster."

"Am I to understand you've refused this gallant gesture?"

"Yes. I hardly wish to marry a man inspired to wed me out of pity."

Ailis raised her eyebrows. "I would wager 'pity' has little to do with it, but 'tis your own affair. Marriage is a rather dismal business in any event. But love-play—ah, now that is a different matter altogether. If you lust for Quentin as I think you do, then make him your lover."

Remembering her pathetic efforts already in that vein, Caragh laughed out loud. "Let me assure you, Ailis, I have no skill whatsoever in enticing a man! Besides, Quentin will always see me as his virginal, gently-born maiden neighbor. Should I succeed in seducing him, his honor would demand that he marry me afterwards. Which is almost as revolting a reason to propose to me as pity."

"You must do as you wish. But I still say if you want him, do what is necessary to get him." Ailis winked at her. "I can give some advice, if you like."

Before Caragh could decide whether or not she wanted to avail herself of that offer, from the room beyond she heard a clock strike the hour. "Heavens!" she gasped, "I completely forgot the time! Thank you for the tea, but if I'm not to be late for dinner, I must get back."

With a shrewd look, Ailis waved her toward the exit. "Yes, better return before Aunt Kitty misses you. Higgins will summon a hackney. Wait a moment before you walk down, though. I have something I think you must have." Ailis jumped up and strode to her workbench.

Moving by rote, Caragh put on her pelisse and gloves. Her body still tingled and her thoughts stopped and stuttered as she tried to assimilate the incredible information—and images—revealed to her over the last hour.

Ailis caught up with her by the door, surprising her with another quick, fierce hug. "I'm glad we've reached an understanding."

"So am I," Caragh replied, and meant it. After tonight, she would carry with her a radically different image of her sister. No longer the strong-willed, selfish child who needed her sister to tend her, Ailis had become a self-absorbed but independent woman with, Caragh realized with a touch of humility, a worldly experience far greater than her own.

"For you," Ailis said, handing her a folded piece of drawing paper.

Caragh would have thought she'd received too many jolts already this evening to be moved by anything else, but as she unfolded the gift, a bolt of surprise—and desire—flashed through her.

The pencil drawing, apparently a study for one of her sister's commissioned works, featured a naked man reclining on his side—displaying an impressive full erection. A man who smiled seductively at her from Quentin's face.

"Ailis, how could you?" she cried, torn between outrage and amusement.

"Oh, it took me but a moment to alter it to Quent's features," her irrepressible sister replied. "Keep it—and dream about him."

At that moment, Higgins skipped up the stairs to tell her the hackney had arrived.

Ailis tugged the drawing free and refolded it, then held it out. "Come visit me again."

After a half-second's hesitation, Caragh took the sketch back. "I will."

Bemused and unsettled, Caragh followed the maid to the waiting hackney. After the great blow her sister had dealt her, her affection for Ailis would be forever altered. But the gaping breach between them that had so blighted her spirit was a fair way to being healed.

Caragh felt a warm expansiveness, a new hope flooding her. Anything was possible, she thought jubilantly. Perhaps even— her thumbs caressed the drawing—seducing Quentin Burke.

CHAPTER THIRTEEN

LISTENING with half an ear to her aunt's chatter, Caragh sat through dinner, her mind still churning over the events of the late afternoon. But after the footman came to clear the plates, her aunt's cheery voice wavered, recalling Caragh's attention.

Obviously thinking about the variety of entertainments which, several weeks previous, she would have been readying herself to attend at this hour, Lady Catherine put on a brave smile. "Should you like to try a hand of whist in the parlor, dear? If not, I have that chair cover I've been meaning to finish this age."

Guilt jabbed at Caragh. Now that her mission here was nearly accomplished, she really must stop putting off a discussion of her future and reveal to the kind relative who had supported her so valiantly what a viper she was still nurturing in her bosom.

"Let's just have a comfortable coze, shall we?"

Lady Catherine's face brightened. "I should love it! I understand how…distressing this whole affair must have been for you! Your hopes for Ailis so cruelly dashed, and as for your own…" Her aunt heaved a sigh. "I hadn't wished to press you into discussing it until you were ready, but I think it an excellent idea for us to begin redesigning your future."

Knowing how her aunt was likely to feel about her plans, Caragh's resolve almost wavered. But her dear aunt deserved better of her than to learn her intentions at the last moment. "Shall I bring us more wine?"

Lady Catherine nodded. Girding herself, Caragh poured two glassfuls and followed her aunt into the parlor.

"I know we've suffered some...reverses, but you needn't be too cast down," Lady Catherine said as she seated herself. "I am still Somebody, after all, and more important, I can count at least two of Almack's patronesses as bosom bows. What we must do first—"

"Aunt Kitty, I know you would willingly trade upon your well-deserved reputation to ease me back into Society, but I really feel I must take a...different path."

"Oh, dear." Her aunt's smile faded and she took a quick sip of wine. "I'm not going to like what I'm about to hear, am I?"

Caragh smiled, her eyes misting. "I'm afraid not—at least, not initially."

Lady Catherine took a larger gulp. "You'd best open the budget and tell me the whole, then."

"You know Papa has given me free rein to manage both the house and estate at Sudley for years. Since a husband would probably wish to take over my finances and my stables and relegate me to household affairs, I believe I prefer to remain unwed. I'm happiest working with my horses. In fact, I'm about to expand the breeding operation. I came back to London to arrange the purchase of additional land."

"But Caragh, you were hardly in town long enough to meet anyone before Ailis...well, my dear, let me assure you, when you make the acquaintance of the right gentleman, all thought of who manages what will go right out of your head! Please, give it more time before you convince yourself that marriage will not suit you."

Caragh offered a rueful smile. "I'm afraid the rub is that I've already met such a man, Aunt Kitty, but…but he does not return my regard. With my feelings already fully engaged, I cannot envision developing a *tendre* for someone else. So it's best I resign myself to spinsterhood."

"My poor darling! But you mustn't give up! There are ways to…move such a situation along. An intimate tête-à-tête unexpectedly interrupted—"

"Oh no, Aunt Kitty!" Caragh cried, torn between amusement and gratitude. "If he does not wish to wed me willingly, then there is an end to it."

"Few gentleman ever wish to wed *willingly*," Lady Catherine countered with some exasperation. "Most have to be…assisted to that decision! I promise you, taking a husband will be infinitely more pleasing than residing with your father. And though I was never so blessed, there is always the possibility of children. Besides, what shall you do after Archibald inherits? You cannot imagine that he will leave you in charge of the Sudley stables."

"No." Fidgeting with her wineglass, Caragh took a deep breath. "I expect I didn't make myself perfectly clear. I do not intend to remain at Sudley with Papa. I shall be moving all my horses to the land now being purchased—of which I shall be sole owner. So Cousin Archibald inheriting Sudley will have no effect on me."

Her aunt's eyes widened as she comprehended the full implications of that speech. "Y-you will live there without your Papa? And operate—a breeding farm? But Caragh, your clients will be almost solely—gentleman!"

"Yes, I suppose they will."

"Once word of this gets about, your reputation will be ruined almost as effectively as Ailis's!" Lady Catherine wailed.

"It won't be quite that bad," Caragh tried to appease her. "I shall be immured in the country, and you know the ton cares little for anything that occurs outside—"

"Breeding *horses!* Oh, this must be all your mama's doing!" Aunt Kitty burst in. "But how? I screened the letters you received most particularly, just as I promised your Papa!"

"Mama's doing?" Caragh echoed. Had the distress of envisioning a second social disaster overset her poor aunt's mind? "Now Aunt Kitty, you know that…"

As she watched her aunt's indignant face, the incredible suspicion crystallizing in her head made her lose track of her sentence. "You can't mean Mama is…still alive? But…but I thought she died of influenza when Ailis was in short skirts!"

"Would that she had, the unnatural creature!" Lady Catherine said crossly. "Especially as it appears she has inspired both her daughters to behave almost as badly as ever *she* did!"

"Mama truly is alive, then? Does Ailis know?"

Her irritation fading, Lady Catherine looked suddenly uncertain. "You mean Aurora…has not contacted you?"

"No! Until this moment, I thought her dead these fifteen years."

"Oh, dear," Lady Catherine said faintly. "Then I'm afraid I have been vastly indiscreet. Your Papa will be so vexed with me!"

Caragh waved an impatient hand. "He will never learn of it. So tell me, where is my mother? Where has she hidden all these years? And what did she do that caused everyone to tell us she had died?"

Lady Catherine took another sip of wine. "I suppose it is too late to insist I know nothing about it?"

"Much too late. Granted, she figures in my memory only as a beautiful lady who occasionally deigned to visit her grubby offspring, but still, I'm curious. And I *am* her daughter, little acquainted with her as I was. Do I not have a right to know?"

Lady Catherine sighed. "I suppose you do. But I fear there will be quite a dust-up when Michael discovers what I've let slip."

"Unless the details have somehow become embedded in the original Greek of the *Iliad,* you have nothing to worry about. Have another sip of wine and tell me everything."

As if in need of more than just a sip, Lady Catherine drained her glass. Setting it down, she began, "Aurora was stunningly beautiful, you know—Ailis is her image."

"Which is why Papa has always favored Ailis," Caragh said drily.

"Michael was just down from Oxford, a hopeless scholar, his head stuffed full of poetical nonsense. What must he do but take one look at Aurora Wendover, riding neck-or-nothing to the hounds at some hunt, and tumble head over heels! The most frivolous chit in the ton, and he's declaring her to be the very embodiment of some heathenish deity."

"Aurora, goddess of the dawn? Or the huntress Diana?"

Lady Catherine waved a hand. "Goodness, how should I know? Since Michael was handsome and his verses celebrating her perfection quite superior to the drivel generally spouted by her court, she deigned to consider herself in love with him, too—for a time."

"It didn't last?"

Lady Catherine uttered an unladylike sniff. "I tried to tell my brother how unsuitable a match it was! But he wouldn't listen—and Aurora had long since learned to manipulate her papa into allowing her whatever she wanted. They married and Michael bore her off to Sudley, eager to craft a new folio of verses in her honor. I suppose for a time, with their mutual love of horses, they may have been happy. But Aurora Wendover was not created to live quietly in rural obscurity. As soon as she recovered from her confinement with Ailis, she began pestering your papa to take her back to London. The spring before Ailis turned five, he finally did."

"Where she once again conquered the ton."

Lady Catherine nodded. "Yes, despite being a mother and quite old! Between the court of dandies hanging about her drawing room and the crowd trailing her wherever she went, she drove poor Michael to fits of jealousy, especially over some count in the Italian ambassador's retinue. When the Season ended and Michael insisted they return to Sudley, there was a dreadful row. The next thing I knew, Michael was at my door virtually incoherent, and Aurora had run off to Italy with her count!"

"Did she divorce Papa to marry him?"

"I don't believe so. As a papist, the Italian couldn't have married a divorced woman—and he may have already had a wife, for all I know! In any event, Aurora didn't remain with him long. Ever skilled at manipulating, she managed to coax her heartbroken papa into settling a handsome income on her. I understand she hired a villa in Rome and bought a country estate in Tuscany. She lives there now, spending the season in town, patronizing the arts—and taking lovers half her age."

"She sounds fascinating!"

"She has a most unsteady character and I am heartily sorry that you and Ailis share her blood." Lady Catherine said roundly. "My poor brother never recovered. He found what solace he could in his books, gradually withdrawing from the world until now I believe he scarce notices anything that did not transpire some ten or twenty centuries ago."

Suddenly Caragh was arrested by the memory of her father's melancholy face. No wonder his eyes were always sad, his thoughts turned from a painful reality to an inner world he could order and control. "Poor Papa."

"Well, now you know the whole. If you are set on burying yourself on this horse farm, I suppose I can comfort myself with the knowledge that, though you are bidding fair to be as unconventional as Aurora, at least you'll not create quite so public a scandal."

Impulsively Caragh reached over to hug her aunt. "Thank you, Aunt Kitty! For taking me on to begin with, given my history. And for loving me despite my faults."

Her aunt hugged her back. "I might deserve your thanks, if only I'd managed to get you respectably settled. But if you will not allow me to attempt that, at least promise me you'll be happy, child."

"I shall certainly try to be."

"Now, if you'll excuse me, dear, I believe I shall go up to bed. I'm feeling a bit...overwhelmed."

"I'll take you up."

After leaving her aunt with another hug, Caragh continued on to her bedroom. She let the maid help her into her night rail, but once the girl departed, her mind racing with too many ideas and observations to find sleep, she abandoned her bed and curled up in the wing chair by the fire.

Never in the wildest flights of fancy could she have imagined what she'd learned this day! That Ailis, who had taken a lover at sixteen and seduced Lord Freemont, would be earning her living—sketching erotic art! That their mother, very much alive, was leading a still-scandalous existence in Rome. Though her sister—as she had bitter reason to know, Caragh thought with a muted pang—seemed to place scant value on familial ties, she still ought to tell Ailis their mother was not, as they'd grown up believing, among the Dearly Departed. But since her sister had little interest in anything that did not directly touch on her art, there was no urgency in conveying the news.

Caragh shook her head and laughed. At least she and Ailis came by their unconventional behavior honestly.

She stilled, listening carefully to confirm all was quiet and the household abed. Then she went to the desk, unlocked the top drawer, and drew out the drawing Ailis had given her. A wave of heat that had nothing to do with the fire in the grate washed over her as she studied it.

What if Quentin were here with her now, lounging nude on her sofa? She grinned at the possibilities. How would his… endowments compare with what Ailis had sketched?

Make him your lover, her sister urged. Being her scandalous mother's unconventional daughter, perhaps she should.

THE FOLLOWING DAY, Quentin set out for London. After Caragh's refusal of his suit and her unexpected departure, he'd returned to Thornwhistle to take the one rational action he'd managed to filter from their turgid confusion of an interview. Though he had not yet given up hope of dissuading Caragh from her disastrous notion of running a farm, it was high time he ensured his property was being properly run by his own estate manager, without benefit of advice from his neighbor.

But though that work kept him occupied for several days, it did nothing to soothe the queasy mix of uncertainty, anger and concern that still troubled him. Until Caragh had disappeared, some alien spirit taking her place within the outwardly familiar body of his friend, he'd not realized how much he depended upon her level-headed intelligence, how much he enjoyed her wit and warmth.

To put it simply, he missed her.

His immediate reaction, of course, after having been rebuffed in absentia that second time, was to let her go her own way if she valued his opinions so little. But by the second day after her departure, the pride-driven desire to hold himself aloof began to crumble. By the time he'd assured himself of Manning's competence, he'd decided to set aside his hurt and seek her out.

Perhaps, he told himself as he journeyed back to London, her unprecedented behavior was merely the product of shock and distress after being pitched so unprepared into Ailis's scandal. Quite understandable under the circumstances, and a lapse he'd willingly forgive.

To determine how best to approach her, he needed to ascertain how serious she was about carrying through this plan to expand the Sudley breeding farm. Then he could figure out how to persuade her that marrying him would be the right choice, whether or not she went through with it.

For he'd found, once he got himself over the hurdle of actually framing a proposal, that he rather liked the idea of contracting a sensible, practical marriage of convenience with his best friend. Or at least he had until that stranger back at Sudley had coolly rebuffed him.

Surely, having had time by now to recover her normal

composure, the Caragh he called upon in London would be the same Caragh he knew and valued so highly. They could discuss the matter of a future together rationally, and with the addition of the right lover-like words, he would induce her to agree it was in both their best interests to combine their resources in marriage.

Combine their bodies as well. But he'd best put that distracting thought out of mind until he'd obtained her consent to his proposal.

He had another, previously postponed reason for returning to the metropolis. At his first opportunity, he intended to seek out Ailis Sudley and tell just what he thought about her self-centered lack of appreciation for her sister's efforts and her callous disregard of Caragh's feelings and reputation.

He reached London in the late afternoon and, still uncertain whether to seek out Caragh immediately or send a note announcing his return to town, he decided instead to call on Ailis. He felt no uncertainty whatsoever about what he needed to tell *her*. Besides, Ailis might have some news about Caragh that would give him a hint about how to approach her.

As soon as he refreshed himself from the journey, he set out for Ailis's studio, where a maidservant led him through a small anteroom to an open chamber whose large north-facing windows telegraphed its purpose as eloquently as the clutter of paints, canvas rolls and brushes that dotted every level surface. Clad in an outmoded day gown, her sleeves pushed up, Ailis sat on a sofa to receive him.

"Quentin, how kind of you to come visit."

A note of irony colored her voice. He cast her a sharp glance, but she was smiling pleasantly. Though the words of the diatribe he'd come to deliver pressed heavily upon his tongue, he ought to be civil and exchange a few pleasantries before launching his attack.

"What a handsome studio! I imagine the morning light is splendid."

She nodded. "It is, and holds well into afternoon. I've been able to make great progress since moving here."

"You've obtained work?"

"Yes, I'm just finishing a very lucrative commission." Her smile deepened. "I shall have to show it to you sometime."

"Caragh approves?"

"She was a bit shocked at first, but I believe she enthusiastically supports it now. She has visited me here, you know, and I'm pleased to say we are once again in perfect charity."

"I don't doubt it—Caragh being ever generous to those she loves." Unable to keep the edge out of his voice, Quentin continued, "I do wonder, though, after Caragh championed your art for years and attempted to arrange your future to accommodate it, how you could have played so low a trick on her. I grant that you are young and blinded by your muse, but surely you've noticed how hard she works at Sudley, always putting everyone else's needs before her own. Was it really too much to ask to let her have a whole Season to enjoy herself before you did this—" he gestured around the room "—and destroyed it all for her?"

While he spoke, his voice rising in volume as he proceeded, Ailis's smile faded and her eyes turned hard. She listened to his jobation in silence, making no attempt to reply until he stopped for breath.

"Have you finished yet?"

Her coolness, her total lack of remorse, incensed him. "No, I have not! How could you hurt her so? You do at least understand that you hurt her, I trust! She's been looking after you with a mother's devotion since she was barely more than a child herself, and how did you repay her for that loving concern? With deceit, scandal and disgrace!"

Ailis arched an eyebrow. "My, my, and who appointed Quentin Burke judge and jury? Before you become too assiduous about examining the log in my eye, perhaps you'd better look in the mirror and examine your own."

"And just what do you mean by that?"

She rose from the sofa and walked over to glare at him. "Just that it isn't only at Sudley that Caragh worked hard all these years. I seem to recall her traveling quite often to Thornwhistle, too. Rearranging her schedule to accommodate your calls when you deigned to visit, toiling late to finish her own tasks after you'd left. If I selfishly received the care she freely gave without offering a return, have you done any better? Did you ever look beyond the obliging friend to determine what the woman beneath might wish? Perhaps, my lord, you should answer *that* question before you accuse *me* of taking advantage. Now I must change. Higgins will show you out."

Without giving him a chance to reply, she turned away and, as Quentin stared after her in disbelief, for the second time this week, a Sudley female walked out on him.

Rising to his feet with such vehemence that his chair rocked on its legs, he stalked to the door.

How dare Ailis accuse *him* of selfishness and insensitivity! he fumed as he pounded down the stairs. Caragh had assisted him on many occasions, it was true, but he helped her as well. They were devoted friends who always sought the best for each other!

At the echo of Ailis's strident question, Quentin's pace

faltered. Out of memory bubbled up Caragh's soft voice asking if it might not be possible to add passion to their relationship—a possibility he had firmly rejected.

An uneasy feeling settling in his chest, he continued down the stairs. Could there be at least a germ of truth to Ailis's accusation? Had he ever truly asked himself what *Caragh* wanted from their relationship?

Or had he only considered how to maintain their friendship in the fashion most acceptable to *him,* arbitrarily accepting as a given that Caragh wanted the same thing he did?

By the time he reached the street he'd slowed to a walk, his anger muted to a slow burn. Perhaps he had been a little…forceful…in insisting on the terms of their relationship. For the best of reasons, of course—to keep that precious bond intact. But he had decided on that course rather…unilaterally.

And he could have seized more opportunities to express his appreciation for the care she expended on Thornwhistle, as well as his admiration for her intelligence and wit.

Frowning, he paced down the street. Surely he could discount most of Ailis's speech as merely a way of parrying his verbal onslaught by mounting a counterattack of her own.

Caragh couldn't think of him selfish and dictatorial… could she?

Still, the possibility that Caragh might entertain even a muted version of the opinion of him expressed by Ailis was deeply troubling. An even more unpalatable thought followed hard upon that.

Had she refused his suit not out of the confusion and distress engendered by the scandal, but because she found him in his own way as selfish and unappreciative as her sister?

He simply couldn't believe it. But little as he credited it, the notion was too disturbing to dismiss out of hand.

He must call upon Caragh first thing tomorrow and lay that anxiety permanently to rest.

CHAPTER FOURTEEN

AFTER A RESTLESS NIGHT, awakening at intervals from vivid dreams in which she and Quentin replaced the models in Ailis's sketches, Caragh awoke, her body still tingling, a dull throb pulsing between her thighs.

She pushed herself to a sitting position, the friction of the night rail's linen against her taut nipples sparking a thrill of sensation. Ah, if that glancing caress had come from Quentin's fingers!

She fanned her heated face. Could she overcome modesty and upbringing and find the boldness that would put his hands there? Equally important, could she trespass upon their friendship to trick Quentin to it? For if she were sure of nothing else, she knew beyond doubt that Quentin Burke would expire from lust before he would bed a gently-born virgin.

Her mother had destroyed a family to pursue what she wanted. Caragh would never go that far, but with her reputation already lost and the man she desired unmarried, she could follow her desires without hurting anyone.

Except perhaps herself. But could the anguish of Quentin leaving her after lying in her arms be any worse than the anguish of living without him, forever bereft of his touch?

If she succeeded in seducing him, she would have the memory of that closeness to cherish. She would have relief from the fire smoldering within her and a personal knowledge of the powerful, inexplicable force that bonds men and women together.

And she would have been very clever in disguising her identity, for if Quentin ever succeeded in uncovering her ruse, his anger and his honor would force him to coerce her into marriage. The only outcome she could envision that would be worse than her current misery would be to trip herself into wedlock with a man who didn't truly love her.

Was a night of Quentin's love worth taking that risk?

Caragh leaned back against the pillows and drew Ailis's sketch from beneath her pillow. Her body flamed anew as she traced a fingertip down the outline of the bare shoulder and torso, across the length of the taut erection.

To have her hands touch not cool parchment but warm flesh, her fingers—and lips—explore not an artist's sketch but the man out of her dreams, would, she decided, be worth every risk.

She would have to be very careful. But before she left London to begin her new life, she would seduce Quentin Burke.

Laudable audacity, she thought with a sigh as she carefully refolded the sketch and rang for her morning chocolate. She still hadn't the faintest idea how she could bring it about.

But Ailis might. So this evening, Caragh would pay her sister another visit.

Shivering against the morning chill, she threw on a wrapper and drew a chair close to the hearth. After the maid delivered a tray, she warmed her hands over the steaming brew and glanced at the morning paper.

Sipping chocolate, she read in a desultory fashion, her thoughts frequently distracted by flashbacks to last night's torrid dreams, speculation about how she could engineer a seduction, and curiosity over how her sister had produced those amazing…figure studies.

She'd skimmed the political news and several pages of society gossip when a small advertisement caught her attention—the announcement of a Grand Masquerade Ball to be held at Vauxhall Gardens on Friday next, with Refreshments and a Superior Orchestra to Delight the Discerning Guest.

A masquerade ball! As her mind focused on the possibilities, a knock sounded at the door.

"Beggin' your pardon, miss, but Lord Branson is waiting below to see you. Will you receive him?"

Though she could have wished for more time, the outlines of a plan were already forming. "Tell Lord Branson I will be down directly."

HEARTENED when the maid returned to inform him that Caragh would receive him—for he'd half feared, if Ailis's accusations had any merit, that she might refuse to see him—Quentin rehearsed once again what he intended to say.

Avoiding any mention of his previous offer, inquiring about her plans and expressing once again his appreciation for her efforts on his behalf would do for a start, he decided. He would then take his cue from Caragh on where to proceed next.

Hearing voices approach, he straightened and wiped his suddenly damp palms on his pant leg. Oh, that the lady who walked through that door would be *his* Caragh, rather than the chilly stranger he'd encountered at Sudley!

A welcoming smile on her face, Caragh came toward him, hands extended. "Quentin, what a delightful surprise! I thought you still at Thornwhistle."

Joy and a relief so intense he felt momentarily light-headed washed through him. *His* Caragh was back.

He seized her hands in a punishing grip and kissed them fervently. The immediate punch of contact as their gloved hands met, as his lips grazed her knuckles, rocketed through him. For a moment, all he could think was how much he'd missed her—and how much more he craved of her touch.

Finally pulling his mind back to the moment, he said, "I've only just arrived. I regret that our…visit at Sudley was so short. You must tell me how your plans are progressing."

If she wished to make some explanation—or apology—for the manner in which she had received his proposal, he'd just given her a perfect opening.

He braced himself, but with no discernable constraint or embarrassment, she answered, "Quite well, thank you. And I am doing much better, too, so you'll have no need to amuse me with absurdities, as you did that day at Sudley."

"Amuse you?" he asked cautiously.

"Yes—with that spurious offer of marriage! I must admit, you fooled me at first into thinking it a legitimate offer, which made me quite angry, until upon reflection I realized your intent. After all, you couldn't have truly called yourself my friend and made a serious offer."

"I…I couldn't?"

She laughed. "Of course not! To suggest, after all the years I've managed Sudley, that I was not capable of suitably handling the masculine attention inherent in expanding the farm—most of which would come from clients who are already well acquainted with my family—would have been insulting, to me and to them. And to offer marriage because you felt sorry for my situation would have been unsupportable…had you been in earnest, of course."

"Of…of course."

"If I've learned anything about you over the years of our friendship, Quentin, it is that you judge by what you know to be true, not by the artificial dictates of Society. You've assured me on several occasions that you admire my skill at estate management and respect my independence. How silly of me, even for a moment, to think you would suddenly begin to question either! I can only attribute it to the…distress I was experiencing at that moment."

"Yes, I could see you were…distressed."

"After all, had we not, just a bare week previous, decided that—" she turned her head away, her cheeks coloring "—that passion and friendship would not mix? To have taken it upon yourself to alter those terms unilaterally, without consulting *my* preferences, would have been arrogant, presumptuous and insensitive."

"Arrogant, presumptuous and insensitive?" he echoed, inwardly appalled. "I suppose you could say that."

"And I know you are none of those," she affirmed, pressing his hand warmly.

Once again, as her fingers lingered on his, that immediate connection between them fired his senses. He fought the effect, knowing he dare not risk another blunder.

"I hope you also know," he said, struggling to find the proper words, "that however…unfortunately I may have expressed myself, all I ever sought was your happiness."

Her breezy smile faded and her face grew almost…sad. "I know," she whispered. For a moment she let her fingers rest in his. Then, withdrawing her hand with a slow, lingering caress that he felt down to his toes, she said in a bright tone, "Now, let me tell you where things stand on the expansion of my enterprise."

Arrogant? Insensitive? Presumptuous? Shocked to discover how Caragh had viewed his offer, Quentin only half heard the details she rattled off about her land purchase. Though he had certainly not intended to be any of those things, after examining that ill-fated proposal from her perspective, he had to reluctantly admit there might be some justification for her viewing it that way.

He *had* rather blindly proceeded according to the social convention that proclaimed an unmarried maiden must always be gratified by a proposal of marriage, regardless of its reason or wording. Nor had he accompanied his offer by avowing any tender feelings. And were Ailis to once again pose her pointed question, he would have to admit that in this instance, as the first time he'd discussed the nature of their relationship with Caragh, he had failed to consult her opinion, presuming to decide for them both that marriage was the best course.

"I did wish to ask for one favor, Quentin."

He jerked his attention back to the present. "A…a favor? Ask what you will, and if 'tis within my power to give, it is yours."

For an instant her glance caught his. "Would that it were," he thought he heard her murmur. But before he could ask her to repeat the comment, she seized his arm, once again rattling his concentration.

"Nothing too arduous, I assure you," she continued. "It's just…well, as you know, my social schedule is rather…restricted at present, and soon I shall be back in the country, where entertainments are even more limited. I should very much like to attend the masquerade ball at Vauxhall Friday, but of course, I could not go to such an affair without an escort."

A deep wave of sympathy welled up to war with the sensual pull. Of course, banned from balls and parties as she was, she would pine for some amusement. "I should be happy to escort you. Will Lady Catherine go also?"

"I don't think so. She, ah, does not care for masquerades. I'm to meet with the lawyers that afternoon to finish details of the land purchase, so I may need to meet you directly at Vauxhall—I'll send a note. Speaking of which, I have an appointment with them shortly, so I must bid you good-day."

She rose, once again giving him her hands to kiss. He covered them with his own, relishing the contact and loath to break it. "Until Friday, then."

She curtseyed. Reluctantly he released her and bowed. As he reached the door, she called his name. He turned back with an inquiring look.

"Thank you for being my friend."

He smiled, his blood still humming at her nearness. "You can count on me," he assured her, and walked out.

That had not gone too badly, he told himself as he climbed into the hackney Evers summoned for him. He'd avoided a repetition of the disaster at Sudley and, he hoped, moved them further down the path of restoring to their friendship its previous comfortable intimacy.

He looked down at his still-tingling fingers. Well, almost comfortable.

Though he was nearly certain she'd known his proposal to be genuine, she'd pretended otherwise, allowing them to proceed beyond her refusal with a minimum of awkwardness and recrimination. She'd even given him a way to retreat from the shoal-filled waters of renewing his suit.

All he need do was continue to acquiesce in the charade that his proposal had been merely an attempt to amuse her out of her distress, and he had every reason to believe they would eventually recapture the same warm and easy relationship they'd shared before the upheavals that occurred after Caragh brought Ailis to London.

There remained the thorny problem of dissuading her from abandoning her father and moving to her new farm alone, but since he'd evidently offended her so deeply by suggesting a marriage of convenience, perhaps that too could be finessed under the guise of friendship.

Which should have relieved and pleased him—except that by now, he was almost sure a platonic friendship with Caragh Sudley was no longer what he truly wanted.

JUST AFTER DUSK, after sending Aunt Kitty into palpitations by informing her she meant to visit Ailis, Caragh arrived at her sister's studio. To her relief, her sister had already finished her day's work and reclined on her sofa, a glass of wine in hand.

"Sorry to burst in on you unannounced," Caragh said as she walked in, "but I must tell you—I mean to do it! And I shall need your advice on how to make my plan succeed."

Ailis's eyes lit with comprehension. "You propose to seduce Quentin? Bravo! Let's drink to that resolve, and you shall tell me how I can help."

While Ailis called for another glass, Caragh paced, too nervous to sit. "There's to be a masquerade ball at Vauxhall Friday, and I've obtained Quentin's promise to meet me there. Now I must determine where to meet him, in what disguise I should appear, and how I shall convince him to…to ravish me."

"Must you be disguised?" Ailis asked, handing her the wine.

"Certainly! Should I succeed in making us lovers, and he somehow recognized me, you know what that would mean."

"Ah, yes, the gentleman's sense of honor. He'd have you riveted as soon as a special license could be bought. We cannot have that! One of my models is an actress at Drury Lane—she can help with the disguise. And we must think where you are to take him. Though trysting in the open can be delightful—" Ailis winked at her "—Vauxhall is much too public for you to be comfortable seducing him there."

"Indeed not!" Caragh cried, her cheeks pinking at the very idea of performing the acts shown in Ailis's sketches in a location, however dimly lit and secluded, into which other people might at any moment wander. "What do you suggest?"

"Let me think about it. Surely Max or one of his friends will know of some suitable place."

Her embarrassment deepening, Caragh took a sip of wine. "What I most need you to advise me about, though, is how I…get him to that point. I have no experience with men, you know. If I can't entice him, arranging the disguise and the rendezvous will be wasted effort."

"True, although I doubt you will have much difficulty persuading him—he's a man, isn't he? But you must know more than just how to entice." Ailis looked at her thoughtfully. "Whatever persona you choose, for your deception to succeed, you shall have to appear experienced in the giving of pleasure. In fact, it would be best if you were to inflame his senses and then satisfy him so exquisitely, he will cease to think at all, much less have the wit to connect the siren who seduced him with the proper, virginal maiden she vaguely resembles."

The notion of bringing Quentin Burke completely in thrall to her sensual control made her dizzy with delight—and desire. "That sounds wonderful. But how can I learn to do that? Do you," she could feel her blush deepening, "have more… more…sketches I could study?"

Ailis grinned. "Though I consider myself fairly skilled, I think for this, you need the advice of a master! I've just contracted to do a portrait of Lady Belle Marchand. Do you know of her?"

"Lady Belle? Isn't she the courtesan Lord Bellingham has had in keeping for years? The one the Duke of York offered him ten thousand pounds to relinquish—and he refused?"

"The same. If her reputation is any indication, I wager she knows more about bewitching a man than any female living. And she really is a delightful lady."

"You've met her?" Caragh gasped, scandalized to think of her little sister actually consorting with this most infamous of the Fashionable Impures.

"How else could I decide whether or not I wished to paint her likeness? I shall send her a note asking her to come by early tomorrow evening. Rachel can stop by before her performance as well. So let us toast to tomorrow, sister dear. With our expert assistance, you shall soon give Quentin Burke the most erotic night of his life!"

CHAPTER FIFTEEN

AILIS ANSWERED the door the next evening upon Caragh's first knock, glass of wine in hand. "Let the transformation begin!" she cried, passing the glass to Caragh and sweeping her into the room.

Already nervous about the undertaking, Caragh downed a large gulp. "Have my...tutors arrived?"

"Rachel is here. Lady Belle shall not stop by until later, once we've perfected the disguise. You shall need to be wearing it when she gives her instructions, to insure you can follow them while garbed in different dress." Ailis laughed and whirled Caragh around. "This shall be so entertaining!"

"Let's hope it's not a farce," Caragh muttered, downing another gulp of wine.

"Nonsense, you shall be perfect. That is, you are still sure you want to do this, aren't you?"

Caragh smiled wryly. "Do I want to? Yes. Am I sure I can manage it? No. Am I frightened out of my wits about failing? Absolutely!"

As they walked into the studio, a curvaceous brunette rose from the sofa. "Fail to seduce a man? My dear, 'tis almost impossible! Seeing that most of 'em think of little else, a smile and a wink is usually enough."

"Caragh, meet Rachel DuVollet, currently of Drury Lane. Rachel, my sister Caragh."

"You are performing with Edmund Kean, are you not? I thought your Lady Macbeth particularly fine."

The actress looked at her with heightened interest. "I'm flattered that you noticed. With Edmund on the stage, the rest of us have a tendency to be ignored."

"Is he very difficult to work with?"

Rachel laughed. "We thespians are a rather selfish breed at best. If Edmund weren't so remarkable an actor, I doubt he could induce anyone to take the stage with him. Speaking of acting, what role shall you play to bedazzle your gentleman?"

"It will be dark, you will be masked and Rachel will help us alter your appearance, but you shall still need some convincing persona if you wish to avoid his recognizing you," Ailis said.

Caragh crossed her arms and struck a woeful pose. "Ah, *chérie,* I am but a poor widow, forced to flee *la France* with my darling Phillippe, who later gave his life *en combattant* Boneparte, that monster Corsican."

"Magnifique!" Ailis cried, while the actress clapped her hands. "Since you can hardly accomplish this mute, I worried he might know your voice. But your French is excellent and that accent delightful. He shall be charmed—and completely taken in."

"I sincerely hope so," Caragh said with a sigh.

"Widow's black is a good choice for gown and veil," Rachel said. "Especially at night, 'twill mask your features better than any other color. Muffle your voice, too. Add a wig, and your own sister won't know you." She waved Caragh toward the sofa. "I brought several wigs and an assortment of gowns from the theatre. Let's see which become you the best."

Before Caragh could utter another word, Ailis and Rachel began stripping her out of her afternoon gown. For the next hour, the two women dressed and undressed her like a manikin, finally deciding on a black velvet gown with matching cloak, a soft velvet toque with a figured black veil to mask her face and a wig of short black ringlets. Having chosen the ensemble, they made Caragh walk, kneel and lie down on the sofa to make sure the wig would stay in place.

"The wig feels secure, but I cannot say the same for the gown," Caragh said. "Are you sure the bodice isn't too low?"

"Dearie, you want the gent to be thinking of bedding, right?" the actress asked. "Give him an eyeful of you in that ensemble and trust me, the only thing he'll be wondering is how fast he can peel off that last inch of cloth." She looked over at Ailis and giggled. "Worked for me with the Earl of Gresham, anyways."

Ailis grinned at Caragh. "You can't dispute proven success." Taking Caragh's arm, she marched her over to the cheval glass. "Behold, I give you…Madame LaNoire! The Black Lady," she added for Rachel's benefit.

Through the obstructing veil, Caragh peered at herself in the glass. "Oh, my!" she said weakly.

Gazing back at her stood a slender woman, dusky curls escaping beneath her jaunty toque, her face tantalizingly obscured by a mist of black veil. With the cape pulled behind her shoulders, even she had to catch her breath at the dramatic contrast between the midnight velvet of the gown and the ghostly paleness of her skin. The high, tight waistline pushed up and accentuated the voluptuous roundness of her nearly-bare breasts, which did indeed appear as though they might at any moment burst free from the extremely brief bodice.

"He won't be able to take his eyes off you," Ailis promised.

"Nor will any other man that gets a peep, so you'd best keep the cloak fastened until your gent arrives," the actress advised. "Now, I must go. Don't want to be late getting into makeup and give Edmund the Ego a reason to shout at me."

While Ailis walked her guest to the door, Caragh stared at herself in the glass, then held up her arms and made a slow pirouette. Though the material was heavier than the silks and muslins to which she was accustomed, it draped beautifully and the nap was as soft as a caress against her skin. Seeing herself peeping naughtily through her veil, dressed like an enchantress, made her feel like one.

I shall actually be able to do this! Giddy at her boldness, she threw back her head and laughed. As she doffed the bonnet and cloak, Ailis walked back.

"First, the disguise. Next—" Ailis went over to scoop something off her work bench "—the key to your pied-à-terre." With a flourish, she presented it to Caragh.

"Where? And whose is it?"

"Darling Max suggested it—I knew if love-play were the purpose, he would know how to arrange it! An artist friend of his, now traveling in Italy, has a flat nearby. Before Friday, I'll take you there so you can familiarize yourself with it—and rearrange things if you like."

"Italy!" Caragh exclaimed. "I nearly forgot! Ailis, did you know that Mama is still living?"

"*Our* mother? I thought she died of a fever ages ago."

"So we were told, but Aunt Kitty let slip last night that the story was a ruse to cover up the fact that she ran off with an Italian gentleman when you were still a babe. Did you truly not know?"

Ailis shook her head. "No, why would I?"

"Aunt Kitty said she's become quite a patroness of the arts. I thought perhaps Mr. Frank might have met her on his travels."

Ailis burst out laughing. "If she supports galleries in Rome or Florence, he's probably seduced her!"

"From what Aunt Kitty says, she probably seduced him," Caragh said drily. "I expect she goes by some other name now, so he wouldn't have made the connection."

Ailis clapped her hands. "Famous! While you're enticing a gentleman into the artist's rooms here, our long-absent mater may be enticing its owner into her suite in Rome. You see?" She flung an arm out at Caragh, as if closing the argument. "With such blood in your veins, how can you fail?"

Ailis laughed again. "No wonder Aunt Kitty never wanted to let me of her sight!"

"I think Papa understood. When I told him about your studio, he said something about the inevitability of doing what the gods within compel you."

Ailis shrugged. "Well, I think we would all have been much better off if, instead of burying himself with his books in the countryside grieving, he'd have found another wench to replace her."

Could she find another buck to replace Quentin when their stolen night was over? Caragh wasn't so sure. "I think, in spite of everything, he still loves her."

"'Tis his life to waste," Ailis said with a sniff. "I would have chosen to move on."

She would have no choice but to move on, Caragh thought with a flash of sadness. But before then—she would have the magic of her night with Quentin.

Provided she could, in fact, entice him to the rooms—and escape undetected. "How shall I manage it if…if I can persuade him to escort me there? I don't suppose we could…you know, still fully clothed."

"It can be done," Ailis said with a grin, "but I don't recommend it. Skin to skin is so much more…satisfying."

Her words softened to a sigh and she closed her eyes, obviously remembering. Caragh felt a tremor of desire, just imagining the feel of Quentin's skin—hands, lips, body—against hers.

"I shall have to leave the lamps low—or dispense with them—to keep him from recognizing me."

"Light just one lamp when you arrive and insist on blowing it out before you remove your veil. We'll make sure the room is arranged so you'll not be caught in the moonlight. And require him to leave you in darkness. You are Madame LaNoire, *n'est-ce pas?*"

Caragh looked down at the low bodice of the wicked gown that emphasized the proud thrust of her breasts. "*Oui, c'est vrai.* Now—what do I do to ensure this is an evening he will never forget?"

"Let us defer to the expert. I believe I hear Lady Belle at the door."

They walked to the entry as the maid ushered in their visitor. Growing up with her sister, Caragh had become inured to physical loveliness, but the woman who glided with sensual elegance into the room was beyond doubt the most beautiful creature Caragh had ever beheld.

Her face, a profile of Grecian perfection framed by ringlets of purest gold, her skin the smoothness of white marble, she turned toward them a bow-shaped mouth that smiled in greeting, while eyes of an intense gentian blue inspected them.

No wonder, Caragh thought, her mouth agape, rumor reported that gentleman had offered enormous sums to lure this woman from her long-term protector.

"Lady Belle, thank you for visiting on such short notice," Ailis said.

"One must humor the whims of so talented an artist," Lady Belle replied. "And this is your sister, I presume?"

Surprised to hear in the woman's husky voice the cultured tones of a gently-bred lady, Caragh found herself sinking into a curtsey deep enough to do honor to a royal. And truly, this woman held herself with the noble bearing of a queen.

"Lady Belle, I only wish I had half Ailis's beauty! But thank you for agreeing to come."

Lady Belle nodded, handing her pelisse over to the maid, along with a coin the startled girl pocketed with alacrity before hurrying off. The evening gown revealed once her wrap had been removed—of a deep blue silk almost the color of her eyes—was cut in the latest fashion and obviously expensive. Yet the bodice, unadorned by jewels, lace or furbelows, was only moderately snug and almost modestly cut, higher than those sported by most of Society's ladies and much higher than that of the gown Caragh currently wore.

Of course, as the lady's bust and shoulders were as perfect as her face, she had no need to display them nearly naked to rivet the attention.

"Won't you join us in here, Lady Belle?"

The courtesan took a step, then halted. "Oh, dear!" she said in vexation. "I wished to ask you about the preliminary sketch you made, but I've left it in my reticule. Could you fetch it, please?"

Ailis nodded. "I'll be right back. Please," she said with a wink to Caragh, "make yourselves *comfortable*." She waved them toward the sofa in the studio.

Which was obviously a jab at how *un*comfortable she was likely to find this interview, Caragh thought, tempted to stick her tongue out at her sister as she took a chair opposite Lady Belle.

Caragh's composure wasn't helped by the penetrating gaze the courtesan focused on her. "So, you wish to seduce a particular man?"

Caragh found herself blushing. "Y-yes, ma'am. But I fear I am woefully ignorant of how to go about it."

"You are a virgin, then?"

Caragh's blush deepened. "Y-yes."

"You are sure you wish to do this? You will likely ruin your chances of wedding, should you succeed. It would be…infamous for you to be coerced into it."

The almost bitter intensity of her tone distracted Caragh from her embarrassment. Was that how this woman, who looked every inch a lady, had ended up a byword for carnality?

Intriguing as the answer might be, she couldn't possibly make so personal an inquiry of a stranger. "I am sure," she said, returning to the original question. "The man I would bed is also the man I love. But as he feels for me only a tepid affection, marrying him would end in misery. I should, though, like just one chance to lie in his arms."

With a graceful gesture, Lady Belle indicated the wig. "Hence the disguise?"

"Yes. Should he recognize me, he would insist that we wed, and I couldn't bear that."

"You have some means of support if you do not marry?"

"I manage a horse-breeding operation—in my own name."

Lady Belle nodded. "That should provide you a good income. Very well, I shall help. First, you must take precautions against conception. A vinegar-saturated sponge is best. I expect Ailis can get you a supply. Now, what do you wish to know?"

"I'm told this gown will focus his interest. What else can I do to…attract him?"

"You will be veiled?"

Caragh redonned her toque and wrapped the figured veil over her face. "I shall meet him at a masquerade ball in Vauxhall Gardens, dressed like this."

"Good. Night, shadow, a bit of aloofness will add to the allure, challenge him to master your mystery. You'll wear that cape?"

Caragh plucked the cloak off the sofa arm and tossed it on, tucking it behind her shoulders as Ailis had instructed. "Like this."

Lady Belle studied her for a moment. "The whiteness of your skin under the torchlight will capture his attention, entice his eyes to linger. You can further inflame him by leading his gaze on the journey his hands and mouth will already be thirsting to follow. Come here, please."

After Caragh obediently approached her, the courtesan picked up one of the tasseled cords that tied the cloak beneath her chin. "With him watching you, retie the cloak and then release one of the cords like so."

Beginning at the hollow of Caragh's throat, she slowly traced the silken tassel down the naked skin of Caragh's chest, over the swell of her bosom, then whisked the soft bristled tip over Caragh's breast before releasing it.

Caragh caught her breath, feeling her nipple stiffen in response to that subtle caress. Heat sparked in her stomach, pooled between her thighs. "Oh, my!" she gasped.

Lady Belle smiled. "A squeeze of his arm when he offers it to escort you down the path, a brush of your torso against his in a waltz—and he will be more than ready, my dear."

"I shall contrive an excuse to have him escort me to the apartment. But…how do I—persuade him to come in?" She felt her face heating again.

"You are presenting yourself as a married lady?"

"A widow."

"A *French* widow," Ailis said, returning with the sketch.

"Ah, then he will be prepared for some boldness. Simply tell him you want him."

"That's…all? It's that simple?"

At Caragh's incredulous tone, Lady Belle laughed. "Generally—yes."

"But…but I'm not a beauty like you or Ailis."

"My dear, sheer physical attractiveness often has little to do with sensual allure. If you have done all I have described, you can be sure he will want you. That is, you have no reason to suspect he finds you…unappealing?"

"No. Quite…quite the contrary."

"Then he is yours for the taking."

"Well…I shall need some assistance there as well. I want this to be a night he will never forget."

"Do you know how intimacy progresses?"

"In general terms."

"She has seen my 'Seduction' series," Ailis inserted.

Lady Belle nodded. "That would be a good sequence to follow. You remember each phase?"

Caragh smiled. "I assure you, each pose is etched into my brain!"

Ailis grinned. "I don't doubt it. I'm quite a superior artist."

"Nonetheless, it would be well to review the process, if you could fetch the sketches, please?" While Ailis went to the work bench, Lady Belle turned to Caragh. "If you have never been with a man, you must prepare your body as well. Since some women bleed the first time, to maintain your pose as an experienced woman, you will want to avoid that. And depending on his size, the stretching necessary for your body to accommodate his may be painful."

"I have the solution!" Ailis said. Handing Lady Belle the portfolio, she walked over to rummage in a side table, returning with a large, smooth piece of solid whalebone—in the shape of a male member. "Many women use a dildo to obtain satisfaction in the absence of their partner, but using it—as a lover would use his—will accustom you to the size and feel of a man."

Her cheeks on fire, Caragh took the object gingerly. "So I prepare myself in advance. But Friday night, how do I... begin?"

"Disrobe for him...or let him disrobe you, as he prefers," Lady Belle advised.

"He will find watching your pleasure stimulating," Ailis said. "While you experiment with the dildo, touch yourself to see which areas of your body are most sensitive, how much pressure is most pleasurable." Taking the portfolio, she flipped to the sketch of the girl standing naked before her lover, her fingers at the junction of her thighs. "With the lamp still lit and your veil in place, let him watch you touch yourself like this. It will fire his blood, do you not think, Lady Belle?"

"Assuredly. Most men find it titillating for the lady to take charge. Forbid him to touch you until you give him leave. Explore his body first, using your hands and lips to find his most sensitive places."

"Then take him in your mouth," Ailis said, "like this." She displayed the sketch to Caragh.

"'Tis very effective," Lady Belle agreed. "Do you think you can do that?"

The idea of baring her body to Quentin, touching him intimately, *tasting* him, made Caragh's mouth dry and her pulse race with eagerness. "Oh, yes."

"Sliding your tongue along the length of his member, then suckling it gently, especially here—" she pointed at the sketch "—where the tip joins the shaft, will create the most exquisite sensations for him. Massaging him here at the same time—" she indicated the plump sacks suspended below the rigid shaft "—will intensify the sensations even further."

"He will probably wish to do the same for you," Ailis said, indicating the sketch in which the couple pleasured each other.

Imagining Quentin doing that to her, while she did the same for him, effectively deprived Caragh of speech, even had she been able to think of something to reply.

"When you are ready, let him recline against the pillows and mount him from above," Lady Belle advised. "Watching you taking him within you, being able to fondle your breasts and touch the point of your joining while you move with him, will also heighten the experience for him."

"And when the act is completed," Ailis added, "let him linger beside you, reliving and savoring each moment."

"I shall certainly do that," Caragh said. Indeed, if intimacy with Quentin proved to be as exquisite a sensual and emotional experience as she anticipated, it was going to be very difficult to send him away at all. But she would worry about that later.

"Anything else I should do?" she asked.

"That should be sufficient for the first time. After all," she added with a touch of self-mockery, "you are a widow—not a courtesan."

"Lady Belle, I know you have an engagement, so we will not keep you longer. Caragh," Ailis said with a wicked grin, "you should review the sketches again while I discuss Lady Belle's portrait with her."

As the two women moved to Ailis's work bench, Caragh flipped through the drawings, recalling with each pose the advice she'd been given. Imagining herself and Quentin in those positions soon had her skin sheened with dampness, her pulse throbbing and her body quivering in a low buzz of anticipation.

She wished their rendezvous were tomorrow rather than Friday—and yet, at the same time she wished the time might never arrive, that she might savor this delicious sense of anticipation forever. For after the searing crucible of union would come the devastation of parting.

But first, she promised herself, she would experience the full height and depth of love's ecstasy—and transport Quentin Burke to that heaven with her.

CHAPTER SIXTEEN

AFTER CHECKING his pocket watch, Quentin once again scanned the throng of merrymakers strolling through the colonnade before the Vauxhall Gardens orchestra. Queens, knaves, jesters and medieval knights mingled with patrons dressed in more normal fashion, their only concession to the masquerade the dominoes worn over their faces.

Although it was not yet late, there were already a number of tipsy gentleman swaggering about, loudly accosting an assortment of "ladies" in scandalously brief gowns, who, after much giggling and tapping of fans, accompanied them into the shadows down one of the infamous Dark Walks.

Viewing the increasingly rowdy behavior of the crowd, Quentin could well believe Lady Catherine had no taste for attending the masquerade here. He was somewhat surprised that she was allowing Caragh to come, even with his escort.

Probably that kind lady had allowed compassion for her niece, so unfairly barred from more conventional amusements, to overrule her caution, a lapse Quentin could readily understand. Nonetheless, he'd already decided that once he found Caragh, after a few dances and a taste of the Arrack punch and wafer-thin ham, he would hustle her back to the safety of her aunt's house.

It was now almost half an hour later than the time she'd

indicated for their rendezvous, he noted uneasily. The note she'd sent him indicated that, with the session at the lawyers expected to run late, she intended to bring her costume with her and meet him directly at the Gardens. She'd assured him Smithers would dispatch one of his clerks to watch out for her until she found Quentin.

He was wishing he had insisted on meeting her at the lawyer's offices when he caught sight of a lady of Caragh's size and height, standing by the orchestra with her back to him. A second look confirmed she was gowned in the black Caragh had written she'd be wearing.

He sprinted toward her, his immediate relief succeeded by vexation. Neither the promised clerk—nor any sort of escort that he could see—appeared to be hovering in the vicinity to protect her. He would certainly send a few sharp words to her lawyer!

Coming up from behind, he placed his hands on her shoulders to turn her toward him. "Caragh, I'm so relieved—" he began, only to release her and spring back when the lady uttered a little shriek.

"Monsieur! Qu'est-ce que vous faites, alors?"

"Excuse me, ma'am!" he cried. "I thought you were…"

As his gaze swept down the figure of the woman he'd inadvertently accosted, the rest of his apology went straight out of mind. From the back, this slender lady might have resembled Caragh, but from a hand's breath away, he could see that the curls tumbling from beneath a jaunty toque were not a soft golden brown, but deepest ebony. And though the lady was garbed in black, never would Caragh have worn so scandalously—and enticingly—revealing a gown.

In fact, his body, unconcerned about the true identity of the

lady possessing such delicious curves, was already rising in
enthusiastic appreciation. Even his more responsible brain
was having difficulty ordering his eyes to cease devouring the
visual delight spread beneath them and lift instead to the
veiled lady's face.

"Je m'excuse, madame!" he said, recapturing the power
of speech. "Pardon me, please! I…I thought you were someone else."

She appeared to regard him through the veil for a moment,
then nodded. "Since you were gentleman enough to release
me *immediatement,* I accept the apology, monsieur."

At that moment, a boy approached Quentin. "You be Lord
Branson, sir? A lady from Mr. Smithers's office done sent me
with this message fer ye."

Quentin took the note and slipped the lad a coin. Squinting in the flickering light of the flambeaux, Quentin scanned
Caragh's message. By the time they'd completed their trans-
actions, she wrote, she'd developed one of her headaches and
felt compelled to return straight home. She ended with pro-
fuse apologies for having inconvenienced him.

A bit annoyed at having wasted his time, Quentin refolded
the note. Still, with this gathering already bordering on the dis-
reputable, he was really rather relieved he'd not have to shep-
herd Caragh through it.

When he looked up, the veiled lady was still facing him.
He thought again that, except for that display of bosom, somehow she reminded him strongly of Caragh.

"It was not distressing news, monsieur?"

"Not at all, madame. Just that the friend I was to meet will
not be coming after all."

He was about offer a final apology and bid the veiled lady

good night when one of the revelers staggered over and seized her by the shoulder. "How's about a kiss, sweeting?"

With an inarticulate cry, the woman tried to twist out of the drunkard's grasp. Incensed, Quentin seized the man's arm, jerked his hand off the lady's shoulder and forcibly returned it to the ruffian's side. "The lady isn't interested. Be on your way, man."

For a moment, it seemed the drunkard would protest his intervention. But after owlishly noting Quentin's height from head to boot tips, he apparently decided against it. "Meant no harm," he muttered, backing away.

The lady put a hand to her bare throat. "*Mille fois merci,* sir!" With a little shudder, she readjusted the silken cords that held her cloak in place. In spite of himself, he could not help watching as she tightened the knot, then smoothed the tasseled ends down the front of her bodice, across the peaked tips of her breasts… He stifled a groan as heat flushed through him.

"It isn't my place to say so, madame, but you shouldn't be in Vauxhall alone." *Certainly not in that gown,* he added silently.

"*Vraiment,* I did not wish it, monsieur! I was walking with my friends, there—" she pointed a slender hand "—when a large party pushed past us. Almost they knocked me down! When I found my balance, my friends had disappeared. So I wait here for them. This place, *il me fait énervée*—how you say? It makes me nervous."

For a gentleman, there was but one reply. "Since I no longer need to wait here, let me help you find your party."

"*Comme c'est gentil,* monsieur! But I cannot ask it."

"Nonsense. I could not have it on my conscience that I left so pretty a lady unescorted in the midst of so unruly a crowd."

Once again, the lady studied him from behind her veil. "I

should not, sir, for I do not know you. But you have twice been the gentleman, and truly, I cannot like to stay here alone."

"My word as a gentleman, madame, I will not take advantage. Though 'tis not exactly proper, allow me to introduce myself. Lord Branson, at your service." Quentin bowed, trying not to notice as he bent down how close that action brought his lips to her enticing bosom.

She bent her head and curtseyed in return. "Madame LaNoire, milord. Many thanks for your noble rescue." Tentatively, she offered her hand.

More conscious than he wanted to be of those warm fingers resting in the curve of his arm, Quentin led the lady along a circuit through the Gardens. But although they checked in every gathering spot, they did not find her friends.

At length they returned to the area by the orchestra. "So dark it is, I fear we missed them. But I cannot keep you longer. Surely, they will come back for me."

"No more than before could I abandon you now, madame. Should you like a glass of punch? Perhaps by the time we have some refreshment, your friends will return. No, truly it is no bother!" he said, forestalling her protest.

"You are sure? *Eh bien*, then I accept with gladness, milord."

Keeping an eye on her to make sure she was not accosted again—and really, 'twas no hardship to keep an eye on that luscious display—Quentin obtained punch and some sandwiches of slivered ham. A few more coins given to the attendant, and he was able to lead the veiled lady into a box with a clear view of the passing crowd.

"You are French, Madame?" he asked after they had sipped some punch.

"*Oui*, monsieur."

"But your English is quite good."

"*Merci,* monsieur. I have had years here to learn it. *Mon cher* Phillippe was a royalist, so we were forced to flee our home. His dearest wish was to see that monster Corsican driven from *La France*. And for that—" her voice softened "—he gave his life."

"My condolences, ma'am. Have you no family here?"

She shook her head and gave a soulful sigh "Some friends only. I do not go out often, *moi,* but tonight, they beg me. They say the music here is lovely and ah, I do so adore *la danse*. But it was mistake to come."

The melancholy of her tone touched him. Despite the riveting display of bosom, she seemed a proper matron. Bereft of support from the men of her family, cut off from her world…in truth, her circumstances were very like Caragh's.

He wouldn't be able to offer his neighbor some diversion tonight. But perhaps he could give this sweet lady a brief respite from her grief.

Quentin put down his mug. "You must dance with me."

"Milord, I could not!"

"Why? You just said you came here for the dancing. You must know by now I shall not harm you, and in any event, this is the most crowded, well-lit place in all of Vauxhall. You can still watch the revelers, and I promise to release you the instant your friends return."

"*Vraiment,* milord, I should not."

Sensing her resolve weakening, he made her a deep bow. "Would you honor me, madame?"

Though she shook her head at him, she held out her hand. "You are very bad, monsieur."

"On the contrary," he said, smiling as he lead her onto the

dance floor, "I am very good." *Oh, that I might show you how good,* the thought flashed through his head before he could suppress it.

She seemed to enjoy the first dance so much, he immediately asked her for a second. Which, since it turned out to be a waltz, was probably a mistake.

She fit a bit too nicely in his arms. He couldn't stop thinking of her nearly bare breasts brushing his chest, separated from his flesh only by the linen of his shirt and a flimsy bit of velvet. His fingers itched to see if the ivory skin glowing in the dimness would be as soft as the plush of her gown. And the subtle pull of that fabric as the nap dragged against his coat and trousers as they danced, heightened his unwanted arousal.

By the time it was over, his breathing was labored and sweat beaded his forehead. He had, he told himself grimly, been much too long without a woman.

His partner, mercifully in ignorance of his heated thoughts, clasped his hand fervently. "Ah, monsieur, that was *magnifique!* Not since the last ball with my dearest Philippe have I danced so! *Merci, merci encore!*"

Quentin bowed. "My pleasure, madame." *Both more and less than I would have liked to give you.* "I take it you have not yet seen your friends. Shall we make another circuit of the grounds?"

"No. Perhaps they are still here, but *moi,* I am *fatiguée.* I would go home. But ah, milord, I cannot say enough how *gentil* you have been! I…I had forgotten what it is like to be with a true gentleman." She made him a deep curtsey, then turned to go.

"Wait!" he cried, catching her arm. "You cannot mean to travel at night alone! I don't wish to be presumptuous, but you must allow me to escort you."

She shook her head. "No, I already trouble you too much."

"No trouble, I assure you. After all, I too must cross the river and find a hackney to convey me to my lodgings. It would be no trouble to drop you on the way."

She hesitated, looking toward the river, then back at him. "I would feel safer, I cannot deny. You are sure it is no bother?"

"Not a bit." He offered his arm. After another moment's hesitation, she took it.

Quentin walked her to the quay and engaged a boatman to oar them across. But once they were seated side by side on the narrow seat, the sway of the boat rocking them together, he grew all too conscious of her slim figure tucked beside him.

It was even worse in the hackney. In that closed space, the scent of her perfume teased his nostrils, her dusky curls tickled his cheek…and he simply couldn't stop thinking of those outrageously tempting breasts beneath her cloak, a mere brush of his hand away.

Being French, she probably did not realize what havoc that lavish display of skin played with English sensibilities, he thought, surreptitiously tugging at his over-tight neckcloth. He was both relieved and sorry when the jarvey pulled up before the address she had given him.

When the carriage stopped, she looked over at him. "I…I should not ask, but…my hallway is very dark. Could you walk up with me?"

"Of course." Giving the driver a coin to wait for him, Quentin followed her up.

Inside the entry, she located a candle and matchbox, then lit a taper. Carrying it to illumine the gloom of the stairs, she led him up to an apartment on the top floor.

Moonlight from a tall window on the landing outlined her figure in silver, cast in relief the figured pattern of the veil covering her face as she drew a key from her pocket and unlocked a door.

Quentin watched her, wondering with a touch of whimsy how the rest of her life would treat her, this gentle widow cast adrift so far from her homeland. Suddenly he wished he might pull aside the veil and kiss her goodbye.

She pushed the door open, then turned back to him. Hesitantly she put a hand on his arm. "I…I wonder if—but no, I must not. You will believe me…wanton."

A frisson of excitement zipped through him at the word. "N-not at all," he stumbled. "What is it?"

"It is just…I am widow, *vous savez.* I miss, ah so much, the loving with my Philippe. *C'est curieux,* but you…very much resemble the man I love. So much, I ache to leave you."

His heartbeat leapt as she took a ragged breath, her voice quieting so he had to lean closer to hear her words. "Just for tonight, I wish not to be alone. Just for tonight, I wish to know again what love is. Ah, *mais, c'est impossible!*" She dropped his arm and stepped away. "You have a wife, *oui?*"

"No!"

"A lady you are promised to?"

He shook his head. "There is a lady I wished to marry, but she…she refused me."

She remained silent, as if pondering that revelation. "Foolish lady!" she murmured at last. "Just for tonight, we console each other, eh? You will…stay with me?"

Desire swelled in him, restrained by a touch of guilt. But as he'd told her, Caragh *had* refused him. There were no promises between them, no bonds but friendship.

So how could he refuse this sad, sweet lady?

When she once again took his hand, he let her lead him within.

SHE SET the candle down inside and lit a single lamp, then beckoned him to follow her through several shadowy rooms. His pulses leapt again when beyond the threshold of the next, she halted—beside a large canopied bed.

Setting the lamp down on the bedside table, she turned to take him eagerly into her arms. But when he raised his hand to grasp her veil, she caught it.

"No, my love. Now I show you all of me but my face. Later, when the light is dim, I remove the veil."

"Why?" he whispered. "You know I will not harm you."

"I know. But with my Philippe gone, I must work to survive. I teach French and music to the children of your ton. One who influences innocents must be, as you say, 'above reproach.' If you know my face and see me later, on the street—"

"I would never betray you!"

She put a finger to his lips. "Ah, *non*. But seeing you, knowing what you know, I might betray myself. Now if I see you, it will be for me a secret joy."

"A joy I may not share?"

"You have another life. For us, there can be only tonight. You…understand?"

He nodded reluctantly. "If I must."

"Then, let us begin."

She shrugged out of her cape and tossed it on the bed, then turned her back and indicated the tapes to her gown. *"S'il vous plaît, monsieur?"*

CHAPTER SEVENTEEN

OH, DID IT please him! *"Certainement,"* he murmured. Fingers clumsy with eagerness, he loosened the tapes, then struggled to free the long line of tiny buttons securing the back of the gown. As the fabric released, he lifted it away, drawing the sleeves down her arms, letting the heavy full skirts fall to her ankles.

Beneath the gown she wore stays and ruffled petticoats over a thin linen chemise, through which peaked nipples now, at last, showed clearly. He wanted to rip the linen aside, view with no further impediment those full plump rounds that had titillated him all evening, but she gently pushed his hands away.

While he watched each movement, she slowly dropped one strap, then the other. He heard himself groan as bit by bit she peeled down the remaining inch of cloth. Cupping her hands beneath her breasts, she lifted them, massaged them, rubbed the stiffened nipples with her thumbs. "Do you like what you see, milord?"

"Yes." His voice sounded hoarse, guttural.

"You would see…more?"

"Yes. More. Everything."

She laughed softly as she unlaced the stays and tossed them aside, then stepped out of the petticoats. Straightening, she stood before him, breasts bare, the fine linen now barely veiling her body from stomach to calves. She ran her hands down her sides, over her belly, letting them come to rest on her thighs, her thumbs grazing the dark triangle at her center. "More?"

He was nearly frantic with the need to touch her, taste the pale skin and dark puckered nipples, but this slow unveiling was too enrapturing to resist. "M-more."

She wrapped her fingers in the linen beneath her breasts and drew it down her ribs, tugged it an inch at a time over her belly and hips, little by little revealing the tight dark curls beneath. "More?"

"Ah, yes!"

She turned her back to him and teased the fabric lower, let it whisper down her legs. Bending over, she gave him the arousing vista of her naked back and buttocks as she dropped the chemise to her feet and kicked it away.

Languorously she straightened and turned back to face him. "More, milord?"

Beyond speech now, he nodded.

She eased her bottom up onto the bed and sat back, then drew a leg up, gripped garter and stocking and pushed them down, arching and withdrawing her foot. While he stood, breathless at the glimpses she allowed him, she removed the other stocking. Leaning back, she parted her thighs to give him a fuller view and ran a fingertip over the nub at her very center.

Over the roaring in his ears, he heard her say, "Come to me."

But when he rushed to the bedside, his eager fingers reaching for her, she sat back up and once again caught his wrists. *"Pas encore,"* she murmured. "Not yet."

Placing his hands back at his sides, she wrapped her legs

around him and drew him close, until his straining breeches were pressed to the spot her fingertip had caressed. "Now, let *me* see *you*."

He wanted to indicate his approval, but his voice seemed to have stopped functioning. Apparently taking his silence for approval, she loosened the knot of his cravat, unwound the cloth and tossed it aside, then plucked open the buttons of his shirt until she had bared him from throat to chest.

"Comme c'est beau," she murmured, running her fingers from his breastbone up to the hollow of his throat and back while he stood motionless, in thrall to her touch. She clutched him tighter with her legs, bringing him even closer into her heat while she struggled to free him from his tight jacket. After stripping him of his shirt with the same teasing slowness with which she had removed her chemise, she set to work on his bare torso. Using fingertips and the pads of her thumbs, sometimes barely touching him, so that the tiny hairs of his skin bristled in electric response, sometimes massaging with deep and powerful strokes, she caressed every inch of skin.

By now he was ablaze with need, desperate for her to remove the rest of his garments and subject his lower body to the same thorough exploration she had given his arms and chest. And once again, she drove him nearly to madness with her slow deliberate pace. Yet so exquisite was the torment, he could not bring himself to disobey her command that he remain motionless, submissive to her control.

One by one she unhooked the buttons of his trousers, until his throbbing erection sprang free. Nestling him against her moist warmth, she leaned forward until her breasts just grazed his chest, then inched his breeches down his backside, caressing his buttocks with her fingers as she went.

By now restraint was almost pain. Every instinct urged him to seize her and plunge himself deep within the slick canal so excruciatingly close. When she bent to tug his breeches lower, her face near enough to his rigid shaft that he could feel the warm breath through the veil, he nearly lost control altogether.

Fortunately she seemed to sense how close to climax—and collapse—he was hovering. She untangled her legs and slipped off the bed. Urging him up on it, she tugged his boots and then his breeches off, treating him to a wonderful view of bare backside and bouncing breasts.

After she'd stripped him completely, she ordered him to recline against the pillows. Once more stilling his hands, she climbed back up on the bed and straddled him, positioning herself so his rigid erection almost touched the cleft between her parted thighs. "Would you see more, milord?" she whispered.

"Y-yes," he gasped, beyond anticipating what she might do next, carried away by wonderment. And so he watched as this time, she traced her hands from his forehead down his nose, teasing apart his lips and pausing to allow him to suckle her fingertips, then trailing her moistened fingers down his chest, circling his nipples, slowing her pace as her hands descended.

His breathing erratic and his heartbeat thundering in his ears, he watched her fingers trace down the now acutely sensitive skin of his abdomen, pausing just above the point he most wished her to stroke, then flaring her hands out to his hips, fluttering them over his buttocks.

Nearly growling with equal parts of gratification and frustration, he struggled to keep still. A few moments later his patience was rewarded when, while still caressing his backside, she moved her other hand up and slowly, so slowly anticipation squeezed his chest until he could no longer breathe, with the barely perceptible pressure of one fingertip, stroked him from base to tip.

He shuddered violently, his penis leaping beneath her finger. She encircled him with her hand, steadying him, then drew her hand down his length and back once, twice.

"Parfait," she murmured. *"Absolument parfait."*

He wanted to tell her she was perfect, absolutely the most divinely perfect lover he'd ever known, but his words seemed like wild creatures fled before the coming of the earthquake, unable to be recalled into speech. He could not articulate, he could only feel. And watch.

"You observe still, *mon cher?"* she asked. Despite the veil that obscured her face, she must be able to see that though his tongue was mute, his eyes remained riveted on her hands… which gently caressed him. And, at last, guided him to that place he most longed to be.

He gritted his teeth and closed his eyes, groaning with the effort to hold back as her wetness dewed the tip of his erection until, unable to stop himself, he thrust into her.

She gasped, her arms going rigid on his shoulders. Alarm restoring his control, he withdrew. "Did I hurt you, *ma belle?"* he whispered.

"N-no, *mon cher,"* she whispered. "Only…it has been so long, *vous savez.* Almost it is like the first time again."

"Then we will take it slowly," he promised.

And so he did, though the slowness was almost torture to him. She moved her hips to take him in a fraction at a time, until at last she'd drawn his length completely within her moist warmth.

"It is good now for you, my sweet?" he asked.

"*Vraiment,* it is h-heaven," she said, her fingernails biting into his shoulders as she rocked herself forward.

That bold movement unraveled the last of his control. With a hoarse cry, he seized her buttocks and drove deep. She cried out as well, matching his rhythm and meeting him thrust for thrust until, with an inarticulate wail, she shattered around him.

Satisfaction at her pleasure swelled in his chest before his own climax erupted within her, robbing him for a few heart-stopping minutes of breath and sight.

He awoke to find her slumped against him, their bodies slick with sweat, her heartbeat rapid against his chest. For a long time he was too full of delicious satiation to be able to move or speak. Finally, with a supreme effort, he found her hand and managed to bring it to his lips.

"You, *ma belle dame,* are perfect."

She murmured and with a languid movement, pushed to a sitting position astride him, setting off a series of exquisite aftershocks. Raising her hands above her head, she arched her back and stretched, angling her full, high breasts close to his face.

Catching her shoulders, he eased her forward until he could capture one pink nipple. She moaned as the captive hardened under his tongue and her inner muscles contracted, sending another burst of sensation through him. With one hand he circled and massaged her other breast, brushing his thumb over the tip, as she had shown him earlier.

By the time he had thoroughly sampled each breast, her breathing had gone ragged again and he could feel himself hardening within her. She began to rock, small, gentle thrusts that soon brought him back to full erection.

He observed only her this time, listened as her breathing turned from pants to gasps, noticed as her arms went rigid and her hands clutched on his shoulders, suckled in rhythm with her increasingly rapid thrusts. Just as he felt his own control unraveling once again, she arched into him and cried out. Her body spasmed around him, demolishing the last of his resistance, and once again, his world exploded into a soaring starburst of sensation.

Afterward they both dozed. He awoke languid, conscious of the pleasant burden of her soft body cradled against his chest. Awe and amazement welled up in him, and unable to resist the temptation to peek at the face of the lady who had brought him twice to paradise, he tugged at her veil.

She jerked awake at once and caught his fingers. "*Pas permis,* my naughty one," she reproved. Disengaging from him, she slid off the bed and stood beside it, beautifully naked but for her veil, her breasts dappled pink with the marks of his possession.

He sat up on his elbow, and for a few moments she allowed him to feast on the sight of her. Then she blew out the lamp, leaving the bedchamber in inky darkness, silent but for a soft rustling he realized must be madame at last removing her veil.

Excitement swept through him. He leaned forward in the darkness to meet her, pulled her onto the bed beside him and back against the pillows. "At last I shall see you," he whispered, and felt her lips curve into a smile as she allowed him to trace first his fingers, then his lips over her naked face.

But when he moved his mouth lower to nip at her tender neck, she pulled away. "*Pas encore,* milord," she said, urging him once again back against the pillows. "You have seen. Now, you shall feel."

And before he could imagine what she intended, she began her slow journey of exploration again, this time using her tongue.

ANOTHER BLISSFUL interlude later, he awoke again. Smiling into the darkness, he stroked the shoulder of his dozing lover, wondering which had been more intense—his pleasure when he'd watched as well as felt her guide him to completion, or the pleasure produced when he was focused only on her touch?

While he pondered that sweet dilemma, she stirred beside him. He bent down to capture her lips—lips whose contours he wished to memorize, that should his lady not permit him to see her unveiled, he might still be able to recognize her should they pass by chance on the street.

As if suspicious of his intent, she drew away. *"C'est tard, mon amant,"* she whispered. "Much too late. You must go before the sky lightens. I cannot risk that anyone see you here."

He wanted to protest, but she had already slipped from the bed. By the sibilant sounds in the dark chamber, he knew she must be gathering up their clothing. A moment later he dimly perceived the pale outline of his shirt as she guided it over one hand.

Soon, too soon, he thought. Though, given the circumstances she'd described, he understood her caution, still he sought to put off the moment of parting. Interrupting her with a long slow kiss, he ran his hands over her peach-soft skin, interfering with her determined efforts to get him into his shirt, then distracted her by bending to suckle those firm, sweet breasts.

"Méchant!" she groaned, pushing him away. "No more delay." But though, whether from the chill or to escape temptation, she threw on a thick satin dressing gown, she showed herself not quite as committed to hurrying as her words might indicate.

After fastening him into his shirt, she paused to once again caress his buttocks before tugging up his breeches. Then she kissed his spent member so enticingly he nearly insisted they linger longer before, with a sigh, she drew away and firmly rebuttoned his trouser flap.

When she brought him boots and jacket, he stayed her with a hand to her shoulder. "Will you let me see you?"

She caught his hand and kissed it. "Nay, love, I dare not."

Disappointed, but not surprised, he asked, "Will you let me see you again?"

She hesitated, making his heart leap. "That, too, would not be wise."

Sensing her waver, he pressed harder. "But you will allow it? I beg you, *ma belle dame,* please say yes."

Without answering him, she moved away into the darkness. A few moments later he blinked against the sudden brightness and jerked his gaze to her face.

She stood beside the candle she'd just lit holding his jacket and boots—her face once again obscured by the veil. Swallowing his disappointment, he walked to her and ran his finger over the soft patterned fabric that masked her features. "You still do not trust me?"

"Please, you must go now."

She seemed already a bit distant. Sensing that pressing her to reveal her face would only make her withdraw further, he did not persist. Instead, he let her assist him into his jacket and boots and lead him to the door, where she dropped him a curtsey.

"Thank you, milord."

She rose, clearly expecting him to walk away. Yet he could not seem to make himself take the first step. What sorcery she had worked on him, he marveled as he dawdled on her doorstep? Never before had he been so reluctant to end a romantic interlude.

"Can I return here tomorrow?" he found himself asking.

He tensed as he awaited her answer, suddenly realizing he desperately needed her to agree, not sure what he would do if she refused.

Finally, with a shuddering sigh that rippled through her slender frame, she whispered, "*Oui. Vraiment,* 'tis madness, but yes. Come at midnight."

His drooping spirits revived on a surge of delight and wild anticipation. "I promise to make it a madness you will never regret. Until tomorrow at midnight, then."

She opened the door and after peeping into the hallway, motioned him through it, allowing one last kiss to her hand before shutting it behind him.

For a long moment after that portal closed, he stared at it, listening as the soft pad of her footsteps retreated, lost in awe, curiosity and wonder.

Finally he forced himself into motion. After tonight, he must concede the French deserved their reputation as masters of seduction. If only he could see her! How he thirsted to look upon the face of this lady with the tragic past and the magic touch!

But even should she never permit that, the splendor of the night they'd shared far surpassed his craving to view her features. And he had tonight still to anticipate. How many hours until midnight?

Smiling in the dimness, he fingered his pocket watch and with an eager step, trod down the stairs.

HOURS LATER, Caragh sat on the divan in her sister's studio, sipping hot chocolate. After dismissing the maid with an impatient wave of her hand, Ailis turned to Caragh. "So, did I not tell you 'twould be delightful?"

Caragh smiled. "Aye, you did."

"And viewing him in the flesh after having studied the drawing did not…disappoint?"

Caragh chuckled. "Oh my, no!"

Raising her eyebrows, Ailis laughed too. "I think I shall have to have him model for me—if only so I may make you a more accurate sketch to remember him by!"

"I'm not ready to be reduced to memories just yet. The reason I called—beyond thanking you again for all your help— is to beg more…supplies. I've asked Quentin to return to the flat tonight."

Ailis's amusement faded. Regarding her sister thoughtfully, she sipped her tea. "Are you sure you are not committing more of yourself to this than you ought?"

Caragh gave her a wistful smile. "I'm not sure of anything," she replied, mastering the wobble in her voice before it told Ailis far more than she wished to explain.

Her midnight excursion, so much more magnificent than anything she could possibly have dreamed, seemed to have dissolved the careful hold Caragh had been maintaining over her emotions. During those stolen hours in a borrowed room, the lust, curiosity and wistful need to hold Quentin close that had driven her to that outrageous masquerade had both strengthened and evolved into something almost beyond her ability to control. Physical rapture had deepened her love for him, while love in turn, she suspected, had intensified her physical pleasure. Sending him away had been nearly impossible.

Her resolve not to see him again, one of the fundamental tenets upon which she'd permitted herself this rash undertaking in the first place, had faltered upon the mere repetition of his request that they meet again.

Other emotions she'd not anticipated assailed her as well. Guilt at deceiving Quentin, using his body under false pretenses and eliciting his ready sympathy for a creature who did not exist. Shame at probing the depth of his allegiance to her, though—mercifully or not, she wasn't sure—she'd been too cowardly to pursue the matter to its end and baldly ask if he loved the girl who'd refused him.

If he loved *her.*

"Foolish lady" indeed!

"Are you going to tell him the truth?"

Ailis's inquiry startled her back to the present. "No!"

"If your activities last evening were as vigorous as I imagine, you are probably lucky that the wig—and your anonymity—survived the night intact. How much longer do you expect such luck to hold? If you would keep Quentin as your lover, 'twould be much simpler to abandon pretense."

"You know I cannot. If Quentin discovered I am Madame LaNoire, he would insist that we marry." She took a deep breath, voicing aloud the truth that had become more painful minute by rapturous minute of their time together. "Delightful though it be, the…arrangement cannot become longstanding."

Ailis shrugged. "If you enjoy him that much, I don't see why not. Simply refuse to marry him. 'Tis what I do every time Holden pesters me about wedlock. He cannot force you, after all."

For a moment, Caragh was diverted from her own predicament. "Holden is pressing you to marry? The confirmed rake, brought to his knees at last? Famous!"

Ailis waved a nonchalant hand. "I daresay he only asks because he's so certain I'll refuse. I like him well enough and he's a charming lover, but no man is charming enough to persuade me to trade independence for the iron trap of matrimony."

Matrimony with Quentin could be heaven, not trap, Caragh thought wistfully. But only if he truly loved the lady who'd refused his suit—and he'd given Madame LaNoire no hint that he would have affirmatively answered the question she'd not been brave enough to ask.

Caragh wanted only what he willingly offered her—or rather, Madame LaNoire. One more glorious night.

"Well, sister, is advice all I can pry from you? Or may I take more of those clever little sponges as well?"

"Both, of course." Ailis set down her wineglass and went behind the screen that concealed her bed, returning a moment later with a small pouch. "Remember to use them properly," she said as she handed it over. "I still think it best for you to reveal the truth—I know, you won't," she said before Caragh could protest. "Should your disguise somehow slip, however, don't say I didn't warn you."

Caragh took the pouch and tucked it in her reticule. After one more stolen evening, she would let Quentin go, then get on with her life and refuse to look back. "Nonsense, 'tis but for one more night. In so short a time, how could anything go wrong?"

CHAPTER EIGHTEEN

TWO DAYS LATER, Quentin sat at the desk in his London study, staring sightlessly at estate documents he'd ostensibly been reviewing for the past hour. Instead of the prosaic details of materials purchased and funds expended, though, in his mind shimmered indelible images of the two nights he'd spent with Madame LaNoire.

She'd not allowed him to remove her veil during their second evening either. But, after extracting his promise not to touch that forbidden item, she had agreed to his request that, reversing roles, they repeat the love-play of their first night. He had thoroughly enjoyed inspecting every inch of her body in the lamplight, driving her to the brink of ecstasy with the same extreme slowness with which she had tortured him, before plunging them both over the edge to fulfillment. And knowing this time, *she* watched *him* as he explored her, from the curve of her toes to the velvet folds beneath the dark curls at her center to her pink-nippled breasts, made the journey even more erotic.

Or had his senses been more stimulated the second time, after he extinguished the lamp, removed her veil, and retraced that journey with his tongue, both of them enveloped in a cloak of darkness that intensified every touch, every scent? Certainly he'd been able to tantalize her to climax several times before finally heeding her ragged pleas that he sheath himself within her.

A knock on the door interrupted that arousing speculation, plummeting him back to the uninspiring vista of the estate ledgers stacked atop his desk. Even after he dealt with this tedious array of paperwork, the evening stretched bleakly before him. Though he'd pleaded with all the persuasion he could muster, the bewitching Madame LaNoire had sadly but firmly refused to let him return.

With a catch in her voice, she'd asserted that despite the certainty of delight they might share, his visiting again would be too risky—for them both.

Knowing thoughts of her had already monopolized far too much of his time and attention, he had reluctantly bowed to her decree. It appeared likely he would never see her again— without ever having really seen her.

Should they chance to pass on some Mayfair street, would he recognize her? Or, as she had predicted, might she pause to gaze covertly at him, recalling the rapture of those nights, while he walked on oblivious?

A mingling of protest, regret and something disturbingly like dismay stabbed in his gut.

The knock sounded again. "Enter," he barked.

"Begging your pardon, my lord," his butler bowed himself in, "are you intending to dine at home? Cook was not given instructions."

Was it as late as that? He glanced at the mantel clock, startled to find it late afternoon. Yesterday, in sated splendor he'd slept through most of the daylight hours. Inspecting the nearly untouched stack of papers on his desk, he realized he had daydreamed away the better part of them today.

"No," he said, suddenly restless and weary of his own company. "I shall dine at the club as usual. Summon me a carriage in half an hour."

The end of so unexpected and magical an interlude was bound to leave him feeling somewhat melancholy. A few convivial hours of wine, political commentary and companionship at White's would be just the thing to restore his spirits—and distract him from recalling that tonight, no veiled lady waited to enrapture him.

He entered the club an hour later to find it as bustling as he'd anticipated. Lord Andover, seated in his usual spot by the bow window, spotted him as he entered and waved him over.

"Been rusticating again, old fellow? Haven't seen you at dinner of late."

"No, sir. Busy, I expect," he replied noncommittally, the knowledge of the sort of rusticating in which he had been indulging burning like a bright flame within him.

"Come, sit down! You'll broach a bottle and share a few moments with an old man, eh?"

Regretting the quest for information that had led him to ingratiate himself with his father's friend the previous week, Quentin took the seat indicated. Though a recitation of the latest society gossip no longer appealed, he couldn't see a way to refuse without slighting the old gentleman, who had, in truth, proved helpful.

Andover looked him up and down, eyes shrewd in his wrinkled face. "Now you have the appearance of a man who's been well-satisfied." The old gentleman cackled. "Been calling on your old neighbor, that Sudley artist chit?"

Irritated, Quentin ignored the first remark to concentrate on the second. "Yes, I did call on Miss Ailis. Despite what

rumor claims about artists, I interrupted no orgiastic revels-
in-progress. Nor did I find a lover hiding in her armoire—just
a quantity of canvases and paints, and a rather unconventional lady set upon using them to make a living."

"Make a living—bah!" Lord Andover dismissed that pronouncement with a disparaging wave of his hand. "A real Diamond, they say, and living alone now?"

"She is a beauty, yes. But not quite alone—there's a maidservant in residence."

"I'd wager the cost of Prinny's next extravagance that she'll
never earn enough to fill a teapot. Since she's betrayed her
birthright and given up any claim to gentility, stands to reason she'll soon be taking a protector. I hear Freemont's already dangling after her, so what are you waiting for?"

The old man poked Quentin in the side. "Being a close
friend of the family, you have a decided advantage in winning
her favors, if you make your move quickly!"

"Being a close family friend," Quentin said stiffly, "I
couldn't consider such a thing. Damme, Andover, I've known
the chit since she was in short skirts."

"Think how much better she will look in—or out of them—
now," Andover said, chuckling at his own witticism.

Quentin wasn't amused. "I hardly think her aunt, Lady
Mansfield, or her sister, Miss Sudley, would appreciate such
conduct toward their near relation by someone they trust to
be both a friend and a gentleman."

"Lady Mansfield's above reproach—courted the gel
m'self, years back—but the elder Miss Sudley had better look
to her own reputation," Lord Andover said. "I hear she's been
visiting the artist chit and mixing with her low-bred friends.
Siblings and all, I understand, but if she does that overmuch,

Miss Sudley will find herself featured alongside her sister in the latest print shop broadsides. Both fillies bred from the same mare, eh?"

Before Quentin could make a sharp rejoinder about the unfairness of slandering the Sudley daughters because of their mother's ancient scandal, a voice from behind him said, "What is this about Miss Sudley?"

Quentin turned to see Alden Russell approaching.

"Russell, pray join us," Andover invited. "Know the Sudley chits, do you?"

"Never been introduced to the Diamond-turned-artist," he replied, taking the chair offered, "but Branson presented me to the elder—a lovely, intelligent lady. Quite a knowledgeable estate manager too, as he can also attest. In fact," Russell said, turning to Quentin, "my solicitor has just completed the sale of some land to her family—that parcel I mentioned to her."

"Caragh—Miss Sudley is buying the old Reynolds farm?" Quentin echoed.

"Wants to expand their horse-breeding operation, my lawyer said. I'm delighted to see the land go to a purpose for which it is so well-suited—especially when I hope it will frequently bring the lady herself there to oversee it!" He grinned at Quentin. "Of course, I shall have to call frequently to offer my assistance whenever she visits the neighborhood."

The hot light in Russell's eye as he announced that intention, added to Quentin's knowledge of just how often—and just how well-chaperoned—Caragh would be at the new property, nearly made him choke. Bad enough that, should she proceed with this mad intention of running the farm alone, she would leave herself open to just the sort of speculation and innuendo Andover was already bandying about, as well as potential insult from the clients who patronized the operation. But to know his erstwhile friend, who'd already offended Quentin by making randy remarks about the lady, would be able to lie in wait for her not five miles outside her gate was outside of enough!

He must, Quentin swore with a murderous glance at Russell, immediately begin redoubling his efforts to persuade Caragh not to relocate there alone.

Before he could master his irritation to make a reply light enough not to engender Russell's suspicions, several newcomers joined them and the conversation became general. Although Quentin normally would have enjoyed the heated discussion that ensued about the several bills just introduced into Parliament, he soon found his attention wandering. Restlessness claiming him again, as soon after dinner as possible without arousing comment, he took his leave of the club.

Eschewing a carriage, he elected to walk. His mind needed clearing, and with the whirlwind of events the last few days, he had neglected Caragh. Indeed, so caught up had he been in his interludes with Madame LaNoire, after scanning the note of apology Caragh had sent for failing to meet him at Vauxhall, he'd not thought about her since.

The unwelcome information that the property she had bought for her new enterprise adjoined Russell's land had swiftly cleared what remained of that sensual distraction. In its wake remained the troubled uncertainty that had plagued him ever since a coolly distant Caragh had refused him at Sudley Court.

He had missed her acutely after that episode, missed the easy camaraderie of their friendship. Not until it was suddenly withdrawn did he fully realize how much his emotional well-being had become anchored to the deep abiding warmth of their relationship. Indeed, he was fast coming to believe that persuading Caragh to marry him was imperative not just to protect her future, but to secure his happiness.

Especially when he considered the unappealing possibilities inherent in her having Alden Russell as her nearest neighbor.

As for his most recent source of pleasure… A pang of guilt touched him. At the time he'd succumbed to Madame LaNoire's blandishments, there had been no commitment between Caragh and himself—at Caragh's own insistence. He had not broken her trust. Had matters already been settled between them, he would have resisted the veiled lady's entreaties, however tempting.

What was he to do about that lady, whose sad plight still whispered at the edges of his consciousness? If he were not contemplating a future with Caragh, he might be tempted to woo for his mistress the lady who had, silhouetted by moonlight that first night, seemed so hauntingly like his good friend.

Who was she, this lady so fiercely driven to hide her face? A governess as she claimed—or the actress from the Green Room her masquerade costume seemed to indicate? Whatever her true identity, it seemed clear she lived in precariously straitened circumstances.

Despite the subtle physical *something* about her that reminded him of Caragh, in character there could hardly be two women more dissimilar.

While Madame LaNoire eked out a bare subsistence in a private household, Caragh directed a lucrative breeding operation in the public arena. A refugee from her own world, the French lady seemed fragile, in need of protection, whereas

Caragh, after being rejected by her class, had with courage and spirit decided to forge a new future of her own design. One lady was reticent and submissive, the other independent and self-assured.

Though they did share one characteristic. As he'd lately come to appreciate, Caragh possessed a sensuality as deep as Madame's own. In fact, at the hands of a sensitive and knowledgeable tutor, Caragh might well become a lover as creative and responsive as the veiled lady.

That conclusion burst into his brain with the attention-riveting power of an exploding fireworks, halting him in mid-step. Faith, what an amazing amalgam that would be—to have in one woman the courage, strength and competence that was Caragh wedded to the passionate sensuality of Madame LaNoire!

Add sensual power to the hold Caragh already had on his affections and he'd be in imminent danger of falling completely under her spell. One lazy trace of her finger along any part of his anatomy could reduce his rational mind to mush. And her lips—a spiral of desire coiled through him at the mere thought of what Caragh's lips, trained in Madame LaNoire's sweet witchery, might do.

Caragh had already shown that she would prove a willing pupil. Indeed, had she not once tried to urge them down this very path? An overture he—fool that he was!—had firmly rejected. Since he'd never known her to fail in mastering any skill she attempted, could he but convince her to marry him and perfect her in this new art, she might make them both deliriously happy for a very long time.

Wooing her to such a course entailed risk, for once they changed the terms of their friendship, there could be no going back. But as he was fast becoming convinced that they must marry, which would alter the parameters of their friendship in any event, the prospect of gaining a best friend who was also his warmest erotic dream of a lover seemed to far outweigh any possible loss.

Especially after having just experienced the glimpses of heaven given him by Madame LaNoire. The idea of experiencing such delights with Caragh filled him with both joyful anticipation and a sense of awe.

Mille fois merci, madame, he said silently, *for opening my eyes to the possibilities within my grasp.*

As he entertained visions of that exalted future, the uneasiness that had plagued him dissolved, along with the last of his lingering reservations about marrying Caragh. Once he persuaded her to it—and he intended to persevere until he did—he could proceed to turning those enchanting visions into reality.

Grinning, he picked up his pace. Although another tiresome visit to that pesky new estate outside London would prevent his calling on her tomorrow, he would reply to her previous note this very night, begging leave to visit her the day after. And then begin his new campaign to swamp her objections and sweep her into his arms.

But as he paced along, a lingering concern nagged at the edges of his euphoria. Though he'd known her but a few hours—and still did not know the truth of her story—Madame LaNoire had touched him deeply. Was she truly the widowed governess she claimed, her employment uncertain and her financial reserves almost nonexistent?

If so, it didn't seem proper, somehow, that while he confidently proceeded toward a bright future with Caragh, the woman who had inadvertently led him to conquer his doubts remained so unprotected and at risk.

If she were who she claimed, he ought to repay the gracious gift she'd offered him by rectifying her precarious situation—and insure, should her capricious employer dismiss her, that she was not forced to choose between compromising the virtue she seemed to prize so highly by taking a protector, or starvation.

Outright financial assistance she would most certainly refuse. But surely she would not reject an offer of a legitimate, but more secure, position. Among his network of relations and business associates there should certainly be someone who could employ as a companion or governess a foreign widow of gentility and refinement.

After a few moment's reflection, he recalled hearing from his solicitor that his mother's Aunt Jane, an elderly spinster, had requested that he find a replacement for her recently-deceased companion. A sweet-tempered, gentle woman esteemed by both friends and servants, Aunt Jane suffered from poor eyesight and particularly missed, she told the solicitor, having a companion to read to her.

With her governess's background and quiet melodic voice, Madame LaNoire might be the ideal candidate for Aunt Jane's new companion. Such a position, at his relation's house just outside London, would offer permanent security without requiring the lady to move far from the few friends she had in England. And its salary, discreetly augmented by Quentin, would permit her to accumulate a modest sum for her retirement—or as dowry for another marriage, should she cease grieving her lost husband and wish to wed again.

Of course, before promoting her for such a position, he would have to discover the truth of her circumstances. Regardless of the debt he might feel he owed her, he could hardly in good conscience seek to introduce into his great aunt's household a woman of whom he knew for certain only that she was apparently French, seemingly genteel, and supposedly widowed.

The easiest way to discover it would be to call upon Madame LaNoire herself. So it appeared he would have to go against that lady's wishes and visit her again—though not this time, he acknowledged with a pang of regret impossible to squelch, with midnight interludes in mind.

A few minute's conversation with them both concentrated on the matter of legitimate employment should establish whether she was in fact a virtuous widow—or an actress who'd toyed with playing an amusing new role.

It would also obviate the need for secrecy. He would finally be able to view her in full light—without the veil.

His curiosity fully piqued by that prospect, he halted again and pulled out his pocket watch. Was it too late to stop by tonight?

A glance at the timepiece confirmed that the evening was not yet far advanced. Visiting now might well offer his best chance of catching her at home, for he must be out of the city tomorrow, and in any event, she most certainly spent the daylight hours at her employer's residence.

He would try it, he decided.

As he hailed a hackney, he had to admit that however platonic his intentions, a fever of anticipation was licking through his veins. Committed as he now was to claiming a future with Caragh, some indefinable *something* still bound him to the veiled lady, drew his thoughts back to her plight and person like a lodestone seeking north.

Probably, he assured himself, 'twas merely the same rigid sense of responsibility that had led him to toil for eight years to redeem his heritage. Naturally, until he knew Madame LaNoire to be safely situated, he'd be unable to dismiss her from his thoughts. Once that task was accomplished, he could focus solely on Caragh.

By the time he'd reached the landing outside her door, his heart was pounding, not just from the exertion of half running up three flights of stairs. Holding his breath, he rang her bell.

When she opened the door and spied him, would she gasp, her eyes wide with shock? Would she shut the door in his face, seeing his intrusion as a breach of her trust and an unwarranted invasion of her privacy? Or hold out her hands and welcome him warmly?

Though he sought to squelch it, another enticing possibility kept squirming back into his consciousness. If Madame LaNoire was as moved at seeing him as he expected to be at seeing her, might she suggest they share one final night of intimacy before forever severing their connection?

His mind alternately rejecting and entertaining that prospect, he waited. After several minutes, during which no sound of approaching footsteps emanated from behind the door, he rang again.

His excitement dimmed as the minutes passed and the door remained stubbornly barred. Might she be already abed and asleep? She'd told him she rarely attended evening entertainments. Surely by this hour she should be home.

Knocking again, he called out her name until, not wishing to rouse the neighbors, he felt compelled to cease. Still there was no response from within.

A sharp disappointment scalded him. Short of breaking the

lock, which he would rather not do, there was no way for him to enter and ascertain whether she was in fact within.

Loath to give up on his purpose, he lingered, administering several more sharp raps. Eventually, though, he had to acknowledge that Madame LaNoire was either not at home, or sleeping too soundly to rouse.

As he descended the stairs, he cheered himself with the reflection that he could still accomplish one bit of business tonight. As soon as he arrived back to his rooms, he would pen Caragh that note.

CHAPTER NINETEEN

My dear Caragh,

I regret the business that takes me from town, robbing me of the delight of your company.

I hope you suffered no recurrence of the headache that plagued you the night of the masquerade, and look forward to calling on you as soon as I return.

Until then, I remain
Your very devoted Quentin.

FINGERS TREMBLING, Caragh set the note, which retained a faint lingering scent of his shaving soap, back on the breakfast tray beside her hot chocolate. Seizing the cup, she took a gulp, but the savory brew seemed to have turned to chalk.

Quentin was coming to see her. Soon. Panic rose in her chest. Thrusting the tray aside, she hopped to her feet and began pacing the room.

He would lounge on the sofa in Aunt Kitty's drawing room, expecting her to pour him tea and sit beside him while they conversed about the continuing problems at his new estate or plans for moving her stock or her sister's shocking career.

Sit. Beside. Him. Heaven have mercy! she thought, putting hands to her hot cheeks.

She now knew how Pandora must have felt, trying to stuff

back into that box all the unexpected devils her rashness had allowed to escape.

How could she look at Quentin and not remember seeing every inch of his skin as she slowly undressed him—as he had seen hers? Or hand him a teacup without their fingers touching—fingertips that had caressed *his* body colliding with fingertips that had explored *hers?*

Not that she regretted a second of the two glorious nights they'd spent together. Indeed, so splendid were those interludes, it had been terrifyingly difficult to resist his pleas for yet another night. Her palms still showed the crescent marks of the nails she'd dug into them to keep herself from turning that "no" into a "yes."

Though this note did put an end to her secretly entertained and impossible hope that the bond between them was so strong he had somehow recognized the veiled lady to be her— and now realized beyond doubt that they belonged together. Having deliberately played upon both his chivalrous instincts and his masculine desire, she couldn't fault him for succumbing to the seduction of this supposed stranger. 'Twas ridiculous to feel disappointed—had she not deliberately created a persona so unlike her own that it would be nearly impossible for him to connect the two?

For the best of reasons. Should Quentin Burke discover his midnight lover was not the experienced widow he'd been led to believe, but his previously virginal neighbor, she'd find herself quick-stepped to the altar by a man whose keen sense of honor would not allow him to do otherwise, no matter how furious he'd doubtless be when he discovered her deception.

Given the depth of her love and the beauty of the intimacy

they'd shared, she could not bear to contemplate living with the enmity such a forced marriage must create.

How stupidly innocent and blindly arrogant she'd been when she chose to proceed down this path, thinking to assuage her curiosity and indulge her senses with a few stolen nights of pleasure.

By that second night, their minds and bodies had become so well attuned that she and Quentin were able to anticipate, savor, prolong each other's enjoyment. The power of their mutual attraction seemed to create an almost audible hum between them.

How could she sit beside him in a drawing room and deny that pull? How could they be close enough to exchange teacups, and he fail to perceive it?

For nearly half an hour she paced, trying to think of some arrangement by which they might meet and maintain sufficient physical distance. She could not. When he called, he would surely take her hands as she entered the room, would expect to sit beside or directly across from her as they conversed.

And when he did, she simply could not carry off the pose of congenial friend. Not with the memory of his hands, his mouth on her, the feel of him sheathed within her still so vivid. The very hairs on her skin prickled at the thought of being near him.

Perhaps later, given time for the intensity of these feelings to fade—and surely, if God were merciful, they would!—she could manage to cobble back together the pieces of the serene demeanor she'd been able to present to him the previous six years. Teach herself to accept his arm or his hand and not yearn for more.

But not by tomorrow or the day after.

What reason could she invent to delay his visit?

She paced to her desk, thinking rapidly. She'd signed the deeds this morning, completing the final step in the purchase of her new property. She could write Quentin a reply and claim that, as she'd already sent instructions for Sudley's manager to begin the moving process, a complicated business that would likely require all her time and attention for the foreseeable future, she was on the point of leaving London. She could ask him to call on her at her new farm, delaying the visit until she'd finished setting up the operation so she might be able to show it off to him proudly.

He would honor such a request—wouldn't he?

Walking to the window, she stared out at the gray dawn and examined the plan, searching for potential flaws. After several minutes, she concluded it offered both a reasonable excuse for quickly departing the metropolis and her best chance to delay Quentin's inevitable visit until she was better prepared to deal with it.

Though the idea of fleeing shamed her, that humiliation paled beside the dire consequences of having her deception uncovered.

Feeling a bit calmer, she strode to the armoire to withdraw her portmanteau. She'd pack the essential items, let Aunt Kitty's maid finish the rest and be on the road to Sudley by this afternoon.

Moving stock, equipment and personnel would indeed keep her too busy to fret over the dilemma she'd created. Then, while she set all to rights at her new property, she could begin once again armoring her heart against Quentin.

Against his kindness and caring. The engaging sense of humor that always lifted her spirits, the exhilaration of racing their mounts across a meadow, or vying over billiards, or debating the best way to resolve some problem on one of their estates.

Against the touch that had awakened her body to desires and responses she'd never dreamed she possessed, a pleasure that had liquefied her bones and swept her away on a flood-tide of delight, to subside in ecstasy later within the safe harbor of his embrace.

Against the devilishly seductive thought that her great love for him, combined with his genuine liking for her, would be enough to make a marriage work.

She took a ragged breath, the irony of it forcing her to a rueful smile. It appeared Quentin had been right to resist attempting to add passion to their friendship.

With her loss of innocence had come a vastly magnified physical awareness of Quentin, a knowledge of how addicting was the pleasure he could produce in her. Denying that hold was shattering her heart and reducing to splinters the stout defenses behind which she'd previously managed to resist him.

Tears stung her eyes. Angrily she swiped them away.

She would not, she vowed, become like her father and play Orpheus, who, when his bride was stolen from him by a viperous seducer, shut himself away from the world, forever mourning his loss.

Every man had flaws—even Quentin. Perhaps while she toiled to assemble her new enterprise, she could create a list of his faults, use it to school herself into considering it fortunate they would never marry. Let dispassionate reason pry loose the hold Quentin had established over her heart and soul, a hold she'd stupidly allowed passion to strengthen.

Once she had the farm running well and could demonstrate how successful and content she was as a single lady in control of her life, he would see there was no need for him to "salvage her future" by making her his wife.

And perhaps by then she would be able to meet him and feel only the tepid platonic friendship that was all Quentin Burke wanted from Caragh Sudley.

QUENTIN RETURNED to London in the early evening to the news, conveyed to him in a note from Caragh, that she once again had left the city. In fact, she requested that he not visit her until after she'd finished the move to her new property and had the farm functioning properly.

In addition to disappointment, a vague sense of…hurt pierced him as he read the note. Urgent as her business was, could she not have lingered just one more day and delivered her message in person? That emotion was swiftly succeeded by a niggling sense that perhaps Caragh was avoiding him.

But the facts didn't truly support such a suspicion. She'd been completely open and cordial at their last meeting. Excited as she was about her plans for the new venture, it was hardly surprising she was impatient to begin carrying them out.

Much as he burned to follow her immediately, as an estate manager himself, he understood both the complexity of the task facing her and the pride that had her urge him to postpone visiting. No more than she would he relish a friend calling at one of his new properties until he'd had time to staff, organize and begin running it efficiently.

Since the farm was located in a rural corner of Hampshire, it was unlikely anyone in the ton would discover her new venture for some time. With her reputation safe for the moment, he had little excuse not to honor her request.

It appeared he must contain his impatience for a few weeks at least.

The only sweet note in that otherwise sour conclusion, Quentin was confident after last night's discussion, was that Russell did not realize how soon his new neighbor intended to take up residence. Even so, in his current state of frustration, Quentin wasn't sure he could maintain a suitably friendly demeanor toward the man if he happened to encounter him over dinner at the club. He decided to stay home and order a cold collation.

Rather than brooding over what could not be changed, he told himself as he made short work of a beefsteak and ale, he should instead concentrate on settling a matter that could. Directly after dining, he would pay another call on Madame LaNoire.

A hot flash of anticipation washed through him, followed by another wave of guilt. He had to admit, this lingering…fascination with the veiled lady was a bit disturbing.

'Twas merely an attraction based on sympathy magnified by a healthy dose of lust, he reasoned. Once he married Caragh, with whom he shared a much deeper bond, and had *her* in his arms to beguile his senses, memories of Madame's allure would fade to the insignificance of a candle's glow beside a raging bonfire.

The sooner he secured Madame LaNoire's future, the sooner he might focus all his efforts on settling his with Caragh. After instructing a footman to summon a hackney, he allowed his valet to help him into his greatcoat.

A short drive later, he found himself once again mounting

the stairs to Madame LaNoire's apartment, his nerves simmering with anticipation and grimly suppressed desire. Once again he knocked repeatedly, to no avail.

This time, however, he had come prepared. Squelching the protests of conscience, he produced from his pocket a long iron key. He had noted on his previous visit that the heavy oak door sported an old-fashioned lock. Before leaving his rooms tonight he'd rooted through his belongings to unearth a key the blacksmith at Branson had fashioned to open some long-neglected storage rooms for which, they'd discovered during Branson Park's renovation, the original keys had somehow become lost.

It was still early enough that he was certain Madame was away from home rather than asleep. Since finding her in residence was proving more difficult than anticipated, if the key chanced to work, he could leave her a note explaining his purpose and begging the favor of a reply.

He'd not yet decided what he would do, should he leave such a message and she fail to contact him.

Dismissing that thought, after peering down the staircase to insure he was not being observed, he inserted his key into the lock. After some jiggling, he managed to turn it and heard the latch click open.

Heartbeat speeding, Quentin pushed open the door and entered the apartment.

Calling her name as he walked, he proceeded from the small antechamber through the sitting room into the bedroom. Given the lack of response to his knock, he was not surprised to find no one at home.

What did surprise him, as he retraced his steps more slowly through the deserted rooms, was the palpable sense of emptiness that struck him, sharp as the click of his boots on the bare floor. Not only was Madame LaNoire not at home, it appeared she had not been home for some time.

The parlor hearth was cold, containing neither ashes from a previous fire nor the kindling necessary to start a new one, while the table beside the wing chair before it was barren of newspapers or needlework. No dishes cluttered the dry sink in the small kitchen; no cooking pot sat ready on the stove. Even in the bedchamber of which he had such warm memories, the bed linens were cold and creaseless, as if no one had lain upon them in a long time.

He wandered across that dim chamber, to halt beside a dressing table in the opposite corner. Recalling the clutter of bottles that had always adorned his mama's, he noted with surprise that not a single vial of perfume or box of powder sat upon the table's surface—not so much as a brush or a hairpin.

In growing dismay, he hurried to the armoire and jerked open the door. The space within was as bare as the dressing table.

Impossible though it seemed, the conclusion was inescapable. Madame LaNoire was not just out—she was no longer in residence.

Dismay intensified, laced with an edge of panic. Had their tryst been discovered and she dismissed, compelling her to abandon her lodgings? Given her lack of resources, where could she have gone?

Surely nothing so dire could have occurred in the space of just a few days! But whatever the reason that had led her to leave home, Quentin felt compelled to find her, make sure she was safe—and verify that it was not their stolen interludes that had brought her to harm.

Unable to explain even to himself the urgency that drove

him, he hurriedly relocked the door and trotted down the steps. As expected, what appeared to be landlord's apartment occupied the ground floor.

His knock was answered by an unkempt older woman, straggly gray hair escaping from beneath a stained mobcap. The surly look with which she opened the door faded as she took in his fashionable dress, and she belatedly dropped a curtsey.

"What kin I do for ye, m'lord?"

"I'm sorry to disturb you, ma'am, but I'm looking for one of your tenants, a Madame LaNoire?" Improvising rapidly, he continued, "My sister, who has engaged her services as a governess, sent me to fetch the lady, but she doesn't appear to be in. Might you know of her whereabouts?"

The matron peered at him, frowning. "Don't have no tenant by that name, m'lord."

So the name she'd given him was false, Quentin thought without surprise. That fact, added to her insistence on retaining the veil, only reinforced the likelihood that she was exactly what she claimed—a virtuous widow intent on keeping her reputation free from any taint of scandal. Which would make it all the more likely that his hopes of placing her in Aunt Jane's care would be realized.

After, of course, he found her.

"Perhaps I did not get the name aright—my sister's handwriting is sometimes difficult to decipher. Surely you've seen her, a slender, dark-haired lady with a pronounced French accent? My sister assured me she lived in this building."

The matron shook her head, setting the tattered lace of her cap bobbing. "B'ain't never had no furriners living here. Be ye sure ye've got the right house?"

His clandestine inspection of Madame LaNoire's flat left him certain of that, though he hardly wished to confess that excursion to the landlady. Since he knew beyond doubt this was the correct building, why did the landlady disavow all knowledge of her? Could it be Madame LaNoire's accent had been false as well?

"I believe I am correct," he said slowly, his mind still scrutinizing possibilities. "I am quite certain my sister indicated she resided on the top floor."

The lace fluttered again with another denial. "Got no lady on the top floor. In fact, 'tis nobbit up there now. Flat is let to an artist gent, but he's off traveling in some rubbishing place—Rome, I hear."

Quentin shook his head, trying to make the disparate pieces fit. One explanation occurred, so awful he felt compelled to ascertain forthwith whether it might be true.

"Does that gentleman have a w-wife," he stumbled over the word, suddenly realizing the bitter implications should it turn out his veiled lady was *not* a widow, "who might have returned before him?"

The lady shrugged. "I wouldn't know, m'lord. Long as a tenant pays the rent on time so's I can turn it over to the owner and keep me own flat, I don't put my noggin in nobody else's business."

He took a ragged breath, relieved to at least not have that possibility confirmed. "Do you know when the artist plans to return?" he persisted.

Once more the mobcap bobbed as the lady shook her head. "He didn't say, but the rent's paid up until autumn."

Which left Quentin exactly—nowhere. Unable to think of any further questions that would not arouse still further the curiosity of the matron, who already showed signs of suspicion about his interest in the artist, he judged it prudent to retreat. Regardless of what she might know—and unless she were a better actress than he could credit, it appeared she knew little—he would learn nothing further about Madame LaNoire's whereabouts from her.

"I must have misread my sister's note after all. Pray excuse me, ma'am," dropping into her hand a coin that elicited a gap-toothed smile and a flurry of assurances that Mrs. Jeffries be ever at his service.

Trying to stomach his second major disappointment of the day, Quentin wandered to the street to summon a hackney, his mind awhirl with speculation. Could Madame LaNoire be the artist's errant wife? She must have some association with the man, or she would not have had a key to his flat.

A more palatable possibility presented itself as he journeyed back home—that she was a friend asked by the artist to watch over the property during his absence. Who, when she determined upon seducing Quentin, decided to further protect her identity by borrowing the premises for their tryst.

How much of what she had told him was real, how much invention? With her face masked and the dwelling she'd taken him to belonging to someone else, he had to acknowledge that her name, her story and even her voice might have been equally false.

The only thing he knew to be true was the intensity of the passion they'd shared.

Given his determination to wed Caragh, that was hardly a memory on which he needed to dwell. He would do better to wash his hands of the mystery that was Madame LaNoire and get on with his own plans. The care with which she'd obscured

the truth of her circumstances argued that she felt in no need
of his assistance.

And yet…if her story were true, she might well be in difficulty, possibly because of their brief liaison. Unable to rid
himself of that persistent worry, he decided to allow himself
one more evening to ponder how he might discover her current whereabouts before abandoning his efforts to assist her.

The idea came to him just as the hackney reached his
lodging.

The artistic world was a small one. Possibly Ailis or her
mentor Mr. Frank knew the painter who'd rented the rooms
Madame LaNoire had borrowed. At the least, he should be
able to determine that man's identity, perhaps discover
whether a friend—or wife—was watching the property.

He might even learn the identity of his veiled lady.

Once again, excitement and an irrepressible desire stirred
at the prospect.

Would he find her to be a virtuous governess in real need
of his assistance? Or an artist's model, an actress or courtesan who had amused herself by weaving a tall tale to hood-
wink a gullible gentleman?

It hurt to consider that his lovely veiled lady might have
been laughing up her sleeve at him the whole time they'd spent
together. And yet, as he forced himself to face the possibility,
when he recalled her air of gentility, her voice, her carriage,
he simply couldn't believe her to be less than a lady born.

In any event, learning the truth about her was fast becoming such an obsession, he suspected he would never rid himself of this fascination unless he followed the trail to its end,
whatever that turned out to be.

The hour was now too late for social calls, he decided, re-

gretfully refraining from banging on the roof to redirect the jarvey. But first thing tomorrow, before she became enmeshed in
her work, Quentin would drop by the studio of Ailis Sudley.

CHAPTER TWENTY

QUENTIN WOKE EARLY, driven by a sense of expectation. Today he might finally unveil his mystery lady!

He jumped from bed and strode to the window, pulling aside the heavy curtains. The dawn appeared clear, with just a glaze of high clouds—the sort of day that would provide the steady north light in which an artist preferred to work. Doubtless Ailis Sudley would be up and at her easel early to take advantage of it. If he wished to speak with her, he'd best snare her before she began painting, for he knew she wouldn't hesitate to have her maidservant send him away if she were deep in the throes of artistic creation when he called.

As soon as he felt she must be awake and about, he presented himself at her studio.

Fortunately, he caught her still at breakfast. Accepting her offer of coffee, he took a chair in the sitting area she'd screened off from the open workroom. Ailis lounged on the sofa, clad in a thin wrapper that accented her ample curves.

Odd, he thought, noting dispassionately the voluptuous outline of her bosom as she raised her arm to drink her coffee, that her striking blond beauty left him unmoved, while her less conventionally pretty sister inspired in him a deep physical attraction.

Would Madame LaNoire turn out to be a beauty, once he was finally able to gaze upon her face?

"To what do I owe the honor of this early visit?" Ailis asked, pulling him from his reflections. "Whatever it is, be quick about it, for I mean to be at work within the hour."

So much for a gracious hostess's manners, Quentin thought, grinning. "Perhaps I just wanted a few moments of scintillating conversation."

"Then you would certainly not have sought me out," Ailis returned, not at all offended. "Come, Quent, cut line. What is it you want?"

"Some information. I'm trying to trace an artist and thought you, or Mr. Frank, might know him." Now that he was so close to possibly solving the mystery, Quentin had to work to keep his tone light and mask the urgency that stretched every nerve trigger-tight.

Ailis raised an eyebrow. "And what need would you have of an artist?"

Having anticipated the question, he replied smoothly, "Now that Branson Hall is restored, I'm looking for still life paintings to adorn some of the rooms."

"Fortunately, neither I nor Max do still life, else I should be much insulted that you did not consult us first. This artist specializes in them, then?"

"So I've been told."

"Ah. Who recommended him? One of your aristocratic acquaintances?"

"Really, Ailis, does it matter?" Quentin replied, exasperation cracking his calm facade.

"A bit impatient, are we?"

Controlling himself with an effort, he replied, "'Tis you who wished to conclude the interview quickly."

She nodded, though her eyes sparkled with an amusement he had learned over the years to mistrust. "So I did. What is this esteemed individual's name?"

"I'm afraid I don't know. When I admired the work and asked the owner, he could not recall."

As he'd hoped, this lack of appreciation for the artist succeeded in diverting her from speculating about his interest in the matter.

"How typical of the rich!" she exclaimed, her eyes firing up. "Completely oblivious to the importance of the genius who creates the masterwork!"

"Lamentable, I know," he soothed. "He did, however, recall the location of the man's studio—a top-floor flat on Maiden Lane, not far from here."

"Maiden Lane?" Her indignation subsiding, Ailis grew thoughtful. "You're quite certain it was Maiden Lane? I don't know of any artist of repute living there, but I'm newly come to London. If you wish, I can ask Max."

So he must leave no more knowledgeable about the veiled lady than when he'd arrived. Once he'd controlled his disappointment—which was far keener than it should be—Quentin replied, "Yes, I should appreciate that."

"He's away at the country home of a client now, finishing up a portrait, but I shall ask him directly when he returns."

He clenched his teeth to prevent an oath of frustration from escaping. "When do you expect Mr. Frank back?" he said instead.

Ailis gave a graceful wave of her hand. "I'm not certain. Completing the final details should occupy several weeks, I should guess. It's fortunate I have a commission of my own to finish up, for which he's already approved the preliminary sketches, else I should sorely resent his absence."

Several weeks! After spending the last few hours in ardent expectation of perhaps learning the identity of his veiled lady today, several weeks seemed an eternity. Fuming inwardly, Quentin rose to his feet.

"I've taken up enough of your time for today, then. Thank you for the coffee."

"Should you like to see some of the sketches before you leave?" Ailis asked, rising as well.

Despite the choking sense of frustration that made him want to pound a fist into the studio wall, it would only be polite to agree. Besides, he was curious to see what commission Ailis, as both a fledgling artist and a female, had managed to wangle.

"I should be honored."

She led him around the screen to the workbench. "The initial sketch was a figure study I'd done for Max, which he thought handsome enough to hang in his studio. One of his clients liked it so much he commissioned a series."

"Does the patron know you are the artist?"

"Max told him it was the work of his most promising student," she told him as she opened a leather portfolio and leafed through its contents. "The client was thrilled, apparently thinking to purchase the series for much less than he would have expected to pay Max. But being the exceptional mentor he is, Max secured a very fine price for it. I shall have no need to draw upon my reserve funds for quite some time," she finished, a note of pride in her voice.

"My congratulation, Ailis! It sounds as though you've

made a fine beginning." Having long considered her to possess a superior talent, Quentin was genuinely happy for her. And it dampened somewhat his still-smoldering anger toward Ailis to learn that the career she had wounded her sister and ruined Caragh's future to secure at least showed promise of being successful.

"I decided not to include this sketch in the series, so you may have it. In fact, thinking I might one day offer it to you, I recently made a few changes." She held out the parchment, a little smile playing at her lips.

"Thank you, that's very kind. I shall treasure it."

Ailis chuckled. "I'm sure you shall."

As Quentin glanced down at the sketch Ailis handed him, shock sucked the air from his lungs and the conventional compliment he'd been about to utter evaporated off his lips.

His eyes riveted to the drawing of a slender woman reclining on her side, one arm masking her face, a tumble of dusky curls cascading over her shoulders and down to frame her breasts. Her naked breasts.

The utter relaxation of her limbs and the sheen of perspiration glistening on her nude body conveyed the impression of blissful satiation. Indeed, her lover reclined behind her, his face in shadow as he kissed her shoulder, his arm over her hip, his hand on her belly, his fingers resting possessively over the curls at the juncture of her thighs.

Shocking as it was to realize the creator of this erotic tableau was the little girl who'd grown up his neighbor at Thornwhistle, what stole his breath was the woman's startling resemblance to his veiled lady.

Memories came flooding back—of lying tangled in the bedclothes after lovemaking, his lady reclining just so, satisfied and pliant in his embrace. The sketch's suggestion of the subtle stroking by which he could rouse her responsive body and begin the magic spiral again sent a blast of desire and longing through him.

He must have been staring for some minutes before he managed to pry his gaze from the image and his mind from the memories, for when he at last looked up, Ailis was smiling broadly.

"You like it, I can see."

"I…it…confound it, Ailis, how could you—" he broke off, heat flooding his face, nothing in his previous experience equipping him to discuss so intimate a matter with a female, much less a gently-reared, unmarried one.

She laughed, her voice rich with amusement. "Honestly, ton gentlemen are such hypocrites! They think nothing of reveling in the embrace of courtesans or mistresses, but are rendered speechless by viewing the *image* of such pleasure when in company with a female." She shook her head. "Even Holden, as wicked as his reputation is, was shocked when he first saw the sketches."

He wanted to argue something about a gentleman's discretion and the need to protect a lady's tender sensibilities, but couldn't quite get his tongue around the words. Besides, such a speech was probably wasted on the creator of this startling drawing.

"Are…all the sketches in the commission like this?" he managed at last.

"Oh, no! Most are much more explicit…but I didn't wish to shock you overmuch."

Quentin could only be glad she'd decided to refrain. The very suggestion of what else she might have drawn propelled his thoughts back to Madame LaNoire's bedchamber, tightening his body with another flush of need, leaving him once more speechless.

She laughed again at his obvious befuddlement. "Come now, Quent, don't be such a rustic. 'Tis considered quite normal for a *man* of my age to have experience. Indeed, had I been wife these last five years to some complacent husband and had already produced the requisite heirs, you must admit that your compatriots would now be vying to put *me* in just such a position as the girl in the sketch."

Quentin opened his lips to object, then closed them. Recalling the bawdy comments already being tossed around concerning her at the gentlemen's clubs, he could not with veracity protest that assessment.

"Thank you for not insulting my intelligence by attempting to deny it," she said, patting his hand before taking his arm to lead him to the door.

She halted with him before the entry. "You will take good care of it," she said, a naughty gleam in her eye.

"Of course," he replied a bit stiffly, still striving to regain his shattered composure.

"I'll be in touch with you when Max returns," she said as she plucked his greatcoat from the clothes tree. As she pulled the heavy garment off, though, it snagged on the adjacent pegs, knocking several items to the floor.

Ailis exclaimed in annoyance. Before she could reveal any more of her charms by bending over in her flimsy wrapper, he thrust the sketch into her hands. "Allow me," he said, kneeling down to retrieve the fallen garments.

"Thank you, Quent," she said as he straightened to offer her a pair of gloves and a long trailing scarf.

Something about the touch of the latter item caught his attention. Grabbing the end, he drew it back and stared. For the second time that morning his breath suspended.

The long, filmy rectangle fashioned of black velvet had a pattern of fleur-de-lis burned into its surface—the same design he'd traced with his fingertips, trying to map the features of the face hidden behind it.

"Wh-what is this?" he gasped, his heartbeat now loud in his ears.

Ailis raised an eyebrow. "Quite evidently, 'tis a lady's scarf."

"Yes, yes," he said impatiently, "but where did you get it?"

"'Tis Caragh's. I thought the pattern so pretty, I asked her to lend it to me to use as a drape in my figure studies."

Caragh's? Incredulity, delight and consternation pulsed through him. But 'twas preposterous! Patterned scarf or no, Caragh could not possibly be his veiled lady. Still…

"How long have you had it?" he demanded.

Ailis's eyebrow lifted higher. "Two days. I kept it when she came by to tell me she was leaving town to begin the move to her new property. Oh, she did tell you she's bought land to expand her farm—"

Quentin scarcely heard her after the first riveting words. *Two days…* As he ran the veil through his fingers, the soft fabric whispered under his thumbs in patterns he'd memorized in the lamplight and traced lovingly under the erotic spell of darkness. He took a deep, gasping breath. "Y-you are sure it is *Caragh's?*"

Ailis gave him an odd little smile. "Positive. Why do you ask?"

He shook his head. In character, experience and conduct

the two women could not be more dissimilar. Surely there was some other explanation. "I...I've seen something similar. Lovely, isn't it? It must be quite a popular style in the shops."

Ailis shook her head. "As it happens, I was with Caragh when she bought it and can attest we saw nothing remotely like it. The pattern is burned into the velvet by hand, so even should others have been produced, I don't expect any two could be identical. Does it matter?"

"N-no, not especially." Numbly he handed it back.

While he shrugged into his coat, Ailis folded the scarf neatly—and inserted the sketch in it. "Since you seem to like it so much," she said, holding the items out to him, "keep the scarf, too. Or return it to Caragh when next you see her. When will that be, by the way?"

"I'm...not sure. She asked that I wait to visit, ah, until—later." Like a river at flood tide, his thoughts were boiling over each other in a mad chaotic rush of speculation, making it extremely difficult for him to concentrate on conversing with Ailis.

He needed to get away, examine the scarf more closely, consider the implications of this startling development.

Mercifully, the traditional courtesies of leave-taking fell automatically from his tongue. And then he was alone, walking back down the stairs, clutching against his chest the velvet scarf—and Ailis's scandalous drawing.

In the brighter daylight of the street, he gave the scarf a minute inspection. After studying the graceful swirl of pattern, closing his eyes and tracing his thumb across the plush crests and silken valleys of its surface, his conviction intensified that this was indeed the covering that had veiled his lady's face those two nights.

The conclusion made him dizzy, as if he were standing at

the end of a long tunnel, watching his life spiral away from him, out of control. He took a steadying breath.

He'd return to his rooms, pour a strong brandy and ponder this again, slowly.

But the facts as he examined them in the unhurried privacy of his chamber led him back to the same conclusion, absurd and impossible as it first seemed.

He must take a trip to Bond Street and make a survey of the ladies' scarves. If that visit confirmed Ailis's contention that the scarf was indeed one of a kind, it must inevitably follow that...*Caragh* was Madame LaNoire?

As he tried to get his mind around the enormity of that conclusion, other details floated up out of memory.

When he'd first approached the veiled lady at Vauxhall, he recalled suddenly, he had mistaken her for Caragh. Even after two nights with her, something about the soft, fluid sound of her French syllables, her carriage, the angle of her body as she moved continued to whisper to him of Caragh.

And it was Caragh who'd begged him to attend the masquerade, Caragh whose failure to appear had left him alone and unoccupied—at the precise moment he encountered Madame LaNoire.

Coincidence? Or calculation?

Yet, convincing himself that Caragh was his veiled lady appeared absurd on the face of it. How could a gently-born virgin—for he would stake his life on the fact that Caragh was an innocent—have played the knowing widow?

The answer occurred, so simple he wondered why it had taken him so long to make the connection. Caragh might be innocent, but, he thought grimly, gazing at the sketch Ailis had given him—her scandalous sister was definitely not.

If Caragh were indeed Madame LaNoire, it was certainly Ailis who had helped her plan and execute the deception.

Anger welled up. How dare Caragh abuse his trust by perpetrating such an outrage? The heedless, unconventional Ailis he could well believe capable of it, though his mind boggled at imagining her actually instructing her sister in the arts of seduction.

He recalled the veiled lady's curious mix of carnality and hesitance, especially on their first night together. At the time, bewitched by her, he'd accepted without question her explanation that, having been celibate so many years, she was experiencing again the ways of a man with a woman as if for the first time.

Experiencing again—or for the *very* first time?

Into his mind flashed the image of the coy little smile Ailis had given him as she handed him the sketch—the *recently altered* sketch—of the sleeping woman who so closely resembled Madame LaNoire. His suspicion of her duplicity strengthened.

Who else might so easily access the key to another artist's studio? Or have at her disposition, given what she'd inferred to be in the rest of her series of sketches, a veritable pictorial guide to seduction with which to tutor an innocent?

If his suppositions were correct, Ailis had known all during their meeting this morning what he really sought. No wonder she'd drawn out the questioning, delighting in his discomfiture. *She knew of no artist of repute in that studio,* indeed!

He gritted his teeth against a choking swell of fury. If the infuriating wench had been to hand at this moment, he'd have been seriously tempted to strangle her.

And yet, as he gazed back at the sketch, some of his emotion shifted into burgeoning desire as, against his will, the deft lines of her drawing elicited vivid memories of those two evenings in Madame LaNoire's bed.

How could he murder someone who'd helped to produce two of the most glorious nights of his life?

Another thought occurred, and he slammed his glass down in agitation. No wonder Caragh had fled London before his return! Confronted face-to-face, she'd never been good at dissembling. If she were truly Madame LaNoire, she might have managed to fool him with an opaque veil and an untraceable accent, but after what she had done to him in candlelight and darkness, she would never be able to meet his gaze squarely in the unrelenting light of day without blushing. Nor, had *she* been his midnight lover, would she be able so much as to enter the room without them both becoming immediately conscious of the powerful physical bond created by two nights of thorough and passionate lovemaking.

Though he still could not truly believe it, if Caragh *were* Madame LaNoire, what was he to do about it?

Fury and desire to repudiate her friendship forever for deceiving him warred with exhilaration at the notion that the inventive, passionate lady who'd so captured his mind might be the lady who already held his affections.

He'd have to marry her, of course, but as he'd already decided on that course some time ago, that would hardly be a sacrifice. At the notion of having a lifetime of Caragh to titillate his mind and Madame LaNoire to inflame his senses, a delighted anticipation filled him.

Except…a strong stirring of caution quelled his delight. Would it not be folly to wed a woman who had behaved like a veritable hussy? Having shown herself capable of planning an elaborate seduction, how could he be sure after they were wed that Caragh might not take the notion into her head to entice some new lover?

Still, even if events proved she was indeed Madame LaNoire, Quentin simply couldn't believe Caragh a wanton. Every instinct told him she would never have permitted such intimacies, much less sought them out, were her emotions not completely engaged.

Which brought him to the perplexing corollary. If Caragh *were* Madame LaNoire, *why* had she done it?

Despite his anger, he had to feel flattered at the great lengths to which she'd apparently gone to make him her lover. Still, the whole charade had been unnecessary. He'd already asked her to marry him. She had only to say yes, and his body would be hers. Permanently. Why concoct this elaborate deception?

He took another fiery sip of the brandy, struggling to understand the impenetrable labyrinth of female reasoning. She'd professed herself insulted that he would offer marriage merely to salvage her reputation, although that was an eminently sensible reason to marry. Also practical and logical was the desire to wed someone for whom one already entertained a warm affection.

Unless… The only reason he could imagine to explain why a virtuous lady would sacrifice her honor and perpetrate such a ruse was that Caragh didn't just like, but loved him. Loved him too much to agree to marry for merely practical or logical reasons. She wanted his love in return—or nothing at all.

Convinced mild affection was all he had to offer her, had she decided to sample how glorious passion could be before devoting herself to her horses and turning her back on marriage forever?

Glorious it had certainly been!

He jerked his mind back from the temptation to focus once again on recalling those arousing interludes. He needed to decide what he meant to do now.

First and foremost, before he wasted any more time in uninformed speculation, he must determine whether or not Caragh was in fact his veiled lady.

He might return and baldly ask Ailis—but she'd had ample time this morning to reveal what she knew. Since she'd not chosen to avail herself of the opportunity, even if it were true, she was likely to deny the connection, after extracting the maximum entertainment value from mocking his delusion.

Better instead to follow the trail of the veil. Once he was able at last to confirm or refute the incredible notion that Caragh might actually be Madame LaNoire, only then would he confront the puzzle of what to do next.

THREE WEEKS LATER, Caragh leaned back in her chair in the small library she'd taken for her office and flexed her tired shoulders. The east-facing window before her desk looked out over a pleasing vista of scythed lawn, behind which stretched the newly erected fences of the paddocks for her stallions. The west and north sides of the small manor house were also surrounded with verdant pastureland partitioned off by fencing to contain the herd of mares.

She'd found the stone buildings of the original farm in excellent condition. Not having to expend funds on repairs, she noted with a pleased glance at the ledger, would leave her the necessary capital to construct all the additional barns she'd planned this very first year. There was even sufficient cash remaining to update the manor house and put in a new cook stove, which was certain to delight the few servants she'd brought with her from Sudley.

The move itself had required a full week, and she'd spent the next two with carpenters, stonemasons and grooms supervising the beginning of the additions and inspecting the new stock she'd had sent over from Ireland.

So serene were the vast meadows now dotted with grazing horses that she'd decided to call her new venture Hunter's Haven. The horses here would breed strong; her clients would find the stock so superior that the Haven would indeed become the refuge of choice for those seeking the finest in horseflesh.

She hoped it would prove a haven for her as well.

Her days were long, intense and exhausting. But as satisfying as it was to guide her longtime dream into reality, the best part of the move thus far was that the hectic pace kept her too busy to think about Quentin.

Most of the time, she amended with a sigh. In odd moments between tasks, as now, his image persisted in muscling its way out of the background of her mind to seize center stage, however much she resisted thinking of him and the halcyon hours she'd tricked him into spending with her.

She still vacillated between cherishing those evenings and regretting she'd ever conceived the bacon-brained idea of making him her lover. But she now knew with absolute certainty that fleeing London had been wise.

Beyond the difficulty of meeting him with the knowledge of their intimacy burning like the illicit secret in her breast, the ache of missing him was so acute that, were he still near enough, she knew she would break down and seek him out, however great the danger that he might uncover her deception.

Stronger still was the hunger for his touch, for the incredible sensations he could summon with his cunning hands and knowing tongue. Her will would certainly not be strong enough to resist the temptation to redon her veil and, in the guise of Madame LaNoire, summon her lover back for yet another night of bliss.

Passion, she was discovering, was a Pandora's box indeed. The powerful need he'd unlocked in her refused to be contained, clamoring instead for additional fulfillment.

As she had each previous occasion when thoughts of Quentin refused to be subdued, Caragh drew from beneath her ledger a now-worn sheet of vellum. Upon arriving at Hunter's Haven, she'd followed through on her London resolve and begun a list of Quentin's faults. A list she was supposed to review until she overcame her useless unrequited love for Quentin Burke.

"Managing" had been the first entry. He was certainly that. But like her, his intentions when he took on a project—or a person—were always pure. He wished not to control or subdue, but to improve, and he usually succeeded. His bringing his estate back from the verge of ruin was proof enough of that.

She ended by crossing it off the list.

"Arrogant" was the second item. But after pondering the matter, trying to recall when he had imposed his will or opinions on her, she concluded he had never tried to dictate her agreement or disregard her feelings. Certainly he was an ardent advocate for what he believed, but he had always sought, and listened patiently to, her opinions. Occasionally he even changed his views in favor of hers.

She'd drawn a long dark line through "Arrogant."

And so it had gone with "Insensitive," "Conceited" and "Humorless." The only item she'd penned on her list that she had not eventually crossed off was "Does not love me."

She touched her fingertip to the words again, her eyelids stinging. Even that was hardly a failing. As she knew only too well after living for more than two decades with her father, even with the deepest desire and after the sincerest of efforts, you could not *make* someone love you.

Perhaps she should just concede defeat and tear up the list. It seemed that rather than convincing her how lucky she was to escape Quentin's spell, reviewing it only made her ponder him and his qualities at greater length, leaving her missing him all the more keenly.

Enough self-pitying nonsense, she told herself crossly, thrusting the paper back under the ledger. List or no list, as her memory of the seductive pleasures of his body faded, the hold he had over her mind and heart would dissipate, too. Then she would finally master this unacceptable weakness for him, extinguish once and for all the pathetic longing for his touch.

She had better, she thought grimly, make progress in that direction quickly. She'd already penned him two notes, chatting of her progress and referring vaguely to when she expected to have Hunter's Haven presentable. She couldn't hope to stave off his visit much longer.

And how she wanted him here, despite how dangerous his nearness would certainly prove!

A knock at the door set her heart racing.

Idiot! she told herself as she bid the supplicant enter. It would surely not be Quentin, too impatient to wait any longer in London for her summons. Silently chastising herself for her fixation on the man in terms crude enough to have impressed her stable boys, she turned toward the door, struggling to master her hopeless hope.

Standing behind the butler on the threshold was not, of course, Quentin. Instead she saw his London friend and the former owner of her new property, Lord Alden Russell.

"Your nearest neighbor, Lord Russell, Mistress," the butler intoned.

Smiling, Lord Russell walked past the servant and swept her a bow. "The very warmest of welcomes to our county, Miss Sudley! Had I known you intended to take possession of the property so quickly, I'd have been much more gracious about bowing to Mama's wishes that we return to Hillcrest Manor for a short respite from town."

It was quite impossible not to smile back at his open friendliness. "Thank you, Lord Russell," she replied, curtseying. "Please, do come in."

"I'm not interrupting?" He gestured to her desk with its stack of account books.

"Not at all. I needed a break—" *from more than just account books,* she thought "—and was on the point of ringing for some tea. Won't you join me?"

"Alas, I cannot stay. I was on my way to do an errand for Mama when I saw your sign and felt compelled to discover if the new owners had yet arrived."

"Another time, then," Caragh replied, nodding a dismissal to the butler, who left them with a bow. "You will stay a few moments, I hope?"

"Finding you at home, I cannot deny myself that pleasure," he murmured.

Surprise and a warm gratification flowed through Caragh as she walked to the wing chair before the fireplace. Since Ailis's debacle, she had spent so much time armoring herself for criticism and rejection that Lord Russell's warm friendliness fell like soft rain on parched ground. "So your mama is a lover of country living, but you are not?" she asked, gesturing him to the sofa.

Before seating himself, he caught her hand and brought it to his lips. "I am now," he murmured.

A subtle current flashed between them. Before her masquerade as Madame LaNoire, she might not have noticed— or identified—what the pressure of his fingers, the tenor of his voice, were telegraphing. *He's attracted to me,* she realized in surprise.

That novel thought was followed immediately by a new and rather gratifying sense of feminine power. Not sure what she meant to do about it, she ignored the innuendo under his words.

"I should think you would be, given the beauty of the land hereabouts. By the way, I'm very grateful to you! I found the property in just as excellent a condition as you and your lawyer described it. It shall do wonderfully for my enterprise."

"'Hunter's Haven,' the new sign said," Lord Russell replied, accepting her tacit rebuff of his flirtatious overture. "You specialize in that breed?"

"Yes, as I believe I told you when we first met. Sudley produced some excellent horses, but with insufficient pasturage to maintain them, I was forced to sell all but a few. An impediment to expansion of the breeding operation that shall no longer hinder me, given the vast amount of prime pasturage here. With the addition of the superior Irish stock I've just purchased, I'm quite excited about our future."

"It sounds promising indeed. I always thought this would be a perfect property for horse-breeding. Once you have the operation organized and running to your satisfaction, I should love to tour it."

"I shall be happy to show you around. But if such an enterprise interests you, why did you sell the farm?"

Lord Russell shrugged. "I haven't the talent for horses I understand you possess, and I've enough other acreage to manage. Now, I've interrupted you long enough," he said, rising. "I just wanted to extend a welcome and assure you that, should you need anything while you're settling in, please don't hesitate to call at Hillcrest."

"That's very kind," Caragh replied, rising as well.

"When do you expect your father?" he asked as she walked with him to the door. "By rights, I should have postponed my call when your butler informed me he was not yet in residence, but I must confess, I was too impatient to heed the proprieties. Oh, and Mama bade me invite you to dinner tomorrow, just a small gathering. She plans a more formal affair to introduce you and Lord Sudley to the neighbors once you've settled in."

Heat rose in Caragh's face. She might return an evasive answer, put off revealing that her father would not be coming to join her. But it would be shabby to bask in the warmth of the hospitable gestures of her new neighbors while leaving them in ignorance of her true status.

She cleared her throat. "My father is a classical scholar of some note. I'm afraid he is far too immersed in his studies to have time or interest in supervising a farm. He…he intends to remain fixed at Sudley."

His bright smile dimmed. "Now that is a disappointment! Not only will we be deprived of his acquaintance, but I had hoped you would be making your residence more or less permanently among us. However, an enterprise as vast as you envision will surely require you to make frequent visits." Winking, he gave a theatrical sigh. "I shall have to content myself with that, I suppose. Please do join us for dinner tomorrow, even without your father." Reaching for her hand, he said, the caressing undertone back in his voice, "I must make the most of my opportunities."

She allowed him to kiss her fingertips, noting once again that small quiver of physical attraction. He was quite a handsome gentleman, she thought dispassionately.

All the more reason to set him straight from the outset. "Lord Russell, before I accept your mama's obliging invitation, you should know that my visits here will be more than frequent. I…I intend to reside here. Without Papa," she added, once more feeling the color rise in her cheeks but determined to make sure there could be no misunderstanding.

His eyebrows winged upward, and for a moment he stood silent.

Even without Quentin's warning, she'd known that by flouting convention, as a single woman living alone she would leave herself open to criticism, ribald conjecture, perhaps even dishonorable offers. She braced herself for the appraising look, the intensifying of his sexual innuendo once he realized the full implications of her disclosure.

Faced for the first time with actually dealing with that potential reaction was more humiliating and distasteful than she had ever imagined. Grimly she set her teeth and lifted her chin.

"What an immense undertaking!" he said at last, bowing with perfect propriety. "Mama and I shall certainly look forward to your telling us all about your plans when you come to dine."

Caught off guard, she let out a gusty breath she hadn't realized she'd been holding and looked up into his face. Could it be he had *not* understood? But no, he would have to be dim-witted indeed not to have comprehended her meaning. Both from Quentin's descriptions and her own dealings with him, she knew him to be quite intelligent.

"You…you are sure? I should not wish to embarrass your lady mama."

He laughed. "Mama is made of sterner stuff than that—as are you, I'll wager. Or so Quentin has led me to believe.

'Flashing-eyed Athena, wise and fair' indeed! Until tomorrow evening, then?"

He did understand…and meant to befriend her anyway. Gratitude and humility brought her shockingly close to tears. "You are both indeed kind, then. Until tomorrow."

Once more he kissed her hand, his lips lingering on her bare knuckles long enough for the current running between them to intensify.

Pulling her hand away, she wondered if she should revise her previous impression. Was friendship all he was hoping for from a woman who'd just announced herself gentry-born but not gentry-behaved?

And what coercion would he have to exert over his poor mama to keep her from withdrawing her invitation once she learned the shocking truth about her new neighbor?

"I'm deeply indebted to Lord Branson for introducing us," Russell said, pulling her from her thoughts, "and I hope to become much better acquainted."

She curtseyed in return to his final bow, then watched him walk out, an odd mix of feelings—gratitude, suspicion, uncertainty—jostling within her. Just what sort of acquaintance did he wish for with his unconventional new neighbor?

Although inviting her into his home to dine with his mama argued against his harboring any ignoble intent, she didn't yet know him well enough to be sure.

Ailis would probably say his intentions were irrelevant, advise her to use the attraction he obviously felt to smooth her way in the neighborhood. Perhaps even take him for her lover.

That would certainly be one way to distract herself from longing for Quentin and quiet the body still clamoring for his touch. She felt a surge of warmth within at the thought.

But her stolen nights with Quentin had taught her several hard truths. She had no intention now of taking another lover, even were she to develop a warm enough friendship with Lord Russell to envision such a step.

She was having difficulty enough coping with the first experience. Loving Quentin as she did, their intimacy, for her, had truly been a merging into one flesh. Having to send him away had been like ripping her soul in two. She didn't think she could survive a second such experience.

Besides, she was discovering, she was not as much her mama's daughter as, in the throes of hurt and heartache, she'd originally assumed.

The social upheaval which still buffeted her had been Ailis's doing. She herself had no real wish to defy the ton's rules by spurning wedlock and traipsing from lover to lover, as her mother—and Ailis—seemed inclined to do. Nor, after nearly a month of isolation at her new farm, was she finding it quite as much a blessing as she'd envisioned to live totally removed from society.

From her girlhood, she'd assumed the reins of a large household and taken up corresponding responsibilities in her rural society. In addition to her work with the Benevolent Association, she'd participated in a continuous round of calls and consultations with her neighbors. At home, she had her father and Ailis to look after, their company at meals and in the evenings—even if the company of two such self-absorbed individuals was often less than stimulating.

Though her work here was satisfying and occupied nearly every minute, for the first time she was living totally cut off from both family and local society.

She was, she had to admit, lonely.

She missed the almost daily business of calling and receiving calls. She'd grown to dread the silence of meals where she dined alone but for the attending footman. And after dinner, on some evenings where the only sound in the room was her even breathing and the hiss and pop of the fire, she even missed the fractious ladies of the Benevolent Association.

And what of holidays? With whom was she going to share the warmth of the Yule log, the excitement of Boxing Day or the festivities of midsummer?

It appeared Quentin had been right when he'd urged her not to hastily make so irreversible a decision as cutting herself completely off from society.

Having, in addition to a successful farm, a home that included not just servants but also friends, a husband and eventually children on whom she could lavish her love had, she now realized, a deep-seated appeal.

It wasn't pride that would keep her from confessing this discovery to Quentin when he finally made his visit. She dare not admit it to him, lest he be quick to suggest it was not yet too late to have both her farm and the family she longed for—by accepting his offer of marriage.

Even now, the desire to do so pulled at her with frightening strength. After her nights as Madame LaNoire, she knew they would share passion as well as friendship. Would such a union be so impossible to bear?

But she knew her world too well. Ton couples often went their separate ways once the necessary heirs were conceived. Indeed, it was thought odd for a married couple to live in each other's pocket. As long as a husband supported his wife and children and treated them with courtesy—sometimes even when he did not—society considered it acceptable for him to pursue relationships elsewhere.

When the initial fiery heat of Quentin's passion for her faded to the tepid warmth of companionship, would he be able to resist the temptations their world would inevitably present to a handsome man of his wealth and position?

Discovering that the husband she loved with such intensity had lain with another woman would devastate her.

Her only real chance of avoiding that fate would be if the friendship Quentin felt for her were buttressed by a love as deep and abiding as her own. A love he had, up until now, shown no signs of harboring.

And if, after knowing her these six years, he had not yet developed such an attachment, it seemed unlikely he ever would.

The misery of that conclusion was a familiar one. Before melancholy overwhelmed her, though, a more cheering thought occurred.

She couldn't marry Quentin. But if, despite her status, Lord Russell persisted in befriending her—and that friendship proceeded into courtship—might she envision wedding him, should he turn out to be as kind and honorable as he seemed?

Not in the near term, of course. Her heart and mind were still too full of Quentin. But perhaps once she'd had time to extinguish that love, the yearning for a family might permit her to foster affection for someone else.

Considering that prospect, she suddenly understood why Quentin had felt confident about pressing her to marry him. She now saw the appeal of pledging one's troth to a partner for whom one felt nothing more intense than shared respect and friendship. Such a union might not engender heights of bliss, but it was also unlikely to plunge one into valleys of despair as deep as those she'd recently been plumbing.

Sighing, she turned her gaze out the window in the direction of Hillcrest Manor.

Regardless of his ultimate intent, the attentions of her new neighbor had already brought warmth and a glimmer of hope into her isolation. Perhaps Lord Alden Russell would prove just the antidote necessary to cure herself once and for all of the malady of loving Quentin Burke.

IN THE EARLY EVENING, Quentin sat at the desk in his London study, idly flipping through a stack of invitations. After three long weeks of attending functions ranging from Venetian breakfasts to dinners to musicales to come-out balls, none of the delights promised tonight by London's hostesses held the slightest appeal.

When they'd first arrived in London and he'd wanted to be available to offer Caragh his escort and support, he'd been pulled away repeatedly to address a continuous stream of small concerns at his new property. Naturally, he thought sourly, now that he most needed work to occupy his mind, no further problems had occurred. Even his paperwork had slowed to a trickle.

Yesterday, desperate for some activity, he'd ridden to the estate outside London to find, as he expected, that the new manager he'd just installed was doing splendidly. Indeed, upon his departure, after thanking him for the visit, the man had rather pointedly remarked that as he had matters well in hand, my lord needn't waste any more of his valuable time traveling out from London.

Without the Sudleys' affairs and his own business to distract him, he'd been experiencing for the first time the full measure of attention Society accorded a bachelor considered by the ton to be an extremely eligible parti.

He had to admit, he'd reveled a bit at first in the triumph of being sought out by matrons who, before his transformation of the Branson fortunes, would have steered their precious daughters well clear of him. For a few evenings he'd found it rather amusing, wondering if the ambitious mamas had all studied the same course at their female academies on "Pushing Eligible Daughters to a Gentleman's Attention."

As his connection to the scandalous Sudleys was well known, he was now finding the performance increasingly distasteful. After Lady So-and-So cornered him over dinner or dancing or cards and prevailed upon him to let her present her "darling Marianne," she would invariably opine that, given the distress he must have suffered over those "unfortunate girls," he would doubtless find it refreshing to meet a young lady whose breeding was as matchless as her countenance. She would then gesture toward the daughter, who, after lowering her eyes demurely behind her fan, would glance up with an unmistakable "come-hither" look.

He was having a hard time of late restraining the strong desire to cut off Lady So-and-So's effusions about her progeny by informing her just what he thought of a "lady" who would malign persons not present to defend themselves.

Perhaps Caragh was wiser than he'd thought in deciding to forego Society.

Ah, Caragh. Longing, confusion, impatience and the bite of repressed desire scorched him anew whenever his thoughts strayed to her, as they did all too frequently.

Impatience that had chafed him every moment since he'd

made a thorough search for velvet scarves, from the elite establishments on Bond Street to the peddlers crying their wares on the streets, without finding another similar to the one draped around his bedpost.

He was now virtually certain that Caragh had to be Madame LaNoire.

After three weeks of wallowing in a most atypical stew of indecision, he was still uncertain what to do about it.

His first thought had been a fierce desire to disregard her wishes and ride to see her immediately, to confront her before she had a chance to prepare herself for the meeting. If she reacted with awkwardness and hesitancy, her cheeks rosy with embarrassment at the memory of their intimacies, surely that would prove her to be the innocent he wanted to believe her.

He had nearly convinced himself of the gratifying notion that love for him must be what had driven her to such unprecedented conduct. Desire to claim the man she loved without obligating him to marry her had spawned the deception. To convince her to admit the truth and come to him openly, he would have to avow his own love in return.

Could he offer her that?

Just imagining Caragh's dear face on Madame LaNoire's responsive body caused powerful emotion to bubble up from deep within him, a fiery amalgam of desire, affection and tenderness. Awe and euphoria swelled his chest.

What an amazing woman! Intelligence, courage, honor he'd already known she possessed. But the outrageous impudence that would lead her to create a deception of this magnitude and the passionate audacity with which she'd carried it off illumined a side of his good friend he'd never suspected.

Small wonder he'd had such a difficult time trying to get

the veiled lady out of his mind and senses! He could envision no more exciting a prospect than sharing his life with a woman who could in the space of a single day ride, shoot and manage property like a man, keep house, entertain guests and attire herself with the elegance of a lady—and in his private chambers, drive him delirious with the skill of Madame LaNoire. He was likely to become completely besotted by such a creature.

In fact, he conceded, most likely he already was.

Recalling the joy she brought him, he was hard-pressed not to summon his horse and ride to her farm this instant.

Hunter's Haven, she was calling it.

Heaven, he would name it, if the two of them might be there together...

Which was the crux of the problem.

Every time he told himself to dismiss worries over her possible wantonness and abandon himself to anticipation of their imminent union, the image of the cuckolded husband— a fabled figure of fun in both literature and society—rose out of mind to give him pause.

He couldn't really believe Caragh would serve him such a turn. Every instinct and years of association argued that, in deciding to seduce him, Caragh had acted out of love rather than lechery. But then, he would never have predicted that the Caragh he thought he knew so well could have masqueraded as Madame LaNoire.

Innocent or doxy, he was honor-bound to marry her. The only question was whether he could do so with a full and open heart, or still harboring an unsettling suspicion.

The simple truth was he missed her, and even with his worries about her character, he wanted her.

Hoping time would resolve his doubts, he'd swallowed his frustration and impatience and remained in London awaiting her summons. Waiting, and wasting his time on these damned idiot entertainments.

A wave of frustration welled up, escaping the rapidly fraying bonds of his patience. With an oath he swept the trayful of invitations to the floor.

To hell with matchmaking mamas! He would spend the evening at his club. And give Caragh exactly three more days before, bidden or not, he would go to her.

Suitably re-attired, an hour later he entered White's to find old Lord Andover already at his favorite post by the window. Having little desire for company, Quentin bit back an oath. Resigning himself to the inevitable, he pasted a smile on his lips and approached.

"Ah, Branson, good to see you!" Lord Andover hailed him, waving his cane in salute. "Been missing you. Engaged in cutting a swath through this Season's young lovelies, I hear."

"Not nearly as large a swath as you would, my lord, should you ever decide to thrill the ladies by abandoning this masculine stronghold."

Andover chuckled, his cheeks pinking with pleasure at Quentin's remark. "Damme, I'm much too old to trouble myself doing the pretty! Now, there was a time in my youth…ah, but I've never been much in the petticoat line. Not like you!" The old gentleman poked his finger at the paper on his lap. "*Morning Post*'s society column asserts that 'a certain Lord B, too regrettably absent of late on his estates about London, returned to set several feminine hearts fluttering with his assiduous attentions at Lady L's come-out ball last night…'"

Quentin waved a deprecating hand. "I'm merely the latest raw meat being offered the Society hostess wolves."

"Yes, several of their usual favorites have decamped," Andover agreed. "Russell, for one. Smoke of the city bothers his mama's lungs, he told me. Said Lady Russell was insisting he take her to the country to recuperate."

Quentin, who had been only half listening until he might politely take his leave, suddenly whipped his gaze back to Andover. "Russell has gone out of town, you say? To Hillcrest Manor?"

"He didn't specify, but 'tis his mama's favorite property, so I expect that's where she dragged him. He was kicking up quite a dust over it…"

Russell was at Hillcrest Manor—a mere five miles from Caragh's new property?

"…not like you," Andover was saying. "The Russell lad prefers London to some rubbishing rural backwater full of livestock and bumpkins. I expect he'll not remain long."

If Russell had gone to Hillcrest, he would soon learn through the infallible network of servant's gossip that the new owner of Hunter's Haven had taken up residence.

The lovely new owner, whom he'd already ogled on several occasions, would certainly soon become the object of his assiduous attentions. Attentions that, Quentin thought, a surge of fury rising in his breast, he would not bet on remaining honorable once he discovered that Caragh intended to live there alone and unchaperoned.

The very idea of Russell luring a lonely and responsive Madame LaNoire into his arms and her bed flamed Quentin's long-smoldering frustration into fury, curled his fingers into fists he hungered to clasp around Alden Russell's throat. He jumped up, nearly knocking over his chair.

"Excuse me, my lord, but I must leave on the instant," he said, sketching a bow. "Urgent business." Ignoring the astonishment on the old man's face, he strode away.

He'd pack his bag tonight and be on the road to Hunter's Haven first thing tomorrow.

Not that he didn't trust Caragh. But if she felt as lonely and dissatisfied as he did, if her body ached for his touch as much as his did for hers, she might be vulnerable to a handsome, charming devil like Russell.

Wanton or innocent, she was *his* lover and would soon be his wife. Doubts be damned, it was past time for Quentin to claim the lady who had stolen his heart as completely as she'd bewitched his senses.

Having gone to such lengths to conceal her identity, Caragh might well, at first, deny the deception and reject his suit. But if she should prove a little slow to believe in his love or to accept the proposal he was more eager than ever to tender, he now had a few more tools in his arsenal of persuasion.

Fortunately, he thought, his lips curving in a smug grin, he knew just where Madame LaNoire was most vulnerable to his touch. Should Caragh prove resistant to reason, he would simply lure her into his arms where, if he repeated his offer at the right moment of intimacy, she would be helpless to refuse him.

Besides, the cardinal rule in assuring that a woman of passionate temperament was not tempted to find another lover was for her current lover to keep her well satisfied.

A task to which Quentin was looking forward with great enthusiasm. Even if he had to strangle Alden Russell first.

CHAPTER TWENTY-TWO

PEERING INTO the dull tin mirror as he shaved five days later, Quentin reflected he'd been right to set out without his valet. Not only would the modest accommodations, much less exalted than the man would deem fitting for a gentleman of Quentin's stature, have pained him, the journey had been an exercise in frustration from start to finish.

After exchanging his own mount for a job horse at a busy inn the first afternoon, he was halfway to the next posting stop when the animal threw a shoe. He'd led the lame beast for over five miles, only to discover at the first hamlet he encountered that the town smith was gone for the day and the inn had no mounts for hire.

Not until nearly noon the following day, having with a liberal infusion of gold coins persuaded the smith to put aside his other tasks, was he back in the saddle. Soon after, the dull gray clouds dissolved into steady rain which intensified to a ceaseless torrent, turning the road to a river of mud and limiting visibility to within a few feet. Though every delay rubbed his ragged patience like a burr beneath a saddle, he knew 'twas insanity to try to gallop his mount through dense fog along an unfamiliar road in hock-deep mud. He spent his second night drying his sodden clothing before a smoking fire at a modest inn, still far from his destination.

He made better progress the third day, but it was not until late afternoon of the fourth day that he finally turned the last hired mount into the streets of the village nearest Hunter's Haven. Rather than ride up to Caragh's gate bone-weary and mud-splattered, he decided to endure one final night apart and stay at the inn in the village.

In addition to rubbing his temper raw, the dawdling pace of his journey had given him entirely too much time to worry over what Alden Russell might be doing with *his* lady.

With a sigh, he put the shaving water aside and rang for a servant to remove it. Taking up one of the clean cravats the inn's maidservant had just pressed, he set about tying it.

In the first heat of jealousy, he'd unfairly suspected his friend might take advantage of Caragh's unusual circumstances. Upon more reasoned reflection, he'd decided that, regardless of Caragh's situation, Alden was unlikely to make improper advances toward a lady he knew to be gently born.

However, despite her assertion that she intended to renounce Society—and her rejection of his suit, for which he thought he now understood the reason—he did not believe someone as loving as Caragh would be content to spend her life alone. She might not, he sincerely hoped, easily succumb to the blandishments of a man who wished to *seduce* her, but she just might be persuaded to *marry,* should some other eligible and presentable gentleman press her.

A handsome, charming, persuasive gentleman like Alden Russell. A man who'd been attracted to her from the outset, who had heard Quentin sing her praises, who was intelligent enough to weigh her excellence of character more than her sister's indiscretion.

A man not blinded by years of friendship, who had seen

immediately upon meeting her that the girl Quentin held in such esteem had become a desirable woman.

At that conclusion, he gave one end of the cravat such a tug he nearly ruined the knot.

Still, though Caragh might eventually decide she had erred in deciding to remove to Hunter's Haven, she probably hadn't yet had sufficient time to begin regretting her self-imposed isolation.

And, Quentin reassured himself again, dropping his chin to crease the cloth into perfect symmetrical folds, as far as he knew, Russell wasn't hanging out for a wife. Most likely he'd only be interested in engaging Caragh in an agreeable flirtation to pass the time while his mama held him captive at Hillcrest.

How likely was he to have fallen in love in the short space of…a week?

It had only taken Quentin two magical nights.

Just thinking of Alden discovering love the way Quentin had was enough to bring his rational musings to a halt and fire the primitive jealousy smoldering beneath.

He gave a final nod to the scuffed mirror and strode from the room. If Alden had become enamored of Caragh, that was regrettable. But if Quentin discovered Russell had been hovering about her—or daring to lay hands on *Quentin's* lady— he was going to murder him.

Now to find Caragh and persuade her to finish the unfinished business between them with a wedding.

Once on the road, desire and impatience to see her swelled to such a pitch of anticipation he had difficulty refraining from kicking his horse to a gallop.

He hoped the shock of his unexpected arrival would send Caragh running to him before she remembered all the paltry reasons she'd used to convince herself to keep him at arm's length. And once he had her there—ah, he'd give her no opportunity for regrets! He intended to kiss her until she had just breath enough to say "yes" to his proposal of marriage.

Thoroughly warmed by envisioning that happy scene, he turned his horse in through a stone gateway bearing the sign Hunter's Haven and spurred his mount down the drive. After a few moments, the wooded border of the carriageway gave way to newly-fenced pastureland. Then the manor itself appeared in the distance, mullioned windows sparkling in the morning sun.

In just a few moments, he thought, heedless of his clothes as he kicked the horse to a gallop, he would be kissing her hands, her lips…

Reaching the manor, he turned his horse over to a servant and hurried up the entry stairs, heart pounding and hands trembling with eagerness. His enthusiasm was checked by the butler, however, who informed him Miss Sudley was not in the house, having departed at first light to supervise the ongoing construction of some new barns.

Stifling a curse at this further delay, he swallowed his disappointment and followed the footman the butler summoned to lead him to the construction site.

He'd hoped to bribe her butler into letting him come into her presence unannounced. It was unlikely, with him approaching down an open lane, that he'd now be able to use the element of surprise.

With her forewarned of his approach, he feared he'd probably need to apply some intimate persuasion to get her to admit her deception and accept his hand—which he could hardly do in the middle of an open field full of interested

workmen. Fortunately, his guide informed him the new barns
were being constructed beside an existing structure. He would
have to persuade her to give him a tour, then look for an estate office or tack room—given the height of his impatience,
even an unoccupied box stall would do—for the privacy in
which to press his argument.

Once he confronted her, might she admit everything and
fall into his embrace, as eager to be back in his arms as he
was to have her there? Or would she have used these weeks
of separation to armor herself against him?

Rounding a curve in the lane, he saw straight ahead a knot
of workmen around a frame structure, masons at its base setting a first course of stone. Unable to wait any longer, he paced
past his escort, searching for her.

As he trotted by a stack of lumber and building stone, a
flash of light blue caught his eye. He slowed, then skidded to
a halt.

On a cloth spread on a bench of stone blocks sat Caragh,
gesturing toward the toiling workman. Pressed close behind
her, his hand on her shoulder—was Alden Russell.

He must have uttered some sound, for Alden glanced over.
In his eyes, Quentin saw the same desire he felt welling up
within himself.

The gladness flooding him at the sight of her steamed immediately into rage. For a moment he couldn't trust himself
to speak or move, so strong was the impulse to charge over,
rip Alden's hand off Caragh's shoulder and plant him a facer.

While he struggled to master it, Caragh turned toward him.
Through the red haze clouding his vision he saw her eyes
widen, a smile of delight spring to her lips. She half rose, only
to sit back at the restraining pressure of Alden's fingers.

Quentin's gaze narrowed to the hand that prevented Caragh from coming to him. He was going to break every bone in it.

"Quentin, what a surprise!" Russell said, his unwelcoming tone and the unfriendly glint in his eyes confirming Quentin's suspicions that his friend was as little delighted to see him as he was to see Russell.

"Y-yes," Caragh echoed, her voice uneven, "I was not expecting you. Have you other business in the area?"

Even then, he might have carried off the meeting with some aplomb, had not Russell stepped in front of Caragh, as if to deny Quentin access to her.

The courtly veneer of civilization disintegrated under the primal hostility of a man who sees his mate coveted by another. Sidestepping Russell, he grabbed Caragh's arm and pulled her to her feet. "I have business with *you*," he all but snarled.

"Quentin, what in the world?" she exclaimed.

"See here, Branson, that's no way to greet a lady!" Russell protested, seizing his sleeve.

Quentin jerked his arm free and gazed into Caragh's eyes. "Come with me, please, Caragh! It's important."

Russell stretched a warning hand toward Quentin. "Miss Sudley, if you wish me to send him to the right-about, I'd be happy—"

"Thank you, Lord Russell, but that will not be necessary. I...I'll rejoin you in a moment."

After one speaking glance, Caragh followed Quentin silently as he led her toward the stone barn. He knew he'd annoyed her, rushing in like someone demented, but the feel of her flesh under his fingers at last, following swiftly upon the shock of finding her with Russell's hands on her, was making it very difficult for him to think.

Her docile silence ended the second they entered the barn. "Quentin Burke, what in blazes was that all about?" she demanded, shaking her arm free of his grasp.

He opened his mouth, then closed it. The clever little packet of an address he'd intended to deliver seemed to have smashed itself to bits on the unexpected shoal of Russell's presence, leaving him at a loss for words.

After all, he couldn't shout "How dare you let him touch you?" or "Why did you keep me away so long?"

Instead, he fumbled in the pocket of his waistcoat, dragged out the figured veil and flung it at her. "This!"

She gasped, her eyes widening and her face going pale, then crimson. Having given him all the proof he needed, Quentin stepped toward her, eager to sweep away every misunderstanding in the heat of the passion they'd shared.

She sidestepped his advance and backed away toward a stall, her arms crossed before her. "I fail to see what *that*—" she jerked her chin at the scarf that had come to rest on the stable floor between them "—has to do with you dragging me off like a Bedlamite."

"Come, Caragh, you can't mean to deny it!"

"Deny what?"

"Vauxhall! Madame LaNoire!"

She sniffed, the picture of hauteur. "Not having gone to Vauxhall, I have no idea what you are talking about."

"Come now, haven't you tortured me enough, practically nestling in Russell's arms? Need I remind you what you did to me that first night at Mercer Street? Then again, I should be delighted to show you." He stepped closer.

"N-no!" she cried, holding up a hand. A tell-tale crimson came and went in her cheeks, but her glance didn't waver.

"What nonsense are you spouting? Indeed, I begin to believe you *are* a Bedlamite."

"If I am, 'tis you who've made me one!" he nearly shouted. Grasping for control, he exhaled a gusty breath. "Faith, Caragh, I know I'm making a hash of this, but I've never known you to tell an untruth. Surely you don't mean to start now by denying that, under the guise of Madame LaNoire, you lured me from Vauxhall to Mercer Street and made me a gift of your virtue—and what a beautiful gift it was! But you must agree, sweeting, 'tis now imperative that we marry."

For a long time she made no reply, merely gazing at him, her breath coming quickly, her face guarded. He longed to cross the space separating them and pull her into his arms, assure her everything would be all right as long as they were together, but her hostile stance warned him not to attempt it.

Hugging her arms more tightly about her, she said at last, "Even if…what you said were correct, I see no reason to marry. A man does not feel obliged to wed a woman just because they shared…intimacies. Why should I?"

"That sounds like your sister speaking. Has she had the tutoring of you? Caragh, I'm not that sly cur Holden Freemont, and you're not Ailis!"

"Indeed I am not!" she flashed back. "If I were, I'd have my servants haul you off my property for embarrassing me in front of my friends and staff, dragging me from my work and then verbally harassing me!"

"I don't mean to harass you!" He groaned and ran a hand through his hair. "I admit, I suppose it seems I am. But if ever a matter needed settling speedily, this—"

"Enough!" she broke in, shaking her head rapidly "I'll not hear another preposterous word."

With that, she straightened her shoulders, jerked her chin up and marched past him, treading the velvet scarf into the mud of the stable floor.

He snatched up the crumpled material and shook it off, then ran to grab her arm. "Caragh, we are not done yet!"

She ripped her arm free and whirled to face him. "How dare you presume to dictate to me?"

He reached out a hand, desperate, appealing, but she batted it away.

"Touch me again," she said, her low voice trembling with emotion, "and I *shall* have you evicted."

"Because you can't ignore what happens between us when I do?" he threw back.

In response, she turned her back on him. "Good day, Quentin," she said as she walked away. "Kind of you to stop by, but I'm still too busy to entertain company. I hope your business in the neighborhood prospers."

For an instant he considered calling her bluff, but the reason struggling to emerge from the chaos of jealousy, hurt, disappointment and anger warned him trying to hold her by force would only alienate her further. Better to let her go, for now at least.

He'd chosen his ground poorly and then made mice-feet of his advance. Caragh was too much a fighter to succumb meekly to what she saw as an attack—even if she secretly agreed with him—as, despite her stance today, he knew she must. Why else would she not trust herself to allow his touch?

He'd not been able to detain her long enough to reconstruct the pretty, persuasive speech that his rage at Alden Russell had driven out of his head. He would have to come back later, apologize, plead with her to listen to him one more time.

How he was going to lure her into meeting him after having just blundered so badly would require some ingenuity. But he hadn't pulled himself up from near-poverty to impressive wealth by quailing at a challenge.

He wasn't about to give up the woman he loved either.

Slowly he walked from the barn. Caragh stood beside a stonemason, her eyes focused on the workman's face, nodding as he talked. The surrounding laborers listened silently, their approving glances and respectful attitudes showing she had already won the local craftsmen over to the novel idea of working for a woman, a significant achievement in the few weeks she'd been at Hunter's Haven.

Pride in her character and abilities washed over him, cresting to a swell of love and admiration.

Gently he brushed the drying mud from the tufted scarf and slipped it back into his waistcoat.

He thought at first she would ignore him as he walked by. But with admirable graciousness, considering the rancor of their brief meeting, she stayed the stonemason in mid speech and turned to him.

"Good day, Lord Branson. Thank you for your visit." Though a subtle blush stained her cheeks, her cordial tone gave no hint she'd threatened to have him forcibly ejected just a few moments previous.

"Miss Sudley," he replied, bowing to her and nodding at Russell. The triumphant gleam in Russell's eyes nearly overset Quentin's resolve to retreat with whatever dignity he could muster. But knowing he must not further prejudice his case by giving in to the desire to mill down his erstwhile friend, he managed to keep his back straight and his feet marching away from her.

As he trudged, he raised his hand to touch the crushed velvet inside his waistcoat. No, by heaven, he would win her. The consequences of a future without Caragh were so bleak he refused even to contemplate them.

A LONG, chore-filled day later, Caragh finally reached the sanctuary of her office at the manor. After weeks of wrestling with the problem of her love for Quentin, she'd developed a real appreciation for Hercules's struggle with the nine-headed Hydra.

Just when, under the soothing balm of Lord Russell's attentions, she felt she was at last making progress in her attempt to cut off and cauterize the many threats Quentin Burke posed to her emotions, the immortal center of the beast—the man himself—arrived, overthrowing all her efforts. Instead of dismissing him from her mind as speedily as she'd dismissed him from her property, she'd been impatient all day for the privacy with which to contemplate how she meant to deal with his unexpected reappearance—and unprecedented behavior.

She drew from its hiding place beneath the ledger the crinkled list that she had not, in the end, been able to make herself destroy. Shaking her head in bemusement at her folly, she read through the familiar words again.

After his performance at the building site, she ought to restore "Arrogant" to the list—and add "Presumptuous" as well.

But given that he'd evidently discovered the truth behind Madame LaNoire's disguise, what could she expect? Tempted as she'd been to refute his assumption, he'd been correct in believing it went too much against the grain for her to lie. Though she'd not actually confirmed his assumption, he would surely construe her evasion for the admission it was.

Perhaps what had impelled him to seek her out was the possibility that their interludes might result in a child. Since she now had evidence it would not, she could put to rest that argument for forcing a ring on her finger.

Despite the wording of her dismissal, she knew quite well that one paltry reverse wouldn't send Quentin Burke scurrying back to London. Sooner rather than later, he'd be returning for another skirmish.

Hopeless gudgeon that she was, an immediate surge of anticipation filled her at the thought.

What good would it do to meet him, talk with him any further? Seeing him only meant taxing her mental reserves by pretending herself indifferent to his appeal, as well as courting the danger that he might use her physical yearning for him against her.

After all, he'd given her no indication that anything else had changed between them. He'd certainly not vouchsafed the declaration of undying love she secretly craved—and without which she refused to marry him.

Sighing, she started to thrust the paper back under the ledger when another memory stilled her hand. Quentin had given no sign his feelings for her had changed, except…there had been a *look* on his face when she first saw him. His eyes narrowed on the fingers Alden Russell was resting on her back, that look had said he would derive great pleasure in separating Lord Russell from those digits.

Passing in review both his words and his actions, her startling suspicion wavered toward certainty. Slowly a smile curved her lips, and for the first time since Madame LaNoire had watched the lover she adored departing, she felt a stirring of hope.

Taking up her pen, she scrawled "Jealous" on the list.

A flaw, to be sure. But perhaps, if she were clever enough to manage the matter of Lord Russell, one that might at last bring her more joy than she had ever believed possible: having both her enterprise and Quentin Burke on his knees, delivering a *heartfelt* declaration.

LATE THAT EVENING, Caragh finally transferred the last of the week's totals for labor and materials from the craftsmen's bills into her ledger. Closing the leather journal with a thump, she sighed and stretched her tired shoulders. She'd sent the servants to their beds hours ago, so after lighting a single candle to guide her to her chamber, she blew out the rest and headed for the stairs.

She was, she had to admit, just the tiniest bit disappointed that Quentin had not come back to spar with her again today. She really was hopeless, she thought with a despairing shake of her head, when even the idea of clashing with him sent a burst of energy and excitement flowing through her. But the sooner he appeared—particularly if he encountered Lord Russell when he did—the sooner she could begin testing whether Quentin's apparent jealousy sprang from a paternalistic desire to protect his "innocent" friend from a man's carnal advances—or because he wanted no man but himself to make such advances.

As she entered her chamber and set down the candle, a shiver of delight escaped the prudent hold she was trying to maintain over her emotions. Oh, that she might drive him to distraction with jealousy! If he truly feared she was tempted by another man, perhaps that shallow emotion could be the catalyst to transform his affection into a deeper, genuine love.

She was smiling at that happy prospect when she was seized from behind and a thick gloved hand clapped over her mouth.

Unable to scream, she struggled like a madwoman, twisting and lashing out with hands and legs. But hampered by her skirts and a long cloak that protected her assailant from her blows, she found herself being pushed inexorably toward the bed.

She landed face-first on the soft surface and tried to twist free, only to have her attacker sit down and swivel her into his lap. As he did, she caught a glimpse of a tall figure swathed in a black cloak, his face obscured by a black domino.

"Ah, *cherie,* listen to me! *Vraiment,* you must not struggle so," a deep masculine voice in a lilting French accent breathed into her ear.

A *familiar* deep masculine voice.

"Quentin!" she shrieked, the sound muffled by his glove. "Let me go!"

"But I dare not liberate your lips, *ma jolie,* unless it is to cover them with my own. Only hear my sad tale, *je vous implore.*"

"Madness," she muttered into his glove, amused in spite of her anger at him for frightening her. But since she was clearly no match for his strength, better to cease struggling and allow him to say whatever he wished—before the heat of his body against hers melted will and resistance into nothing more protective than a puddle beneath his boot.

Though she went still, he bound her even more closely, as if he wished to meld them into one body. A possibility that, acutely conscious as she was of his hard chest behind her and startlingly prominent male member beneath her, did nothing to improve her ability to concentrate on outwitting him at this game, whatever it turned out to be.

"I was a man given a great gift, *ma chère,* the gift of a young girl's love. Yet foolishly, I was too blind to see the gem she offered. Even when the girl changed before my eyes, her loveliness enhanced by a woman's passion as a diamond cut by a master jeweler takes on brilliance, I was too cautious to claim this prize. Now I may have lost that which I have come to love so deeply. Please, will you not end my suffering, *bien-aimée,* and tell me it is not too late?"

At last he removed his gloved hand, but before she could utter a word or even take a breath, he jerked her chin up and covered her mouth with a kiss.

At first his lips on hers were hard, demanding, as if to stifle protest before it began and channel any anger into fire of another sort.

But by the time her greedy senses rallied in response, fogging her brain and robbing her of any desire to object, the kiss gentled, became coaxing, almost reverent, as if she were a priceless object too delicate to be roughly handled. At the tenderness of the slow, lingering brush of his lips against hers an ache of love and longing swelled in her chest. *This is where I belong,* her heart whispered.

In spite of the dizziness afflicting her when at last he released her lips, she could feel his heart thundering in his chest beneath her. *As rapidly as my own.*

"Quentin," she groaned as she sagged against him, "that was not fair. And how dare you invade my chamber in the dead of night and scare me witless?"

"Who are you to talk of fair?" he demanded, cupping her face in his hands. "You took what you wanted, hid the truth from me, then disappeared before I had a chance to say what *I* felt or wanted. After my stupid jealous fit this morning, I feared you might never do so. I had to come up with some way to insure you'd let me speak to you."

"Well, you now have my full attention," she replied wryly,

"so say what you wish." *And quickly, before the joy of being in your arms again makes it impossible for me to refuse whatever you might ask.*

From the pocket of his long cloak, he drew out the black velvet scarf. "You *were* Madame LaNoire?"

Since there was no longer any point in denying it, with a sigh, she nodded.

"Why did you do it, Caragh?"

"Because…because I longed to be close to you. But just because I pretended to be Madame does not mean anything must change between us. Certainly you don't need to marry me! No one but we two—and Ailis, of course—knows of this and there…" she felt her face heat in the darkness. "I know for sure there will be no…consequences."

"Ah, but there have been—exceedingly grave consequences, my sweet. For if an audacious and lovely lady had not embarked upon so scandalous a course, I might have drifted along forever, too complacent to recognize the truth."

He resettled her closer into his embrace and continued, "You were little more than a child when we first met. Not until I finally put the puzzle together and figured out that the friend I valued so highly was also the Madame LaNoire who had so bedazzled me did I realize that you are the one woman, the only woman, I shall ever want. Surely you love me, too, or you would never have embarked on so outrageous a course. That is, you're not going to make a practice of seducing innocent Vauxhall revelers?"

Incensed, she jerked away from him and attempted a punch to his jaw, which given her proximity and the poor angle of its delivery, merely glanced off his chin. "Certainly not!"

Chuckling softly, he captured her hand and kissed it. "You relieve my mind. So you *do* love me, my dear Caragh?"

"Since that first morning you rode down our drive," she admitted. Oh, how liberating it was to say those words at last! Still, she must be wary. "But you say Madame 'bedazzled' you. Is it truly a life with Caragh you want—or simply more nights in the bed of Madame LaNoire?"

"You doubt that what I feel is love? I confess I was slow to recognize it myself, nor can I put my thumb on the precise moment when I decided that marrying you was essential to my happiness. But if love is wanting to spend the rest of my days with you, a joy that wells up whenever I am near you, and a hunger to take you here and now and never let you go, then I swear by my sacred honor that I truly love you."

"You…you are that certain?" she whispered, not daring to believe it.

He nodded. "I came here intending to persuade you into accepting my proposal by seduction, if necessary. But that wouldn't be a proper way to begin a life together. You must accept me willingly, with a clear mind—not befuddled by passion—much as I long to befuddle you again."

His ardent eyes compelling her gaze, he held out his palm. "Caragh, will you give me your hand?"

When without hesitation she placed hers on his, his face lit in a smile. He lifted her fingers to his lips and kissed them tenderly, then laid her hand against his heart.

"Caragh Sudley, will you marry me and make my life a joy for the rest of my days?"

He wasn't down on his knees, but given the strength of the commitment evident in his eyes, the passion of his tone—and the hardness of the anatomy pressing so invitingly against her bottom—it was good enough.

"As long as you haven't any stuffy notions about waiting to act on this—" she rubbed her derriere against him, eliciting a groan "—until after the vows are formalized, then I accept. After all, I am my mother's daughter."

"So long as you agree to become my wife as well as my wanton, there is nothing I'd like more. After all, I did come prepared."

At that, he nudged her off his lap and stood. Swiftly he began unfastening his cloak to reveal first his bare throat, then his naked chest…

He stopped, the cloak still masking him below his waist. *"Il vous plait, Madame?"* he murmured with an exaggerated French accent.

"Tu me plais beaucoup," she replied, laughter in her voice. And then sought his lips as, tugging the cloak from his shoulders, she dragged it free and pulled him back into bed.

* * * * *

The Wedding Knight

BY JOANNE ROCK

In joyous celebration of the historical romance writers who have preceded me, this book is dedicated to one writer heroine in particular. For fabulous Teresa Medeiros, whose medieval stories transported me hundreds of years in a matter of minutes. Many thanks for the wonderful tales and personal inspiration!

And for Kentucky Romance Writers, an endlessly talented and supportive group. Thank you, ladies, for sharing your wisdom on everything from plot development to Derby Day recipes.
I am eternally grateful.

Chapter One

Spring 1250

If Lucian Barret had been a righteous, God-fearing man, he might have trembled at the thought of kidnapping a nun.

Fortunately his faith in God had died two years ago, along with his foster father in a stale sickroom. Stealing Melissande Deverell posed no moral dilemma for him now.

Lucian dragged in a breath of thin mountain air and pulled a length of white muslin from his saddlebag to wrap around his face. Although he would reveal himself to his captive eventually, he didn't want her to recognize him too soon and inadvertently betray his identity.

The good sisters of St. Ursula's would not appreciate his plans for Melissande.

He peered through the generous chink in the loose rock enclosure to spy on the young nun. After spending days observing the rituals of the convent's inhabitants, Lucian had narrowed his focus to this particular female.

Studying her profile as she read from her book, he searched

for affirmation that she was the object of his quest. The graceful woman in the severely cut habit bore no similarity to the hellion he recalled from childhood.

Her demeanor radiated contentment and fulfillment, as if divinely called to life behind silent walls.

The Melissande Deverell of ten years ago had screamed herself hoarse the day her parents announced she would enter a convent. She'd been rumored to have sobbed halfway to France once she departed England.

Confirmation of her identity came when playtime began.

Lucian watched his quarry frolic with three children in the sun-filled gardens. The scene reminded him of his childhood with his brother Roarke and their neighbor, Melissande— two boys and one mischievous girl to lead them on a merry chase. After reading to the little sprites for most of the afternoon, Melissande now allowed them to run and romp. Flashes of his old devil-may-care friend became apparent as the young woman tumbled laughing to the ground under the gleeful attack of her small charges.

A glimpse of vivid red hair peeped from beneath the black wimple when she sprawled on the new spring grass. The grin playing about her lips spoke of vibrant life trapped within her Spartan cloak.

Melissande.

There could be no mistaking the woman Roarke had demanded he retrieve from her convent hideaway in the secluded French Alps. The same woman whose deliverance would fulfill Lucian's long debt to his brother.

Roarke would not be disappointed.

As beautiful a maiden as he had ever seen, Melissande had blossomed into a prize who merited stealing. If Lucian were worthy to carry on the Barret family line, he would leap at the chance to possess such a wife to bear heirs.

But that job he left for Roarke. Lucian would continue to pay his penance for the life he had taken with his sword. In spite of those who had labeled the deed an accident, he blamed himself.

Remembering the need for swiftness in his plan, Lucian jerked the fluttering white muslin about his head to secure it.

A sudden stillness permeated the convent garden.

He wrenched his gaze back to the happy group sprawled on the ground and discovered Melissande had gone stiff and wary while the little ones continued their play. She peered with intent eyes toward the crevice in the wall, as if she saw beyond the fractured rock to the danger lurking there for her.

I am saving her, Lucian told himself, needing that peace of mind to counteract the contented picture she presented as a nun.

Obviously startled by whatever movement she might have detected, Melissande spoke in a hushed voice to the children, hurrying them indoors.

The time had come to act.

Melissande Deverell had known many lonesome moments in her convent exile, but until now she had never known fear.

Heart racing as she struggled with her skirts and willed her children safely inside the sturdy walls of the schoolroom, her hands foolishly gripped the leather binding of the book she'd been reading to them.

Suddenly another set of hands gripped *her.* Impossibly big, strong hands.

No.

She tried to scream, but one of the massive paws smothered her mouth while the other reached around her belly to slam her backward into a rock wall.

"I will not hurt you." The rock wall spoke.

She kicked and jerked at her captor, wondering how a human body could be made of such hard substance. Even as she feared for herself, she winged a prayer of thanksgiving heavenward that at least Andre, Emilia and Rafael had made it safely inside.

Oblivious to her struggles, the man who restrained her scooped Melissande up as if she were no more than a feisty kitten. Still flailing any portion of her body that would move, she watched in growing panic as her tormentor kicked open the convent gate and left the towering protection of St. Ursula's in their wake.

My babes! Melissande's heart wrenched at the thought of those three dear faces waiting for her in the schoolroom. She fought even harder, screaming behind the hand smothering her mouth and nose.

Her shouts reverberating in her brain, Melissande didn't hear her abductor's commands whispered into her ear. All she could think of was the pain and disillusionment her absence would cost the three little orphans who were finally learning to love and trust again.

The madman who held her released her mouth, apparently needing a free finger to aid in the whistled call that now pierced the air.

"Please!" Her sudden cry rang out with startling conviction in the quiet Alpine forest.

Hesitating only a moment, Melissande launched into a torrent of urgent pleas to the man she still couldn't see. "I am the guardian of three young children. I must not leave them. I am their only stability, their—"

A horse galloped out of the woods, a fleet-footed gray beast with a dappled body and black mane. "They will be taken care of," a deep masculine voice growled in her ear, the rumble of which Melissande could feel against her back. He spoke slightly accented French, as though a foreigner to the land.

She screamed. A blood-chilling, forest-shaking screech that scared birds from their perches and caused the gray horse to rear in displeasure.

If the nuns were alerted to Melissande's absence soon enough, the abbess could possibly track her down before any harm came to her. Abbess Helen commanded a modest army, after all.

And if shrieking helped Melissande escape her captor, then by Ursula's sainted slipper, she would raise a holy terror.

"Quiet!" the voice behind her ordered, though the man could not cover her mouth while his one hand was sorely taxed to hold on to the nervous horse. Yet before she could shriek again, Melissande was hefted high onto the frightened animal's back, her forgotten burden ripped from her arms.

"My book!" It occurred to her she might have fought him off with more success if she'd dropped the manuscript.

"You cannot hold it while you ride," the man returned, shoving the heavy volume into a saddlebag.

"I do not know how to ride," she protested, though her hands instinctively sank into the thick mane when the animal reared again.

"The hell you don't," growled the voice.

Shocked, both at the curse and at the man's risky assumption that she would be able to keep her seat on a temperamental horse, Melissande braved a glance backward to look at him.

The flash of white, she realized, taking in the intricate wrapping of the man's exotic head covering. She had spied the material through the crevice in the convent wall.

Steely gray eyes stared back at her. A long, textured scar from his temple to ear gave him a sinister visage. Dark skin around his eyes and his uncovered hands conjured an image of a desert sheikh.

Was she being abducted by an infidel warrior?

Terror clenched cold fingers around her stomach and squeezed. She knew the bloodthirsty ways of men who chose to kill for a living.

Perhaps her captor read her renewed commitment to escape in her eyes, for he suddenly materialized at her back, mounting the horse quicker than a blink. Shouting to the animal, the warrior kicked the gray mare's sides, launching them headlong into the forest.

"No!" Wiggling in her seat, Melissande cried out, thinking it would be better to fall from the mare than to submit to the heathen.

Yet as she slipped in the saddle, one strong arm caught and lifted her, yanking her down onto her captor's lap with amazing speed.

"Be still," he rasped. "You'll hurt yourself."

His muscular arm anchored her against the broad expanse of his chain-mailed chest. The tiny links of the metal tunic pulled at her woolen habit while his hand clamped the narrow space between her ribs and hip.

She had scarcely been touched in her ten years at the convent. To be held thus now seemed cruel fulfillment of her secret wish for human contact.

True to his warrior nature, the beast used his strength with reckless abandon. Melissande could not move if she tried.

"You're hurting me," she gasped, her words breathless with the effort.

To her surprise, his grip softened at once, though the heathen still made certain she could not fall—or jump—from the galloping mare.

Perhaps he was capable of listening to reason. If he would relax his hold at her behest, mayhap she could still convince him to release her altogether.

"You're making a grave mistake, sir. I belong to a holy order of women who—"

"I know who you are."

The husky whisper sent tremors down her spine.

"Then you know I must go back to the cloister where I belong." She breathed deeply, steadying herself against the nervousness his presence wrought. Melissande had not so much as spoken to any man save a priest these last years. And never had she touched a priest's body in such a manner.

"You will not be going back." His words fanned over her ear, his cool assurance at odds with the warmth of his breath.

Never see her home again? Anger surged through her, keen-edged and volatile as the fear she'd felt earlier.

Before she could frame a suitable response—a scathing tirade to put the heathen in his place—the stranger spoke again.

"But you will thank me one day." Scarcely slowing the horse as the forest grew more dense, he rode the rough terrain with reckless speed.

"Thank you? I would be hard-pressed to ever forgive you!" Outrage filled her. "You've stolen a novitiate right out of her convent!"

"You are not an avowed nun then?"

The hopeful note in his voice made Melissande regret she had not yet taken her final vows. "I will be *very* soon."

"No, lady. You will not."

He held her more tightly than strictly necessary as the landscape passed in a blur. Perhaps he'd given some credence to her claim that she could not ride after all. She'd never been so firmly anchored to another person, as if they'd been hewn of the same stone in a living statue atop the huge horse.

They were pressed so close she didn't need to turn around for him to hear her words.

"Yes, sir, I will. My abbess is one of the few to command her own army. She will hunt you down and demand my release." Or so Melissande hoped.

"My research found the good abbess heads a minimal force of men to protect her convent, but perhaps you know something I don't." The crinkles in the corners of his eyes deepened as if he smiled.

He knew the abbey's resources? He'd obviously exercised more forethought to capture her than she'd first realized.

Indignation brought a hot flush to her cheeks.

"Hellfire awaits you, sir. I hope you know that. This act denies your access to the Kingdom of Heaven for all eternity."

The man's gaze shifted to hers above the clean linen hiding his face.

"Then I shall add this to my long list of sins, Angel."

Chapter Two

Silence reigned in the aftermath of Lucian's declaration. Perhaps Melissande was finally so shocked she couldn't speak.
Good.

The last thing he needed was someone asking the whys and wherefores of his past. Better that Melissande be intimidated enough to leave him alone until they reached the time for him to unveil himself. Then there would be no hurry.

Although she sat still and outwardly tranquil, Lucian felt the tension reverberate through her slender form. Her stiff posture reminded him of the fear she surely struggled to hide.

She's frightened.

A moment's regret whispered through his consciousness, stirring a bit of emotional empathy he'd thought long dead. It seemed rather cruel to allow Melissande to suffer under the delusion he was a faceless stranger with harmful intent. He should reveal himself so her mind might be eased. Once she knew who held her, and for what purpose, she would willingly submit herself to his protection. Indeed, she would no doubt be grateful to him for rescuing her from a life of isolation.

Yet, Lucian waited.

Putting distance between her and St. Ursula's was critical to his success. The powerful abbess did indeed possess a small army for her personal use and would no doubt dispatch men to find Melissande.

If Lucian wanted to keep his prize, he needed to move quickly. That meant Melissande would have to remain ignorant of his identity awhile longer.

A contrary part of his brain reminded him that once she knew who he was, he would have no cause to ever hold her this way again. The knowledge should not have bothered him half so much as it did. Melissande was to be his brother's wife, not his.

Yet he would have to be a dead man not to notice the sweet curves his hands cupped beneath her coarse habit.

He was a damned man for so many reasons. Lusting over a convent-bred bride meant for another man would be a small transgression compared to his other sins.

How would she react when he revealed himself? Would the darkness of his soul be all too apparent to one as pure and unspoiled as her?

He could not pretend to be the Lucian Barret she had known. When confronted with the truth of his identity, she might be disillusioned at the stark changes. She might question what had turned the quiet boy into a cold, hard man. Worst of all, she might pity him.

And that, he could not bear.

Her youth and innocence brought to mind the life he might have had if his sword had not found its way into his foster father, Osbern Fitzhugh. Perhaps Lucian would now be securing a bride such as Melissande for himself instead of his brother.

Cursing foolish thoughts, Lucian dismissed all notion of

marriage and Melissande from his mind. He could not alter the fact that in the heat of anger, he'd raised arms against a man who'd loved him like a son. Nothing would erase Lucian's sins—or erase the debt he owed his younger brother for safeguarding his most grave secret.

For now, he longed to shorten the distance between his captive and England as much as possible. The quicker he delivered Melissande to the man who awaited her, the sooner he could return to his penance and the savagery of war.

'Twas what suited him best.

The sun sank early in the mountainous forest region, leaving in its wake a brisk evening and a journey fast growing hazardous in the approaching dusk. A vast outcropping of rock closed in on them to one side, while a cliff dropped off to nothingness on the other.

Melissande's sore body and chilled skin cried out for rest, yet she feared sliding off the horse and having to face her captor once again.

Her back ached as if it would break under the strain of keeping her body away from the beast who held her. Though she could do nothing about the heavy arm wrapped around her waist, she found she could avoid more intimate contact with the silver-eyed man if she remained ramrod-straight in front of him.

In spite of her best efforts to evade his touch, however, she could not escape the brush of his strong thighs bracketing hers as they rode. The smooth leather of his braies slid against the coarse wool of her gown in a most unnerving manner.

He reined in their horse abruptly, slamming her backward against him.

In a heartbeat, he righted her in the saddle, forcing the

space between them again as if he desired it as much as she did. But he showed no inclination to dismount. Instead he lifted his head into the wind, like an animal scenting danger long before its arrival. A predatory stillness came over him.

"We are not alone, lady." Though whispered through the layer wrapped around his face, his words were distinct in her ear.

The road they now traversed accommodated little more than horseback travelers or perhaps a rugged cart. Melissande had given up hope they would meet any passersby on the route, but in the distance she heard the drum of quick hooves.

Someone to save me. She opened her mouth to scream, but her captor's muffling hand stifled the sound.

"You do not want to do that, Melissande. Trust me."

After a long moment, the sound of her name penetrated her brain. *He knows me.*

Cautiously she turned and raised her eyes to his, her lips still covered by a huge, warm palm. Drawing still closer, the echoing hooves beat an urgent rhythm to her fears. She watched, fascinated, as her captor reached to unwind the concealing layers from his face.

"I am your friend." His features revealed, he looked more European, less foreign somehow. His hair grew as dark as any infidel's, yet its shorter length was the same as that favored by many Englishmen. The sound of horses beating the hard ground closed in on them. "Your former neighbor."

Yanking the rest of the cloth from his head, he stared back at her with intent gray eyes. The hard planes of his face, the quiet intelligence of his gaze, loomed above her with haunting familiarity.

Lucian Barret.

Recognition hit her a scant second before the other riders came into view around a mountainous pass. Though she did not see the newcomers, her peripheral senses alerted her to their presence as she gazed dumbfounded into the eyes of a childhood friend.

A boy she'd once fancied her hero.

Her relief lasted only an instant before fury took its place. How dare he steal her away?

The horses halted on the dirt path in front of them. Lucian's hand slid from her mouth before he turned to the riders. The touch struck her as more intimate now that she knew her captor's identity. Her lips burned with the touch.

She fumed silently though her curiosity compelled her to greet their visitors. "Good evening to you, gentle knights."

They wore the sign of the cross, Melissande noted, yet they had that haggard look of long travel about them. Their beards were dirty and unkempt, their shields dulled with lack of recent care.

Crusaders.

"Good eve to you, sir." The first knight directed his words to Lucian, then turned to Melissande. Noting her habit, he bowed his head more deeply. "And you, Sister."

Now was her chance. All she had to do was to say something. Anything. Decry her abductor, proclaim her captured status.

Yet despite their pretense of respect, the men looked at her with disturbing boldness. Some demon lurked in their brazen stares, as if they would gobble her up at the first opportunity.

Never, in all her years at St. Ursula's, had she met a warrior knight whom she admired. The battle hungry sought shelter on their way to war. The battle weary sought food on their way home from war. If they did not bring obvious bloodlust to the convent table, they brought vainglorious tales of their prowess on the field. All of them brought boorish manners and lice.

She'd been aware of their bawdy ways, but none had dared lust after a nun. Warrior knights were apparently more bold outside the convent walls.

Melissande nodded in acknowledgment of their greeting, holding her tongue until she determined the best course of action.

"You go to Acre?" Lucian asked the question naturally enough, but Melissande could feel the edge of tension in his body where it surrounded hers. The thighs embracing hers no longer seemed like cold stone. The knowledge that this hard masculine form belonged to Lucian Barret infused the limbs with warmth.

Or was it her limbs that grew so heated and…aware?

"Outremer." The first man answered in French, though the second knight never took his attention from Melissande.

She shook off her odd response to Lucian to take note of her situation. The Crusader's silent appraisal deflated all hope that she could ask the newcomers for help. The devil she knew, at this point, seemed safer than the two she didn't know.

Even if the known devil seemed to be causing a quiet inferno within her already. She edged forward slightly, needing the extra space between her and Lucian.

"Your king has great need of you," Lucian told them, tightening his grip on Melissande's waist before she could go far. "His wars do not go well."

As twilight fell, the men spoke of faraway battles and the French king's recent captivity at the hands of the infidel. The exotic place names and foreign events held little meaning for Melissande, though she had read many Eastern texts in her work as a copyist at the abbey.

One thing became quite clear from the exchange, however. Lucian himself had been a Crusader.

It didn't recommend him, in Melissande's eyes. In fact, it made her all the more wary. But he was still Lucian Barret, for St. Ursula's sake.

He must have some compelling reason for taking her. News of her family, perhaps. Maybe one of her sisters needed her. Once she explained to him how much she belonged at the convent, he would return her. He had always been an honorable person, even as a young man.

With a respectful nod, the first knight spurred his horse forward to ride past them to the south into the dark swell of forest. "God speed you, sir."

"God speed," Lucian returned, his gaze falling to Melissande now that the threat of danger had diminished.

Distant gray eyes seemed to forbid her unspoken questions, inspiring Melissande to shiver with their blatant lack of human warmth.

"Lu-Lucian?" Her voice caught in her throat. It seemed silly to fear an old friend—an honorable one at that—yet anger for what he had done still boiled in her blood.

"We need to ride a bit farther, Melissande." The terseness in his tone cut off any hope of further interaction. "We'll talk then."

Ordinarily, Melissande would not have submitted to a high-handed directive, especially from a man who'd kidnapped her and purposely kept his identity a secret knowing it would have lessened her fear to know it.

But by now she was so cold and uncomfortable she had little thought for anything other than a warm fire and a seat anywhere but perched atop the mare.

Inky darkness surrounded them by the time they reached a vacant cottage in the middle of nowhere. Ice already forming in her veins, Melissande knew she would not sleep a wink in such drafty quarters with naught but thin wooden walls between her and the frigid night air. As Lucian helped her from the horse, Melissande slumped with weak relief into his arms.

"You are unwell?" Lucian asked, carrying her into the cottage.

"Only tired, I think." There was no need to mention her susceptibility to lung fever. The years of hard Alpine winters had given her more cases than she cared to count.

He looked skeptical as he settled her on a low bench before a dank fire pit in the one-room shelter.

"And sore. I have not ridden a horse in many years." Her legs ached with the truth of the statement.

"You will be warm in no time," he promised, though she hardly heard him through the veil of fatigue that quickly overcame her.

She didn't realize she'd slept until she awoke a short time later.

True to his word, Lucian had supplied a brightly burning fire for Melissande while she'd slumbered. One heavy woolen blanket covered her. Another was propped beneath her head with a thin sheet of white muslin thoughtfully tucked between her cheek and the scratchy wool.

Running idle fingers over the muslin, Melissande recognized Lucian's head covering from earlier in the day.

The tender care evident in her warm cocoon eased Melissande's spirit. Lucian Barret did not seek to harm her, even if he was a warrior.

Lifting her gaze to his seat a few hand spans away, Melissande watched him unwrap a linen sack and pull out a loaf of bread and some cheese. A large wineskin followed.

"Has my family asked you to seek me out?" Her voice sounded throaty and thick with sleep.

Lucian stared at her for a long moment, keen gray eyes roving along every detail of her missing wimple and bed-rumpled hair.

A curious prick of heightened awareness darted through her, faintly akin to embarrassment, but not quite.

This was only Lucian, after all.

She had never been shy with the boy who had taught her how to fish and never pulled her braids. Although he was much bigger and infinitely more intimidating than the skinny boy she'd known ten years ago.

"Drink this." He thrust the wineskin in her direction.

Melissande shook her head, determined to learn the truth behind his scheme to abduct her. There must be some vital reason he had frightened her half out of her wits. "Is it one of my sisters? Are they—"

All the other Deverell daughters had been married off long since. Only the youngest had been destined for the convent. What if one of them had taken ill or had trouble birthing or...

"I do not know the status of your family since your parents died. I didn't come on behalf of your kin." He cut the cheese into smaller portions as if it were the most important task before him, as if he didn't have a woman hanging on his every word, waiting to know her fate at his hands.

Melissande struggled for a measure of calm, recalling Abbess Helen's favorite admonishment from the Book of Proverbs. *The fool blurts out every angry feeling, but the wise subdues and restrains them.* "Then why?"

Handing her a portion of cheese and bread, Lucian regarded her with stern eyes. "Eat well, Melissande, and I will explain as much as I can."

She tore off a small piece of bread and ate, too tired to be contrary.

Lucian took a deep breath, then raised the wineskin in casual tribute. "I have saved you from a life behind the cloister walls so you might marry the man you love."

Saved me? Melissande tried not to panic as she pulled her blankets more closely about her shoulders, watching Lucian drink deeply from the skin. The muscles of his neck contracted in intriguing rhythm with his swallow. Melissande found herself fascinated to watch him.

A man.

"And who might that be?"

Lucian raised a dark brow at her ignorance. The thin, pale scar near his eye caught her attention in the flickering firelight. A jagged line that marred his temple from brow to ear, the mark was one of the reasons she had not recognized him earlier.

"You've forgotten the man you claimed you'd love until your last dying breath?"

Heat flooded her cheeks as Melissande recalled the horrible scene she had caused the day she'd left for the convent. She had screamed like a harridan, ranting and raving that she did not want to be a nun, that she would find a way back home…and that she would love Roarke Barret until her dying day.

"Roarke?"

Lucian almost smiled. Amusement definitely quivered around the corners of his lips before his face fell into more serious lines once again. "Aye, lady. Roarke."

"You traveled all through Europe and braved the Alps to retrieve me…" The thought staggered her, knowing how difficult the roads were. "For Roarke Barret?"

"I hope you are well pleased," he managed to say between bites of his apple.

Her curiosity quenched, Melissande's good sense returned. She snatched the fruit from his hand. "Nay, I am not pleased, sir. I demand you return me to my abbey at daybreak."

Only the crackling of the fire broke the stiff silence of the room.

"You do not wish to wed Roarke?" His voice told her he was genuinely surprised.

"Of course not."

At his look of utter confusion, Melissande sighed.

"How many things did you yearn for at eight years old that you no longer want or need as a man full-grown?"

"None." He grabbed his apple back and devoured half of it in one crunching bite.

Recalling the serious sort of boy Lucian had been, Melissande realized he probably spoke the truth. "Well, you are unusual. Most people have unobtainable dreams during childhood."

He furrowed his brow before he schooled his features into the mask of patience a teacher might use with a difficult child. "Your dreams are not unobtainable."

"But they are no longer my dreams!" Melissande heard her voice reverberate through the cottage with satisfying volume. When was the last time she had raised her voice? "Don't you see? I am happy at the convent, Lucian. I care for the abbey's orphans. I read books few people in the western world will ever lay eyes on. It is a blissful life!"

"Blissful?" He took back the wineskin from where it lay forgotten in her hand and sipped its contents thoughtfully.

The warm brush of his hand unnerved her.

"Yes, blissful." In the most secret regions of her heart, she knew that might be stretching the truth, but she loved St. Ursula's. She certainly would not chain herself to a knight who would be off fighting ten months of the year, and then train her sons for the same dangerous profession.

"Fickle woman."

"Pardon?" Melissande could not have heard him properly.

He pinned her with a cold steel gaze. "You are most fickle, lady, to claim you love Roarke and to pledge yourself to him in tortured screams as you left England, then decide you do not love him and want to live in a convent."

"I was eight years old!"

"Old enough."

Could he be serious? "I can assure you it is not uncommon behavior for a child's passions to alter as he or she grows."

"And I can assure you with equal authority that some people possess the same passion their whole lives."

She flushed, although she wasn't sure why. His words confused her, taunted her in ways she couldn't understand.

"I am sorry you have changed your mind, Melissande. The fact is, I am bringing you back to England to marry Roarke."

"I will not go to England and I will not wed anyone." Melissande might just as well shout into the Alpine wind for all that he seemed to be listening.

"Ah, today you do not wish to wed, but who is to say what you will feel tomorrow?" He brushed a weary hand through his hair. "I am hoping your fickle nature will turn to my advantage by the time we get home."

Dear God, he was serious. A small twinge of panic shot through her. "Lucian, I cannot go with you. I won't."

"You can and you will. I have promised Roarke you will arrive in England by midsummer."

"But—"

"And I always keep my vows." Hints of pride and warning mingled in his voice, his cool gaze level with hers.

Melissande stared back at him, feeling no glimmer of friendship or empathy with the man across the fire from her.

Similar to his childhood self only in his quiet seriousness and obvious intelligence, Lucian Barret had changed drastically in the past ten years.

The raven's-wing hair he used to keep so closely shorn now touched his collar. The sharp planes of his face seemed even more dramatic now that his visage had lost all traces of youthfulness. Of course his huge warrior frame bore little resemblance to the lanky youth she remembered.

Darkness pervaded him, where once Melissande could tease a grin from her somber friend. He kept her at arm's length now, as if being too friendly might shake his resolve to accomplish his own goals.

His utter commitment to those goals, even if it involved kidnapping a woman devoted to God and ignoring her pleas for return, unnerved her. Ruthlessness lurked behind his words. And no wonder—he was a warrior. He would do whatever necessary to drag her back to England.

Yet Melissande could not allow him to proceed with his scheme to "save her."

She gauged her opponent, wondering how best to attack as he stored the leftovers of their dinner. Firelight danced over his intimidating form, making him appear even larger and more forbidding in the tiny cottage.

With little hope the ploy would work, she tried one last time to appeal to the heart he seemed to be lacking.

"Three children depend on me to care for them—"

"There is an abbey full of kindly nuns to watch over them." He did not even bother to glance in her direction as he settled a few feet from her. His protective armor hit the dirt floor with a dull clink where he laid upon it.

The man slept in chain mail?

The impropriety of their closeness struck her, but her main

concern remained with the children, not Lucian's unorthodox proximity.

"I must go back in the morning," Melissande informed him, hoping with all her heart he would agree but knowing he would not.

With him or without him, she would return.

"Go to sleep, Mel." He yawned.

Though he used the nickname from old habit, it brought to mind the loving way her little charges called her Mel. Or Angel Mel. Or Rafael's ridiculous combination of AngMel.

Her heart lurched with a sudden, empty pang. Her arms ached for her children. Could any mother love them more, these babes of her heart?

"Don't you want a blanket?" she asked, realizing he meant to sleep on the hard floor with no covering to warm him. As soon as she asked, she felt embarrassed by her solicitous concern.

"Nay."

Her maternal nature forced her to pull off one of her numerous woolens and toss it over him anyway.

He flung it back with angry impatience. "I said nay, lady." Then, as if realizing his appalling manners, he managed a stiff, "No thank you."

Odd.

Melissande watched him close his eyes, one hand propped under his head for a pillow. He had to be excruciatingly uncomfortable, but she would certainly make no move to offer him any reprieve. She left the blanket he tossed aside between them, however, just in case he changed his mind.

As she watched and waited for his breath to even into the smooth pattern of sleep, she wondered what had happened to Lucian to turn him into the cold, hard man before her.

She prayed she could be stealthy in her escape, because she had no doubt his wrath would be formidable when he discovered her missing the next morning.

Chapter Three

Perhaps he had been too hard on her, Lucian thought, listening to Melissande fidget in the pallet he'd made for her. She'd been raised to become a nun, after all. A sheltered, delicate creature, she would be unacquainted with the harsh side of life. She did not deserve his continual reminders that she could not return to her convent. Since leaving England, he had lost all notion of how to deal with a woman.

Maybe not quite all, he amended, recalling the faceless females who had slaked his most basic need for feminine flesh over the past two years. But he no longer possessed the finesse necessary to deal with a sensitive noblewoman, let alone a cloistered would-be nun.

Regret stole through him when he thought of his crass refusal of the blanket she'd tossed him. Of course she wouldn't understand his deep-seated need to suffer, to sleep on the hard floor, to allow the cold to permeate his skin in the early morning hours.

Her action had been thoughtful and he'd rewarded the effort with boorish behavior. She was a sweet soul, incapable of understanding the darkness driving him to his acts of penance, acts of guilt.

Even now another kind of guilt flooded him for the inappropriate thoughts he'd experienced in regard to his brother's future wife. The coarse woolen habit she wore didn't begin to hide the pleasing form of the woman Melissande had grown into. She looked like a walking sacrilege with those voluptuous curves straining her habit in all the right places.

But in spite of Lucian's poorly placed fantasies, Melissande Deverell would wed his brother by the moon's next cycle, and she deserved Lucian's polite respect. He wouldn't be caught leering at her like the lecherous Crusaders they'd met on the forest road.

As his future sister-in-law, Melissande deserved a bit more freedom under his protection. He didn't need to watch her as if she were his prey.

She wasn't a prisoner, but a bride.

Breathing deeply, Lucian promised himself he would relax his watch just a little. Heaven knew his tired body cried out for a good night's rest. He had not slept in two days, and fitfully on the road before that. She did not need him breathing down her neck, and Lucian could use some sleep.

Melissande shivered in the warm nest of woolens Lucian had given her. Now she shuddered not from the cold but from her fear and unease at the thought of escaping him.

Certainly he meant her no harm, in spite of the fright he'd given her when he'd stolen her from St. Ursula's. He would be furious to discover her defection, but there could be no help for it. Lucian would just have to tell Roarke she didn't want any part of marriage.

Slipping silently from her blankets, she waited for any change in his breathing.

Nothing.

Steady, even sighs greeted her ears.

The intimacy of the sound wound around her, drawing her back to where Lucian lay with hypnotic pull. Long accustomed to nights spent in a hard bed with naught but her own thoughts and a warming brick to keep her company, Melissande found the experience of lying in the warm cocoon between a fire and Lucian oddly comforting.

For years Melissande could not sleep at the convent. After sharing a room with two older sisters at her home, she had found it impossible to slumber alone in the darkened cell at St. Ursula's when she'd first arrived. How peculiar that she would rest easily in the company of a warrior knight.

She would leave in a moment, she told herself. Now, gazing on the dark mass of chain mail and muscle lying in a perfectly straight line on the cottage floor, curiosity consumed her.

Would Lucian look as cold and forbidding in sleep as he did awake?

Driven by the innate inquisitiveness ten years of convent education still hadn't overcome, she knelt beside the knight who had stolen her. Fading firelight played over his features, casting half his face in shadow. The scar glared; the one patch of white in an otherwise deeply bronzed complexion attesting to long battles fought under a scorching desert sun. Brow furrowed even in sleep, he still bore an aspect of cold harshness.

Instinctively, Melissande reached to touch the vaguely wrinkled place across his forehead. He radiated warmth despite the chill of the room. Amazingly, the skin beneath her fingers smoothed as she touched it. Lucian's whole countenance slowly relaxed into a less fearsome visage.

She drew her hand back, surprised at the change in him, but even more astonished at her brazenness.

Immediately the furrow returned to his fac̲ ̲ ̲ ̲breathing hitched.

Oh, no.

She counted each measured inhalation to assure herself he would not awaken. Finally she tiptoed away, tying her loose habit more snugly about her.

The sooner she left behind the strange pull of Lucian Barret, the better.

With slow caution, she lifted the heavy blanket over the shelter's one window and hopped across the sill. Replacing the rock that secured the covering over the opening, Melissande prayed she would not regret her action.

Many hours later, as first light hovered, Melissande murmured proverbs to herself as her tired body longed to collapse in a heap on the frosty ground.

The way of the lazy is a thorny hedge, the path of the honest a broad highway. She hoped her determination to do the right thing would render her path more highway-like and less thorny.

A village had to be around the next rise, although she had told herself the same thing for the last fifteen hills she'd climbed.

A stranger to such grueling exercise in the thin mountain air, Melissande knew her lungs would burst from her efforts. The thought of returning home to Emilia, Andre and little Rafael kept her feet moving in spite of the burning in her chest.

"You need help, Sister?" a small French voice called out in the hazy light of predawn.

Dragging her eyes up from the ground, Melissande caught sight of a young girl, no more than eight or nine, with a large bucket in her arms.

Blinking in surprise, Melissande wondered if she hallucinated.

"Yes!" She thought she'd weep with relief.

After helping the girl procure a bucketful of water from a nearby stream, Melissande accompanied young Linette to her family home, which really was just over the next rise. A simple wooden structure, the house was a neat square with two plain windows flanking the doorway like eyes in a face. The stubs of empty rose vines poked through the snow at intervals across the front of the dwelling, and Melissande could envision the cottage as it must be in the summer, covered with roses and sweetly fragrant.

"My papa is away until next week, but you may speak with my mama." A dark-haired imp full of energy despite the early hour, Linette spoke musical French that warmed Melissande's heart.

Melissande helped the girl open the door to the sparsely furnished home. A single chair graced the one room dwelling, a prized possession for the family, no doubt. Several other wooden objects filled the small cottage—a set of spoons hung on the kitchen wall, a polished box near the fireplace that probably contained a store of salt and a carved cross above the table.

"My papa is a carpenter," Linette told her proudly. "Would you like to sit in our chair?"

Linette's mother hurried over from her sewing beside the window, the worried lines in her face telling Melissande she looked a sorry sight. The woman—a sturdy blonde whose Nordic features seemed at home in the wintry landscape—appeared scarcely older than Melissande herself.

"I apologize, ma'am," Melissande began, gratefully accepting the arm the taller woman held out to her.

"Just rest, Sister," the lady of the house admonished as she guided Melissande to the chair before the fire. "I am Mistress Jean, but we may speak later."

Heaven. The chair, the warmth, the generosity of Linette and her mother...Melissande could think no further. She closed her eyes, overcome with fatigue and gratitude now that she sat still for a moment.

She needed to relay her story to these strangers, but grogginess overwhelmed her after the unaccustomed exertions of her snowy trek. The cold weather had never agreed with her...

Melissande didn't realize she'd drifted off to sleep until a small gasp awakened her with a start.

"A knight approaches, Mama!" Linette's childish tone grew shrill in her excitement, prompting Melissande to lift an eyelid.

"And he rides the most beautiful speckled horse!"

Melissande's eyes flew open, her fingers clutching the smooth wooden arms of Mistress Jean's lone chair. Cold dread sank down her spine.

Lucian.

How could he have found her so quickly? All hint of exhaustion evaporated. She jumped to join the girl in the doorway.

Sure as she breathed, there he was—a walking weapon of war come to impose his will upon her. Why did he insist she marry Roarke? For that matter, what did Roarke care about a woman he hadn't seen since childhood?

"You know this man," Mistress Jean observed, her assessing blue gaze flicking over Melissande.

"He stole me from St. Ursula's convent yesterday, but I escaped him." Melissande dug into the small sack tied around her girdle and removed a tiny cheesecloth parcel.

If there had been a man in the home to help her, she might have called upon him to protect her. But she could not put Linette and her mother at risk. They had been so kind.

"We could hide you," Mistress Jean suggested, her eyes already flitting about the inside of the cottage for a suitable place.

"He will know. My footprints must be obvious for him to have found me already." She pressed the small bundle containing a short missive and a signet ring into the woman's hand as they watched Lucian vault from the gray mare's back. "But if you know a way to get this to Abbess Helen at St. Ursula's, I will be forever in your debt."

They locked gazes over Linette's head. Melissande could see the woman's hesitation. Yet at the last moment, just before Lucian reached the doorstep, Mistress Jean withdrew the bundle from Melissande's hand and shoved it into a pouch among the folds of her gown.

Her words were a tense whisper beneath the heavy fall of Lucian's boots on the cobblestone walkway. "I will try, Sister."

Melissande breathed a sigh of relief. Even if Lucian dragged her away with him again, she could at least count her mission somewhat of a success. If the abbess received the note and signet ring, she would launch a search party. Failing that, the abbess could always proceed straight to Barret Keep in England. Melissande had revealed her captor's final destination.

"Good morning, mistress," Lucian called from the doorframe, his uncommon height filling the entry. "Good morning, Melissande."

Although he kept his tone utterly neutral, there could be no mistaking the anger seething just below the surface.

"I have come to escort you home." His gaze froze her in place. "I trust you do not want to cause a frightening scene in front of the little one."

Linette looked back and forth between them with wide, scared eyes. Mistress Jean skittered closer to her daughter and looped protective arms about the girl's shoulders.

Lucian certainly knew how to wield a weapon effectively, Melissande thought. Just like a man who killed for a living.

The beast.

He couldn't have put her in motion any faster than by threatening that sweet girl with a scare.

Melissande made a move to stand beside him, but he halted her with one raised palm.

"First, I'd like to see you dressed in more appropriate travel clothes." Glaring at her habit with disdain, he pulled a sack from the belt at his waist. "Perhaps you have something, madame?" He jingled the coin-filled sack as he turned inquiring eyes toward Mistress Jean. "I am willing to pay handsomely for warm garments to replace the habit."

The woman glanced nervously between Lucian and Melissande. "I could spare her a few things if she really wants them—"

"She does." He gave Melissande a prodding shove. "We need to hurry, Melissande, to recover the time you've cost us." Turning his back, he waited just beyond the cottage door.

Gratefully, she accepted the comforting squeeze Jean gave her as she steered Melissande toward the wardrobe. Blinking back her frustration, Melissande concentrated on the small wooden chest and not her disappointment.

The thought of removing her habit after all these years both troubled and tempted her. It symbolized everything she held dear, and she valued its practical warmth. Yet, as Linette and her mother dug through the clothes, Melissande could not help a rush of pleasure to see colored garments in less coarse material than her woolen habit.

She crossed herself and prayed for forgiveness for her worldly wants.

Soon, Melissande stood outfitted in the modest but pretty garments of a merchant's wife. Although not richly decorated, her new surcoat boasted a finely woven wool in a dull shade of forest-green.

The white undertunic brushed her skin in a silken caress, its soft muslin fabric the most decadent material to touch her skin in ten years.

She noticed Lucian with his back still turned and hesitated. A flush stole through her as she realized she had never faced a man without the barrier of her habit in place, at least not since she had become a grown woman.

Melissande cleared her throat to gain his attention. "I'm ready."

"Very well then, we—" He stared at her. His gray eyes widened as he took in every detail of her new garb.

Self-conscious under his scrutiny, Melissande hurried to drape a shawl about her shoulders.

With a soft clink of silver, Lucian laid a bag of coins in the woman's hand and turned to leave. "Come, Melissande."

"I apologize for the intrusion," Melissande murmured to her hostess, following Lucian out the door into the cool morning air. "And thank you."

"God go with you, Sister," the woman returned, her blue eyes sympathetic.

Lucian tugged Melissande's arm, obviously impatient to go. She longed to fling herself around Mistress Jean's neck and to plead for shelter from her fate, but she did not.

With the submissive grace pounded into her at every opportunity at St. Ursula's, Melissande allowed Lucian to pluck her from the ground and seat her before him on the horse.

Again.

"Goodbye, Sister Melissande," Linette called from the doorway of the cottage.

Melissande waved and made a vain effort to smile even though her thoughts strayed to her children at the abbey who never got to say goodbye to her.

Now she sat trapped between Lucian's thighs; the leather of his braies against her new, soft garments did nothing to ease her jumpy nerves.

"Children seem fond of you, lady," Lucian remarked as he spurred the horse to a run.

"They are trusting souls."

"I, however, am not." Gray eyes flickering with an anger he didn't bother to hide, Lucian looked down at her.

"I am sorry I could not go with you willingly." As soon as the words were out, Melissande regretted having said them. Why should she be sorry? "But you must understand my refusal to wed."

"I do not understand it at all," he remarked as he reached behind him to pull a length of rope from a satchel. "But I do know I cannot allow you to roam the forest unprotected."

Words clipped, movements tense, Lucian radiated impatience. Tying the horse's reins around the pommel, he allowed the mare to choose their path while he adjusted the rope, tying and retying it. What in St. Ursula's name could he be trying to accomplish?

"Can I help?" she offered, growing nervous when the horse raced beneath a particularly low branch.

"Give me your hand."

With one wary eye still cast toward the mountainous trail, Melissande reached to assist him.

No sooner had she extended her palm than the heavy rope looped around her wrist.

"What?" She jerked back instantly, but she was too late. The bond held her fast. Its other end, she now realized, had been secured to Lucian's waist. "Just what do you think you are doing?" Outrage simmered in her veins.

"Protecting you." With methodical movements, he untied the bridle and regained control of the mare.

Man and horse alike seemed to relax, their tension dissipating now that Lucian held the reins.

Melissande, however, had never felt further from calm.

"Your idea of protection is imprisonment?" Her well-modulated convent voice evaporated. She shouted like a termagant.

"I gather yours is, too, lady, if you are so fond of your home at St. Ursula's." Ruthless control back in place, Lucian glared at her. "You are as imprisoned as you are protected within the cloister."

"But there, I am not tied to a man!" She yanked the rope for emphasis, but the movement did not budge him.

"Become accustomed to it, Melissande," he counseled. "You will be tied to a man once you wed Roarke, though mayhap not with such a tangible bond."

Over my dead body.

"I will never marry Roarke, or any other man who kills for a living." Crossing her arms, she stared up at him in rebellion.

Lucian's gaze fell to her crossed limbs.

No, she realized, to her chest.

Unaccustomed to her new garments, Melissande had not taken into account the more snug fit and low cut of secular clothing. Her defiant action succeeded only in squeezing her breasts together and thrusting them upward in vulgar display.

Embarrassed to her toes, Melissande let her arms fall to her sides, though his gaze did not budge from her body for a long moment.

When he did look up, his gray eyes glittered with an unfamiliar light.

"Nevertheless, Angel, you certainly were not meant for the convent."

Chapter Four

⸭

This was all Roarke's fault.

If Roarke hadn't been so hell-bent on having Melissande Deverell for a wife, Lucian could have crossed Europe at his ease. He fumed as he picked their way toward the Alpine lowlands, trying to ignore the sweet scent of Melissande's hair beneath his nose.

If not for Roarke, Lucian wouldn't even be returning to England. Why should he? He'd given up his claim to the Barret lands long ago. There was naught for him there anymore.

Melissande shifted sleepily in his arms, her feminine curves brushing against him with startling clarity now that she wore regular clothing instead of the flour sack she called a habit.

His request that she trade in her convent attire ranked as his most stupid move of the day. He had a difficult enough time keeping his eyes off her when she remained dressed as a nun.

But now…

Lucian gritted his teeth as his sleeping passenger finally settled her head on his chest, burrowing as close to him as humanly possible upon horseback.

Damn.

Lucian had known, even as a boy, that Melissande would transform into a raving beauty one day. Her unruly red braids and freckles hadn't fooled him. Her ready smile and warm brown eyes had won his heart the first time she'd clamored to go fishing with him.

Roarke had been the dolt who'd never noticed her. No matter what tricks little Mel tried, Roarke had ignored the youngest Deverell daughter, oblivious to her tender feelings for him.

Until now.

Roarke had written to him during the wars and asked Lucian to retrieve Melissande on his way home from the fighting. He had not planned to go home at the time, but couldn't refuse his brother's request.

And the more he thought about it, the more he realized Roarke must have finally come to his senses. Melissande was a noble lady and a strong woman. She would make any husband proud. Although the idea of her as Lady Barret inspired a small twinge of jealousy, Lucian enjoyed the notion she would help rule their family lands.

Reaching a small clearing in the trees, Lucian reined in his mount. He still needed to hunt for their dinner and to build a shelter of some sort. Alpine nights were none too forgiving to unprepared travelers.

As they stopped, Melissande lifted her head from his chest. The late-afternoon air felt more chilly without the warmth of her body against his, his arms strangely empty without her in them.

"Where are we?" The throaty rasp of her voice reminded him of a lover's morning greeting.

"We're camping here tonight." Shoving aside the inappropriate thoughts, Lucian slid from underneath her and jumped off the horse.

Melissande looked bereft atop the animal. "Here?" she

squeaked. She rubbed her wrist where the rope still bound her, though she seemed too sleepy to wonder about it.

Lucian had removed the other end from his waist and now held it, wondering where to put her so she would be safe.

Unwillingly, he held his hands out to her. She fell into his arms without a thought.

The brief contact sent a jolt of awareness through him, tantalizing him with sensations he ruthlessly suppressed.

He set her at arm's length before she noticed anything amiss. "I need to catch our dinner and start a fire." He began pulling out the necessary equipment from his saddlebag and tossed her a large cheesecloth. "Perhaps you could warm the bread when the fire is ready. The merchant's wife kindly packed us a bit of food for our journey."

Melissande drew her shawl more tightly around her. Scooping up the cheesecloth, she seemed to accept the chore.

"You will not continue to bind us together, then?" She looked faintly hopeful.

Hardening his heart, needing to protect her from her own impetuous nature, Lucian carried his end of the rope to a nearby tree and cinched it. She'd put herself in grave danger when she struck out on her own. He still could not believe his stupidity at not tying her up when they had lain yesterday. He had known he would slumber like the dead after two days without sleep while he observed the convent routine, searching for Melissande.

He would not indulge her comfort at the sake of her safety again. "I have much to do and cannot take you with me. You will be safe tied here."

"To a tree?" She lifted a disdainful brow at the idea.

"You have made it abundantly clear that I cannot trust you to remain with me, Mel. You leave me no choice."

The flexing of her delicate jaw hinted at the inner war she waged. "Roarke's wishes mean that much to you then, that you would kidnap a holy woman to please him? Are his desires so much more important than your own that you risk hellfire and damnation to give your spoiled brother what he wants?"

Her words, shot through with accusation and bitterness, were aimed to wound him. Everyone in his family had catered to Roarke, sometimes to the younger son's detriment. He had not turned into the most responsible of men, yet he had helped Lucian when he'd needed it most.

"I am willing to risk damnation because delivering you but scratches the surface of my debt to Roarke." He hitched a light crossbow over his shoulder, his eyes never leaving hers. It irritated him to explain himself to this woman, yet he owed her something for what she'd been through.

Roarke had found a way to protect their mother from the ugly truth that her eldest son had killed his foster father while learning the skills of knighthood from the country nobleman.

It hardly mattered that Lucian had been defending himself against one of Fitzhugh's legendary rages. Lucian couldn't help that the man's fury had been out of control. But he could have helped his own emotional reaction. He could have remained in control rather than allow his own anger to erupt.

Never again.

"The ruination of my life is repayment of your debt?" Lifted by the wind, her red hair fanned behind her in a righteous banner of indignation.

Lucian stared at her across the clearing, sorry she would come to despise him. Yet, as he felt the inevitable draw of her siren's body, the appeal of her vibrant spirit, he realized this was best. Her enmity would erect a much needed wall between them.

"The fulfillment of your childhood dream is what I sought, Mel," he admitted. "But even if you've come to equate that dream with your ruination, I cannot pretend I will not see it through." He turned to leave, eager to escape the censure in her eyes, the betrayal in her voice.

With a twinge of regret, he resigned himself to her hatred.

Melissande watched his retreating back in disbelief. Unable to tamp down the helplessness that rose like panic in her throat, she screamed at him as he left, calling him names no convent-bred woman should have known.

When it became clear he would not return to engage in a verbal sparring match, she stamped her foot in frustration.

She hated not being listened to.

Lucian's charming brother, Roarke, had ignored her no matter how she tried to capture his attention as a girl. Her parents had ignored her cries of refusal when they'd announced she would enter a convent. The nuns had ignored her pleas for release when she'd arrived.

Even Abbess Helen did not truly listen to her. As much as the elder woman seemed to care for Melissande, their relationship was not the sort where she could speak freely. Abbess Helen's position demanded that she be the teacher and Melissande be the student, the listener.

Perhaps that explained why she loved her children so much. They thrived on her stories and her attention. They listened.

Frustration made Melissande yearn to throw the cheesecloth bundle in her hands, but she'd given in to enough childishness for one day.

She was trapped, and she wouldn't be leaving Lucian anytime soon. For now she would make the best of a bad situation, and with any luck, the abbess would soon come to her aid.

Unwrapping the food, she felt a moment's pleasure at seeing a flint stone. She had not started a fire since girlhood, let alone prepared her own meal. That kind of work remained in the hands of a lower class of holy women who did not come from families as wealthy as the Deverells.

Scurrying about the clearing as far as her rope would allow, Melissande gathered kindling to start a fire, eager to try her hand at the task.

Oddly, a fond memory stole through her.

Plucking up the stone, she knelt over the pile of wood and recalled the instructions of a long-ago voice.

You have to be patient with it, Mel...

Young Lucian Barret had taught her to make a fire on a fishing trip. Melissande had tackled the new skill with more enthusiasm than competence before throwing her hands up in disgust.

A small spark interrupted her recollections. Leaning over the dry sticks, Melissande fanned the spark with a soft breath.

Crack.

Snap.

The fire caught one twig after another, until the blaze burned merrily at her feet.

You did it!

Lucian's youthful voice, deep and rich even as a teenager, praised her in her memory. Patient as stone, Lucian had a way of encouraging her past her temper and soothing her prickly pride.

Funny that scene would come back to her now, so vivid she could almost touch it.

"You did it." The masculine voice rang through the clearing, deeper and less animated than she remembered, but with the same words as the ghost of his youth.

Lucian stepped into the ring of firelight, rabbit in hand. The years had rendered him cold and distant where he used to be merely patient and reserved.

"You taught me well." Melissande rose to her feet.

Laying his weapon on the ground, he lifted a brow in silent contemplation. "I am surprised you recall."

Turning her head as he skewered the rabbit, she shrugged. "I've never had cause to light a blaze since our fishing expeditions."

"In ten years you've not needed to lay a fire?" With smooth efficiency, Lucian set the rabbit to cook and cleaned his hands with water from his wineskin.

"The work is rigorously divided at St. Ursula's." Melissande slid to the ground to wait for their meal while Lucian collected more wood. "Because of my noble ties, I was given more exalted chores than cooking and cleaning."

"I would think most women would be grateful." After propping a long log against a thick elm tree, Lucian lashed the two together with a short rope. The peaked wood made a framework to lay other sticks across.

"I was. That is, I am, grateful." Melissande gestured across the clearing. "I collected some long pieces over there."

Lucian peered through the dark behind her and started dragging over the other branches. "You certainly kept busy."

It wasn't exactly praise, yet Melissande warmed at his words. She made no reply, absorbed in the fluid grace of his movements.

"Your more exalted duties included supervising the abbey orphans?"

Melissande turned the rabbit, wondering if he sought to make fun of her. "Do you not agree that nurturing children is one of God's most exalted tasks?"

"It is work I could never pretend to be equal to, Melissande. I am merely curious to learn if you had any other responsibilities."

Mollified, she returned to watching him complete the shelter. "I was only recently put in charge of the orphans. My other main task is translating manuscripts in the abbey scriptorium."

"Translation?" Lucian dusted his hands off and joined her at the fire. He sounded impressed, but Melissande was too busy sizing up the small sleeping quarters he seemed to be finished with.

"You're not done with that, are you?"

"I think it will be sufficiently warm." He turned back to look at it with a critical eye.

Melissande swallowed her embarrassment. "Aye, but not large enough for us both."

"You can't expect me to erect a keep for you each night on the journey home."

Leave it to Lucian to be utterly reasonable.

She took a deep breath and prepared to deal with him in an equally reasonable way. She had not spent ten years at a convent only to let her temper get the best of her. "I realize that. However, I am a novitiate, and I cannot conscience sleeping in such close proximity to a man."

"Neither can I conscience allowing either of us to catch our deaths because we're too self-righteous to sleep near one another."

Oh, how she envied his even tone, his facade of perfect sensibility. "I am sorry, Lucian, that my ideals lead you to believe I am self-righteous, but I will not have my reputation compromised by our sleeping arrangements."

"Trust me, Mel, your reputation will not be compromised. Roarke has complete faith in my ability to keep my hands off you." His tone made it sound as if he found the idea of touching her abhorrent.

She did not consider herself a vain woman, but it hurt to think the world viewed her as unattractive. Even more offended, Melissande fumed openly. "I am not concerned with what your brother thinks of me, Lucian!" Her voice rose to a perilous pitch. She would have to repent on her knees for this display, yet she could no sooner curb her anger than touch the sky. "I only care about my reputation in the holy sisters' eyes. Do you think they will allow a fallen woman to care for the abbey orphans?"

Lucian edged closer. Gently imprisoning her arms in the vise of his hands, he demanded her attention.

Melissande went still. Not that she was scared, just…intimidated.

"You will have no cause to care for the abbey orphans again, because your arms will be full of your own children. You will not be going back, Melissande. Ever." Gray eyes burned into hers as surely as his touch heated her arms.

She could never be a mother, much as she might secretly long for such a fate. After all, what did she really know of mothering when she'd been torn from her own mother's side at a tender age?

"You are so sure that what you want will come to pass," she responded. "Will you not at least consider the idea that I might refuse to wed your brother, and that he will gladly send an unwilling woman home?"

Lucian's grip on her tightened. She might have felt fear then, had not his expression softened at the same time. "Wait until you see your home, Melissande. Have you not missed it?"

Home.

She had learned through the years it was better not to recall the small Deverell property that had been as much a part of their family as she had. To mourn the loss of what she would never regain would have been foolhardy.

"Think on it, Mel." He moved closer, holding her gaze in his own. His voice lowered a notch, adjusting to persuade and seduce. "The soft slope of endless green hills. The cheerful gurgle of the brook you so loved to cross barefoot. Spring will be almost summer by the time we return."

His features glowed with the light of fond remembrance. Even the scar at his temple seemed to fade into the small wrinkles around his eyes as he smiled.

Her heart ached at the mental picture he created. Nostalgia almost choked her. It had nearly killed her to leave her close family as a child to take up residence with strangers. Her mother had begged her father to reconsider his decision to send their youngest to a convent, but in his haste to settle his youngest daughter his will prevailed. As it always had.

"And nary a snowcapped mountain in sight," Lucian continued, as if he sensed another one of her weaknesses.

Dear Lord, but she detested snow. A few bouts of lung sickness in the cold alpine winters had quickly cured any admiration she once had for the white gift of the mountains. Lucian eyed her expectantly.

"You miss it as much as I do," she observed.

His fingers released her at once.

"Nay." The word was harsh and cold. And an obvious lie.

He busied himself with removing the rabbit from the fire and dividing the portions equally between them. Strong, capable hands worked easily at the mundane task.

Melissande's belly rumbled, but she did not allow his diversion to distract her from her cause. She forced herself to eat several bites before asking the question that gnawed at her brain. "How long have you been away from home, Lucian?"

"Two years." He didn't even look up.

Wait. Curbing her impatience wasn't easy, but she suspected it would be necessary with him. She didn't want him to close the conversation altogether. "You've been in the Holy Lands all that time?"

"It is a misnomer to call that particular patch of land 'holy' anymore, Melissande." Lucian stared into the fire, lost in thought. "An untold number of men have been murdered there to secure that ground for one greedy ruler or another. I cannot imagine a place more profane."

She crossed herself. "How can you blaspheme God's purpose?" She knew that war gave men an excuse to indulge their bloodlust, but at least the purpose of the Crusades was noble.

"'Tis man's purpose to hold the land, not God's."

"Why would you go crusading if you don't believe in the effort?" She almost could not believe her ears. All the women of St. Ursula's devoutly supported the efforts to reclaim the Holy Land.

Abruptly he stood. Flinging the clean bones far into the woods, he effectively announced the end of the meal. "It is past time we should be abed."

All thought of foreign wars dissipated in the fear he wrought with a single pronouncement. Melissande sat rooted in place.

"We have a long ride ahead of us this week." He took out a pile of tightly folded linens from his bag and laid them out beneath the makeshift shelter. "It will be difficult enough for you as it is. I want you well rested."

The firelight, muted by the passing hours since they had stopped, flickered over him as he worked to straighten the blankets. Cast half in shadow, half in warm bronze light, he embodied the two contrasting aspects she could not reconcile—blasphemous heathen who would kidnap a would-be nun and patient childhood friend who would never harm her.

He stopped suddenly, as if reading her silent thoughts, and regarded her long and hard.

"I am sorry, Mel."

He closed the space between them with such purpose, she momentarily feared he would pick her up and toss her into the bed. But he walked right past her to the tree that held the other end of her rope. With quick efficiency, he untied it. "There is a creek not a stone's throw from here. You may ready yourself for sleep alone, but if you are not back shortly, I will have to retrieve you myself."

Requiring no more urging, she hurried out of the clearing toward the water. There was no sense trying to escape him now anyway. Much as she feared sleeping next to him, she wouldn't sacrifice herself to the wolves in her haste to depart.

Cautiously she picked her way through the dark, plagued by the knowledge that the nuns would never take her back if they knew she had spent so much time alone in a man's presence. Rather, they would take her back, but she would never be permitted to supervise the children again.

She scrubbed her face and hands, the icy water spurring her to work quickly.

Only one solution presented itself. She could not, under any circumstances, share such a small space with Lucian Barret.

Trudging carefully back toward the newly stoked fire, Melissande took deep breaths for courage as she thought how she would explain herself to him.

"Here, Melissande, you'd better take the inside." He waited for her near the pile of logs he'd crafted into a shelter for their night's sleep.

"You are welcome to tie me to this tree again, Lucian, but I think it best for us to sleep further apart than that refuge allows." She halted on the other side of the blaze.

The old Lucian, the one she'd known as a child, would have at least listened to her. The new Lucian, the steely warrior who could kidnap her and keep her bound to him, crossed the camp in a blink and scooped her up in his arms. "We cannot afford to lose sleep to arguments, Melissande."

She had a brief impression of his body, that wall of rock, pressed against hers before he tossed her into the far corner of the moss-covered sanctuary.

"The fact is, you will freeze to death if I allow you to sleep unprotected from the mountain winds." He lifted one end of her rope and tied it about his waist, then lay beside her.

Melissande's heart thrummed in her ears. It wasn't right for him to be so close.

Pulling more blankets over her, he carefully tucked them all the way around her until she was wrapped in a woolen cocoon. He stared down at her without a hint of remorse for her distress. "I will not allow you to be harmed in any way, Angel."

The endearment hung between them, creating even more intimacy than their shared linens. She closed her eyes to shut out the kindness she saw on his face. His gentle care surprised her into compliance when she should have stood her ground.

She perceived the covers shift slightly and sensed Lucian relaxing beside her.

Releasing a breath she did not know she had been holding, Melissande allowed the warmth of their pallet to lull her to sleep.

As she drifted between waking and dreaming, it occurred to her she could not recall the last time she had felt so protected.

Chapter Five

Upon awakening the next morning, Melissande enjoyed a moment of utter contentment before recalling her whereabouts. In that instant she appreciated the peace of being well-rested, the joy of breathing fresh mountain air while still wrapped in cozy blankets, and the knowledge of her complete safety.

Then the sounds of Lucian breaking camp penetrated her brain.

Sweet Heaven, how had she ended up in such a predicament?

Melissande remained still, needing a moment to gather her thoughts before she faced him again. The warm feelings still lingered, taunting her with the knowledge that she wasn't as removed from her worldly desires as she would have hoped.

Obviously she was not as self-reliant as she presumed, or she wouldn't have slept so blissfully at the notion of having a man beside her to protect her. She found the idea highly disturbing. Not in ten years had she slept soundly at the abbey, yet one night by Lucian Barret and she awoke completely refreshed.

She should have been busy worrying about her immortal soul last night instead of resting contentedly in the presence of his strength.

"Come along, Melissande." Lucian called to her across the camp.

Perhaps if she feigned sleep, he would allow her to lie here a moment longer. She still had not planned her next move.

Suddenly he stood beside the shelter, leaning down over her. The nearness of his voice startled her. "If you want time to go the creek, you must arise. You've already slumbered too long."

As soon as she heard his boots depart, Melissande darted from the pallet toward the creek, the rope around her wrist dragging after her. She wouldn't be deprived of that moment of privacy. Wearing one of her blankets like a robe, she hastened through the trees to the water's edge.

The sun sat well above the horizon. Normally she had to awake for the day's first prayers in utter darkness. No wonder she'd arisen so rejuvenated today.

She washed her face and rinsed her teeth, then considered her options for escape. The further she strayed from St. Ursula's, the less hope she had of finding her way back alone.

But no matter how much she told herself to focus on a plan, the beauty of her surroundings kept intruding on her good intentions. Birds sang in the trees, a few hardy spring flowers fought valiantly for a bit of morning sunlight, and the creek burbled a happy rhythm as it made its way down the mountain.

Despite her circumstances, Melissande felt curiously alive. Patting her face dry with a corner of the blanket, she promised herself she would find a way to escape today. And this time, she would take the horse and let Lucian worry about finding his own way home. After all, he was a strong, grown man.

Very strong, and very grown in fact. There was something oddly appealing about the breadth of his shoulders, the uncommon height of his body.

Lucian regarded her with his shrewd gray gaze as she approached.

"I am ready to break the fast," she noted, trying to keep her voice light. Morning would have been the best time to escape, if only she hadn't slept so late.

Lucian pulled the blanket off her shoulders and quickly rolled it up. "Late risers must take their bread on horseback." He shoved the woolen roll into the saddlebag and pulled out a heavy crust of bread. "Hold this, and I will hoist you up."

"We cannot leave yet!" If they departed now, she would have no hope of slipping away until nightfall.

His arms fell to his sides. "And why not?"

He suspected something—that much was clear from the cynical lift of his brow and the too reasonable tone of his voice.

Melissande wished for a good lie to inspire her, but her mind concocted only feeble excuses. "Eating while riding makes me ill." Her cheeks burned. She felt as if their high color branded her a liar to all the world.

Lucian lifted the corner of his mouth in a pale shadow of a smile. "Your constitution has weakened considerably then. I believe I once watched you devour a whole batch of apple biscuits while seated upon that fat little pony of yours."

"William." Her heart wrenched at the memory of the sweet creature.

"Yes, William." He snorted. "What a sorry excuse for horseflesh. How many biscuits did you slip the poor animal when no one was looking?"

"I'm sure I don't know what you mean."

"Just as I'm sure I don't know what *you* mean when you say you cannot eat while riding." He reached for her and, before she could step back, hoisted her in the air and seated her atop the gray mare.

So much for her plan. She had just lost any hope of a day-time escape. She noticed, however, that Lucian had forgotten to tie them together. That would surely make it easier to slip away if she found an opportunity tonight.

He handed her the bread before vaulting onto the horse's back behind her. Melissande was too hungry to pout over having to eat while riding. Eagerly she took the bread and tore into one of the crusts.

"Do you know where we are?" Melissande asked between bites. "Or how far we will travel today?"

He remained silent so long she assumed he did not hear her.

"Lucian," she started more loudly, wondering if the years of war could have affected his hearing abilities, "do you know how—"

"I heard you." He turned the mare down a steep grade.

"Surely it cannot tax your concentration too much to an-swer a simple question," she observed, hoping she could be as unflappable as Lucian today.

Watch kept over mouth and tongue keeps the watcher safe from disaster, she counseled herself in Abbess Helen's absence.

"Nay, it does not tax my concentration." As the horse picked its way down the sharp incline, Lucian's body pressed tightly against hers.

The solid breadth of his chest reminded her of his much greater strength, tempted her with thoughts about his body she knew she shouldn't be entertaining.

Distracted by their intimate contact, Melissande almost overlooked the fact that he did not answer her. "Then why can you not satisfy my question?"

She waited a long moment for him to answer. As the horse swayed, Lucian's body brushed across hers, creating a wave of oddly pleasant sensation in her breasts and belly.

"I could answer you, Mel, but I won't." His words were disconcertingly close to her ear, heightening the shivery awareness that Lucian's touch had ignited.

She swallowed the last bit of bread, her mouth suddenly dry at the effect of his warm whisper. Struggling to appear unaffected, she cleared her throat. "And why not?"

"Because the only reason you wish to know our plans today is so that you may calculate a plan to run away from me."

Was she that transparent? Melissande opened her mouth to dispute the truth, but before she could speak, Lucian continued.

"I am astounded that a clever girl would continue to plot such a rash scheme, Melissande."

His stern words halted the musical dance of tingles down her spine. Which, she told herself, was definitely for the best.

"Leaving me now would be more than foolish, it would be downright dangerous. If you are so convinced Roarke will release you when he learns of your unwillingness to wed, why not bide your time with me until he returns you to the abbey?" He sounded reasonable, yet for the first time, Melissande wondered if Roarke really would let her go.

"I have thought of that," she admitted. It seemed silly to equivocate with him when he could practically read her mind. "But I am worried about my reputation if I am gone for that long. I fear I will not be put back in charge of the orphans under those circumstances."

She also feared marriage to a warrior who possessed the power to give her precious babes and the frightening ability to take them away again at his will. She would not mother children destined to be pawns in any man's elaborate schemes for power. Just as she had no wish to become part of a family that could be torn apart again.

The horse stumbled just then and Lucian's heavy arm

snaked around her waist to steady her. Heat licked through her whole body.

"Your charges obviously adore you. The good sisters of St. Ursula's would be remiss if they did not put you where you would do the most good."

"Do you truly think so?" Her heart lifted. Maternal pride filled her. She turned around to see his face, wondering if he believed his own words.

"Absolutely." His gaze held hers, steady and unblinking. He meant it.

"That is not to say I think you will be going back," he cautioned her. "I don't believe you are the kind of woman who is made for convent life. My guess is you will quickly remember what you used to love about England and find yourself happy to be home."

Melissande tried not to listen. She could never seriously contemplate life outside St. Ursula's. The orphans aside, she would not form a family with a power-hungry warrior who would have no concern for her wants.

"But if you should ever return to St. Ursula's," Lucian continued, "I have the utmost confidence the nuns will put you where you will do the most good. And that is with the children."

Warmed by the sentiment, she shifted in her seat to look up at him. Their gazes connected, locked, stole her breath.

She forgot all about their conversation and what she might have said to him. Lucian's nearby mouth captured all of her attention. Dangerous thoughts, yet so tempting.

Lucian's eyes strayed to her lips, a curious light in their gray depths. If she closed her eyes would he...

A noisy rustle in the trees jolted her from her sensual musing. A flash of red soared through the sea of evergreens surrounding them.

"Oh, look, Lucian! A bird!" A harbinger of warmer weather, she rejoiced at the return of the more brightly colored fowls—and the distraction from the absurd notion of kissing Lucian Barret.

She needed to redirect her thoughts. Fast.

Watching the bird until it flew out of sight, Melissande thought about what Lucian had said and sighed. "You are kind to compliment my abilities with the children, Lucian, but perhaps you do not understand the rigidity of convent life. The keeper of the future generation must have the most pristine record."

"You mean to tell me *you* had a pristine record at St. Ursula's?" The horse reached more level ground and Lucian allowed the mare to amble along at her own pace.

She couldn't stifle the laughter that rose in her throat. "Fortunately, Abbess Helen did not hold my earliest years at the convent against me."

"You were a child, Mel." He pointed high into the trees toward a fluttering patch of color. "There's another one."

She watched the red bird hop from limb to limb, surprised at the easy rapport she shared with Lucian today.

Perhaps she ought to wait until they reached England, then she could speak to Roarke directly. Much as she wanted to return to St. Ursula's, it seemed futile to fight Lucian and highly dangerous to escape.

She forced her thoughts back to their conversation. "Plenty of children go out into the world at tender ages. Most pages are younger than eight summers. Yet I childishly fought the nuns at every turn."

"You expect too much of yourself."

"So do you," she ventured, surprised to realize they shared that much in common.

"I need to expect much of you, lest you disappear whilst I sleep."

"Nay. I mean you demand much of yourself, as well."

He stiffened behind her. "I am not sure what you mean, Melissande." He slapped the reins lightly across the horse's back to gather speed. "But I suspect we have endured enough idle chatter for one day."

Quelling the urge to vent her frustration, Melissande wondered what nerve she had struck to make Lucian Barret retreat so fast. But she would sooner be struck by lightning than utter one more bit of "idle chatter" for him to denounce.

Sealing her lips, she settled in for the long ride.

Lucian couldn't make the mare go fast enough. With two people riding such rocky terrain, the horse could only cover a limited amount of ground in a day. Yet he needed the pound of hooves in his head to drown out Melissande's words. *You demand much of yourself.*

How had she seen so much, so fast?

The woman was more clever than he'd realized.

Lucian recalled her vibrant spirit from their youth. The fact that she adored spring birds and craned her neck to see every bit of nature did not surprise him at all.

He had been prepared for her loquacity. Melissande had liked to talk as a girl and he could see that much hadn't changed.

But he did not recall such an insightful mind. Or such tempting lips, for that matter.

Apparently the years at St. Ursula's had changed her more than he realized.

As the terrain sped by in a blur of new green grass and melting mountain snow, Lucian wondered how he could keep his distance from her.

They headed west as the sun traveled its arc in the sky. The mountainous terrain slowly gave way to more gentle slopes and low hills. Lucian knew they could encounter other travelers this way, but their journey would be faster and easier.

Several leagues before the next trading village on their route, he spotted a church ruin in the distance. Though the sun was nearly set, the crumbling stone sat on a hilltop that caught the last of the fading rays.

He felt more than heard Melissande's swift intake of breath as she spotted the site. The rosy sunlight painted the ruins in majestic colors, resurrecting a more noble past for the faded little country chapel. Lucian could almost hear her mind at work.

Yet she refused to break the silence he had imposed. It had been thus all day long. She now sat, visibly yearning to see the ancient holy place yet too stubborn to tell him.

It was a bit out of the way, Lucian thought, but perhaps the ruins would keep her too busy to ask him provoking questions tonight.

Shifting his grip on the reins, he guided the mare up the hill.

"Oh, Lucian!"

Her sudden delighted gasp caught him off guard, but it didn't begin to prepare him for the sincere look of gratitude she tossed him over her shoulder.

"Thank you." She smiled.

His heart caught in his chest.

The kindness in her eyes cast a light in his soul as fleeting and precious as the setting sun on the crumbling chapel wall. Then she turned back to the church and the light vanished as if it had never been. The only reminder that it had existed was the race of Lucian's heart, the horror in his conscience.

How could he view his brother's future wife with such fondness? The gentle sway of her body to the rhythm of the horse's walk became suddenly unbearable. The wind seemed to torment him by catching a strand of her vivid red hair and teasing it across his cheek.

Lucian felt certain the gates of hell swung even wider for him at that moment.

He yanked on the rein with little consideration for the dappled mare. "I'm walking." Vaulting from the horse's back as if demons chased at his heels, he rushed to put distance between him and Melissande.

"I'll walk, too," she offered, leaping awkwardly from their mount before he had a moment to protest. "It is a lovely evening."

For you, maybe.

Darkness settled like a thundercloud around Lucian. As much as he had always genuinely liked Melissande, he found he could not enjoy her company with this new strain of attraction mixed into his general admiration for her.

How in Hades would he suffer through the long trip back to England?

They reached the peak just as the last ray of light bathed the ruins in a final streak of pink. Melissande ran to stand in the center of the crumbling walls, as if eager to place herself at the heart of the light.

Lucian told himself to start unpacking the saddlebags, but his body ignored his brain's commands and he stood there staring at her.

"Hurry, Lucian!" she called, smiling and breathless. "You'll miss it!"

Turning toward him, Melissande held out her hand to invite him into the magical place of light she inhabited alone.

Her hair seemed to catch fire in the sun's farewell offering, as if she were touched by Heaven itself. His fiery stolen angel. It dawned upon him that she was utterly untouchable.

Any marriage to his brother aside, Melissande had still declared herself devoted to her faith and her God.

As for him…his faith had died with Osbern Fitzhugh that fateful day two years ago. Lucian Barret was not just forgotten by God. He was—would always be—unforgiven.

Chapter Six

Gut instinct, honed from years in battle, warned him to remain safely outside the chapel. A man so lacking in honor as Lucian had no business enjoying a sunset with a noblewoman.

He had ignored Melissande all day, however, and guilt niggled him.

Leaving the mare to search for new grass, he stepped up onto the remains of the old stone church floor and joined Melissande. Through a moss-covered archway, they viewed the last tiny slip of a brilliant orange sun.

"I've never seen its equal," she whispered with low reverence, her smile beatific. "It is so very lovely."

"Don't they have sunsets at the convent?"

She sighed, oblivious to his sarcasm. "The enclosure walls are too high. Even if you manage to scramble to the top—" she smiled sheepishly "—the trees and mountains obscure the view."

He envisioned her, hellion that she'd been, climbing the sheer rock walls for a view of the world. He'd do well to remember that behind her mild manner, the hellion still lurked.

"You will see countless sunrises and sets when you return

to England." Lucian held her arm just long enough for her to step down from the platform of the stone floor.

Touching Melissande posed risks to his self-control that he could never have foreseen.

He moved to sort through the supply bag, eager to sever the unwanted intimacy of the chapel. He tossed her the remaining food stores before disappearing to hunt for firewood.

Melissande watched him go, wondering how she had offended him this time. She could not endure another evening of silence after their total lack of conversation on the road today. Even at the abbey she spoke her prayers aloud. With Lucian, her pride demanded she not speak to him after he'd chastised her.

How dare he! He had captured her for selfish reasons. The least he could do was—

He had abducted her, and now was her chance to escape.

Although Melissande still wore the rope around her wrist, she had not been tied to a tree or to Lucian or to any other immovable object.

Her eyes strayed to the tired gray mare. It seemed cruel to run the animal into the ground, but what choice did she have?

After dropping the food stores on the ground, Melissande made her way over to the horse. Debating which direction to head, she prayed she could hoist herself up on the tall mare's back.

"I am but a stone's throw from you Melissande," a familiar masculine voice called from the inky blackness surrounding the camp. "You would be most unwise to try."

By Ursula's sainted wimple. Would the man never relax his guard? She stomped her foot in frustration, promptly kicking a root and stubbing her toe.

Curse words bubbled in her brain but she did not give them vent. *In the sin of the lips lies a disastrous trap,* she told herself.

"Are you all right?" Lucian's voice grew louder as he approached her from the shadows.

Just who she didn't want to see.

She hobbled on one foot, annoyed he had witnessed her tantrum and even more irritated that he decided he could talk to her *now,* when she verged on spitting mad. "I'm fine," she returned sharply, hobbling to take a seat on one of the flat stones scattered about the ruins.

"You are injured." He stepped into her vision, which was very close considering the vast darkness of the moonless night. "If you will not take care of yourself, Melissande, then I will care for you."

The urge to be contrary warred with the pain in her toe, but seeing the look of quiet insistence on Lucian's face, she mutinously stuck out her foot.

"Ten years in a convent has not managed to save you from your own temper, I see." He removed her slipper with more delicacy than she would have thought a hardened warrior capable. Warm fingers brushed over her thin stocking, causing chills to chase their way up her leg. He cradled her ankle in his lap.

"Not for lack of trying, I assure you." She rather hoped he would berate her for her temper—an argument would be infinitely preferable to this warm feeling his gentle caress inspired.

"You broke the nail and are bleeding right through your stocking." His thumb stroked its way over the pad of her foot and down the inside of her sole.

Did he even realize he touched her thus? In the dim light, she could only see that he studied her foot intently.

"Oh, dear." Surely she was a wicked woman to allow him to touch her this way. "I'll see to it myself, thank you."

She attempted to pull away, but he held her fast.

"It would be easier for me to wrap." His hand strayed up to her ankle then hesitated.

The unfamiliar touch of a man's hand on a place so sensitive touched off a chain of little sparks from her toe to her thigh. All feeling narrowed to the one point where his fingers paused.

He glanced down at his hand where it brushed over her thin woolen hose. She saw the muscle of his jaw twitch and flex, as if he might be annoyed. Apparently there were no sinful sparks leaping through *him* at their slight contact.

"I'll get it," she insisted, pulling her foot from his lap and swiveling away from him.

He remained there, frozen, making Melissande more nervous with each passing breath. Did he think her a wanton that she would allow him to handle her so intimately? By the saints, he certainly knew she'd tried to protest.

"Perhaps that would be best," he muttered before striding back toward the horse.

Melissande fumbled with her stocking, her foot much colder now that Lucian had gone. Carefully she removed the broken nail and tore a square of her hose to wrap about her foot.

Makeshift bandage in place, Melissande realized Lucian had the fire going right beside the church ruins. He had already hauled over their linens and was rolling them out around her.

Warmth stole through her, having much more to do with the peculiar comfort she found in Lucian's presence than any blaze. She had not realized how lonely she was for human contact and companionship.

Not that Lucian afforded her much companionship, she thought, recalling their quiet day.

But he provided her with a sense of security she hadn't experienced since childhood. For all his gruff manner and resistance to conversation, Lucian had made it clear he would protect her at all costs. He wouldn't allow her to sleep in the cold and catch another case of lung fever. If she escaped, he would be close behind to rescue her from potential harm.

As much as he frustrated Melissande, she had to admit there was a certain amount of honor in the sentiment.

Strange to find such a noble quality in a mercenary knight.

Materializing before her, Lucian held out his arms. "You will be more comfortable over here." He nodded to the blanket closest to the fire.

He offered her his arm but she refused to accept it. His proximity confused her, unsettled her.

"I can manage." She pushed herself up with her arms to keep the weight off of her foot and settled herself on the pallet in front of the fire.

"You look a bit flushed, Melissande." He balled up an extra linen to prop her foot. "Are you sure you are well?"

Of course she wasn't well. Lucian had her thinking thoughts no proper convent-bred woman would ever dare to entertain.

"I'm fine." Except for the skin that still tingled where his fingers had grazed her ankle. "Thank you."

To distract herself from foolish thoughts, Melissande watched him dole out the remaining food, carefully dividing the meat and bread evenly.

"Perhaps we will come across a village tomorrow," she suggested, hoping she didn't sound overly interested.

Lucian looked around the fire for a moment, as if wondering if he should sit out on the ground rather than beside her on the blanket-covered chapel floor.

Melissande acknowledged it was kind of him to consider her sensibilities as a holy woman. Still, the nurturer in her wouldn't allow him to take his meal on the cold ground. She scooted over a little.

"Sit here, Lucian. I think it would be admissible considering the circumstances."

Despite his skeptical expression, he dropped down beside her. He seemed content to eat and stare with brooding eyes into the fire, but not Melissande.

"It must have been a beautiful chapel," she observed, enjoying the dance of firelight over the moss-covered rubble. Like the setting sun, the glow of the flames animated the cool stone and resurrected the divine spirit of the place.

He said nothing.

Perhaps she would have better luck if she formulated a direct question. "Do you think the architecture is native or—".

"Roman." He didn't even bother to look up from his bread.

Disappointed, Melissande sighed. "I don't remember your being so closemouthed, Lucian. Is it just around me that you don't want to talk, or are you like this with everyone these days?" Perhaps she meddled where she should not, but if she were to be in close company with this man for another sennight, she refused to be utterly ignored. She detested not being listened to.

"It is not just you, Mel." The resignation in his words belied the meager grin on his face. "Doesn't your good book tell you, 'In the sin of the lips lies a disastrous trap'?"

Fortunately the firelight would hide the rising color she felt in her cheeks. Abbess Helen had chastised her with that very proverb more times than she could count. Her indignation refused to be cowed by his cleverness. "You think I talk too much?"

"Absolutely."

Anger spurred her on. "Recall, sir, our spiritual teachings also tell us that 'The mouth of the upright is a life-giving fountain.'" She had never dared to try that retort on the abbess. It would have sounded too prideful. With Lucian, however, she did not care.

He pulled a small stick out of the dirt by his feet and tossed it into the flames. "Do not forget the rest of that one, Angel…'but the mouth of the godless is a cover for violence.' I think that says it all quite nicely."

Could she have understood him properly? Either he was really insulting her or… "Are you suggesting that you don't talk much because you think you are godless?"

"You're a smart woman, Melissande. Make of it what you will." Pushing to his feet, Lucian packed away the empty cheesecloth and retrieved a new wineskin from his bag. He held it up for her to see. "Does the mouth of the upright wish to partake of a good Burgundy tonight? Or will sharing a skin with me profane the experience for you?"

She had never seen this Lucian before. Something cold and dark lurked in him—something far more dangerous than the facets she had seen thus far. Lifting her chin, she readied herself for another round of his strange verbal sparring.

"I enjoy a good wine."

Fire leaped in his gray gaze. With his dark hair and jagged scar, he looked like the devil himself. Tempting but dangerous, Lucian Barret was probably not a wise choice for a drinking companion, yet some rebellious spirit within her wouldn't let her say no to the challenge in his eyes.

"There's my girl." Returning with the wine, he sat a bit closer to her than he had before. He smiled down at her with a mixture of pride and some other nameless emotion that forced her to scoot a little further down the blanket from him. "I wondered where the old devil-may-care Melissande had disappeared to."

Melissande accepted the wineskin from him and took a long drink. "She is tempered with a more practical spirit these days." The wine blazoned a trail down her throat and filled her with a delicious sense of abandon. She'd not taken more than the small sips used in communion in ten years.

He reached over her to retrieve the Burgundy. The brush of his arm against hers caused her skin to tighten and tingle right through her heavy gown.

"What you mean to say is that she has been tamed by the convent," Lucian replied dryly.

"Hardly!" She sat up straighter, surprised at Lucian's direct approach. Apparently when the man decided to talk, he didn't waste time dancing around a subject. "I have acquired a fair amount of wisdom in the last ten years, Lucian."

He looked out over the dark hills from their high vantage point. The wind caught his hair and rippled through the fabric of his loosened tunic, yet the man himself remained unmoved.

Melissande wondered if he would retreat into silence again now that she had disagreed with him, but a few moments later he passed her the wine and spoke again.

"I can see your new wisdom, Melissande. Though I'll warrant you've acquired it on your own in the scriptorium as opposed to on your knees in a drafty church." His tone was lighter now, as if he no longer sought to provoke her.

Pride filled her at his easy recognition of her learning. Yet her desire for humility forced her to argue. "I hope I have cultivated equal knowledge in both places." She turned her attention to the wineskin and drank deeply, welcoming its warmth. The fiery drink seemed to invade her bloodstream all at once and spin through her senses.

"You need not be so humble with me. I can see for myself what sorts of intelligence you have obtained."

As he turned to look at her, Melissande felt transparent. He did see.

Entirely too much, in fact. Those gray eyes probed the depths of her soul, recognizing her strengths and more numerous weaknesses.

"You have the advantage of me then." Caught off balance by his scrutiny, Melissande struggled for equilibrium. Too bad the wine had already robbed her of it.

He loomed so close, she could have touched him if she lifted her hand.

"And how is that, Angel?" A surge of emotion kindled in his gaze. He seemed closer still.

"You seem to understand me, yet I cannot fathom you." She cleared her throat, vainly trying to dismiss the heat that curled through her at his proximity. "I have no idea what sorts of intelligence you have gained since I last saw you, but I can tell you have been exposed to some unhappy circumstance."

He loomed no more.

Sinking away from her, Lucian closed his eyes and rubbed his temples with one hand.

She couldn't quit now. Not when she was so near to learning something about him. "Why are you so changed, Lucian?"

When he looked up again, his eyes were shuttered and dull, the devilish gleam she'd spied earlier had vanished.

"I will not dredge up my past to entertain you, Mel, no matter how curious you might be." The muscle of his jaw flexed with obvious irritation, but his eyes reflected a deep pain she knew was not of her making. "Do not ask me about it again if you wish to have any sort of communication between the two of us."

She nodded, recognizing this was not a good time to belabor the point. Whatever troubled Lucian to the point he thought he was godless must be addressed. She couldn't stand to see her old friend consumed by unhappiness, even if he was a warrior.

"Yet I find it rather difficult to fall asleep without talking," she finally ventured, hoping she did not push him too far.

He groaned in protest.

"How did you ever manage abbey life?" He shook his head with slow resignation.

"There was usually somebody praying somewhere at all hours of the day. The chant of it helped lull me to rest." *God forgive me for the slight untruth. I only want Lucian to talk to me.*

"Very well then." Surprisingly he sounded suddenly chipper. "I seem to recall you brought a book with you from the convent."

Oh, dear. This was not at all what she envisioned. "Yes— I thought you put it in your bags."

He grinned, the first smile of genuine pleasure she had seen from the somber Lucian Barret. "Then I shall read to you, and you can fall asleep to the sound of my voice."

Crossing the camp to retrieve the heavy, leather-bound volume, he looked far too pleased with himself.

She wouldn't learn anything about him this way.

"You are no doubt familiar with the work?" he called, yanking her one possession from his bag.

Two years familiar. "Aye. Homer and I know each other very well by now."

Waving the book above his head like a tournament prize, he called, "Why don't you ready yourself for sleep while I choose a spot to start in here? There is some privacy on the other side of the chapel, I believe."

A moment to herself…maybe this could be the break she'd been looking for—

"And don't forget, I will come to get you myself if you are not back with all haste."

How could she forget? The brute also stood two feet from the horse as if to ensure she would not steal it.

Grumbling about the ill effects of being tied to a man, Melissande picked her way through the rubble to the deserted side of the church.

He did it again, she thought as she loosened her gown's lacings for easier sleep. He'd foiled her attempts to draw him out even a little bit about his past. She should have known better than to blurt out her questions with no semblance of subtlety.

Yet curiosity consumed her now. A mystery lurked around Lucian Barret, and she vowed to decipher it. Like one of her more complex manuscripts, Lucian's secrets begged her to unravel their hidden meaning.

Removing the plaits from her hair, she wound the strands into one long braid for the night and considered the man who had abducted her.

Although a soldier of God, he called himself godless. Although the eldest Barret son, he concerned himself with procuring a wife for his younger brother, as if Roarke were the heir. Although a patient, mild-tempered youth, Lucian had transformed into a hardened warrior who hungered for battle.

A definite mystery.

And as long as Melissande remained his captive, she considered it her duty as a religious woman to help him face his demons and recapture the heart he seemed to be lacking. Any God-fearing person would do the same for a childhood friend, she assured herself.

Certainly it wasn't just curiosity, although that particular character trait had brought the childhood Melissande one piece of mischief after another.

Maybe her interest had more to do with the glimpses she'd seen of Lucian's still generous spirit. She had to admit it had been rather kind of him to trek up to the chapel ruins to camp tonight just because he knew it would please her.

Unfortunately she suspected she would not accomplish much confronting Lucian in the guise of religious counselor. She might have a better chance of reaching him if she appealed to him as a friend. Secular logic would work more effectively with her self-proclaimed "godless" companion. He'd had made it very clear he did not hold the church in high esteem these days.

But could she set aside the convent teachings that had become such a part of her and simply talk to Lucian, woman to man? The idea held a note of danger, but she had to approach him in a way he could respect.

Gathering her courage about her like a protective shield, she picked her way through the crumbling ruin before she changed her mind. Could she do it?

Not giving herself a chance to reconsider, she stepped into the ring of firelight where Lucian sat thumbing through her book. Tonight, she would employ all her subtlety to extract a hint of Lucian's mysterious past.

Tonight, she would seek to recapture the camaraderie they'd known as children.

Lucian looked up and her heart pitched in unsteady rhythm. He had grown considerably in ten years. Why hadn't she noted his raw masculine appeal before now?

He did not have the face of a classically handsome man. Rather, Lucian possessed a visage impossible to look away from. He fascinated her on some simple, elemental level.

The realization stole her breath.

Melissande saw him through new eyes—a woman's eyes.

In the soft flow of firelight she absorbed every detail of Lucian's broad shoulders and muscular arms, his thick black hair that brushed the collar of his tunic.

She swallowed.

Hard.

Yet as their gazes met over the leaping fire, Melissande knew her instincts for approaching him were correct. If she hoped to understand him, the time to encourage conversation was now. Tonight. While he was sipping a good wine and already amenable to talk.

She closed her eyes against the dark appeal of the man and told herself that he was still the same person underneath it all—the same honorable young man—just as she was still the same girl inside.

And she missed him. Perhaps she missed her old self just as much.

Tonight, to learn the truth about Lucian, she would resurrect the bold and brazen Melissande.

Chapter Seven

Melissande Deverell could have tempted a saint with that fiery red hair and siren's body. When she stepped from the shadows, Lucian saw a ghost of her former self, the rash-and-reckless Melissande grown to a spirited woman.

Definitely a dangerous combination. How could a woman who looked like Melissande be a nun?

The Almighty must have a sense of humor.

Now, to top off the Lord's evening of fine jests, Lucian found he couldn't read Melissande's damn book.

"This is in Greek." He swiped the blasted volume through the air.

"Yes, most copies of Homer are—"

Lucian could see the exact moment realization dawned. The moment she recognized the flaw in his otherwise extensive education.

"It only makes sense, of course," he returned. "However, I cannot read Greek." The confession did not come easily to a man who had little left to pride himself on but his academic achievements.

She took the book from his hand and sat beside him, her

unbound hair brushing over his arm. Her gentle, composed air warned him she would try to comfort him. He didn't think he could sit still through it.

Many failures weighted Lucian's shoulders, but intellectual flaws were not usually among them.

"No one can read every language," Melissande observed with studied nonchalance. She flipped through the pages to avoid eye contact.

Which was just as well. He might strangle her if he saw even a twinge of pity in her gaze.

"I draw the line at Sanskrit." She shuddered, her hair dancing an accompanying shimmy to her movements. "I cannot begin to interpret it, though I do a fair job of copying the letters."

A little of the weight lifted from Lucian's shoulders. She couldn't possibly know what a balm the words were to his spirit.

"I speak a passable Sanskrit." He couldn't have held that admission back if he tried. It seemed important that she not think him completely uncultured.

Admiration lit her brown eyes even more than the leaping blaze at their feet. "Truly?" She clapped her hands in delight. "I wish you could see some of the books at the abbey, Lucian. The illustrations look so interesting, but I cannot comprehend the text that goes along with them." Her brow furrowed in frustration. "Can you imagine how vexing it is to spend months copying a manuscript you cannot interpret?"

"I have a fair idea." Lucian tapped the giant Greek volume in her hand.

"At least you do not have to stare at these pages, day after day, knowing you are destined not to understand them." Her face clouded, her voice hinting at well-guarded bitterness. "It is a cruel torment to mindlessly copy books without being able to ponder their ideas as you work."

He found himself curious about who would force her to do a job she clearly resented. It was the only remotely negative sentiment she'd uttered about her beloved abbey.

"You have no choice in the matter of what books to copy?"

"Sister Eleanor chooses what I shall copy as a matter of whether she is pleased with me or not. When she is most spiteful, she gives me Sanskrit, but sometimes—" She crossed herself in obvious horror at her own words. "Father, forgive me."

Poor Melissande. Although she had always been a touch temperamental, Lucian had never met a more good-intentioned soul. Surely she never did anything so wrong as to deserve a job she detested.

He took an instant dislike to Sister Eleanor. "Melissande, you need no forgiveness to speak the truth."

She wrung her hands together. "It is wicked of me to call her spiteful."

"She sounds spiteful to me."

Melissande cast him a scathing glance.

At least she didn't look so guilty anymore. But it couldn't hurt to rile her a bit more to be sure. "Besides, I could call you temperamental and you wouldn't think *me* wicked."

"Temperamental?" Indignation straightened her shoulders and lifted her chin.

"Since you have a temper to match that flaming red hair, I don't feel like I need to ask forgiveness for pointing out the obvious."

"Ooohh!" She clenched her delicate fingers into a fist. The fire in her brown eyes leaped and sparked.

Lucian knew her youthful counterpart would have slugged him.

All too soon, she calmed herself, however, and adopted the

practicality that seemed so at odds with everything he remembered about her.

"Well, it may be true that I have my fair share of temper, but it is unkind to point out people's failings." She smoothed the leather cover of Homer, then straightened her skirts. The busy flutter of her hands suggested she was not as resigned to quiet acceptance as her words intimated.

"That is why I prayed for forgiveness for pointing out Sister Eleanor's shortcoming. Surely she does not mean to be spiteful."

Some demon pushed him to spar with her. Some downtrodden part of his own pitiful soul longed to see her at her most feisty. "Like hell she doesn't."

Her fist flew at him from the far side of her body. He saw it coming—expected it—but he made no move to stop it. Curiosity made him wonder what kind of punch she could muster after all these years.

With a sound "smack," her knuckles connected with his upper arm. He couldn't help but feel proud at how much muscle she managed to leverage into that punch.

He grinned.

In fact, a strange sensation washed over him that he hadn't experienced in years. He let his head fall forward with the weight of it.

Laughter.

"Are you all right?" Gingerly she touched his arm where she'd just pummeled him. "Lucian?"

He could no longer keep it in. As her questing fingers ran up his shoulder, the laughter bubbled up from a long neglected place in his heart.

"Lucian?" She did not sound so concerned this time. Irritation mingled with the last vestiges of her worry. "Are you laughing?"

Good Lord, she was a prize. Propping his elbows on his knees, he held his head in his hands to keep from falling over as good humor assaulted him.

"How dare you!" She now shoved at his shoulder, full of righteous anger. "If you think that was a paltry attempt at a punch, Lucian Barret, let me assure you, I can do better."

He laughed harder. "I don't doubt it, Angel." Reaching across her body, he plucked up her hand and lowered his voice to a conspiratorial whisper. "Too bad you didn't try it out on Sister Eleanor."

She stared at him for so long, Lucian thought she might get offended all over again.

Then, like the sun venturing out after a long rainy spell, Melissande giggled.

And giggled.

"You're horrid!" She jabbed him with her elbow. Once. Twice. Three times, before collapsing in giddy mirth against his shoulder.

Something warm unfurled in Lucian at the unthinking friendliness of her gesture. Something tender and precious and completely misplaced clutched at his sorry excuse for a heart.

Oh, God.

He froze, but Melissande didn't seem to notice amidst her laughter. She held her belly in joyous abandon, head thrown back and eyes closed.

Her pose was far too replete, too satisfied, too…sensuous.

"Melissande." What had he been thinking, baiting her like that? He knew better than to resurrect the woman of his dreams.

Didn't he?

"Melissande." He half shouted at her now, unable to bear the torture of her sweet body against his for even a split second more.

She righted herself immediately, resuming the contrite look that he'd sought to banish only moments before.

Damn.

Thinking fast, he sought his mind for a diversion, a way of putting some space between them without invoking the rule of silence he'd forced upon her today. "Perhaps you could read to me tonight, in light of my lack of Greek?"

The dubious look in her wary brown eyes told him she sensed some ulterior motive on his part. Yet her naïveté prevented her from seeing his real inner struggle.

His body was still warm where she'd touched him, a burning imprint of her vibrancy against the stark backdrop of his cold existence.

"Certainly." Dutifully she opened the book and Lucian had a brief impression of her at the abbey two days ago when she'd read to the children. She had laughed and frolicked then, too.

No wonder she loved the children with such devotion. They answered the suppressed longings of her heart, giving her a place to bestow all that vividness and life she had to offer.

"We might as well start at the beginning." She smoothed a page of parchment with reverent fingers while Lucian's heartbeat slowed. "Perhaps we can read as we ride tomorrow."

"If you like." Perfect. It would save him from infernal conversation that only led him into revealing more of himself than Melissande should know.

She launched into the *Odyssey,* translating the text easily as she read.

As she wove the tale of the Greek hero Odysseus, Melissande wondered at Lucian's peculiar behavior tonight.

Obviously he did not want to forge any sort of friendship with her, else he would not have pushed her away after teasing her into such merriment. Like a well-defended keep, Lucian erected stolid borders around himself to discourage any infiltration.

Still, he sat near her as she read, warming her far more than the lively blaze by their feet. He could not be all that displeased with her if he was willing to sit idly by and listen to her read.

The stars winked in the heavens, rendering the perfect setting for a story. The cool night air above them and cold stone floor below them provided a pleasing contrast to the crackling fire that burned alongside the crumbling stones where they rested.

Melissande relaxed into her role as storyteller, welcoming the chance to indulge in a well-loved pastime.

Was it vanity to enjoy the sound of one's own voice? She sincerely hoped not as reading out loud ranked as one of her dearest pleasures. The trip of Homer's gorgeous images off her tongue thrilled her anew.

Lucian interrupted her early in her tale. "You see how constant and faithful Penelope is?"

Jerked out of the story, Melissande blinked to clear her thoughts and lowered the book. "Faithful, indeed, to wait twenty years for her husband to return from war."

"Yet your heart is so fickle you forgot all about the man you claimed to love in a mere ten years."

Did he mean to tease her, or did he condemn her? Annoyed, Melissande lifted her book again. "Shall I continue?"

He leaned back on the blanket and propped himself on an elbow to listen. "By all means, lady. You are a natural-born troubadour."

The compliment tickled her to her toes. Deep into the night, Melissande read. As the fire waned and cooled, Lucian tossed her a blanket to wrap herself in, but not once did he suggest they put the book away.

Lost in the magic of the narrative, Melissande found herself adopting voices for the characters and theatrics for the gestures. When the hero Odysseus landed on yet another ancient island, she acted out the part of Nausikaa, the foreign princess who fell madly in love with the wandering Greek and begged him to remain by her side for all time.

Though he refused, gallant Odysseus departed with the chivalrous sentiment, "All my days until I die, may I invoke you as I would a goddess, Princess, to whom I owe my life."

"Melissande?" Lucian's whisper halted her before she began the next stage of the poetic journey.

"It is beautiful, isn't it?" She loved the romance of the tale, the obvious love between Odysseus and Penelope no matter how much time they spent apart. Yet despite Odysseus' love for his wife, he took care to be gentle with Nausikaa's feelings as he left her.

"You can hardly see the page anymore, Mel." He pointed to the dwindling embers and her close proximity to the tiny flame that remained. "You will fall into the hot ashes if we don't admit defeat and go to sleep."

Reluctantly she closed the book. "But it is a beautiful story, is it not?"

He pulled the volume from her hands and wrapped it in a portion of his woolen blanket. The care with which he handled her prized possession touched her.

"I am surprised Sister Eleanor allows you to read something so pagan." He sifted through the pile of linens around Melissande.

A grin pulled at her lips. "She doesn't realize how fluent in Greek I am."

His wandering hand brushed against her leg in his quest to find something among the wool coverings. Unnerved by the sudden contact, she jumped. "Can I help you find what you're looking for?"

He held up the forgotten rope that trailed from her wrist. "I already found it."

She experienced a moment's hurt that he didn't trust her in the least, although she knew that made no sense. He shouldn't trust her. Melissande would leave him if he gave her half a chance.

No matter how she told herself she understood Lucian's reasoning, the reminder of being forced to travel to England with him robbed the night of its sense of shared adventure.

After cinching the knot at his waist, he met her gaze. They had been sitting close together before, but now that the rope connected them, their bodies were so close they almost brushed against one another.

"I have no choice." Earnest gray eyes dulled in the fading light, Lucian's voice held a note of empathy. "I cannot allow you to come to harm, Melissande, and it is infinitely dangerous for a woman to travel the French countryside alone at night."

He didn't understand. Would never understand. Stung by the realization that they would never recreate the friendship they once shared, Melissande shook her head. "And you must understand that I, too, have no choice. I could no sooner forget my young charges at the abbey than I could give up my own children. No woman would give up her babes without a fight."

"They are being well taken care of, Mel. You know that."

Her heart ached at the thought of her children being well cared for but never loved. "But the person they have come to depend on most has abandoned them. And I am sorry, Lucian, but I do not consider myself replaceable in their eyes. None of the other sisters will love them so completely as I do."

Lucian leaned forward until naught but a hand span separated them. "And you know why that is, Angel?"

She might have offered some reasons, but she knew he did not seriously wish for her to answer him. Besides that, she found it difficult to formulate a thought when his face hovered so close to hers.

"It is because you were not meant to be a nun." Though his words rang with mild frustration, he softened them with a light sweep of his hand across her cheek. "You were meant to be a mother."

Melissande's soul-deep shudder answered his touch. The hardened palms of his hand fascinated her. The delicate brush of his heavy fingers at her temple caused her flesh to leap with tingling awareness.

"You care for those children with your whole heart because you were fated to be a mother and bear little imps of your own."

Her womb contracted in hungry acknowledgment of his words. How could he see the depths of her heart, her most carefully guarded secret, when he had known her but two days since their shared childhood? But no matter how much she yearned for motherhood in her heart, in her mind she acknowledged it could never, ever be. She had been torn from her own mother's side unwillingly because her father had wanted her to serve his own political ends. Bad enough she'd had to leave her own mother. How would she endure having a child taken from her to serve a husband's ends?

Still, she didn't even think of denying Lucian's claim. No matter that it could never be, she could not have disputed the fact.

Looking up into his eyes, she saw Lucian about to retreat. Instead of learning his innermost secrets tonight, he had somehow divined hers.

In the course of an evening, he had stirred the deepest hungers of her soul and now he planned to just roll over and go to sleep without so much as a "Sorry to force you to confront the biggest sorrows of your life, Mel." Just who did he think he was?

Unwilling to weigh the risks to her actions, Melissande drifted closer to Lucian's warmth, his strength. Strange that she would seek comfort from the very man who had unsettled her in the first place. But he had instigated this intimacy and she was not ready for it to end.

A moment's doubt reproached her when Lucian's eyes widened and his huge warrior's frame stiffened to stone. Was her proximity so unappealing? No matter—the wild tangle of emotions Lucian had dared to call forth would not be quelled by any fear of rejection.

She longed for the healing comfort of human contact, needed to assuage the gaping emptiness in her heart.

With trembling fingers, Melissande reached to stroke his face the same way he had skimmed hers. Some inner demon urged her roving touch down to the contours of his mouth, straying on the fullness of his lower lip.

His flesh was warm and surprisingly soft. Perhaps she had discovered the only part of this man that wasn't hewn of rock. Perhaps he was not incapable of tenderness, after all. Surely such a pliant mouth knew how to speak gently—to spout words that would soothe her heart rather than break it with too much insight.

No doubt such a mouth could kiss a woman gently, as well…

For one breath-stealing moment, Melissande envisioned Lucian's lips upon hers, his mouth tasting her with the same delicate care he used when drinking his fine Burgundy.

Heat flooded her cheeks, her limbs. Whether from embarrassment or from desire for that kiss, Melissande couldn't be sure. She glanced up at Lucian, half wondering if he would be able to divine her thoughts now as well as he had earlier. Would he be able to see her hunger for his touch?

His gray eyes glittered almost black in the fading firelight. As their gazes connected, his seemed to absorb hers, and Melissande could feel herself being pulled in by his watchful stare.

Then his eyes narrowed a fraction, jarring her from her sensual thoughts.

What was she doing? Her heart thumped the walls of her chest so hard she thought it might cause the very ground to rumble beneath its rhythm. She had no right, no business, touching Lucian Barret.

Later she would be ashamed by this brazenness. The wildness in her faded under the press of guilt and recrimination, so she moved to lower her hand.

Her fingers had barely left his lips when Lucian braced her forearm in an ironlike grip. He held her there, hand in midair. She wondered at the restrained power she felt in his grasp and assessed the mix of emotions on his face.

Anger. That was there in full measure. Was he angry because she'd touched him or because she'd stopped?

What fascinated her more was the other emotion she saw in his eyes—something hot and restless and akin to hunger that made her feel edgy and languid with heat at the same time.

Or maybe she merely absorbed the heat that emanated from him. Tense and palpable, the waves of warmth rolled off him and around her, drawing her forward in spite of the threat of impending storm in his eyes.

"Angel." He whispered it with husky reverence.

The strange tangle of emotions in her belly twisted and tightened even more hopelessly.

Then his mouth lowered to hers, just as it had in her wayward daydreams, and she forgot to be frightened or intimidated. He grazed his mouth across hers with infinite gentleness, as if she were the most fragile of creatures.

Sparks shimmered behind her eyelids as her breath caught in her throat.

Oh, my.

She slid her wrist free of his loosened grip and placed her hand on his shoulder. In the warmth of the fire, Lucian had loosened his hauberk, leaving naught but his tunic to cover his chest. Melissande slid her fingers across the soft linen, tracing over the wealth of muscles surrounding his shoulder.

She wanted to explore those muscles, to trail her fingers over every hard plane and nuance, but she could not concentrate on the effort while he kissed her, while his thigh pressed against her own.

Sensation enveloped her, dazzled her, fed her hunger for touch and fueled it at the same time. She could only think about pressing closer, and closer still.

A slow melting effused her limbs.

Her mouth opened in a joyous little sigh at the sensory heaven of it all, and Lucian lost no time deepening his kiss.

A flood of heat swept through her, pooling in the womb whose emptiness had started this whole delicious journey.

The scent of him, only half realized until now, filled her nostrils with hints of campfire and leather.

"Lucian." She moaned the name with all the new longing of her awakened body, yet the moment she uttered it, he seemed to regain his senses.

He froze, his arms turning to wooden weights around her and his lips leaving hers to the rapidly chilling night air.

Frustration churned through her.

"Lucian?" She wanted to drag him back to her, though she knew it was already too late. Her body thrummed with sensations both terrifying and glorious. How could he leave her?

"My God."

More damning than the more vitriolic curses she had heard from him, the oath confirmed her fears that Lucian regretted the kiss.

Regretted touching her.

In the sin of the lips lies a disastrous trap... The proverb took on a whole new meaning now.

"I'm sorry," she murmured, wishing she had not called forth her former self on an idiotic mission to win Lucian's confidences tonight. If she had maintained her hard-won reserve and the air of piousness she ought to project, none of this would have happened.

Instead she had simply been herself.

With stiff movements, he removed the blankets from his body and placed them over her in a ritual she now recognized as some sort of self-imposed penance. "It is not your fault, Melissande. Good night."

The clink of his sword settling along with him against the cold stone floor echoed in the night long after the sound itself.

With it, Melissande's recriminations reverberated in her mind, disparaging her for ever resurrecting the girl of her youth. She folded her hands to pray, then beseeched God to send Abbess Helen to her—soon.

The sooner Melissande escaped the enigmatic pull of Lucian Barret, the better.

Chapter Eight

Lying on his back in the chilly air of the decaying chapel, Lucian counted stars until they faded. The roof of the church ruin had long ago fallen to crumbled bits on the ground, leaving him plenty of space to study the heavens.

Watching the gold-fingered dawn claw its way across the sky, he could not decide if he welcomed the new day.

He had not slept all night. Each deep breath Melissande took reminded him of the liberties he had taken with his brother's intended wife.

Two years ago, after Osbern Fitzhugh had died of a sword wound inflicted by Lucian's hand, Lucian did not think he could sink any lower.

Last night proved him wrong. To add to his sins of pride and violence, now he must add the grievous moral wrong of lusting after his brother's future bride.

And Lucian had more reasons than most men to honor his brother. Hell, he owed Roarke a debt he could never repay. Roarke had lied to their mother about the circumstances of Fitzhugh's death to protect her from the ugly truth. Roarke had shouldered Lucian's responsibilities as heir when Lucian relinquished his claim to the title.

Thank God their birth father had not lived to see the day his eldest son would raise arms to a Fitzhugh. The families had fostered one another's sons since the reign of William the Conqueror.

Although the arrival of the new day marked his chance to depart the church ruins full of taunting memories, Lucian could not be certain he relished facing Melissande this morning any more than he'd enjoyed the torment of sleeping beside her last night.

And it had been torment.

He'd had an easier time dodging Saracen blades than he'd had shutting out the memory of Melissande's body pressed to his own, her generous curves straining closer to him with every breath. Hell, it was all he could do even now to keep his hands off her while she slept a few feet away.

As the glimmer of dawn brightened, Lucian struggled to come up with a plan to address the events of the previous night.

Melissande's kiss.

Try as he might, he knew he would never forget her questing touch, the softness of her fingertips as she stroked them over his mouth.

What had she been thinking? No, damn it. He knew what she'd been thinking. He just still couldn't believe she'd been thinking it. About *him*.

For all her attempts to be reserved and her quest to return to the convent, Melissande still possessed the brazenness he remembered in her as a girl. In fact, all evening he had seen her, not as a nun, but a woman.

Lucian imagined what it would be like to wed a vibrant spirit like Melissande Deverell. She would fill a man's days with intelligent discussion and excerpts from the *Odyssey,* and she would fill his nights…

Of course he had no right to imagine that scenario at all. Imagining, however briefly, had only led him to act on his dreams and to accept the kiss her tentative touches had seemed to invite.

No more.

The kiss would remain in the forgotten ruins of the churchyard, and he and Melissande would never speak of it. Perhaps the encounter merely revealed to her that she was not meant for the convent.

The sooner he delivered her to Roarke, however, the better.

"Melissande." He used his most authoritative voice, thinking if she saw no hint of friendliness in him today, she would not broach the subject of what transpired between them. Heaven knew, Melissande loved to talk. "Wake up."

He did not linger over her. A glimpse of red hair springing free of its wayward braid was enough to inspire inappropriate thoughts. Instead, he stalked about the camp, packing the flint and scattering the ashes from the fire while she rose.

Sometime during the night, he had untied her. As wide awake as he had been, he would not have missed any attempt to escape.

If she noticed, she did not comment, but disappeared around the back of the chapel to prepare herself for the day. Lucian moved to the nest of blankets she'd vacated, hoping to roll them quickly and to pack so they could be under way.

He did not count on the scent of her in the still warm linens. He breathed in the lingering perfume of her clean hair and the dried flowers that must have been packed around the merchant wife's clothing.

Disgusted with himself, he dropped the blankets and

started rolling them into tight bundles for the saddlebag, hoping Melissande would keep her thoughts to herself today. He could barely tolerate his own recriminations. He didn't think he could face hers, too.

Melissande watched Lucian from the cover of a crumbled rock wall as he attacked the bed linens with a vengeance.

Combing her fingers through her hair, she wondered how best to broach the subject of their kiss with him. They needed to discuss what happened and to clear the air so it did not hover over them like a rain cloud.

Besides, she needed reassurance that their stolen embraces didn't mean anything. If she examined the events of the evening too carefully, Melissande feared what she might discover—that she really was not meant for the convent, that ten years of her life had not taught her a whit of practicality or quiet reserve.

Judging from Lucian's fierce scowl, however, a discussion with him would not be easy.

Washing her face with the water Lucian gave her, she considered their shared kiss and the night she'd spent at his side. Once again she'd slept better than she had in years, even with the weight of her sins on her shoulders.

Something about Lucian's presence comforted her on the most fundamental level. He gave her a sense of protection, security, she had not known at the abbey. At St. Ursula's she fended for herself. Here, she knew Lucian would fend for her, too.

Braiding her hair more tightly, she fought the softening of her heart toward a warmongering knight. The kiss had been an honest mistake—the result of her tortured feelings at Lucian's learning her deep desire to have a baby. Melissande had not known what to do with the wealth of unhappiness his insightful words had caused and she had turned to him for some measure of solace.

The fact that it had led to a kiss was a mistake, and certainly the fault of her inexperience with men.

It would never happen again.

Mind made up and hair neatly plaited, Melissande marched from behind the church ruins as Lucian finished the packing. The more this festered, the more worried and guilt-ridden she would be about it. If only he would talk to her…

"Lucian, I've been thinking—"

The cold look on his face stopped her midsentence. Distant eyes flashed her a clear warning. "Not today, Melissande. Not now."

They stared at each other a long moment, taking each other's measure. No match for a man of his quiet intensity, Melissande looked away first, uncomfortable under his scrutiny.

"Fine." Her cheeks burned as her embarrassment grew. "But you only make it worse by pretending it didn't happen."

"We'll stop in a village today to trade for two horses and supplies. I expect you to stay close to me and to keep quiet for your own safety. Understand?" Lucian tied the bags to the mare's saddle, his movements quick and precise.

So much for fostering a friendship between them.

"I've been trained to be obedient for ten years, Lucian, I wouldn't think of giving you any trouble." She flashed a bright smile, unwilling to let him silence her again.

His wary look told her he didn't believe her for a moment, and Melissande couldn't have been more delighted. She had forgotten the fun of teasing and laughing. His playful ribbing the night before had reminded her how soul-lifting such merriment could be.

Before their enjoyment of the evening went too far.

Watching Lucian fling one leg over the dappled gray's back, Melissande admired his fluid grace and strength. She felt that easy power for herself when he hoisted her up in front of him.

The brief touch brought to mind a wealth of memories from the fireside encounter—his arms wrapped around her, the soft brush of his fingers on her cheek…

Melissande guessed Lucian remembered the same things, for he yanked his hands back as if burned.

Giving up her habit had been a big mistake. As they began their trek toward the village, Melissande realized she should have fought Lucian on that count. Without that uncomfortable barrier between her and the rest of the world, Melissande felt less like a novitiate and more like an ordinary young woman.

As the morning breeze captured and teased a strand of stray hair over her cheek, Melissande also regretted the loss of her wimple. She had not gone out without her hair covered since childhood. While she didn't exactly mourn the stifling garment, she had to admit a wimple helped keep her in a more somber and reflective state of mind.

There were other, less obvious changes wrought in a mere two days. She no longer woke for matins and lauds, the prayer times between midnight and dawn. Feeling more rested probably called forth her inherent tendencies to make mischief. Melissande never realized how much bleaker life seemed when she was exhausted.

"I have removed the rope," Lucian announced amidst her cataloging of her new faults. "But I plan to resurrect it after we visit the village and get a second horse."

How comforting. "You think I'll run off with your horse?"

"You'd be gone in a heartbeat." His words rumbled against her back as much as she heard them with her ears. "I just don't want you to waste your morning plotting an escape that has no chance of happening."

"Most considerate of you, Lucian." She paused a moment, surprised for the first time at how easily she used his familiar name. "Or I suppose it is 'my lord' by now, isn't it? Your father must have already given you some title or another."

"My father is dead these five years."

"I'm sorry—"

"He died peacefully. There is nothing to be sorry for."

"That means you are the earl?" How could he be off kidnapping women from their convents with such weighty responsibilities to consider?

"I've given over that honor to my brother." He retreated into the rock wall she remembered from the day he stole her away.

"What?" She pivoted in her seat to look at him. Searching his face, she saw no clue, no telltale reason for this unheard of gift. "You just handed over an earldom to your brother?"

"Aye." His jaw set to granite. His lips compressed into a thin, hard line that mirrored the colorless scar at his temple.

"You would make a wonderful earl," she protested, horrified he would relinquish something that meant so much to him. "You had grand plans for your family lands. I remember—"

"They are my lands no more. Any plans I might have had for them died—" His gaze leveled with hers in a clear warning not to pry. "Roarke is handling the responsibilities very well and with my eternal gratitude."

"But—"

"So you see, Melissande, you'll be wedding the earl, after all." Covering her lips with one finger, he silently pleaded for her to drop the subject.

Her heart caught in her throat at a fleeting image of marrying Lucian Barret.

"I will not be wedding anyone." She turned around to stare straight ahead. Or maybe to chase the vision of herself with Lucian from her mind. "And I resent your implication that I would concern myself with marriage for rank and privilege."

"What other reason is there to tie the matrimonial knot?"

How could he be so obtuse? Obviously the years had stamped out any tender feeling in his heart. "Being a nun, I'm sure I wouldn't know."

"You are not a nun," he promptly reminded her, steering the horse toward the small village in the distance.

Melissande gave up talking to him. For now.

Obviously his mood ran to grossly contrary today and she had no desire to bring his wrath upon her head.

The sun had risen to its full height, warming the day to a degree Melissande had never enjoyed in the alpine mountains before.

"We are truly in the lowlands now, aren't we?" She looked around with satisfaction, forgetting her decision not to speak to him.

"The rest of the trip will be easier. We will move much faster on separate animals."

In no time she'd be standing before Roarke Barret, explaining why she couldn't marry him and why she must return to the convent.

Then she would face being censured by the convent community and blamed for something that wasn't her fault. She knew too well how St. Ursula's politics could demand the most unfair punishments.

Once a young girl had been dismissed from the abbey because it had been discovered that a boy who adored her had been tossing notes and little trinkets like flower chains over the wall to the object of his affection. Although the girl had done nothing to encourage such behavior, she had paid dearly for the boy's actions.

Melissande's heart had ached when she learned the girl's family could not afford to take her back after her convent dismissal and she had been cast out on her own.

Melissande prayed, long and vehemently, that Abbess Helen and her army would come for her soon. The more time she spent away from the abbey, the greater the chance that her fellow sisters would think she had been up to mischief of some sort.

Dear God, the longer she spent away from the abbey the greater the chance she *would* get into mischief.

Witness last night's kiss.

Caught in thought, Melissande scarcely noticed their arrival in the tiny trading town.

"We can trade horses here," Lucian announced, reining in beside a small stable. "If you stray from my side so much as a hair's breath, we will leave immediately atop that poor broken-down mare together."

She itched to retaliate in some way, but could not afford a childish indulgence. *A mild answer turns away wrath, sharp words stir up anger,* she recalled, remembering one of the abbess's favorite proverbs.

"As you wish." She fell from the horse into his arms, righting herself quickly to ward off the inevitable twinge of awareness his touch provoked.

He raised a brow, but did not question her professed obedience. Instead he pulled her along behind him toward the back of the stable, looking utterly unaffected by their brief contact.

After haggling with the stable master, Lucian procured two horses for their journey home for a few coins and the trade of the gray mare. Relieved to be excused from the intimacy of sitting in front of Lucian for another day, Melissande looked forward to riding her own mount.

She visited with the new horses, one chestnut and one black, while Lucian bartered for food supplies.

Disappointed that Lucian would tie the reins from her horse to his own, Melissande considered explaining to him that she would not try to escape him again, but thought she would be wasting her breath.

Now that they were so far from St. Ursula's, it would be foolhardy to strike out on her own. Besides, she had faith that Abbess Helen would receive Melissande's message soon and come to rescue her.

Of course, she could not tell Lucian that. It might help the abbess if Lucian were surprised by her contingent's arrival.

She stroked the black filly's nose, hoping Lucian would come to no harm for abducting her. As much as she had been inconvenienced and frightened, she would not want him punished for something he thought she would ultimately appreciate.

He was different from most warriors she had met. His enjoyment of the *Odyssey* hinted at a scholarly temperament at odds with her bloodthirsty image of knights.

The man read Sanskrit, for St. Ursula's sake. There was more to Lucian Barret than killing and destruction.

"We are ready," he announced, stealing up behind her with a sack of food for the journey. He withdrew two strips of beef and two biscuits before securing the sacks to his saddle. "We dine on the road, Melissande." His grin wrinkled the scar on his temple, the pale line practically disappearing in his good humor. "I hope you shall not be too ill to eat and ride at the same time."

Wrenching her portions out of his hand, she stabbed a defiant foot into the filly's stirrup and in the process lifted her knee much higher than she ought. "I'm sure I'll manage somehow."

His gaze narrowed to the short length of leg her action bared and remained there as he boosted her up. "I just hope I will," he muttered, turning to the chestnut mare.

Both horses were quick and light, bred for swiftness and distance. Melissande thrilled to the feel of the wind on her face as they barreled out of town at twice the speed they had ambled into it.

Lucian had indeed tied her reins to his saddle, but her lack of control over the filly hardly tainted her rush of joy at the steady drumming of horse hooves beneath her.

Such a simple pleasure…and one she had gone without for so long.

For leagues they raced over the hills, the towering Alps an impressive backdrop to the east. The spring air swept by them, warmer and heavier than the cool mountain breezes Melissande had shivered through for a decade.

The sun hovered low on the horizon before Lucian slowed their pace. The horses grew tired, and Melissande's legs ached from the unaccustomed activity, but she blessed the day nevertheless.

Her hair had long come loose from its braid. During the wild ride she had gladly let it whip in the wind behind her. Now a tangled mass of curls tumbled over her shoulders in a sensuous fall that tickled her neck and warmed the bare portion of her shoulders.

Life without a wimple had its merits.

She followed Lucian to a copse of trees, watching his back sway in the saddle, his body silhouetted in the amber light of dusk. Unbidden images of their last sunset sprang to her mind, along with the events of the night that followed.

Memories of their kiss had teased at the corners of her mind all day. For Lucian, who had no doubt experienced his fair share of kissing, the event might not have made such an impression. Yet Melissande recalled every heated nuance, every touch and taste they had shared.

Realizing for the first time why the convent preferred virginal members, Melissande could see how the memory of a man's arms could distract a woman from more lofty concerns. She had only experienced so much as a kiss and she found it difficult to concentrate.

Imagine if their shared caresses had led to more.

By the time they stopped, Melissande could not look Lucian in the eye for fear of betraying her musings. Astonished at the vividness of the mental pictures she created, a blush crept up her neck and heated her cheeks when he approached her.

She distracted herself by trying to recite a psalm, but when his hands snaked around her waist to assist her from the filly, Melissande knew she had no hope of distracting herself.

Ever observant, Lucian ducked under her lowered chin to see the expression on her face. "Are you unwell?"

Her heart raced as if he could read her mind. Foolish, perhaps, but Melissande had never been able to lie or to hide her feelings with much success. "I am fine," she mumbled, jerking from his grasp. "Just a little winded… and my foot is a little sore from where I hurt it yesterday."

He looked skeptical, but bent forward to examine her foot.

As he did, a loud swooshing sound streaked past her head.

Even ten years in a convent did not make a woman forget the sounds of death and destruction. The sound of men and battle.

An arrow stuck in the tree where, only moments before, Lucian had stood beside her.

"My God—"

Before she could utter a prayer, Lucian yanked her down to the ground beside him, where he fell to his belly. "Be still."

Fear thudded through her at the watchful, predatory expression on Lucian's face. He peered out into the falling twilight, utterly still and dangerous.

"What was—" she hissed, only to be shushed with his fingers to her lips.

"Arrow," he whispered, his eyes never straying from his smooth visual sweep of the surrounding terrain.

The evidence still stuck ominously in the tree behind them. Short black feathers had been cropped and dampened to give the weapon just the right speed and distance.

And if Lucian had not bent to check the foot injury she'd lied about, he would be dead beside her right now.

Instead of daydreaming about Lucian's embrace, she should have been remembering that his way of life represented everything she abhorred. While Melissande had dedicated her life to God, Lucian had dedicated his to war.

He might be an old friend, but Lucian Barret was also ruthless and dangerous, a trained killer. And no matter how sweetly he kissed her, he was—and would always be—a warrior.

Chapter Nine

Lucian watched Melissande's face go ten shades more pale, then cursed Roarke for getting them into this mess. Why the hell couldn't his brother have married a nice girl from Northumbria and have done with it?

Instead he'd sent Lucian on a fool's mission to retrieve a woman he'd probably tire of in two year's time. Fickle, spoiled Roarke had always been able to charm their mother, winning his own way since he was a babe.

Of course, fickleness aside, Lucian owed him. But, Christ, this had been a lot to ask.

If anything happened to Melissande because of Roarke's sudden hunger for a convent-bred wife, Lucian would personally kill him.

It wouldn't be the first time he had raised arms against a loved one.

Damn.

"I don't see anyone," Melissande whispered, edging closer to him in a rustle of leaves and sticks.

He gritted his teeth in a fresh wave of frustration. Couldn't the woman even be quiet in a life-and-death situation?

At the same time, he grudgingly admitted her incessant chatter was part of her charm. Her cheery demeanor and vibrant outlook made brooding difficult, even for Lucian.

Gently he lifted his fingers and placed them over her lips. His irritation with her grew in direct proportion to the desire that flared in reaction to her soft mouth.

His heart hammered against the ground beneath them, partly in ill-timed longing, mostly in genuine fear.

He had joined the Crusades two years ago on a mission of penance, not caring whether he lived or died. But now that he served as Melissande Deverell's guardian in a dangerous world, he could not afford to let anything happen to himself.

Without his protection, God only knew what might happen to such an innocent.

Her lips twitched beneath his touch. He glanced at her, not surprised to see her wide-eyed and gesturing in clear supplication to speak.

Fortunately she honored the command of his glare, but not without a definite internal struggle. By now he knew she detested being quiet.

Soon a deceptive calm settled over the outcropping of trees, encouraging him to investigate with caution. Signaling to Melissande to stay put, he crept forward through the brush, waiting and watching for the slightest movement.

A sudden pounding of hooves and flutter of birds scattering sent him diving back to the ground to lie over Melissande, the noise startling him into protective mode.

Hand on his sword, ready for trouble, he listened to the horse's hooves recede to the south, unwilling to believe the real threat had departed.

Refusing to move, he waited, every instinct on alert.

After a long, quiet moment, an elbow caught him in the gut from underneath.

"Can we get up now, please?" Her slight wriggle beneath him shifted his focus from fear to lust faster than a Moor's blade.

Their bodies stretched on the ground in one fluid line, his sealed over hers in a manner that called to mind the most primal of procreation positions.

Only the veil of her hair and a few layers of clothes separated their skin.

Heedless of any threat but the one a certain red-haired woman posed, Lucian couldn't scramble to his feet fast enough.

"Of course." Blood pounded in waves through his body, restricting the flow of thoughts to his brain. He stared down at her prone form in the underbrush. *Damn.* What the hell was the matter with him?

Extending a marginally steady hand to Melissande, he helped her to her feet. He dropped her fingers as soon as she regained her balance.

"What do you think that was about?" Her voice trembled through the question, her complexion startlingly pallid as she stared at the arrow protruding from the tree near their heads.

Lucian gave himself a mental shake, willing himself to forget the impression of lying above her. He studied the red marks and black feathers on the instrument of war until a small amount of concentration returned. "It is well shot," he noted, his mind slowly beginning to emerge from the fog of lust. "My guess is an assassin. Perhaps someone sent by the abbess to reclaim you."

"Abbess Helen would never allow one of her men to kill you without so much as speaking to you." She looked unsettled by the suggestion. Indignant even.

He shrugged, wondering if she could be as naive about her convent sisters as she seemed about the rest of human nature. "I cannot think of anyone else who would know we are together."

Her eyes narrowed to shrewd slits. "Unless it is someone who seeks only you."

One name came to mind at her words.

Damon Fitzhugh.

Perhaps Osbern Fitzhugh's true son had finally learned of his father's death and had come to seek revenge.

Of all the timing…Lucian had prayed Damon would find him in the Holy Lands and end the torment of his guilt there. But after two years he had seen no sign of the English knight in the ranks of Crusaders.

"Lucian?"

Lucian had witnessed bloody battle after bloody battle, but always he emerged, healthy and whole except for his heart and soul. And now, when he could no longer afford to indulge his guilty conscience, when he was charged with the most important mission of his life, his former friend-turned-enemy had come to extract vengeance.

It makes no sense.

"What makes no sense?" Melissande asked, her color slightly returned.

Had he spoken his thoughts out loud? "It is nothing." He strode to the tree and yanked the arrow from its lodging with both hands.

"Apparently it is something," she insisted. "Do you have an idea who did this?"

Examining the device carefully, he ignored her. His head still swam with worries he had not foreseen.

If Damon Fitzhugh had finally decided to seek revenge, wouldn't he have done it with his family colors to honor his father? Noblemen did not *hope* their enemies knew who attacked them. They emblazoned their banners, shields and arrows with their colors to announce to the world their identity. To do so was a matter of family pride.

A commodity the Fitzhughs had never lacked.

"No, I don't know who did this," he told her, relieved he could be honest about this much. "If you don't think it is an emissary for the abbess, then I have no idea who would want to kill me."

The suspicion in her eyes seemed to fade as he met and held her gaze.

She trusted him.

The knowledge stung him with his unworthiness.

"But for a moment you thought you had an idea," she wheedled, pinning him with the intensity of her stare.

How did a sheltered woman see so much?

"That has nothing to do with you." Lucian moved toward the horses with determined steps, hoping he could successfully put her off the scent for once. "What does concern you is our new route."

Melissande's breath caught and hitched in her throat as Lucian led her horse over. "What new route?"

His resolve wavered at the thought of touching her again. Her unbound hair draped over her shoulders like a russet robe, both regal and wanton.

"We go back into the mountains." Lunging for her waist in an effort to get it over with, Lucian unwittingly threaded his hands through the veil of hair that surrounded her. Skeins of the silky strands brushed his palms where he held her.

"To St. Ursula's?" Her voice held a gleeful note of possibility.

He strode to his own mount, loathe to squash her hopes

again. "Nay. We will merely follow the alpine route through France until we are much further north."

They needed time to escape into the rocky passes that separated the mountains from the hills where it would be easier to elude an enemy. Lucian hoped the sun would not sink too soon.

"It is even colder as you go north," Melissande returned sullenly. He could almost detect the shiver in her voice.

"Better cold than dead," Lucian observed, unwilling to debate their path.

Dark shadows lengthened before them while daylight slipped behind them.

"So I've tried to tell myself on many a frosty eve," Melissande mumbled, braiding her hair again as they plodded toward the shelter of the Alps.

Lucian hated the thought of backtracking to the mountains, but it took him by surprise that Melissande did, too.

Normally he would let the matter drop. Now, however, after Melissande's fright and knowing she would have to ride for many more leagues, Lucian thought it couldn't hurt to distract her with her favorite pastime—talking. "You have not enjoyed the Alpine views St. Ursula's provides?"

They journeyed slowly up the rocky inclines leading back into the mountains. Cool air descended upon them, as much from the encroaching twilight as the slight rise in elevation.

"The abbey setting is lovely." Her dismal sigh said otherwise. "In fact, I rather appreciate the remoteness of the place, the utter quiet that pervades. The never-ending winters are what depress me. Sometimes it seems like we'll never see the sun again."

As recently as two days ago, Lucian would have used that knowledge to press his brother's suit and to encourage her to stay in England.

Not now.

Her blatant honesty exposed a facet of Melissande he had only guessed at—her deeply hidden misgivings about convent life.

He stared over at her in the growing dark, her pale skin the only part of her that remained visible. Seeing that creamy white skin in the ominous mountain shadows reminded Lucian of her delicate nature. He cursed his brother again.

"Perhaps you have forgotten English weather in your long absence, Mel. The winters are bleak there, too."

Trudging over rock and loose stones, the horses's hooves clattered a dissonant rhythm against the silence.

"I guess," she admitted slowly. "But at least in my father's home, we were permitted to build many a merry blaze to keep us in good health and good cheer." Her voice lowered with nostalgia. "'Twas not considered hedonistic to roast your toes all evening while we told stories and shared cups of warm wine."

A pleasing domestic image of Melissande stole through his mind. For a moment he envisioned himself seated beside her, tipping a cup to her smiling lips…

"The sisters do not get together in the eve to share companionship around a fire?" Lucian had never visited a convent or monastery before. There were many along the land route to the Holy Lands, but he had avoided them like the plague for fear he would further displease God by disgracing their hallowed halls.

She snorted. "Much of our lifestyle has to do with self-denial. We are not allowed to indulge in many things the rest of the world would find pleasurable."

As if hearing disloyalty in her words, she quickly amended them.

"That's not to say we don't find happiness in many of our good works. For example, my joy in my children and their care. But we do not pursue pleasure for pleasure's sake." She looked over at him as their horses brushed close to each other through a narrow pass. "In other words, no companionship around a great blaze to chase away winter's chill at St. Ursula's."

His leg scraped against hers while the animals squeezed between rocky walls. The memory of her body crushed beneath his came roaring back to torment him.

He needed to shut out that particular incident for his own sanity. He needed to keep his mind too busy to remember.

He needed to talk.

Melissande's cherished hobby suddenly became more enticing.

"So what would you do to pass the evenings at the abbey?" By continually speaking of her years at St. Ursula's, his lust-filled body would eventually get the message, right? Melissande Deverell was forbidden to him.

"During the days I worked with the children, but only with the understanding that I could not slack off in my duties to Sister Eleanor."

The dark grew so thick their conversation took on a more intimate flavor, like sharing pillow confidences with a lover in the deep hours of the night.

Keep talking!

"So you worked for Sister Eleanor at night?"

"I had to report to the scriptorium after meals, and could leave only when the prayer bells tolled for matins at midnight. I had to observe the vespers and compline prayer alone at my desk."

Her voice so lacked emotion that Lucian struggled to gather a sense of how she felt about it. Was she bitter at the way the convent drove her to extra labor? Or was she as accepting as she sounded?

"Sounds lonely," he observed, squinting to see through the darkness for a place to make a safe camp.

"That part I did not mind." Lucian heard the smile in her words. "But the scriptorium is notoriously cold. And that part I truly detes—did not like."

Who would? The woman worked herself to exhaustion so she might have a few hours to play mother to a bunch of orphans. Lucian began to compile a clearer image of her blissful life at St. Ursula's.

Melissande and her vibrant spirit didn't go down without a fight. And she had struggled for years to convince herself she genuinely liked being a novitiate so she could retain some sense of happiness in a world turned upside down for her.

She probably would have run into his arms the day he'd abducted her if it hadn't been for the children. They were her lifeline. The one aspect of her existence where she still found real joy.

Well, maybe she wouldn't have run to him, he amended. She did seem to disparage the knighthood and its members.

"Don't misunderstand me," she blurted into the dark. "I may have had an ongoing battle with Sister Eleanor, but the other sisters were wonderful to me."

Should he believe her? He began to get the sense that Melissande deceived herself into thinking she was happy even when she was not.

"Abbess Helen has been like a mother to me since she arrived," she continued, stifling a yawn. "Kind and gentle…a steadfast guiding force for me. Did I mention she's grooming me to be the next abbess?"

Lucian stilled.

"No. You did not." A pretty big omission if you asked him.

"That may be why Sister Eleanor feels threatened by me." She yawned again, distorting her words in her tired stretch. "I think *she* would like to be the next abbess."

The revelation had several repercussions for Lucian. If Melissande was being prepared for the abbess position one day, her absence would be all the more fretted over and investigated. Mayhap the unknown shooter today had really been a member of the abbess's army, despite Melissande's protests to the contrary.

Second, Melissande obviously had a potent enemy in Sister Eleanor, no matter how much she wanted to ignore it. If this Sister Eleanor came from a powerful family, perhaps she could have sent one of her kin to ensure that her troublemaking nemesis never returned to St. Ursula's to take the top slot away from her.

"Lucian, can we stop soon?" Her voice sounded faraway, though she still rode close beside him, her mount tied securely to his.

He scoured the landscape with his eyes, looking for a reasonably secure place to camp.

"Soon, Mel." He wished they could stop, too. How could it have grown so cold so fast? Even the air felt thinner with their increasing altitude.

Something frigid tickled his nose while he hoped with all his heart he spoke the truth.

"Oh, no." Melissande's despairing wail drew him from his thoughts, alerting him to another tickle at his nose, then his forehead.

A haze of white glistened in the light of a crescent moon as tiny flakes danced down from the sky with growing force, blanketing them in a veil of frosty crystals.

Lucian grinned for a moment, caught up in the beauty of the luminescent shower.

"Only in the Alps," Melissande moaned, her voice hitching on a suppressed cough. "Snow in May."

Chapter Ten

*A glad heart is excellent medicine, a depressed spirit wastes
the bones away.* Proverbs 17:22. Or was it 17:23?

Either way, the point remained the same to Melissande.
Don't spread doom and gloom by complaining, no matter how
bone-cold and tired you feel.

And, Lord, she was cold and tired. How long had they ridden since their hidden attacker had shot at them? Three
hours? Four?

Snow piled over them so quickly now that Melissande
didn't even bother brushing it from her shoulders and arms.
The blanket Lucian had retrieved for her had long since become saturated with the cold, wet flakes.

Still, they trudged on. Snaking through narrow mountain
passes, they climbed back into the Alps and into the frigid
weather she had never liked.

If she didn't get warm and dry soon, she would end up with
another case of lung fever. After the first time she'd been
stricken with it, the illness seemed ever easier to catch. A night
in the wilderness exposed to this sort of weather practically
sealed her fate.

She refused to succumb to the lung fever that had threatened her life not a year ago. With no one but Lucian to care for her, she couldn't afford to get sick.

Annoyed with the gloomy thoughts she seemed powerless to staunch, Melissande ventured a comment to her long-silent riding companion. "Will we ride through the night? I do not mean to pester you, only to quench my curiosity."

Perhaps she sounded as pathetic as she felt, for Lucian immediately pulled his horse to a halt and turned on her. "You are unwell?"

She attempted to straighten under his glare. "A bit tired, perhaps."

He wiped a frustrated hand through his hair. "It is almost dawn, Melissande, I am not surprised."

Dawn? No wonder she could hardly see straight. "I only meant to make conversation, Lucian, not to irritate you. I find it exceedingly dull to ride for so many hours without conversing."

"I thought you were sleeping." His glare eased somewhat.

"On horseback?" She had trouble settling down in her convent bed each night. How would one ever fall asleep on a horse?

"It's been done, believe me." He looked tired, too. She hadn't seen it at first when he had scowled at her, but now the lines of concern and exhaustion were apparent around his eyes.

Melissande blamed Roarke for his thoughtless treatment of Lucian and made a mental note to speak to him about it if she lived through their journey to England. "Well, not by me. I cannot fathom a more uncomfortable way to slumber."

Lucian maneuvered his horse a few steps backward and held his arms out to her. "Come here."

The invitation sent a tremor through her. His embrace

tempted her, but falling into his lap seemed like a declaration of weakness. She lowered her gaze to hide her longing.

"I will be fine here, thank you."

"Nonsense." He plucked her off the black mare with no hesitation, hauling her across his body like a child's rag doll. A grin twitched at his lips, a pleasing change from his customary solemn expression. "You have slept successfully in my arms before."

The blush started in her toes and heated her body thoroughly on its way to her cheeks. She did not think she could utter a rejoinder even if she might have formulated one in her embarrassment.

True enough, she had slumbered like a babe in his arms after the day she had tried to escape him. The sleep she had missed during her long trek to Linette's house she had made up for while curled against Lucian Barret.

She heard a rumble in his chest that might have been good humor as he kicked his horse into motion and led her mare to follow behind them. Settled neatly with her cheek flush to his heart, Melissande warned herself about the impropriety of dozing off while held in a man's arms.

"We will ride until I find a real shelter, Melissande. Something with walls and a roof and a place for a fire."

Several hours later, with Melissande sound asleep on his lap, Lucian realized what folly his quest had become.

Daylight granted him visibility for many miles now, but the sight of undisturbed white snow over the landscape only depressed him. No sign of anything with four walls for as far as the eye could see.

Weary as he was, Lucian didn't mind the journey for himself. The exertion suited his endless quest for penance.

But Melissande…

He hated every step of the wretched trip through the mountains for her sake, especially when he thought of how much she'd been through these past few days.

She was more delicate than he recalled. Perhaps her vibrant spirit had fooled him into thinking she was stronger than she was. At first Lucian had been surprised at the frightening cough racking her body in her sleep, as it seemed unlikely to him that one cold spell could wreak such havoc with her body.

Then, as he went over the past few days in his mind, he realized how worn out she must have been before the snow storm—how her utter exhaustion might leave her defenseless against the chill winds.

She seemed warmer now that she was in his arms, but her sodden blanket and clothes couldn't be helping the cough that had come more and more frequently in the last few hours.

Cursed mountains.

Over and over, he wondered if he could have avoided backtracking into the treacherous Alps. Each time, the answer was no.

A killer stalked them. Lucian didn't know who or why, but someone had come damn close to killing him last night, and he couldn't risk injury to himself for Melissande's sake. The girl would surely die without his protection.

He'd never had so much reason to live.

But no matter how much he assured himself of that truth, the fact that she grew more pale by the hour twisted his gut with guilt. If Roarke hadn't asked Lucian to steal her in the first place…

Caught up in the need to blame Melissande's condition on someone, Lucian didn't hear the travelers' approach until they were naught but one hundred paces before him.

Four men plodded toward them on horseback, carefully

picking their way over the treacherous mountain road. After conversing with them for a few minutes, Lucian learned they were not far from a small trading town, a village with a real live inn to house passing pilgrims and nobles.

Thank God.

In his haste to traverse the remaining leagues, Lucian did not spend much time thinking about his unwitting reaction of thanking God, but he noticed it nevertheless.

Odd he should thank God for anything when he had closed all communication with Him two years ago.

He reined in the horse and her eyelids flew open, her gaze bright with fever. "Lucian!" A smattering of freckles stood out in stark relief against her too pale skin. "Where are we?"

"An inn." Gently he sidled out from underneath her and dropped to the ground. When he helped her off the horse, her strange pallor unnerved him. Even her vivid red hair seemed a shade more dim.

"Well done," she announced, smiling feebly up at him.

Lucian tossed coins to everyone he passed on their way, hoping the groomsmen and stable boys would take the hint and care for the horseflesh. Even the innkeeper hastened to do Lucian's bidding, hurrying up the stairs ahead of them to open a door.

"'Tis my best room, sir—um, my lord." The man stumbled over his words as well as his feet as he scampered back to let Lucian enter. "Will you be needing anything else?"

"My wife is ill," Lucian announced, lying her gently on the pallet in spite of Melissande's obvious protest to the words and the intimacy. "We will take our meals here. Bring us something from supper last night, a hot bath and a fire for the grate."

Bowing himself out the door, the innkeeper left them alone.

Melissande elbowed herself to a sitting position. "How dare you share a room with me and allow that little man to assume we are wed!" Her voice sounded scratchy and strained.

He might have been amused at her misplaced indignation if she hadn't looked ready to pass out. Searching through his bag for the wine, he hoped she would lie back down without his having to help her. He did not like the feeling of possessiveness that stole over him whenever he took her in his arms. "You are ill, Mel. I cannot leave you. And if you were not ill, I would not give you your own chamber because you would try to escape me."

"I will not stand for it, Lucian, I—"

She slumped onto the linens suddenly, clutching her chest as she struggled for breath.

"Sweet Jesus, Mel." He dropped everything to race to her side. "Are you all right?" Easing her to recline completely on the bed, he watched a small wash of color fill her cheeks once again.

Nodding, she relaxed enough to let him reposition her. "It is wrong to share a room." More a croak than a sentence, her words fell on deaf ears.

"You damn well know better." How could she be so stubborn about something so insignificant? "Use your God-given sense, will you? Who would protect you from lustful knights if you are in the next room over? Who is going to take care of you if you're down the hall? The innkeeper?"

As if the mention of the man drew him from the air, the innkeeper appeared at the door with a parade of food, water and wood. Four youths, probably his sons and daughters, bustled about the room to enact Lucian's orders. "The tub is on its way up, sir," the innkeeper volunteered. "Is there anything else?"

"Is there a reputable physician in town?"

"The local midwife has some knowledge of herbs." The man smiled with ingratiating affability.

"Send for her." Lucian waved the tub into the room and tossed out another round of coins before turning back to Melissande.

Only when he heard the door close behind the last of the servants did he reach to touch a tentative hand to Melissande's soaked green gown.

The heavy fabric clung to her pale skin, molding itself into every contour and curve of her body, a body he had no right to see.

His hand hovered in midair.

The hell with his rights. If Roarke wanted her alive when they returned home, he would damn well have to forgive the fact that his brother had to play nurse to her on the way.

With more force than he intended, his fingers attacked the toggles down the front of the gown.

Her scream rent the air as she shot off the rope mattress. "Lucian Barret!"

Color suffused her cheeks now. Her breathing heavy and unnatural, Lucian was hard-pressed to keep his wayward eyes from straying to the hint of cleavage he had exposed.

"What are you doing?" Breathless and blushing, she pulled the edges of her kirtle together.

Wasn't it obvious? "I thought you were sleeping."

"So you use that as an excuse to—" Her brows furrowed in consternation. Voice dropping to a whisper she continued, "Undress me?"

The mental image the words conjured rendered him speechless. But damn it, he hadn't meant to leer at her. She looked ready to collapse. He just wanted to get her warm and dry.

He stood, edgy and restless. "Since you are awake, you are certainly capable of undressing yourself." It took a monumental effort, but he moved his feet toward the door, away from her soon-to-be-naked body. "I expect you will address the matter in my absence."

Congratulating himself on his willpower, Lucian shut the door between them and waited, trying not to imagine her movements on the other side of the thin wall.

How would he ever hand her over to Roarke?

As much as he owed his brother for handling everything after Fitzhugh's death, it galled Lucian to think of giving Melissande to a man who would never fully appreciate her.

Roarke merely wanted a wife whose body was untainted, whose children would be his beyond a doubt. When Roarke recently recalled little Melissande Deverell, the adoring shadow of his youth, there had been no quenching his curiosity about how she'd turned out. He'd wanted only her.

But Roarke had paid her no mind when they were children, and Lucian suspected his brother would not understand or appreciate her now, either.

Lucian, on the other hand, had been fascinated with her even as a child. The girl had more grit than most boys twice her age. And smart…he'd only had to show her something once for Melissande to catch on.

Despite the wall of reserve the convent instilled in her, Melissande would never lose her backbone or her intelligence. Hell, as much as it scared him, Lucian thought she might be smarter than him.

Hoping he'd allowed enough time to elapse, Lucian rapped on the door once and let himself back in.

And there she sat.

Right where he left her, still draped in sodden clothing.

Obviously the woman was not as smart as he'd thought earlier.

Melissande didn't miss the thunderous expression on Lucian's face, but without permission from God Himself, there was no way she would remove one stitch of her clothing while he shared her room.

"Perhaps you were confused about the reason I left the chamber," he began, speaking very softly.

"Nay." Weary and sick, Melissande lacked the energy to argue with him. Surely he understood her dilemma.

"Then why are you turning blue in a dress that is no longer fit to wear?" A tic in his eye gave away his growing ire. The scar next to it pulsed in time with the tic.

Melissande shivered. Did he think she *wanted* to freeze to death? "I have no other garments to wear."

She could see him swallow. Her own mouth felt dry.

"I will procure clothing," he announced, his voice low and deep. "Stay here."

He returned in no time and tossed a ball of women's garments in the door. Barking at her to hurry, he left her alone once again.

She needed no further urging. The lung fever did not respond well to wet clothes. Melissande knew the familiar tightening in her chest, the inevitable sting of her own breath in her throat.

Please God, deliver me, she prayed. *Allow me to return to the children.*

The ill-fitting maid's clothes were a welcome change. She donned the stiff cotton kirtle and worn woolen tunic before sliding into bed, heedless of doing so much as plucking her own clothes off the floor.

Weary to the bone, she feared sliding into sleep and not waking up.

Máybe Lucian will talk to me…

A sharp rap at the door preceded his return.

She noticed he had changed garments, as well, though his tunic and braies were obviously his own. He would have a hard time finding a man anywhere close to his size.

Following him around the chamber with her eyes, she watched as he hung her discarded clothing by the fire to dry.

Sleep beckoned, but she refused to give in to it in case death awaited her there. With an illness as severe as lung fever, Abbess Helen said, one never knew.

"Would you like supper now?" Lucian asked, brows furrowed.

Her belly rumbled in response and she nodded, realizing she had not eaten since yesterday at noon.

She could not sit up to take food, but he did not seem inconvenienced. He simply cut her portion into bite sizes and fed her from his fingers while she lay on her side.

Not for the first time, the sense of being utterly cared for flowed over her. She had been independent for so long, had fought to define herself on her own terms at the convent. But just now, it filled her with contentment to allow someone else to care for her. Lucian—the world-weary warrior who already shouldered burdens beyond her ken—appeared strong enough for both of them.

There was more to being a knight than killing, it seemed.

"Lucian." The word slipped out, no more than a sigh, when she had eaten her fill.

"Hmm?"

"Thank you."

She sensed his stillness, his discomfort with her appreciation even with her eyes closed. But she was too tired and too weak to concern herself with his rigid humility.

If she really were to die before she ever regained consciousness, she wanted him to know how much she appreciated his solicitous concern for her. She pried her eyes open again.

"It is nothing," he scoffed, wiping crumbs from his tunic. On a normal day the gruffness of the words would have intimidated her into silence.

But this night seemed too important for her to back down now. She might not be fortunate enough to battle the lung fever this time. Perhaps she would never have another chance to speak to him.

"It is not nothing," she protested, hoping in spite of her exhaustion that she spoke out loud as she thought the words. "These few days have been enlightening for me. You have made me remember much of myself that I sought to forget, fragments of my character that shouldn't be suppressed." Part of her realized she could never confide such disloyal thoughts against the convent unless she was only half-conscious. But another part of her screamed that she had never thought so clearly. "You've made me feel whole again."

Did he answer her or was she dreaming this whole conversation? She definitely heard his eating knife chewing into the cutting board with overzealous swipes.

Lucian did not know how to accept her gratitude.

It bothered her to think she might never know why, but for some reason, the man considered himself unloved by God.

Godless.

Please don't let me die now. I could help him.

"Lucian?"

His presence filled the room around her, even if he retreated from the intimacy of her words.

An urgency filled her as she fought to remain awake a little bit longer—a driving need to deliver an important message to Lucian Barret.

She could not tiptoe around his surly mood today. She needed to tell him.

"God loves you."

Distinctly she heard a garbled moan, as if her words pierced him with the bite of the arrow that missed his head yesterday.

Strangely, Melissande realized she still had more to say. The burning need to confide something to Lucian had not been quenched by her avowal that he was loved by God.

Another rebellious thought niggled her fevered brain, taunting her with a threat to leap from her lips if she opened her mouth.

Hadn't she conquered her wayward tongue long ago? Surely she wouldn't be so foolish as to say the ridiculous words that floated around in her head.

In the sin of the lips...

But what did it matter if she said it, when she would probably never wake up?

"And so do I."

Chapter Eleven

For the next sennight, Lucian poured all his time and effort into his paltry attempts to heal Melissande, knowing if he allowed himself so much as a moment to relax, her haunting words would torment his soul and claw at his insides.

And so do I...

Lucian scrubbed the cool cloth over Melissande's forehead, willing away the lure of her final fevered sentiment.

Foolish girl. She had been so exhausted, she had obviously forgotten the context of their discussion. Although the comment that preceded "And so do I" had been that God loved him, ridiculously implying Melissande loved Lucian, too, her illness must have rendered her mind a muddle of disjointed thoughts.

He repeated the internal diatribe to himself for at least the hundredth time since she'd slipped from consciousness, reassuring himself that a nun would never fall in love with a man. She must have been speaking in the spiritual sense.

The other option presented too tempting a scenario, a dream long abandoned of wife, home and family. He didn't deserve such tender sentiments, certainly not from someone as pure as Melissande.

He rinsed the cloth and scrubbed, careful not to lower the sheet that covered her any more than necessary. For her sake as much as his own, he had hired one of the innkeeper's daughters to cool the rest of his patient.

She looked no better today. Her breathing continued to deteriorate until it became so shallow and raspy that Lucian had started feeding her warm water with honey at regular intervals to ease the sharpness of her inhalations.

It wasn't much, but he recalled the home remedy from his childhood and put it to good use. Certainly the midwife who came to visit couldn't offer anything more substantial.

Useless woman.

Lucian left Melissande's bedside to retrieve heated water from the cauldron above the grate. Pouring a fresh cup of water and honey, he considered the worthlessness of half the midwives in the world.

Some were highly capable, no doubt, but he'd never had any luck with them personally. The healer who had been sought to cure Fitzhugh, in fact, had actually given Lucian false hope that his foster father would recover. When Osbern died, the midwife had left without a trace.

Good thing. In his newly discovered penchant for violence, he might have killed her.

God loves you...

Slamming the cup onto the crude wooden table near her mattress, Lucian cursed her proclamation. What the hell did she know anyhow?

He shouted for the innkeeper's daughter, Tamara, and handed over his nursing duties to the girl. Damned if he was helping anyway.

Raking a restless hand through his hair, he spared one more look toward the bed where Melissande lay. Her cheeks were pale and lifeless, her hair a quenched fire of dull auburn.

After instructing Tamara to send for him immediately if there was any change, he headed for the inn's common room. Ignoring the two other patrons, a scruffy pair of Franciscan friars, Lucian called for a pitcher of ale.

Downing two full horns in quick succession, Lucian waited for some sign of the mind-numbing effect the brew could give.

Nothing.

He stopped counting after four, powerless to resist the temptation to get drunk.

Away from Melissande's side, Lucian could only think of her.

No matter how much ale he consumed, her face swam in his vision—sometimes alight with laughter, sometimes pale with illness or…death.

Shouting for another pitcher, he willed the ache in his chest to go away. The thought of Melissande dead squeezed his insides like a page's petrified grip on his first real blade.

A part of Lucian recognized her death would be the ultimate punishment for his past sin, the punishment he had sought these past two years. Now that the supreme pain of it faced him, however, he did not run to embrace this penance the way he gladly shouldered his others.

This he could not bear.

Melissande was too pure of heart and gentle of soul to die so young. It struck him as hideously unfair that God allowed Lucian the Murderer to walk the earth, strong as the west wind and healthy as a weed, while an angel would perish without so much as a friend to comfort her.

A pang of guilt nipped him. He shouldn't be indulging himself in drink, he should be near her in case she needed him.

What if she wanted to talk before she died?

A hoarse bark of laughter escaped him when he realized he would give his sword arm to hear her incessant chatter.

And in his drunkenness, he did something he hadn't done in years.

God, grant Melissande her life and I shall listen to her prattle morning, noon and night.

Unthinkingly, the prayer slipped out into the common room with the volume only the inebriated use.

He had prayed.

Jesus.

Lucian cursed, as if to negate the invocation he uttered as naturally as his own breath.

Slumping against the rough wooden trestle, Lucian buried his head in the crook of his arm, wishing like hell he had ignored Roarke's request and left Melissande at St. Ursula's where she would still be healthy and happy.

At the abbey, she would have devout women to bend their heads in supplication for her. Here, in the middle of the deserted Alps, she had naught but Lucian's drunken bargains with the God he had alienated years ago.

Lucian knew his sorry excuse for a prayer would not be heard.

A movement from across the common room caught his eye, and Lucian peered up from his ale to see the Franciscans engaged in animated conversation.

Holy men.

Not ten paces from Lucian sat two men that God would listen to. Men whose invocations for Melissande might be answered.

Lucian's gut roiled at the thought of approaching them. In light of his sins, he didn't have any business speaking to men of the cloth.

Yet he owed it to Melissande to swallow his fears and approach them. She had given him so much in the few days they had been together. Her laughter and vivaciousness served as a balm to his spirit, bringing light to an existence that had grown unbearably dark.

Melissande deserved their benedictions.

"Good Brothers, I…" His shout trailed off. What could he say? He wanted them to pray for a nun he'd kidnapped?

The men turned as one, their pleasant expressions clouding with concern as they stared at him.

Lucian faltered, unsure of himself. His head spun with the effort to talk.

"My son?" A man's deep voice suddenly hovered above Lucian's head.

The endearment, a phrase also favored by Osbern Fitzhugh for all the young men he fostered, stilled Lucian. Slowly he lifted his chin.

One of the Franciscans, the older of the two, leaned over him. "Are you all right?"

"Fine." Lucian massaged his temple, turning away from the monk.

Not easily offended, the friar took a seat beside him on the bench. "I heard you call out for your Savior earlier." Good humor threaded through the Franciscan's voice. "A man does not often do so except in times of great distress."

Lucian studied the stranger's salt-and-pepper beard, closely groomed and clean. Though his clothes were coarse and humble, they were not dirty.

There had been a time in Lucian's life when he would have been fascinated to talk to a wandering Franciscan monk about how it felt to forsake home and fortune to follow God's call. Although Lucian had always known he was not destined for the church, he had been nevertheless intrigued with its scope and power and its poor Franciscan brethren who ignored all the fancy trappings to walk the more simple path of Jesus.

Not anymore. If not for Melissande, Lucian would never have called out to this man.

The monk thrust his hand forward in greeting. "Brother William."

With a curt nod, Lucian acknowledged the name without giving his own. The monk's earnestness, his honesty, was apparent in wise green eyes. Lucian wondered what Brother William saw in his. Gathering his courage, he took a deep breath. "I— My friend is ill."

"Perhaps she would benefit from a Christian blessing, my friend."

"What?" How did this man know Lucian spoke of a woman? He held the friar's gaze, daring him to explain how he knew about Melissande. Could William be associated with St. Ursula's?

"Her poor health is the talk of the innkeeper's family," he returned easily. "I wonder if I might bestow my blessing upon her?"

Of course Melissande would want Brother William's blessing. The best Lucian could offer was a drunken invocation that probably amounted to blasphemy in God's eyes.

"Please." Lucian could not begin to express his gratitude for the offer and for Brother William's insightfulness to extend it. "She rests abovestairs."

Pushing back the trestle bench, Lucian rose and led the man out of the common room. Knowing what awaited him in the sick chamber, he moved slowly, fearing Melissande's waxy complexion and unnatural stillness would be worse than when he left.

He hated the long nights of hoping for a raspy breath to know at least she still breathed. He hated knowing that his actions had done this to her. And, dear God, but he hated his brother for demanding Melissande as if she was his cursed prize.

"She's in here." Lucian gestured toward the door, thinking how trusting the friar seemed to accompany a stranger to a sickroom, not bothering to ask if Melissande suffered from something contagious.

Brother William nodded and stepped in front of Lucian, finding courage where Lucian hadn't, and opened the door.

Lucian avoided the sight of Melissande for a long moment, watching William's face as the holy man surveyed the patient.

"She is uncommonly beautiful," William remarked, his voice appropriately dispassionate but sincere.

Lucian looked to the bed, hoping to see some resurrection of the woman he knew. But she lay there as deathly ill as before.

"You should see her when she is well."

A stupid thing to say, Lucian supposed. What did her beauty matter at a time like this? Or any time, for that matter?

Perhaps he merely craved the sight of her fully animated again, her infectious laughter bright enough to lighten even his most somber of moods.

"She is your wife?"

The question startled him. Guilt pinched him. "Nay."

"She should be." The preacher swung from the bed to meet Lucian's gaze.

"She is promised to my brother."

"Does he know of your regard for her?" Brother William lifted a shaggy gray eyebrow and fixed Lucian with a catlike green stare.

Lucian seethed, refusing to be saddled with a sin he had

not committed. His conscience already overflowed with those he had. "I have not touched her, Brother."

Fortunately, Brother William seemed content to let the matter pass, returning his attention to Melissande. "As God wills, my son. I hope you are prepared to claim her if the need should arise."

Trepidation shook Lucian's hand as he pressed it to his forehead. The monk would never suggest such a thing if he knew the sins of Lucian's past. The very idea of marriage to Melissande…

"It won't."

Brother William held his palm to Melissande's temple. "A little fresh air would serve her well so long as you keep her warm. A bit of sun on her face might help."

Unorthodox, maybe, but Lucian would try anything at this point. Before he could thank the friar for his advice, the man launched into prayer, his powerful voice filling the room.

"You shall wander the barren desert, but you shall not die of thirst…"

Lucian knew he should slip from the room and leave Brother William to work a miracle and heal Melissande, but he found his feet would not move. Entranced by the music of the priest's words, he stood there, his hungry spirit fighting for the bit of nourishment the humble Franciscan's words might provide.

"You shall see the face of God and live…"

Tears burned behind Lucian's eyes for the longing the prayer evoked. He would not see the face of God and live. Melissande would. Even if she died this moment, her place in Heaven couldn't be more obvious.

Because of Lucian's rash actions of two years ago, a hand raised against the kindly man who fostered him, he would ever be denied God's comfort. Still, in his selfishness, he yearned that she would not die and seek her heavenly seat just yet.

He needed her, damn it.

He could not bring himself to say the prayer again, now that the ale seemed to have worn off a bit, but he added a hearty amen to Brother William's words.

For what purpose, he could not be certain, but as sure as knew his own name, Lucian knew he needed Melissande to come back to him, healthy and whole.

Her goodness and purity, her inquisitive nature and irrepressible chatter, represented the one thing Lucian had not felt since God had forsaken him.

Hope.

From somewhere far off in the distance, Melissande heard Lucian Barret's deep voice say "Amen."

Did she dream it?

The voice and the word seemed incongruous and yet utterly right together.

Her dreams had been so vivid and frightening. She felt a danger looming over Lucian but she was powerless to help him. A faceless stranger sought to kill him in some of the dreams or else Lucian sought to punish himself for some sin of his past, but turmoil constantly swirled around him.

Hearing him speak that one word of praise and thanksgiving to God heartened her. If he could still say "Amen" with such a depth of feeling, surely all was not lost. Maybe he would see past the self-inflicted penance he wore like a badge of dishonor and find the strength to reclaim his life.

Her lungs burned with the effort of breathing and she longed to be at rest. Yet the curiosity that had plagued her all her life was piqued now.

Was Lucian ready to share a bit of himself with her? Could he forgive himself for his past and return home to take his rightful place as lord of the Barret lands? Could he give up his warrior's world of killing and destruction? His steadfast refusal to participate in life?

Melissande had to find out. Not only that, but she needed to help him. Burning breath after burning breath, she dragged air into her lungs, determined to make certain Lucian Barret did not slip any further astray.

Days and nights passed before the breathing eased. The effort to battle the latest bout with lung fever had been difficult, but one morning Melissande awoke and sensed she'd won.

The room about her was strange and yet familiar. She knew the smells and the sounds of the place, having floated in and out of consciousness for who knew how long.

But she did not recognize the sight of it. Small and crude, the narrow chamber resembled her tiny quarters at the convent, but for the hot grate that kept the space at a reasonable temperature.

The real difference stemmed from Lucian Barret's presence. His tall, muscular body filled the chamber with efficient movements as he hummed over the cauldron on the grate.

She must have made a noise of some sort, for he suddenly dropped his spoon and whirled around to face her.

Then he grinned.

Not the small nod to humor her that he'd given in the past, but a full smile that made Melissande's heart stop.

"You are awake," he announced with foolish obviousness, closing the distance between them.

Suddenly aware of her lack of clothing beneath the sheets and the total disarray of her hair, Melissande held up her hand to halt him. "I must dress first."

He stepped closer. "You may require some help."

Surely he jested. She clutched the linens closer to her body, keenly uncomfortable with her nakedness near him. "Certainly not! I will manage if I can just—"

"Don't be ridiculous." Lucian turned on his heel. "Tamara will assist you."

Light-headed from the effort of moving, Melissande rubbed her temple. "Oh. Tamara. Of course." How foolish she had been to think he would try to help her dress.

After shouting into the corridor, Lucian ushered a young woman into the room whom Melissande did not know.

"Oh, my lady! You are well again," the girl enthused. "Lord be praised, but I did not think you would make it."

The girl seemed to know her. "Tamara?"

"Yes, my lady." Tamara turned to wave away Lucian.

Melissande swallowed her surprise when the hulking warrior meekly ducked out the door.

"I need some help, please." It embarrassed her to have to ask. As a novitiate she had been taught to keep her body private from all eyes, even her own. But she could not afford modesty now.

Tamara did not seem to suffer from such humility. She chatted aimlessly about various visitors at the inn and the kind attentiveness of Lord Barret and the warmer weather that followed the snowstorm all the while helping Melissande into the green dress the merchant's wife had given her.

"Lucian has been attentive to me?" Curiosity drove the question right off her tongue.

"*Oui!* I've never seen a man so solicitous of his wife before." She nodded her head with sagacity beyond her years. "And we get plenty of married couples at the inn. Half of 'em don't care about each other at all."

Melissande wanted to know more, specifically about Lucian, but before she could think of a way to redirect the woman, Tamara reached for a wooden comb and began untangling her patient's hair.

A sharp rap sounded at the door, sending Tamara off the bed. "He is returned, my lady. Call if you need me."

Lucian walked into the chamber, thanking Tamara as she hurried around him. Then he turned to Melissande. "You are prepared to greet me now?" His words somber and quiet, he lacked the broad grin of before.

Melissande found herself wishing for it back. "Yes." She felt awkward around him suddenly. Unsure of herself with a man who had taken care of her the whole time she'd been ill. "How long have I been indisposed?"

"Almost three weeks." He had reached the bed and stood with both legs pressed against it, staring down at her. "I thought you'd never recover."

"It is not such a long time, actually. The first year I had it, I suffered for almost two months." What a miserable winter that had been. Sister Eleanor was so aggravated about the work Melissande missed, she assigned Sanskrit to her helper for nearly a year.

"You've had this before?" Lucian frowned.

"Several times. After you contract it once, you are all the more disposed to sickness."

His brow furrowed. A casual observer might interpret the severe expression on his face as anger, but Melissande realized she knew him well enough to recognize concern. Maybe fear for her.

"What causes it?"

"Exposure to the cold weather, it seems." She yawned, surprised at how weak she felt after the effort of dressing and conversing.

"And you did not confide this bit of information to me?" His voice definitely sounded angry. Perhaps she'd been wrong about thinking he was only fearful for her health.

"I didn't see a reason to mention it when we had little choice between facing the cold weather or confronting a killer." She strove to keep the defensive tone from her words with little success.

Lucian threw his hands in the air before they slammed down against his thighs again. "If I had known I could have made sure you kept the damn snow off your blanket. Or offered you more blankets. Or any number of things." He pinned her with a steely look of cold fury. "You could have died from this, Mel. You need to take better care of yourself."

Waves of anger emanated from him. Melissande inched further into her pillows, too exhausted to confront him just now. Why was he so angry? It was her health, not his.

"I have been taught not to complain, Lucian. It never occurred to me to discuss my health weaknesses with you."

He sank to the bed beside her, his hip grazing her thigh. Although she told herself she was too tired to move, part of her acknowledged she remained still just to feel his solid presence next to her.

"Melissande." He addressed her slowly, thoughtfully, as if speaking to a child. "How long ago did you first contract this illness?"

She calculated the years in her mind. "Seven years ago."

Like a mountain eclipsing the landscape, he rose from her bed to stand before her, inhabiting every bit of her vision. "And they did not send you home?"

"St. Ursula's *is* my home."

"How could they conscience keeping a child in the alpine mountains who was susceptible to a deadly illness exacerbated by cold weather?" He tipped her chin up to look at him, compelling Melissande to open her sleepy eyes.

The rough texture of his sword-wielding hand seeped into her skin, flooding her with his warmness and a sense of being healed. She wondered how it would feel to close her eyes and lean into that strong palm. "The world is dead to those inside the abbey, Lucian. We handle our own affairs."

He drew his mouth into a pale semblance of a smile. "Not any more you don't, Melissande. We are getting the hell out of the Alps and never looking back."

She started to contradict him, but he placed a forbidding finger over her lips. If she hadn't been so tired from the weeks of battling the fever, she would have been more forceful about arguing the point.

Today, she let him have his say. In fact, she allowed herself a lazy fantasy of what it would be like to stay with Lucian. What if he were not taking her to England to wed Roarke, but to marry *him?*

Her heart leaped at the strong temptation the image presented—succumbing to Lucian's kisses as his wife, growing round with his babe, healing the darkness that lurked inside of him.

The vision dissipated as quickly as it had arisen when Melissande imagined Lucian teaching their son how to wield a sword, how to be stoic. She would never raise a warrior or breed another generation of brutal men cut off from their emotions. Her mother hadn't been able to keep her family together no matter how much she'd pleaded with her husband. What made Melissande think she could ever create a genuine partnership with a man, and a warrior at that?

"I don't care what trouble you give Roarke or how much you try to wrangle your way out of a marriage," he warned, shooting her a level glare. "I'm telling you here and now that once you get to England you are staying there for good."

Pivoting on his heel, he stomped across the planked floor and out the door.

She sighed, regretting her lack of strength. When she recovered, she would tell him in no uncertain terms that she would be headed back to France in less than six weeks.

Melissande yawned and reclined on the mattress, wondering briefly what Roarke Barret would be like as a grown man. She hadn't allowed herself to think of the man, choosing to hope she'd never have to face him. But given Lucian's determination to deliver her to England, perhaps now was the time to remember Roarke. He was probably as manipulative as he had been as a child.

Although she hadn't recognized his behavior for what it was until years later, Melissande knew he had taken advantage of her infatuation with him, sending her on small errands for him, cajoling her to pilfer fresh muffins from the kitchen when he was hungry, or coaxing her into catching his portion of the fresh fish Lady Barret sometimes demanded from him. Roarke had always been so different from the rest of his family, a smooth-talking charmer among his blunt, hard-working kin.

Even if he turned out to be a prince among men, Melissande would not marry him. First of all because he would be a knight by now, the same as Lucian. Second, her commitment to St. Ursula's—and God, she amended—was much more important to her than wedding an earl who didn't deserve his older brother's lands.

Besides, three powerful forces drew her back to St. Ursula's, the three reasons she kept her sanity in the abbey despite the Sanskrit and lung fever and Sister Eleanor.

Three precious children held a part of her heart, and she would never give them up for either of the Barret men, no matter how sorely dreams of the elder Barret might tempt her.

Chapter Twelve

After a torturous three weeks at Melissande's side, aiding her through her convalescence, Lucian thanked the Fates when she seemed well enough to ride again. Stealing through the lodging in the predawn hours, he made the necessary preparations for their trip and left another sack of coins for Tamara and her family.

For the initial week of her recovery, it had been easy to care for her. She had been so fatigued from the fever that she slept much of the time, waking only to eat and to read from the *Odyssey* for an hour or two in the evening. But after several days, she had started her campaign to return to St. Ursula's.

Foolish woman.

He walked away the first time she introduced the topic, but as soon as he shut the door between them, he recalled the vow he'd made while she'd hovered near death.

God, grant Melissande her life and I shall listen to her prattle morning, noon and night.

Unwilling to break such an oath, he had returned to her and was promptly rewarded with Melissande's numerous attempts to bargain for her freedom. Not that he would ever consider granting it while a killer might follow in their footsteps. Lucian had made inquiries among other travelers who visited the inn, but had learned naught of their pursuer.

Following a quick stop at the stable to alert the groom they were leaving, Lucian made his way to the tiny room he shared with Melissande.

Their close quarters had become the most compelling reason to get Melissande on the road home. Once she started to regain her health and vitality, Lucian could not concentrate around her.

His hand hesitated on the latch to where she slept. Just knowing she was within the chamber, sleeping peacefully, utterly vulnerable, wreaked havoc with his mind and body.

Gritting his teeth for strength, he turned the handle, determined to protect her from any threat. Including himself.

She had bathed last night. The room still held the fragrant smell of the bath soap Tamara had found for her. As he eased closer to the bed, careful not to wake her yet, Lucian realized her hair radiated the floral scent from where it lay strewn over her pillow in a deep red fan.

As if a vise squeezed his chest, Lucian struggled for a full breath as he stared at her. He squelched the urge to fall to his knees and to worship her with his hands, his mouth…

Was the pain that clenched his chest his lust or his guilt? Seized equally by both, Lucian wondered how grave an error it would be to skim his palm over her cheek and through the skeins of pillow-warmed hair.

He lingered beside her for a long moment, knowing this would be the closest he ever came to fulfilling the misplaced longing he felt for her.

As if she sensed his presence, she turned toward him in sleep, curling on her side at the edge of the narrow pallet. Her blanket edged further down her body, revealing another tantalizing inch of her skin and confirming his guess that she was indeed naked beneath the covers.

The knowledge spurred his hunger for her, edging the clamor of his desires to the forefront of his mind and effectively nudging away the guilt for a moment.

Now settled on her side, Melissande draped one arm across her body to rest beside her head, so close to where his thigh grazed the bedding.

Sinking to his knees, he lifted a tentative hand over her, absorbing her warmth and essence before his skin ever connected with her flesh. Slowly, gently, he let his fingers fall onto her shoulder and curve around the softness of her bare arm.

Heaven.

Her skin was smooth and fragrant and far too inviting. Not for all the world would he nudge aside her blanket another inch to unveil the lush breasts he knew resided there. But that didn't mean he couldn't think about it. Dream about it. Long for it with all his heart and soul.

She sighed, startling him for a moment with the fear that she had awakened. Instead she settled more deeply into her pillow, a satisfied smile rounding her lips at the corners.

Pure torture.

What scared him more than his own lust for Melissande was the fact that she seemed to return it. Her tentative touches in the chapel, the way she'd returned his kiss, the way she smiled at him in her sleep…all suggested she might share his desire.

Of course, she was too young and sheltered to know better.

But for Lucian, the realization that he could lower that blanket and wake her with languorous kisses to her breasts drove him to the brink of insanity.

How could he ever let her go? How the hell could he turn her over to Roarke after having lost his heart to her for the second time in his life?

Melissande had won him long ago. Her spirit, her wit, her quick intelligence had impressed him when he was little more than a boy. And now…now he was more impressed than ever, but he had become a man so unworthy of her that his growing regard would only offend her if she knew the depth of his sins.

As much as his gut twisted at the notion of Melissande in the arms of another man, it was far better than imagining her suffering from a fatal case of lung fever in a nunnery with no one who loved her by her side.

"Melissande." His voice sounded husky and full of unspoken emotion. He cleared his throat and rose to his feet. "Melissande."

Her eyelashes fluttered over her cheeks with the delicate sweep of a butterfly's wing. "Lucian?"

The desire to answer her call was so fundamental, so deeply rooted in his being, that he wondered how and when she had worked her way into the empty places inside him. "We leave this morn," he told her, incapable of gentling the brusqueness in his tone. "Rise and dress and meet me below."

Well, that's a fine way to wake up, Melissande thought miserably, unable to jump out of bed no matter what the high-and-mighty Lucian Barret willed.

Rubbing a lazy palm across her eyes, she remembered the wonderful dream she'd been having where Lucian…

Dear God, she'd been dreaming something totally inappropriate about him. Her face flushed even though she was in the room alone.

What sort of spell had the man cast upon her to inspire such wanton thoughts? In her dream, Lucian had been kneeling beside her bed, running his fingers over her body and it had felt so real and so delicious that Melissande found it difficult to brush away the lingering desire the imagined touch had wrought.

One thing was certain. She would not allow herself to sleep naked again. Although she'd adopted the habit in her weeks of convalescing as a way to conserve on laundry for the already overworked Tamara, obviously sleeping without a night rail encouraged shameless thoughts.

Shameless delicious thoughts that would plague her all day.

Hurrying to dress, she chastised herself. As a novitiate, her thoughts should be directed toward the spiritual and not toward the flesh.

Crossing herself two times for good measure, she prayed for guidance through her current predicament. As much as she knew it was sinful for her to think of Lucian, or any man, in that manner, she admitted to herself that it was not the first time a blatantly lascivious thought had crossed her mind where he was concerned.

Thank heaven they were finally escaping the intimacy of the chamber. She scrambled out the door still plaiting her recalcitrant hair, eager to put the last month behind her.

Her step faltered when she spied him already atop his horse, tying the lead rope for her mare.

His hair blended into his black hauberk, cloaking him in darkness from head to toe. The scar stood out in stark relief on his temple this morning, his every feature as stern and defined as a marble statue.

Even under the layered fabric of his tunic and hauberk, the play of muscle in his arms was apparent as he worked.

Her vision of him as a warrior returned. For the past fortnight she had deceived herself into thinking of him more as her friend, sometimes even as more than a friend when she thought of their shared kiss…

"Good morning," she called.

He stilled, then straightened, staring at her with the distance of a stranger.

"Lucian?"

As if awakening at her call, he broke his gaze and vaulted down to assist her onto her mount. "Sorry," he mumbled, wrapping both hands about her waist to lift her.

A bolt of awareness shot through her at his touch, singeing her nerves and calling to mind the dream she'd been having about him only moments before. Warmth pooled in her belly and effused her limbs, enhancing the feeling of weightlessness as he held her suspended in the air above him.

His gaze locked with hers, distant no longer.

She stared down at him, drawn by the heated promise in his eyes. His mouth was within kissing distance, taunting her with memories of the last time their lips had touched. The result had given rise to a flurry of sensual dreams she hadn't escaped from even at the heights of her illness.

Would he settle his mouth over hers again?

Melissande closed her eyes. Hoping.

Yet as his name escaped her lips in a breathless sigh, she found herself settled firmly onto her horse's back, the distance between them restored.

Had she dreamed the exchange?

Her heart beat so furiously she was obliged to take shallow breaths of the crisp morning air.

Mayhap she was just being fanciful. No matter that they'd shared one stolen kiss those many weeks ago. Lucian was far too honorable a man to harbor romantic feelings for the woman he regarded as his brother's intended bride. Or a would-be nun, for that matter.

Their kiss in the chapel had probably been an accident he regretted—a misstep brought on by Melissande's brazen touches and bold manner.

Annoyed with her traitorous longings, Melissande forced herself to repeat every proverb she could recall before delving into conversation with Lucian. She didn't deserve to indulge in talk until she served some sort of penance for her worldly wants.

Somewhere between the Sayings of Lemuel and the Sayings of Agur, she realized Lucian called to her from his horse. She forced herself to use the smooth, modulated tones of her convent voice. "Yes?"

"You are uncommonly quiet today. Do you not feel well enough to travel?" Swivelled backward to face her, Lucian regarded her with concern.

"I am giving your ears a rest." Summoning a smile, she wondered if she could dispense with her penance early and talk to him. Appealing as it sounded, probably not.

"Please do not. You've had me worried." He turned back around to guide them through a thicket of close trees. "Besides, I've become rather accustomed to you."

Lucian wanted to hear her talk? The temptation proved too much to bear. Perhaps she could finish the penance after lunch.

"Actually, I do have a proposition…"

As Lucian listened to her musical voice fill the clearing, he wished he could afford to focus more attention on her. Technically he was *listening* as she discussed her reasons for wishing to go back to St. Ursula's. His brain, however, did not really comprehend the finer points of her arguments. Right now, Lucian needed to heed the gnawing fear in his gut that they were being followed.

All morning—whenever he hadn't been envisioning Melissande cocooned in the bed coverings as he'd seen her earlier—Lucian had been tormented with a sense that someone stalked behind them, waiting to take a shot at him while he was most vulnerable. The mountain terrain seemed ominously quiet, as if danger lurked nearby and every creature great and small was aware of it except for Lucian. He couldn't say what made the hair on the back of his neck prickle, but he could not deny his warrior instincts.

Melissande's voice soothed his raw nerves and maybe served a higher purpose if they were being followed. The stalker would think his quarry engaged in conversation, hence more vulnerable to attack.

Far from distracted, Lucian was strung so tight he'd snap if the breeze so much as blew across him the wrong way. He would not let himself or, more accurately, he would not let Melissande be unprotected for even an instant. He had to draw out the enemy while the element of surprise was on Lucian's side.

Melissande's words covered his silence, allowing him to brood over the identity of the person who followed them. Perhaps the too-quiet pursuer was simply a fellow traveler, but Lucian knew on a gut level that it must be the shooter from the lowlands who forced them back up into the mountains. With all the time Melissande had been ill, their unwanted guest certainly had time to track them.

With the methodical cunning instilled by war, Lucian formulated a plan for removing the threat. The time had come to act.

After scouting the landscape for safe shelters, he drew her

horse beside his and turned in the saddle to face her, keeping his voice as low as possible. "You need to ride on without me, Mel, to that bend in the trail. There is a predator behind us—"

Before her head could swivel around, Lucian threw one arm out to intercept her chin in his hand and kissed her, hard. Under the guise of nuzzling her neck—strictly for the benefit of whomever watched them—Lucian whispered against her softly scented skin, "Do not look back. We must be discreet."

"What is it?" Her heart pounded wildly under his lips. He forced himself to ignore the sensual draw of that rapid pulse and to concentrate on the threat at hand.

"Not what…who. If I let you go, will you ride straight ahead, no looking back?" He didn't want to let her go.

Melissande nodded and Lucian pulled away, regretting the terror he saw in her innocent eyes. She'd not seen violence as a child, and heaven knew she hadn't seen it in the convent. What would she think if she knew Lucian planned to dispatch whoever lurked behind them?

"I will drop down in a moment, but you must allow my horse to stay in front of you, as if I were still riding. Then take cover on the other side of those rocks." He had no choice but to send her forward, much as he hated the thought of her being alone in this wild terrain for even a moment.

"What will you do?" she whispered, her brow furrowed in displeasure and worry. He could see she struggled not to deluge him with questions, thoughts. He knew her natural inclination would be to talk over every option available.

Lucian also knew they didn't have time for that.

"Eliminate the threat." He double checked the knot on the lead rope between horses. "Stay there until I come for you, and we shall be safely on our way." For a moment he considered what would happen to her if he didn't make it back to her.

That course of action was unthinkable. He wouldn't allow it to happen.

"Lucian—" She worried her lower lip, for once unsure what to say.

"There is no time, Mel. I will be there." He allowed his gaze to linger over her, hoping he conveyed a confidence that would reassure her.

She stared back at him, wide-eyed and frightened, and nodded. "All will be well."

The gift of her trust hit him like chain mail being tossed over his body, cloaking him with invincibility as he went to face an unknown enemy.

Secure in his plan, Lucian slid silently to the ground. To her credit, she did not even glance down as she rode by his hiding place, though the stony set of her jaw told him she was none too happy with the plan.

Damn.

He clenched his fingers about the hilt of his sword, waiting for the horse and rider that followed many paces behind them. He had not so much seen their presence this morning as he had felt it, but he trusted his instincts implicitly.

Melissande arrived safely at the curve in the trail and the rock outcropping at about the time Lucian heard a horse in the distance. Her faith in him overwhelmed him, humbled him, strengthened him to honor the magnitude of her trust.

He would not disappoint her.

With the patience of a man long accustomed to stealth, he waited. The trees obscured the face of the oncoming knight, a man who rode armed to the teeth.

The newcomer seemed to lack Lucian's size and—

Lucian's grip on his sword faltered as the man's face came into view.

Peter Chadsworth.

A fellow knight. A fellow Englishman. A fellow foster son under the tutelage of Osbern Fitzhugh.

Dear God. Half of him wanted to whoop with joy at the sight of an old friend. His smarter half knew this could be no happy reunion.

If Peter Chadsworth followed him through the woods without identifying himself, chances were the man meant to do him harm.

Before he could dissect the matter any further, Peter's mount passed Lucian's chest, near enough to touch. After the head of the horse, Lucian raised his sword and knocked the rider neatly from his saddle. The blow reverberated with satisfying force up Lucian's arms.

Amid much cursing and spitting, Chadsworth rose. Honorable knight that he was, Lucian allowed him to.

"Bastard!" The fallen man lifted his weapon, prepared to defend himself. Encumbered by the quiver of arrows that rode high on his back, now crooked from his tumble, Chadsworth didn't stand a chance in hell of winning a ground battle against Lucian.

No matter. If his former friend meant to kill him, the man posed a threat to Melissande. And that, Lucian would not suffer.

He unleashed a series of blows to set Chadsworth on his heels. Lucian held him at sword point, not ready to kill him but determined to extract some answers.

"Why do you follow me?"

Peter ran shaking fingers over a flesh wound on his thigh. "As if you didn't know." His injury did not keep the venom from his voice. "Murderer."

The word sliced through Lucian with more force than any blade.

"Ah." Lucian supposed he should not be surprised. All of Osbern Fitzhugh's fostered knights had been fond of him. But Peter Chadsworth had been one of the more mild-tempered of the bunch and, truth be told, one of the more simple-minded. Lucian would not have anticipated such a level of vengeance in one so innately kind. "You seek revenge on Osbern's behalf?"

"And for his son." The downed man's hand clenched on air, as if seeking his sword nearby.

"Damon Fitzhugh needs your help in claiming vengeance?" Lucian emitted a short bark of laughter before he kicked Chadsworth's weapon farther away.

"He did not ask for help. I give it out of loyalty to him." For the first time, he looked less sure of himself.

"You would steal his right to kill me?"

Chadsworth was more of a dolt than Lucian realized, though dangerous enough to have nearly killed him once before with his lethal crossbow aim.

"He wants you dead," the man shouted. "He repeats it like a litany every night before we sleep, every morning when we awake."

"You have been at war with him?"

"Aye." He closed his eyes for a long moment, perhaps recalling the same horrors Lucian did when he thought of the Crusades.

"Yet he no longer travels with you?"

"He conducts business on behalf of the king." Chadsworth announced his news with the pride of a younger brother. "He returns to England by harvest time."

Lucian nodded. He still had a few months then.

In the meantime he did not think he could kill young Chadsworth. Instinct told him the man's plan to seek revenge had been completely of his own, simpleminded making. He looked up to Damon like a worshipful squire reveres a knight.

A throbbing commenced in his temple. He would learn no more from this man, yet he could not kill him. Lucian knew he would curse himself to hell and back if he let the man go, and thereby allowed one of the dolt's misguided arrows to hurt Melissande.

Perhaps the risk would not be so great if he could ensure himself a substantial distance over a wounded enemy.

He braced himself. Then squeezed the shaft of his sword as he hefted it.

"God go with you, Peter." Striking a blow with the blunt side of the sword to the younger man's head, Lucian hit him hard enough to keep him senseless for an hour or two, but not hard enough to do permanent damage.

With any luck, Chadsworth would be so groggy and confused upon awakening, he would lose more time finding his horse and hauling his sorry carcass over the animal's back again. And now that Lucian knew of the man's intentions, he could be that much more alert to danger. Assuming Chadsworth would be foolish enough to continue his quest now that he realized young Fitzhugh would not thank him.

"My God." The startled gasp was too horrified to have come from Lucian's jaded conscience.

He turned to see Melissande a few feet away, taking in the scene with stunned eyes in an ashen face.

"What are you doing?" Lucian barked, more harshly than he'd intended. How could she have left the safety of the shelter he had directed her to? A few moments earlier and she could have gotten caught in the middle of swordplay. She could have been injured or—

"How could you do this?" Tears pooled and spilled down

her cheeks as she looked upon the fallen figure of Peter Chadsworth.

She stepped toward the body, but Lucian grabbed her, unwilling to let her discover the man was still alive. "Leave him be, Mel."

Her hand flew to her mouth, maybe to muffle a sob or to quell the queasiness some people experienced at the sight of blood. The skin on her arms felt chill and clammy to his touch. Her words were barely a whisper. "How could you do this?"

He would not put her mind at ease by telling her the man would wake up in the afternoon.

No, it would be easier to distance himself from Melissande if she finally viewed him as the man he had become.

A killer.

As he hardened his heart and lifted his gaze to her condemning one, Lucian knew that, at last, she saw him all too clearly.

Chapter Thirteen

After they rode away from the dead man in the deserted forest, Melissande wasn't surprised that Lucian checked and rechecked the rope that tied their horses together.

If given half a chance, she would leave him now without a backward glance.

How could she have so misjudged him? How could she so grievously misread his character to the point of half falling in love with a cold-hearted killer?

In fact, it had been her deep regard for Lucian that made her betray his wish that she remain safely ensconced in her rocky hideaway while he fought the enemy.

Try as she might, she could not force herself to sit quietly with the horses knowing Lucian might meet his death in a quest to protect her. She had slipped down the mountain, heavy stick in tow, to tip the odds in Lucian's favor and offer whatever help she could.

She had been so relieved to discover Lucian already a victor in his battle. His opponent lay bleeding and beaten on the ground, while Lucian stood over him without a scratch. Before she could make her presence known, however, she'd watched in horror as Lucian raised his sword above his head and killed the man—a defenseless man—with one foul swoop of the blade.

Melissande would have understood if Lucian had struck the blow in combat. But the smaller man Lucian attacked had already been defeated. Lucian's actions broke a basic rule of battle, and an even bigger moral rule.

For hours she shed tears over the young man Lucian brutalized. And, though she did not ask, she knew the person Lucian killed could not have posed any real threat to them on the alpine road. The baby-faced knight looked scarcely out of his squire years, hardly a match for a warrior as well-favored as Lucian Barret.

When they camped that night, Melissande stood unmoving while Lucian tied the rope to her wrists and attached the other end to his waist. She did not protest or comment, and she doubted she would ever find the need to speak to him again.

The silence would surely drive him mad.

He fought daily with the urge to tell her he had not killed Peter Chadsworth. When she looked at him with those wide brown eyes full of disillusionment, he wanted nothing so much as to restore her faith in him.

As they made their way toward the French coast, however, rapidly closing the distance to the Barret lands, Lucian knew he did not deserve her faith or the gift of her conversation. Although Melissande misread Peter Chadsworth's injuries, she had not misread Lucian's character.

"Will we cross the channel tonight?" she called from behind him, startling him with her first attempt at speech in days.

"Not unless you really want to." He would be willing to change his plans to please her. And he couldn't blame her for wanting to end the journey with him as soon as possible. "It is almost dark."

"Nay." She shook her head, her red braids dancing across the green fabric of her tunic as she looked north toward England. "I am not ready to return yet."

Her willingness to linger with him pleased him immeasurably.

"I thought we would seek shelter at the monastery on the hill." He pointed toward an imposing structure overlooking the sea, scarcely able to believe she had broken the sennight of silence.

Following his gaze, she wrinkled her nose. "I hear monks do not look fondly on sheltering women. I would prefer to sleep under the stars again."

"As would I." He steered their horses toward a thatch of trees some distance from the water. "We can camp over there."

She nodded, apparently satisfied, and said no more, leaving him to ponder her words and new demeanor. She seemed more somber somehow, as if the days of quiet reflection had matured her, or maybe saddened her.

Either way, Lucian mourned the change. As much as he knew he should rejoice at her willingness, even eagerness, to distance herself from him, he wished for a reassuring glimpse of her former vital self.

Would Roarke be able to resurrect that vivacious spirit Lucian missed? The thought made him burn with envy. When had he become so possessive of Melissande?

Battling the jealousy that took him by surprise, Lucian untied the lead rope between horses and approached Melissande to retie it between their wrists. The act had become a nightly ritual between them.

Usually she offered him her wrists and turned her face

away as he knotted the rope. Tonight she extended her hand and stared at him boldly, as if defying him to restrain her.

The last rays of sun lit Melissande from behind like a golden halo. The challenge in her dark eyes unnerved him. "It seems we are bound together, whether I will it or nay." Her voice whispered through him, making him recall all the reasons she was far more dangerous to him than he could ever be to her.

He forced a smile to mask the heaviness in his heart. "You shall be well rid of me soon, Melissande. Your captivity ends on the other side of the sea." He smoothed his fingers over her bared wrist, wishing he did not have to compel her to remain at his side.

Her skin was petal-soft and creamy, pale and delicate in contrast to his sun-worn hands. He wondered how that small patch of exposed flesh would feel against his lips, how it would taste on his tongue.

The pulse in her neck fluttered and jumped, as if reading his mind.

"But we will not idle in England for long." She made no move to extricate herself from his touch. "You will accompany me back to St. Ursula's, and we shall be together then. Would you still feel the need to bind me to you then?"

Yes.

"No." He needed to just tie the rope and have done with it. He definitely needed to step away from her and the warmth emanating from her. "I will not escort you, Melissande."

Even if Roarke asked him to do such a thing, Lucian would refuse. He'd have to.

She stared at him a long moment, then shook her head slowly. She stepped closer. "I will not allow anyone else to accompany me."

Lucian's world tilted on its axis. Perhaps his brain did not function properly when she stood so near. "You don't trust me, remember?" Hadn't he proven to her he was a knight with no honor? "You *can't* trust me."

A determined light flashed in her eyes, her delicate jaw set. Stubborn woman. What would it take to convince her?

Forestalling further debate, Lucian made one last attempt to scare her off.

"Do you have any idea how much I want you right now, Melissande? How much I've wanted you every day since that ill-advised kiss in the chapel ruins?"

Her shocked expression told him she hadn't the slightest notion.

He forged ahead ruthlessly to inform her.

"I watch you while you are sleeping and imagine myself lying beside you. In my mind's eye, I am beneath the covers with you, pinning your body to mine with my hands, tasting the curve of your neck with my mouth."

Her eyes were still wide with surprise, but her breath grew shallow at his words. Did the notion of sharing her covers with him hold a certain appeal? As much as the idea tantalized him, he couldn't allow his shock methods to decline into something she found fascinating.

He couldn't risk moving any closer to her. Forget physical intimidation. He was the one intimidated enough he had no choice but to remain as still as stone. One inch closer to Melissande and his control would combust into flames, turning to ashes at his feet.

"But I wouldn't quit there, Mel."

She licked her lips, propelling him closer to igniting with her wickedly innocent mouth.

"Every night I dream of covering your body with mine, spreading your thighs…" Why hadn't she stopped him?

Where was her sense of maidenly outrage? "And entering you. Claiming you. Making you mine alone."

Her furrowed brow suggested she puzzled over this rather than being horrified.

And in the meantime, he was so wound up with wanting her now he didn't dare to breathe the air for fear of catching the scent of dried flowers, the scent of Melissande.

"Do you have any idea how untrustworthy this makes me when you belong to my own brother, Melissande?" He ground out the last words between clenched teeth. "Don't ever make the mistake of trusting me."

She trembled slightly.

Good.

That's exactly what he wanted. What he needed from her. Her friendship was far too dangerous to them both.

But despite the tremble, she met his gaze levelly. "Perhaps that's exactly why I do trust you."

Lucian stifled a curse.

"You've never acted on those feelings," Melissande continued, watching him as carefully as a mouse eyes a nearby hawk. "And you do not allow your warrior status to make you feel entitled to anything you want. I admire that."

Lucian was stunned. Speechless.

"I've considered the matter of the forest road carefully, and I've realized I trust you anyway." She lifted her free hand to lay it gently across his chest. "Explain to me what happened with that man who followed us." Hope flared in her eyes, a testament to her faith in him.

Oh, God.

He couldn't let this happen, couldn't allow her to concoct a fanciful vision of him that he could never live up to.

The delicate brush of her palm on his chest heated his

blood and fired his imagination. Perhaps there was another way to scare her off, to ensure she kept a safe distance between them for the rest of the journey.

Not bothering to weigh the merits of his scheme, he leaned forward, savoring the way her eyes widened a fraction. Her faint floral scent drifted to his nose, stirring his senses and fanning the hunger that had stalked him for weeks.

He kissed her. Hard.

His lips fell upon hers with more force than he'd intended, yet Melissande tilted her head back to accommodate him. Her pulse pounded through her veins at her wrist, where he still held her captive.

There was no finesse, no teasing exploration. He cupped the back of her head to steady her and plundered her mouth with blatantly provocative sweeps of his tongue.

His mind screamed a protest, asking him what the hell he was thinking to kiss her this way. Had he really meant to scare her off? Or was he merely exploiting the moment for a chance to taste her?

Her small moan robbed him of the ability to figure it out.

He dragged her against him, their bodies aligning in a sensuous connection, thigh to thigh, hip to hip, his chest to her high, rounded breasts. Her dress molded to his legs in the breeze, tendrils of her hair wound around his shoulders to stroke him with red silk.

Why didn't he offend her sensibilities with his coarseness? His impudence?

Refusing to retreat until he'd succeeded, Lucian trailed his hands up her arms, over her shoulders to slide down the green-velvet bodice of her gown.

Melissande gasped, he could feel it right through her kiss. Yet she did not pull away.

Blood whooshed through his veins in heated tidal waves, resounding in his ears like the crashing surf. Too bad he couldn't stop himself. Not yet. Only Melissande could stop this insanity.

He was surprised to feel his hands shake just a little as he reached for the ties on her bodice. He'd wanted this so much, dreamed about her for so long. With slow precision, he gauged the knot with his fingertips. He wasn't about to break the best kiss of his life to examine how to best untie her gown.

Somewhere beneath the deafening pound of his heart, he heard Melissande's voice as if far away.

"Wait."

He released her immediately; her body, her gown's ties, all traces of green velvet. But the memory of how she'd felt in his arms—he wouldn't ever let go of that.

He pulled away in time to see her eyelids force themselves open with lazy effort. She blinked back at him, the fire in her eyes barely banked.

Her lips were still swollen from his kiss, yet her brow furrowed in confusion.

"You weren't kissing me because you wanted to just now, were you?"

He couldn't mistake the censure in her tone.

"Trust me, I wanted to." That much was always true.

"But you didn't kiss me to indulge some personal passion for me, did you?" Her arms folded over her chest, as if to shut herself away from him as much as possible. "You want to scare me away more than anything."

How could he deny the truth?

She tipped her chin at him. "Haven't you figured out by now that's the wrong tack to take with me?" Her eyes glittered, locking head-on with his. "Next time you try a trick like that you might be surprised who scares who."

His jaw probably hit the ground. Lucian was too busy staring at her in disbelief to notice.

Had the convent-bred Melissande truly just baited him with sensual threats?

His blood pounded with an unqualified yes.

With considerable effort he peeled his gaze from Melissande as she moved around the camp, focusing instead on the rope that had fallen unbidden to the ground in their kiss. He picked it up and let it dangle from his fingers, knowing he could not bring himself to tie it around her.

Not after all that had passed between them.

Instead he found himself envisioning other, more pleasurable ways of tying her to him. He imagined her ensnaring him in her long skeins of red hair, tying her to him with a lover's silken threads. He imagined tying Melissande to him as his wife, slipping the bond of marriage around her finger instead of the bond of captivity about her slender arm.

Tossing the rope aside, he admonished himself for dangerous daydreams.

Father, forgive me.

Still awkward with his renewed habit of heavenly supplication, Lucian had succumbed to the realization that he desperately needed prayer in his life. If he was to deliver Melissande to Roarke with her virtue intact, he required all the divine intercession he could muster.

"Are you all right?" Melissande straightened her clothing and stared at him with gentle concern.

"Fine." He willed his breathing to a more even pace. He had to put a stop to this, to put space between them if she wasn't going to do it for them.

He stalked toward the saddlebags, urging away the raw sensual hunger in his body. He discovered the flint among the other supplies and pulled out the stones. "Would you care to light the fire?"

She shrugged, but held her hands out and Lucian tossed her the tools.

They worked in silence to prepare the dwindling rations, and Lucian wondered what she was thinking. She didn't say much, even when they ate their meal.

"Perhaps we can finish the *Odyssey*?" He needed something to distract him from Melissande.

"I don't think so." She shook her head, loosening her already precariously tied braid a bit more.

"How fortunate you are to read Greek." He wouldn't normally use her generous spirit to manipulate her, but he wanted to know how Odysseus fared in his adventures at sea. And he had to shift the focus of his thoughts away from Melissande. "You have the luxury of plucking up your book and satisfying your curiosity anytime you choose."

"The ending is awfully romantic. I really don't think—" Melissande bit her lip in indecision.

"Understood." The last thing he needed was another night of firelight and *amour* with this woman.

The *Odyssey* ended romantically? Absently, Lucian drew figures in the sand with a short stick, wishing Odysseus had a more realistic fate. One more akin to Lucian's.

"Odysseus was a great warrior," he observed.

"I guess."

Lucian saw an opportunity to push her away and he took it. "That means he was forced to kill people on occasion."

He sensed her stiffen beside him.

But he could not relent. "There are times a man must defend himself."

"It does not seem like defense to hit a man who has already been downed." Her tone did not seem to censure, merely question.

"Sometimes a man fights to protect more than just himself. A warrior's whole purpose is to protect. Sometimes he protects lands or ideals...or in this case, a person."

He glanced over at her, seeking an expression to gauge the impact of his words. Sensing his stare, she lifted her chin, fixing him with the fathomless depths of her dark eyes.

"You felt you were protecting me?" The disbelief in her words warred with the shades of empathy her gaze projected.

"He sought to kill me, Mel. He would have killed me in the lowlands had I not bent down at the moment he released his crossbow." He picked up her hand and squeezed it between his palms, as if he could further impress his thoughts upon her. "Next time he would not have missed. And where would you be if I died out here, Melissande?"

Slowly shaking her head, she did not agree with him. "The Church teaches me—"

"I know what the Church teaches you." He moved to his knees and planted himself in front of her, blocking her view of the fire, the forest, everything but him. "Are you aware that at the same time they're preaching 'turn the other cheek' to you, they're telling me to take up their cause in the Holy Lands and kill for it?"

"The Crusades save Christianity from the infidel—"

"The Crusades steal land from people as noble and kind as you or I, Melissande, yet I have fought for the ideals because..." How did he arrive here? He had meant only to remind her that he would forever be a warrior. That it came with the territory of knighthood to kill. Oddly, he had succeeded only in circling back to the one death he had not meant to cause.

"Why, Lucian?" She reached to touch his face. Her delicate fingers smoothed over his cheek in a gesture of reassurance, acceptance. "Why would you go into a battle you did not believe in?"

His efforts to defend the knighthood suddenly rang hollowly in his ears. He was a fraud to pretend he hadn't killed without reason. No amount of postulating and theorizing about the nature of battle would relieve the guilt in his murderous soul.

He had been a fool to try.

"My foster father believed in the Crusades with all his heart." The words burned in his throat as they eased past his lips for the first time. The time had come to confess his sins and to set Melissande Deverell safely away from him once and for all.

And, Lucian realized, to a certain extent, his recent return to prayer had unearthed a deep desire for absolution he had not known he possessed. Melissande could not, would not, provide that absolution, but she could serve as his confessor. It was because of her, after all, that he had taken the first step toward God again.

"You mean, Lord Fitzhugh?"

Of course she knew him. Osbern's property neighbored her lands as much as Barret Keep. Lucian withdrew his hand from hers, unwilling to feel her pull away in horror when he confided in her. "Aye. He found the Church a year or two after you left England."

Melissande laughed without mirth. "I should say that was a good thing. No one was in more need of religion than Lord Fitzhugh."

"Why do you say that?" His head whipped up. Everyone at home idolized the man since his death. Lucian couldn't resist hearing an opinion of him that might not be so sainted.

She shrugged. "I thought that was a common sentiment. Even as a child, I recognized the man's ferocious temper. Especially after a few rounds of ale."

"He stopped drinking after he started going to church." Lucian rose and dusted off his knees before seating himself by her side again. Her observation gave him no comfort.

"Did he stop flying into rages over nothing?"

"For the most part." Except when the conversation turned to the Crusades. "Anyway, I joined the wars because of him." Revealing his sins would be more difficult than he thought. Would she be frightened of him when she learned of his deed? He didn't want to scare her, only to open her eyes to who he was.

She leaned forward, closing the distance between them a bit more. Her eyes sparked with curiosity. Lucian thought it ironic that he finally had drawn her out of her week-long silence only to dump his most closely held secret on her narrow shoulders.

"He became like a father to you after yours died, I imagine." Her sharp mind wrapped around the facts and used them to further the story.

"I tried to please him, but ultimately, I couldn't." Lucian admired her intelligence even as he dreaded the conclusion of her efforts.

"You went to the wars because he wanted you to!" She looked indignant on his behalf. "What more did he expect?"

"Nay. I went to the wars because it was my foster father's dying wish." The image of his last conversation with Osbern Fitzhugh flashed through Lucian's mind.

Sympathy softened her features. Her hand reached for his,

but Lucian gently captured hers and set it back in her lap. "There is more." He lifted his eyes to hers. "And it is ugly."

"I'm listening." She frowned. Worry creased her forehead.

How unusual for him to be talking and her to be silent. Lucian wondered if it would be their last conversation. He stared into the fire, trying to forget he had an audience for his tale.

"We had argued repeatedly about the wars. Osbern wanted me to go, spurred me on with flattery that I was the most accomplished knight he had ever trained. His son, Damon, had already left to take up the cause. So had several men whom Osbern fostered along with me. It disappointed Fitzhugh daily that I remained in England, craven and unworthy."

From the corner of his eye he could see Melissande shaking her head. He guessed she would oppose his harsh words, but he could not allow her to interrupt for fear he would not be able to finish his account.

"One day Fitzhugh broached the topic while we were in the practice field—Osbern, Roarke and I." He had to show her why his brother's loyalty was so important to him, why he owed Roarke so much that he would steal her away from the convent. "He flew into one of the rages you remember."

Melissande gasped and Lucian imagined her facile mind had already worked through the rest of the story. But he could not stop now. He needed to tell the tale as much for his sake as for hers. It had lived silently in him for so long, cutting him to pieces again and again…

"I meant only to protect myself from his blows." He turned to her then, wishing he could convince her—himself—that he had not meant to harm the man. "I had my practice shield raised against him, but it did not seem enough. I—" The words cost him. The burning in his throat grew to flaming heat, but he forced the rest of the story past his lips. "I raised my sword against an old man. I, in my prime and completely rational, my opponent nothing but a failing old man in a wild frenzy.

"I killed him, Melissande." Lucian still asked himself how the hell it could have happened. How could the wound to Fitzhugh's arm been life-threatening, delivering his death in naught but a few days' time?

"You—" She faltered. "You raised your sword against him to protect yourself and—"

"Do not make excuses for it. It is common knowledge in Northumbria that I murdered Osbern Fitzhugh."

She blanched and Lucian knew he should have told her this much sooner—before they'd ever kissed. It appalled him to think that he had darkened her lips—so pure and innocent—with his lust.

The memory must appall her twice as much.

"You could not have had much choice…."

He could hear in her voice how desperately she wanted to believe it. Almost as much as he wanted to.

"I had a choice, Mel, and I chose poorly. My instincts for violence cost a man his life. My own brother labeled me a murderer, though he was quick to protect me."

"Roarke saw it." The resignation in her voice reflected the fact that his black deed was beginning to sink in. She could no longer find a way to justify his action.

"Yes. And even though he knew what happened, he helped hide the fact from Mother." Did she understand the magnitude of that act in his eyes? "'Tis why I owe Roarke the world, and why I went so far as to abduct you."

"I am repayment." She sounded unnaturally calm.

"Yes."

Her silence unnerved him, yet he feared if he looked at her

he would see hatred in her eyes. He did not know how to handle this quiet Melissande. What was she thinking? Was she terrified of the violent streak he had unveiled to her?

Gritting his teeth, Lucian turned toward her, knowing the condemnation he would find but needing to see her face.

Worse than outrage, he found pity in her gaze, tears streaking a river down both cheeks. "You have fallen so far."

Regret lodged in his throat, choking him. He imagined she looked at him as an angel would peer down upon mere mortals, sorry for their failings but powerless to change their sinful nature.

"It is not too late for forgiveness, though, Lucian. God loves you." Her pronouncement was choked through her tears before she turned away to hang her head in her hands.

Void of comfort, her words echoed in the air behind her, recalling the declaration that had once followed that sentiment.

And so do I.

This time, silence remained in the aftermath of her words. Although Lucian had succeeded in pushing her away, success came at the expense of the heart he thought he'd lost long ago.

Chapter Fourteen

The English landscape blurred around Melissande as her horse tore through the countryside. Lucian had maintained a relentless course, hell-bent to unload his captive at Barret Keep.

Although her body had grown numb to the days on horseback and nights of camping outdoors after the weeks on the road, Melissande's heart ached with a pain all too real. No matter how far they traveled from France, she could not forget Lucian's confession.

She watched him race over the hills ahead of her. He had retreated to his old self since then.

Silent. Distant.

The return to his former ways made her realize how much he had changed to please her while they were in the Alps. He had talked to her, even though he found such idle chatter uncomfortable. He had listened avidly to her relate the *Odyssey* to him, asking her for more when they went for too long without consulting the book.

No sign of this Lucian remained. Once again he was a man with a mission, a warrior knight intent only on her reunion with his brother.

Lucian reined in abruptly, leading them eastward toward a small stream they'd been following all morning. Melissande caught a glimpse of his stern profile, his chiseled features.

Would he ever make peace with himself? Or would he forever feel responsible for everyone around him?

She should have offered him more comfort when he'd admitted the sin of his past. The abbess would have found just the right thing to say, dispensed the wisdom of a proverb, and helped Lucian find a way to forgive himself. But Melissande had wept freely, like the child she sometimes feared she still was. She had far too little opportunity to act on her own instincts in her life. At the convent, decisions had been made for her. So much so, that now she found it difficult to trust her own judgment.

And no doubt, this time, she had made a poor choice in not saying more to Lucian about his foster father.

They ate another afternoon meal in silence while Melissande sought the nerve to apologize. Lucian's aspect could be more intimidating than Sister Eleanor's when he was angry.

Still, she refused to play the child any longer. Gathering her courage, she cleared her throat to speak, determined to offer him what comfort she could.

Lucian bolted from his place on the grass before she had the chance. "I'm washing up," he announced, motioning to the creek nearby as he started to back away from her. "You are welcome to do the same."

Melissande nodded, but he was already striding across the clearing that looked vaguely familiar. Did they near Barret lands so that he must take time to bathe now?

Or did he simply wish to escape conversing with her?

She looked with longing at the sparkling brook, wishing she could dangle her toes in the coolness, until she spied Lucian shedding his tunic.

The vision of his muscular back imprinted itself in her memory, the way his body tapered down from broad shoulders to narrow hips…Lucian's strength had been apparent fully clothed. It was all the more obvious when stripped of his tunic. The thought niggled Melissande's conscience when she considered the time and effort he had channeled into learning his skills as a warrior, only to have her preach to him that he should turn the other cheek.

Lucian spoke truly when he said the Church called men to fight for its ideals. How could she abhor what he did when it was sanctioned by the same church to which she had dedicated her life?

Driven by guilt at her quick condemnation of him, Melissande's feet shuffled hesitantly toward the brook. The man would not have cast off all his clothing when he had specifically told her she could come to the creek with him…would he?

She sidled closer, still mulling over Lucian's past.

Osbern Fitzhugh had been a good man with a big heart until he indulged in too much ale. Melissande had seen him lose control on two separate occasions during her childhood. Why didn't the rest of Northumbria recall the man had a violent temper?

The splashing of water called her back to reality and Melissande peered down to the creek's edge.

He stood, still half-clothed, his face and hair dripping from a dousing. Her breath caught in her throat at the sight of his bare chest, perhaps even more impressive than his naked back.

She might have lost her nerve to approach him, and would have turned back, had not a twig cracked beneath some subtle movement of her foot.

His head whipped around to confront her and she glimpsed the trained warrior in the tense lines of his body. Relaxing as he spied the source of the noise, Lucian resumed dressing in the shady cover of the surrounding copse of trees.

"I am finished." He ambled over to her while slipping the tunic over his head. "You may have the creek to yourself." The fine linen clung to his wet arms. A bead of water rolled over the scar at his temple and down his cheek.

Melissande fought the urge to reach out to capture the drop with her finger. Lost in contemplation of his masculine form, she startled as he walked right by her, no doubt returning to the horses.

"Wait." She reached out to hold him back, her palm connecting with the solid expanse of his chest. "I would speak with you a moment."

He said nothing, but he waited.

The coolness of his damp body filtered through the thin linen of his tunic. She thought she should let go of him, but found she couldn't will her fingers to remove themselves. The solid strength of him fueled her courage to explain herself.

"I am afraid you took offense at my flood of tears the other night—" she hesitated, wishing she did not have to remind him of something so painful "—when you told me about Lord Fitzhugh."

His jaw set in a stony line. Still, he did not move, nor did he try to extract her hand from its intimate resting place against his heart.

"Perhaps you thought I cried in condemnation of you, but I assure you my tears only reflected the sorrow I saw in your eyes and felt as you felt. 'Tis obvious to me it was an accident. I am surprised and saddened that you cannot see it that way."

The sun shone brightly on the horses and fields beyond them, but here by the water, they were sheltered by the forgiving shade of thick trees. The darkness made confidences seems easier to share, touches simpler to offer.

"I know you would never do anything to purposely harm Lord Fitzhugh." Melissande stepped closer to him, plucking up one of his hands in her free one.

"He died in wretched pain, bewailing my cowardice to the heavens as he went." Lucian peered down at their clasped hands as if that kind of touch was utterly new to him.

"Probably delirious from blood loss." Why did it seem so logical to her while the rest of his friends and family chose to believe the worst of a good man like Lucian? "An infection may have set in his wound."

"A midwife gave him medicine to prevent infection." Lucian shook his head stubbornly. "She arrived almost immediately."

"Since when is a midwife infallible?"

"I still raised my sword and stung the fatal blow."

Melissande spied the years of self-blame and remorse in his eyes. "You raised your sword to defend yourself, Lucian! You expect yourself to have absolute control at every moment, but you are only human. No doubt you were reacting to one of Fitzhugh's fits of rage without clearly thinking through the possible consequences. And who could think intelligibly when they are being attacked by a madman?"

He tipped up her chin as if to study her more intently. With clear gray eyes, he peered down at her.

"You believe in me."

His words were not a question but a dawning realization. He squeezed her fingers in a tightening, urgent fist.

"Yes."

She would have complained on her fingers' behalf when he suddenly released her palm and pulled her fully against him, his eyes never leaving hers.

Melissande stilled. Her body crushed to his, a delicious, fevered warmth spread through her. Thinking became impossible. In the short space of an embrace, her world had narrowed to she and Lucian—a place where feelings and the senses took precedent over logic and reason.

"Lucian…" Her words faded into a kiss when his lips fell on hers in hungry demand.

In the sin of the lips lies a disastrous trap… The proverb circled through Melissande's mind, but the desire to return Lucian's kiss overwhelmed her. Would it hurt to quench the thirst for him that had been growing in her for weeks, no matter how much she tried to deny it?

Perhaps one embrace would satisfy her curiosity, ease the longing. She would return to the convent soon, after she expressed her wishes to Roarke. Melissande would never again know the feel of a man's touch.

She parted her lips in silent encouragement and was rewarded with Lucian's groan and a deepening of their kiss.

Creek water seeped from his garments into hers, suffusing her bodice with his sultry heat.

"No one has ever believed in me," he whispered between trailed kisses down her neck. When he reached the barrier of her gown, he raised his head, cupping her face in his hands. "Why you?" He fixed her with a glare that was part demand, part desperate need for affirmation.

Melissande ignored the demand and answered the need. "I've known you to be an honorable protector and a good person."

He dragged his palm down her unraveling hair and over her breasts through the clinging fabric of the green gown. "You call this honorable?"

His touch ignited the last bit of restraint she might have called upon, torching her resistance to ashes in the space of a blink. Desire kicked through her, oblivious to Lucian's sense of honor.

She refused to analyze the consequences of her actions. Shades of her former bold and brazen self roared back to life with a vengeance. She craved passion.

And she would have it.

She laid trembling hands along the squared planes of Lucian's scarred face and tilted his chin toward her.

"I know who you are, Lucian, and I believe in you."

"Angel." He sighed the word with quiet reverence and drew his fingers down the curves of her hips. "If no one else ever believes me, it is enough that you do."

She might have answered him, but the friction of his palms brushing about her waist and down her thighs jumbled her thoughts. Shivery sensations fluttered the length of her spine and through unsteady legs.

Gray eyes bore into hers with dark longing, yet Melissande could see indecision in the furrow of his brow, feel his hesitation as his hands stopped their quest.

She could not bear it if he did not continue to hold her. What would a few stolen moments hurt before they returned to civilization and left their memories of one another behind forever?

Tracing a light path up his chest with her fingertip, she admired the strength of the man, wishing her touch could banish his constraint as his touch had expelled hers.

Still she was surprised to hear herself whisper to him. "I need you, Lucian."

With a curse and a growl, he curved a hand around the back of one thigh and hauled her leg from the ground to wrap it around his body.

Melissande gasped at the intimacy. The leather of his braies skimmed the velvet of her dress, creating a sensuous slide of fabric around her legs and between her thighs. Waves of pleasure radiated from the places their bodies connected. The damp warmth of his body sealed them together, locking them in a steamy embrace.

The scent of sun-warmed leather, spring grasses and the clear stream behind them surrounded her, vibrant smells absent from her life in the convent. She couldn't absorb sensations fast enough, hungry for pleasures she'd been denying far too long.

Lucian brought his mouth down on hers, his kiss as out of control as she felt. She squeezed his shoulders, needing him to balance herself in the onslaught of new awareness she'd half imagined for weeks.

She rocked her hips against him, eager for more of the tantalizing tremor that pulsed through her at his touch. His answering groan sent shivers racing through her, infusing her with a heightened sense of her own feminine power.

He wanted her—wanted this—as much as she did.

Fire took hold of her belly, her legs. She couldn't fool herself into thinking she would be satisfied with a few stolen moments any longer. Curiosity and desire demanded to discover where this tantalizing trail would lead.

She ventured one palm beneath his tunic to smooth over the muscles of his chest.

"Angel…Mel…" Lucian's whispered words wound through her thoughts, his voice hoarse and anguished.

She pressed kisses to his corded neck, the soft fur exposed by the open ties of his tunic.

The needy flames consuming her were too strong to fathom retreat now. Whatever secrets Lucian's body harbored, Melissande was determined to extract them.

"Please," she whispered, not knowing what she asked for but certain Lucian would.

Lucian lowered her body to the pine-needle-covered ground, murmuring words of encouragement, promises that he would protect her.

Had she ever doubted it?

Although somewhere in her brain, a small voice entreated her to use caution, Melissande trusted Lucian more than she trusted herself. Not only would he never hurt her, he knew how to give her body the most pleasure it had ever experienced.

With each new kiss, each caress, she found increasing fulfillment. And with each touch, the stakes raised for the next one, leading her to believe a shimmering goal of pleasure awaited her at the end of this sensual journey.

With clever hands, Lucian untied laces and released garters until she lay half naked beneath him.

She waited for his caress to resume, the moist heat of his mouth to possess her body again.

Nothing.

Melissande propped an eye open to find him staring at her, his gaze absorbing every detail of her bared body.

No one else had ever seen her body since her childhood, though Sister Eleanor had often chastened Melissande for her less than spare figure.

Curving a hand around one of her breasts, Lucian traced its shape. "To think you hid this body under a nun's habit."

The reverent brush of his hand and open admiration erased a decade's worth of Sister Eleanor's disparaging comments.

Eager to feel his strength upon her once again, she tugged him down to resume their kiss.

Only now his gentle explorations were unencumbered by clothing. His lips did not have to hesitate at a neckline. They journeyed down her breasts, the rough texture of his unshaven chin grazing over her tender skin moments before the flick of his tongue eased the burning path.

Immersed in the scent and feel of him, Melissande allowed no thought to mar her pleasure in his touch. His mouth moved to tease and to taste the crests of one breast, and she moaned with the pure joy of it.

"Lucian…" Sighing his name, reveling in the way it sounded, she twisted her frustrated fingers in his tunic. She wanted to feel more of him, to experience the texture of his body without barrier.

Barely removing his lips from her skin, he worked the tunic over his head and flung it aside.

Equally tempted to look as to feel, Melissande settled for a quick peek at the lightly curled hair on his chest that narrowed into a thin line and disappeared into his braies.

He was beautiful. Despite the numerous scars his bare body revealed, his body was perfect in Melissande's eyes. Hardened by battle, honed with practice, his warrior form epitomized the tenacious spirit of Lucian Barret.

And the danger.

But he had shown her he did not kill without remorse. His choice to go to war was dictated by penance, not by bloodlust.

Melissande wrapped one leg around him to bring him even closer, needing to reassure herself that Lucian could be as tender as he could be dangerous.

She hungered to possess some small part of him, the tender and the dangerous, the scholar and warrior.

His fingers traced a pattern up her inner thigh, his nails grazing her delicate flesh. A curious tension spread through her body and heated her skin, converging in an overwhelming ache between her legs.

She wrapped her hand around the reassuring strength of his arm, waiting for the touch she craved, hoping it would somehow relieve the knot twisting inside her.

When his fingers met the juncture of her thighs, Melissande cried out, scoring his back with her nails. Pleasure knifed through her with a keen edge.

Capturing her cries with his mouth, Lucian kissed her, all the while manipulating the most secret part of her. He whispered to her as he touched her, words both sweet and seductive, as he lulled her nearer to some shimmering destination of pleasure.

The knot inside Melissande tightened and grew. Her mouth watered for the fulfillment he could bring. A fevered flush spread through her body, until at last, one finger slid inside her.

She screamed her response to the heavens, waves of heat breaking over her body again and again, until she was naught but heartbeat and trembling flesh.

With each pound of blood through her veins, she rejoiced at the wonder and joy of Lucian. She had no idea the relations between man and woman would be so utterly fulfilling.

His head pillowed by her breasts, his breath warmed her body in the aftermath of their lovemaking. Melissande ran idle fingers through his hair, wondering how her convent sisters could have complained of the burden of marriage when this was the sort of pleasure it brought.

At the same time, Melissande recalled she was not married.

What had she done?

She gazed down at her exposed body entwined with Lucian's near-nakedness. They would have no choice but to wed now.

They had obviously committed the ultimate act of intimacy. Melissande knew from whisperings she overheard at the convent that once a woman's body was pierced by a man, she had lost her innocence forever.

Could Lucian see it? Would a stranger be able to look at her and know she had just been initiated into womanhood?

Lucian raised himself over her, looking far less sated than she felt. Hunger flared in his eyes as he leaned down to kiss her. His body seemed to come alive against her as he moved, nudging her thigh and belly in the strangest manner.

"Lucian?" she began tentatively, hating to spoil the wonder of what they just shared, but desperate to clarify what this new turn in their relationship meant. She cupped his face in her palm, needing him to look at her. "We are not even married."

He released her as if her body was suddenly poisonous, rolling off her to lay by her side some feet away.

Melissande mourned the loss of his touch although she still felt as if a glow must be apparent all around her.

She hated to end their time together here, but knew a church should sanctify their union. In her heart, she was certain Lucian felt the same way.

"You understand, don't you—" she ventured.

"Of course," he shot back, the words surprisingly sharp for how intimate they had just been.

Melissande reached for her clothing, trying not to sound as stung as she felt. "I just think—"

"I know." He wiped a weary hand across his brow. "It is fortunate one of us came to our senses." This time he softened his words, his voice sounding as tortured as she felt.

It was not in his nature to talk things over to the degree that Melissande liked to. She should be accustomed to his uncommunicative ways.

He sounded sincere enough, anyway, and Melissande thought he must understand the need for him to wed her at once. Now that they had been intimate, there was no choice.

She watched him dress, wondering if he felt the same glow through his body that she experienced. It didn't seem that lovemaking could possibly yield as much pleasure for a man as for a woman.

"I am ready," she said finally, surprised how eager she suddenly felt to get back on the horses and find a place to wed Lucian.

She thought she would never marry or have children—

An abrupt pang stung her heart at the thought of the abbey orphans. Once she married Lucian, she could never go back to them.

A baby of her own would be a blessing. Indeed she had nurtured a secret dream for one all her life, yet even a child of her flesh and blood could not erase the memory of the three she already loved.

Trudging through the small wooded area, Melissande watched their dear faces swim through her memory. What if she could still help them? Write to them, watch over them from afar? Indeed, she would pen them a missive immediately to ease their minds, and maybe Lucian would permit her to send them each a fund to start their lives away from the abbey when they grew to adulthood.

Or…what if she could adopt the children herself?

Her mind bounded forward with the possibilities as she followed Lucian from the copse of trees. He walked so quickly that she was encouraged he was as eager as she to speak their vows and return to their former occupation.

A flush of pleasure stole through her, followed quickly by old fears and doubts. Was she even capable of being a good mother to those children? In the convent, there had been others to help her raise them, other women for the children to love. But she would be on her own with them if she could convince Lucian to bring them to England. Would the upheaval in their lives only upset them?

Heaven knew she had been beside herself when her parents had turned her life upside down to bring her to the abbey. She'd had so little experience being mothered herself, what if she couldn't perform the task well? She couldn't bear the breakup of another family. Not after the loss of her own at a tender age.

They faced each other for a moment when they reached the horses. Lucian's expression creased in worry. And although Melissande still felt the resonant joy of their lovemaking, she knew her face must reflect her fears.

His hands shook ever so slightly as he lifted Melissande onto her mount. He deposited her there with unnecessary hurry, as far as she was concerned.

Something seemed wrong. Even if he was unhappy about their thwarted passion, he should still care for her solicitously. Especially after what just transpired between them.

"We must hurry to make Barret Keep by nightfall," he called over his shoulder, not even sparing a backward glance in her direction.

"We will still go to your brother's?" Melissande had rather hoped they would find a chapel and spend the night at an inn. It struck her as awkward to go to the home where Roarke resided. No doubt he would be angry to find Lucian had wed the woman he wanted to marry.

"Where else would we go?" He kicked his horse into motion, apparently unconcerned over her response.

Maybe he was right. She understood why he would want to be surrounded by family for a wedding. With any luck, he would not be so surly by the time they reached the end of their journey.

Despite the worries churning through her mind, her body still hummed from the pleasure Lucian had owed with his lips and hands. What would it be like to indulge in such passion night after night?

Melissande had not allowed herself to think about marriage in years. Even when Lucian abducted her to wed Roarke, she had not considered it for a moment. Returning to the safety of the convent and the duty of helping the children were more important to her than passion.

But now it seemed she no longer had a choice. She and Lucian had shared the intimacy of husband and wife. They must wed. Would Lucian wield all the power in their marriage the way her father had always been able to overrule her mother? She remembered too well that it had been her father's decision to send her to the abbey despite her mother's objections. And of course, he had his way in the end. She couldn't abide the idea of being overruled. Ignored.

At least in the convent she had learned methods for obtaining her own way on occasion. Perhaps with Lucian, she would not be so fortunate. Her mind reeled with adjustments to her life's new plans in light of the afternoon's events.

In fact, she thought so hard and so much, she didn't even realize they had entered Barret lands until Lucian shouted to her that the keep was in sight.

Odd, his voice still sounded remote these hours later. Perhaps Lucian was merely nervous at the prospect of confronting his brother with the news of their nuptials.

Roarke was sure to be mad.

As they drew up to the main courtyard, Melissande's heart filled with nostalgia. She had so many fond memories of playing here, in the surrounding forest and orchard, and along the riverbank that lay between the Barret and the Deverell holdings.

A sprawling affair, Barret Keep had been constructed in several phases since the Norman invasion. A stout, round keep was flanked by high walks and intermittent watch towers. The stone edifice loomed dull and gray until the sun lit the surface just right and highlighted hidden sparkles in the dark rock. Much larger than the small holding she had grown up in, the Barrets were a more powerful family. Lucian would properly be her father's overlord now if her father still lived.

"Did one of my sisters move into Deverell Keep?" she asked, wishing she'd had a brother who could have inherited the inviting property. She had always been so happy there.

"Nay. The king told Roarke that he would reassign it. It has been vacant for some years." Lucian flung his leg over the saddle and leaped from the horse.

Frowning, Melissande allowed Lucian to help her down. Suddenly self-conscious of her appearance, she tried to tighten her braid and to dust their travels, along with a few pine needles, from her skirts.

Already striding toward the main entrance, Lucian called over his shoulder. "I wouldn't worry about how you look, Mel. Roarke will be thrilled to see you no matter how I deliver you."

His comment unsettled her. It seemed a very inappropriate thing to say. She hurried to catch up with him, wanting a moment to speak to him before Roarke discovered their arrival.

Although she called out to him, he opened the main door as if he had not heard her. Doubly annoyed, she nearly ran to reach his side.

Two servants greeted Lucian immediately, apologizing for not noting his appearance earlier.

Now the picture of chivalrous concern, Lucian extended his arm to her as he waited in the archway, although Melissande noted his eyes held no warmth. She took his arm, but silently fumed at him, frustrated they would have no time to talk privately before facing Roarke.

What would they say to him? How should she behave? Would Lucian expect her to contribute to the discussion?

Her fears converged into panic as a towering, princely man with striking green eyes strode toward them into the hall.

Roarke.

There was no mistaking the man she had adored as a child. Those green eyes had always struck her as sensitive, inviting as a spring day. The arrogance still lurked in the set of his chin, the proud tilt of his nose.

Only now as she stared at the brothers with a woman's eyes did it occur to her how different they looked. From the color of their eyes to the way they carried themselves, the Barret men bore no shared physical traits to mark them as kin. As handsome as Roarke might be, Melissande couldn't wait to escape his company. Surely he had turned out to be a fine man, but she could only think of Lucian and what had passed between them earlier in the day. She inched closer to Lucian, needing to feel his strength beside her.

"You are well come, my brother." He bowed low to them both, but turned his bright green gaze on Melissande. "As are you, Melissande. The years find you more beautiful than my fondest imaginings."

To her discomfort, Lucian released her. Indeed, the brute nudged her forward toward Roarke.

Faltering for words, she merely curtsied.

Apparently that was not enough for Roarke. He picked up her hand to hold it gently in his and, raising her palm to his lips, kissed her.

Why didn't Lucian say something?

She turned around to glare at him, hoping she conveyed her

confusion and desperation in her expression. This was not proceeding at all as she'd envisioned.

"Welcome to my home, Melissande." Roarke smiled, his white teeth as perfect as in childhood. "I hope you will be very happy here."

She wanted to scream at him that Barret Keep belonged to Lucian, as did she, but she knew it was not her place. Mutely, she allowed Roarke to take her arm and to draw her to his side.

Her heart beat wildly. She now stood at Roarke's side, staring across the hall at Lucian, who should be saying something any moment to clarify this mess…

"Brother." Lucian cleared his throat and met Roarke's gaze. "It has cost me more than I ever imagined to deliver your wife to you."

Melissande knew her mouth fell wide open, but for all the world, she could not shut it. Betrayal slammed her in the belly.

Lucian's jaw clenched. "Now that I've abducted a convent-bred novitiate and risked her life and limb as well as my own so she might be your bride, I consider my debt to you well paid."

His cruelty, his callousness astounded her. How could he hand her over to his brother, when only a few hours ago they had lain sprawled together in a haze of passion, baring their bodies and souls to one another?

If she lived to be one hundred, Melissande would never forgive him.

Chapter Fifteen

Lucian could live to be as old as Methuselah and still not forget the anguish in Melissande's eyes when he'd given her into his brother's care.

He glared into the cold grate in his room at Barret Keep and reminded himself she had never wanted to marry, had never wanted to leave St. Ursula's. He'd forced her here anyway. Surely that betrayal accounted for the hurt in her gaze and not any regret she couldn't be with Lucian.

To think otherwise would be foolish.

He had departed the hall in haste after that, muttering some rubbish about allowing Roarke and Melissande to get acquainted again. In truth, he couldn't bear to see them together.

Now, Lucian paced the bedchamber of his boyhood with determined strides, wondering what the reunited couple discussed belowstairs.

Or maybe they did not talk. Maybe Roarke wasted no time sealing his bargain with his soon-to-be wife and even now initiated her into knowledge of her wifely duties.

The thought turned Lucian's gut to ice. If not for divine intervention, Melissande would belong to Lucian right now instead of his brother.

Damn.

Lucian would have taken her innocence then and there, on the cold hard ground in the middle of nowhere, if she had not reminded him she didn't belong to him.

We are not even married.

At the time, Lucian's passion-fogged brain had thought, for one brief instant, that she wanted the sanction of marriage upon them before he consummated their union. He had immediately started plotting where he could take his angel to make her his for all time.

Several long moments had passed before he recalled she was promised to another and no doubt meant her words as a rebuff.

On the remaining ride to Barret Keep, he'd thanked God that he had not gone so far as to despoil her. A miracle had saved him from destroying her innocence and shattering his brother's trust.

Could he help it if a part of him cursed the fact that he had come to his senses? If their relationship had been consummated this afternoon, Lucian would be wedding her tomorrow. Or tonight.

He would be warming the linens with Melissande now instead of fuming in this cold, sterile chamber by himself. With every fiber of his being he wished such were the case.

And damn it, not just because his feelings were a knot of lust for her siren's body. No, somewhere on the road between St. Ursula's and Barret Keep, Lucian had fallen in love with Melissande Deverell.

Hard.

He sank into the room's one chair and allowed his head to

fall into his hands. Closing his eyes, he envisioned her, not wide-eyed with betrayal as she had been tonight, but smiling and chattering as she had on their journey to England.

Perhaps he'd first started to love her when she'd built the fire on her own the first night they camped outdoors. She had been so proud…and so quick to credit him with teaching her the skill. The fact that she even recalled moments shared as youths had warmed his heart.

Her passion for reading had further entranced him. He could pass hours listening to her musical voice and inflections for various characters as she spun tales from around the world.

The woman read Greek, for chrissake. What was not to love?

Above all, she believed in him.

The knowledge awed and humbled him. His angel had offered her faith to him at no cost. Freely, she gave him her trust.

And he had betrayed it beyond repair by giving her to a man she had no wish to wed.

The ache in his heart speared his whole body.

Dragging restless fingers through his hair, he gave up trying to think through the tangle of the day's events and emotions. Sleep was out of the question. Perhaps a ride would help. Anything to get out of Barret Keep—and away from Melissande.

Securing his sword to his hip, Lucian stormed from the chamber. Down the main stairs and across the hall, he kept his eyes trained on the front door that would deliver him from Melissande.

"You would steal away in the night like a thief?" A whispered feminine voice called to him from the shadows.

For a moment he thought—hoped—it was his conscience that spoke. Then a woman stepped from the recesses of the hall, clothed in a white linen wrapper.

Guilt and desire warred within him.

Lucian grabbed her by the arms before he realized the torture simply touching her could wreak. "What are you doing out here? Have you no sense?" She was scarcely dressed for greeting strangers.

Anger emanated from her slight form. "I could not sleep for fear you'd sneak away before I could speak with you." She glared at him with more venom than a serpent's tooth. "I am appalled my fears were well placed."

She seemed to wait for him to speak, perhaps make some excuse for fulfilling his bargain with Roarke despite her wishes. He could not.

"You are angry."

"Furious." Her red hair leaped like hungry flames around her shoulders. Lucian had not seen it undone since…this afternoon.

He recalled the taste of her kisses, the sound of her breathy gasps as if they had just embraced. "You did not think I would really bring you here."

"Not after what happened by the creek." Her hands fisted at her sides.

That caught him off guard. Had she sought to manipulate him through her kisses? She had been the one to initiate a conversation, to touch him. "You hoped that…incident… would make me turn around and take you back to St. Ursula's?"

Judging from the way her eyes grew round as carriage wheels, Lucian guessed not. Her mouth hung open as she gaped at him. "No, Lucian." She shook her head, brow furrowed. "I thought that what happened between us counted as something very intimate."

He could not bear a discussion of their familiarity. Not now when she stood mere inches from him, her body unencumbered by a formal gown, her hair freed to his gaze.

Seeing his lack of response, she pressed forward, crossing her arms defiantly over her chest.

The gesture thrust her breasts provocatively forward. Lucian fought to concentrate on her words.

She bit her lip for a split second, then launched ahead. "I thought that when a man touches a woman in such a manner, it constituted a marriage proposal."

The blow that put a lifelong scar on Lucian's temple had not struck so deep as her accusation.

"What are you saying?" Did he want to know? Didn't he already know, in the deepest recesses of his heart?

"That you are not the man I thought you were, Lucian Barret, if you could so carelessly make love to me, then toss me aside for your brother to wed." Tears glittered in her eyes, though she fairly shook with fury.

"But we did nothing to prevent you from—"

"Nothing?" She threw her arms in the air, then let them fall with a hard thud against her thighs. "You have no honor if you can touch me as a husband touches a wife, then marry me off to someone else. And the fact that you would skulk from the keep in the middle of the night to avoid explaining yourself adds to your wretchedness."

Had she thought they made love? She was so innocent. Chances were she knew naught of what went on between husband and wife.

If Melissande said he was wretched, then by God, he had sinned indeed. Hadn't she been his most stalwart supporter up until now? "I never thought you would want—"

"Exactly." She raised her chin, proud and unbending. "You never gave a thought to me and how I might feel. Heaven forbid you should actually ask me. To do so would require conversing, which you seem to find abhorrent."

"I am not worthy of someone like you, Melissande." He longed to place his hands upon her shoulders and to lower her to a bench for a more civil conversation, but dared not risk touching her. He might never let go.

"Only because you won't allow yourself to be worthy, Lucian." A hint of compassion fluttered through her eyes, though not nearly enough to outweigh her anger. "You are too consumed with your own guilt to free yourself from it."

How could he make her see he had made the best decision? How could she think for a moment she would have been happy tied to a known murderer who had given up his home and title to hide from the truth of what he was? "Roarke is a good man."

He recognized the look in her eyes. She had possessed it once before, just before she had slugged him.

But this was a more mature Melissande. She settled for shaking her head in clear disdain. "So are you, Lucian, but it is obvious you do not want me or the trouble it would require to wed me. I will not marry your brother, however. Even if what we shared means nothing to you, you have made it impossible for me to marry another man."

Her words pummeled him with more force than any fist. He reeled from the blow, unsure how to respond without a full-scale discussion of what true intimacy between man and woman involved.

In a more honorable world, however, perhaps Melissande had the right of it. Even if he had not ruined her according to the letter of the law, he had stolen something precious. Something he had no right to.

"I will return to the convent as soon as Roarke can arrange a suitable escort." She cleared her throat, regaining a measure of the reserve all the years of convent breeding had pounded into her.

Having spoken her peace, she whirled away from him in a blur of white linen and red hair.

Lucian watched her ascend the stairs, her determined stride never pausing.

He struggled to orient himself, to regain his wits in the wake of her confrontation. Recovering from battles with the infidel had not been so taxing.

With more reason than ever to depart Barret Keep, Lucian pushed open the main door and stepped into the sultry night air. There was naught but recrimination and unhappiness left for him here.

He would return to the one place he was useful, the only place where his brutality and unworthiness were fortuitous qualities.

While Melissande tried to argue her way out of marriage to Roarke, Lucian would begin his journey back to the battlefield.

Roarke did not seem the least bit surprised that Lucian departed in the middle of the night without saying goodbye. He told Melissande as much each day when she raised the question of Lucian's whereabouts over supper. Their daily ritual was to argue first about where Lucian had gone and then about the wedding that Roarke wanted and Melissande did not.

So far they had reached no definitive conclusions on either matter.

Roarke claimed his elder brother had left because he wouldn't want to confront their mother, a feat Lucian apparently found difficult since Osbern Fitzhugh's death.

Melissande feared Lucian had left because of her. He might never come back.

Left to her own devices much of the day at Barret Keep, she spent her afternoons in the gardens or in the orchards, often traveling the riverside path that would eventually lead to her family's former holding.

As she wandered aimlessly down the trail for the umpteenth time in a fortnight, Melissande seethed that he could leave her behind so easily.

And, heaven help her, she missed him.

Melissande had enjoyed her first true friendship with Lucian. In fact, Lucian had been her best friend before she'd entered St. Ursula's. There had always been some sort of mutual empathy between them. Now there was a layer of attraction in their friendship that made Lucian's absence all the more painful for her.

Could she love him?

The question lurked in the corners of her mind and leaped out at her when she least expected it. The notion scared her to her toes, maybe because it seemed entirely possible.

Yet it struck her as wrong for a woman who had been a few weeks away from taking her final vows as a nun to fall in love with a man so fast, so simply.

When she had been on the brink of marrying Lucian, or so she thought, she had rationalized the nuptials as inescapable.

But now that Roarke wanted to wed her, Melissande protested at every turn. She cared for Lucian, more than she could admit even now, whereas she didn't feel anything but mild fondness for Roarke.

Turning back once she reached the halfway point on the path, Melissande plucked wildflowers with absent fingers.

She might like Roarke better if he had not accepted Lucian's offer of title and lands in exchange for his cooperation in keeping the details of Fitzhugh's death secret from their mother.

Why didn't Roarke have more faith in his brother's motives? Roarke sounded as though he believed the worst from the very beginning. Had he intended to enhance the view of Lucian as a murderer to put himself in a better social and financial position?

The questions niggled Melissande the longer she stayed at Barret Keep, and they couldn't be denied any longer. She resolved to learn more about the events surrounding Osbern Fitzhugh's death and the ones that followed.

Even though Lucian had handed her off to his brother without so much as a farewell, Melissande knew she owed the man more than she could repay for saving her life in the Alps and protecting her the whole way home. He had given her a taste of the bittersweet joy a man's touch could bring a woman— a gift she knew to be precious even if he thought nothing of it. Indeed, she owed Lucian simply for opening her eyes to the world and to herself.

In return, she could delve into the details of Lord Fitzhugh's death to uncover whatever truths might be buried there. It was high time she asserted herself. Instead of passively accepting everyone else's vision for her and her future, Melissande would forge her own plans and exercise her choices.

Feeling fully alive and almost happy for the first time since she'd arrived at Barret Keep, Melissande hurried home with skipping steps. Ticking off a mental list of people she wanted to talk to when she got back, she was so distracted she almost missed the uproar in the courtyard when she arrived.

One of the servants called out to her before she reached the main doors, however. Turning toward the voice, she noticed a small crowd of castle folk engrossed in conversation, including Roarke.

"Yes?" She walked toward them with slow steps, a foreboding growing at the dark look on Roarke's face.

A man-at-arms with foreign colors stood among them, sweaty and dirty as if from a hard ride.

Roarke clenched his jaw and took a deep breath. For a fleeting moment, the hard aspect of his face made him look like his brother.

He called to her. "It's Lucian."

She hastened the rest of the way over. "Is he all right?"

"He's been shot, Melissande. An arrow in the chest."

The world swayed around her, but Melissande bit the inside of her cheek to take her mind off the swirling queasiness that threatened. She could not faint now. "Is he…?"

"He's not expected to live."

As if an arrow pierced her own heart, the words sliced right through her. It couldn't be true. She lashed out at the nearest target, too overwhelmed with pain to harbor it all within herself. "How convenient that will be for you."

Roarke blanched. The crowd of servants gasped.

"If he dies, you will never have to worry about Lucian claiming what is rightfully his." She referred only to herself as a bride, but Melissande knew everyone else would interpret her words as an accusation that Roarke stole Lucian's earldom. She did not care.

"I am sure you are overwrought, Melissande," he declared through gritted teeth, scowling at the servants until they dispersed with the wind. "You obviously have no idea what you are talking about."

"Where is he?" How could she waste time being petty when Lucian could still be alive?

The man-at-arms stepped forward. "On my lord Wesley's holding close to the French crossing, my lady. He lays in naught but an abandoned crofter's cottage. We were loathe to move a man so wounded."

"You will accompany me there." She turned to the groom, ignoring Roarke's spluttered objections. "My horse, please, and do not dally. Mary," she called to a young maid, "would you retrieve the large book in my chamber and whatever healing supplies the keep maintains, please?"

Satisfied to see both the boy and maid depart with all speed, Melissande spun on Roarke. "I have no choice, my lord. He saved me from death, and now I must do the same for him."

He looked as if he would argue, but Melissande plowed forward, refusing to back down.

"You wouldn't want it said that you aided in your brother's death by not lifting a finger to help him, would you?"

His mouth flattened to a thin line. "I will bring someone to relieve you this evening."

"We need a physician." She shifted her attention to the man-at-arms. "Has someone ridden for one?"

Roarke intervened. "There is no one, my lady. Our last midwife left after—" he eyed her warily "—after Fitzhugh died."

"There must be someone." She knew nothing of nursing. The thought that she alone could be responsible for Lucian's life or death shook her resolve.

"Here's your horse, my lady," the groom called just as Roarke assured her there was no medical help in the area.

Swallowing her panic, Melissande waved forward the maid who used both hands to carry the massive copy of the *Odyssey*.

She would save Lucian.

She must.

Maybe then she could return to the abbey with a clear conscience, knowing she had given back to Lucian a portion of what he had given to her.

The thought gave her little comfort as she rode to his aid.

Chapter Sixteen

Lucian hauled in another sharp breath, knowing he would not live this time. He had escaped death often enough in the past two years to realize he could no longer run from his fate.

The abandoned hut he lay in seemed an appropriate place to die. Cheerless. Alone.

After leaving Melissande he'd spent time gathering his supplies for another trip abroad. He'd been prepared to sail for the continent today, ready to leave England behind him. Justice may have been served this morn when Chadsworth's arrow had finally hit true to its mark, yet Lucian experienced none of the relief he had once anticipated.

He had always been prepared to pay for Osbern Fitzhugh's life with his own. Now that the time had come, however, Lucian felt an overwhelming urge to live.

Melissande had made him want to live again.

Thoughts of her plagued him. His callous manner of passing her along to his brother had upset her, and with good reason. Lucian wished he could go back to remove the look of betrayal from her eyes.

How could a woman as fine and pure as Melissande want

him, with a soul as tainted as Cain's, when she could wed his upstanding younger brother? Lucian couldn't have offered for her. Could he?

The question tormented him more than the searing pain in his chest as he lay on the cold dirt floor of the shelter. He had lost the chance to make her his forever, and now it would never be regained. He wondered if she would mourn his passing.

The rhythmic drum of a horse's hooves shook the ground and interrupted his thoughts.

Perhaps his brother…

Nay. A feminine voice trilled on the summer breeze, sweet and musical as it called to him.

Melissande.

As if he conjured her there by thinking of her, she appeared in the doorway, half running, half tripping into the dim interior of the hut.

Lucian's eyes, well adjusted to the amount of light, could discern her clearly. She carried her copy of the *Odyssey* as she groped her way around the room, searching for him. Curiosity pricked his increasingly hazy mind. Why the hell would she bring a book to his deathbed?

Her hand stumbled over his elbow.

"Lucian!" Tossing the magnificent volume aside, she fell to the floor beside him. She ran her hands gingerly along his still form, certainly because she searched his body for injury and not out of the desire to touch him.

"You came." The effort to speak stung, bitter and metallic in his throat, but not for the world could he lay there in silence while the woman of his dreams manifested before him.

She peered down at him as if surprised at his words, her questing fingers pausing in their work. "I heard your wound could be fatal, Lucian."

"Not for a matter of hours, I'll warrant."

She gasped at his pronouncement, then resumed her tentative inspection of his body, blinking back tears when she reached the pile of soaked rags just above his breastbone. "I will save you."

Her tears wrenched his heart. He did not deserve them. Could not bear to witness them.

"Do not bother, Angel." He grabbed her wrist, unwilling to have her waste energy or emotions on a death that had long been destined.

"Nonsense." She grabbed a wineskin from around her neck, paying him no heed. "I can save you."

"My time of reckoning has arrived." He released her arm to swat away the wineskin.

"You can do your reckoning alive as well as dead, Lucian Barret. Argue the point as much as you want, but you will do it as I sew you together." Her brown eyes lit with an internal flame, though her voice still quivered with her tears.

Melissande scrambled away to gather the wineskin he'd tossed aside. When she returned, she seemed more resolved, more determined than ever. She wiped a stray tear from her cheek. "I brought water in this. You do not have another, containing something stronger perhaps?"

"Aye." Sighing, he tugged at another pouch near his hip. He didn't have the strength to argue with Melissande on his best days. What made him think he could win a debate with her when he lay here half dead? "I will need it if you plan to wield a needle."

"Sorry. Your wound needs it more." She pulled out the stopper from the pouch and poured the contents over the injury.

Lucian could not prevent the wince of his body, but no sound escaped his throat.

"I read it in a medical text I translated," Melissande offered, her voice vaguely apologetic. "'Twill clean it."

Her words sounded blurred and far away to his ears. The alcohol in his wound had nudged him a few steps closer to unconsciousness. He wanted to talk to her, tried to speak, but pain engulfed him.

Through fading eyesight, he watched Melissande lean over his body, several strands of her hair slipping loose from its knot to fall on his chest in a silken curl.

Her breath came in light puffs over his wound as she concentrated with her needle and thread, poised to begin stitching.

When had she become so dear to him?

If he had possessed the strength, he would have drawn her head to his heart and rested it there. In his last moments of consciousness, he wished for nothing so much as to hold her one last time.

Doubt niggled the back of Melissande's brain as she tried to decide how to go about sewing a man's skin. Every other Deverell woman knew how to wield a needle. Her sisters had all been experts, but they were scattered to the four winds now, all of them married to men whose keeps were many leagues distant.

Melissande had not sewn a stitch since early childhood. As soon as the convent discovered her facility with languages, they had put her to work in the scriptorium as much of the day as possible.

Now that she no longer resided at St. Ursula's and must face real life, it amazed her how much practical education she lacked.

"It may hurt a bit," she warned him.

God help me. She prayed as she jabbed the needle into Lucian's skin, but he did not even twitch.

"Lucian?" For one horrific instant she thought he was dead. But the pulse at his neck still throbbed weakly.

Relieved he did not feel the pain of her handiwork, Melissande stitched him up quickly. Even after she finished, she continued to apply pressure to the wound, hoping that might quell the bleeding.

Hours after her fingers grew numb and night had fallen, Roarke arrived at the hut, a maid from Barret Keep in tow.

Melissande watched him struggle to see her in the dim light.

"Melissande?" He eased forward, feeling his way around the darkness to find her.

He was a good man, she decided, if a little misguided. Although he should have been beside Lucian earlier in the day, at least Roarke kept his promise and had come this eve.

"I am here," she called, not moving from her place at Lucian's side.

The maid lit a taper then, raining light and shadow upon their heads.

Roarke knelt beside her, his forehead creased with worry. "Are you all right?"

She nodded, too heartsick and weary to say more.

"Is he…?"

"He lives." For the moment. "He will live," she said more fiercely, refusing to allow Lucian's dire condition to predict his death.

"I have brought Isabel to stay the night with him." He took Melissande's arm. "You may come home with me and rest now."

She remained immobile, her fingers staunchly pressed against Lucian's chest. "I am happy to have Isabel stay with me, my lord, but I will not leave until your brother is healed."

"Think of what people will say." Roarke lowered his voice, his head bowed conspiratorially next to hers. "Surely you cannot mean to spend another night with my brother now that our nuptials have been declared."

"I mean to sit here until Lucian is out of danger—" she gave him a level gaze "—regardless of what people say."

Changing tactics, Roarke raised his head and peered down his nose at her. "As my future wife, Melissande, you will do what pleases me. I expect you to return with me tonight." Then, more gently, he added, "I will bring you back in the morning after you have rested."

She would not change her mind no matter what he said, but it surprised Melissande how vehemently she opposed his dictum of "You will do what pleases me." Hadn't she tried in vain to please him as a child, only to be teased and sent on fool's errands for him? Hadn't she been trying to please the sisters of St. Ursula's for years now? In return, the majority of them resented her friendship with the abbess or struck out at her blatantly like Sister Eleanor.

What had been the point of her endless efforts to please?

She peered down at Lucian. He had not expected her to please him. He had been happy to find pleasure in the things that suited her—like reading or, on rare occasions, talking.

"I will not attempt to please you on this matter, Roarke. I do not wish to wed you, and I will not turn my back on my heart to fulfill your commands. After Lucian is well, I wish to return to the convent."

His mouth gaped wide, though it emitted no sound.

"I am sorry I could not comply with your wishes."

He drew himself up to his full height. "You will change your mind about leaving, Melissande. We are to wed within a fortnight."

"I have never agreed to marry you."

Roarke argued the point while she tended his brother.

Melissande ate a few bites of the supper Isabel had brought her and tried to quiet him so Lucian might rest peacefully.

"Why does it matter so much to you who you marry, Roarke?" she asked finally. He could wed almost anyone with his position as earl.

Roarke tugged a weary hand through his golden-brown hair. "Lucian always fancied you to be Countess Barret. Once he gave the title to me and swore he'd never marry…"

"Lucian swore not to marry?" Why hadn't he ever told her? Was that why he did not ask for her hand after their dalliance by the creek?

"Aye. 'Twould no doubt set our heirs at odds if he were to have children. Any lad of Lucian's might feel compelled to take back Barret Keep."

"As well he should," Melissande muttered. Lucian was evidently too muddle-headed to right the mess he had made of things.

Her mind strayed back to Roarke's earlier comment… something about Lucian fancying her for a countess. She sifted through the bits of information she had, trying to force the pieces into order. "So you want to marry me, because Lucian once wanted to marry me?"

Roarke pinched the bridge of his nose as if to relieve a pain in his head. "I thought it would ease his heart to see you in the place he had once envisioned for you."

"You thought to please him by taking to wife someone he had once admired?" Could Roarke be so stupid? Somehow she didn't think so. "Or…perhaps you thought Lucian would be less likely to change his mind about granting you the title if you were to marry a woman he respected."

Roarke's grimace gave her all the answers she needed.

"Good God, Roarke, you have bumbled this." She hoped

God might forgive her for taking His name in vain this one time. Roarke's foolishness seemed to warrant an oath.

He covered his eyes with his palms, rubbing the heels of his hands into the sockets. "At some point, I really thought I was doing the right thing."

"The moment you realized you were not, you should have stopped." How could the Barret brothers have gone so far astray in her absence? They had both changed so much in ten years.

They had obviously done a lot more living than she had. Perhaps it was easy to judge from the comfortable position of a bystander.

"Mother died six months ago," he confided. "I did not tell Lucian until he returned home with you. But she babbled incoherently at the end. Spoke of things that could not be true." Roarke closed his eyes. Swallowed. When he stared at her once again, dark secrets lurked in his gaze. "I didn't think Lucian needed that burden, too. I let him think she passed peacefully in her sleep a few weeks ago."

"I am sorry." She patted his arm with her free hand. *All the more reason he is in a hurry to wed.* Without the threat of Lucian's mother learning the truth, Roarke probably feared his brother would try to take the earldom back.

"I hate to lose the rest of my family." He gestured toward Lucian, and his big hand trembled just slightly. "Did he say who shot him?"

For the first time, Melissande saw the love he bore his brother. "Nay. I did not think to ask."

"Did you see the arrow?" He peered around the dark room, lifting the taper Isabel had set on the floor.

"Nay, I—"

Holding the object aloft, Roarke had already discovered it. Melissande gasped. She recognized it immediately. "'Tis the same as an arrow launched at him while we journeyed here, only…"

Roarke frowned. "Someone shot at my brother in the Alps?"

"Aye. But Lucian already killed the shooter. I saw him—" What had she seen, precisely? Lucian hitting a man in the head with a sword.

"Yes?"

There could be no mistaking the black-feathered arrow with its red markings on the shaft. Identical to the one in France, it could have only come from the man who'd targeted them abroad. But why would Lucian have allowed her to think he had killed the man, if he had not done so?

The answer sprang to mind almost before she finished formulating the question. It had to be part of Lucian's web of penance, his quest for the world to recognize the depths of his sins.

"Lucian made it appear as though he killed the shooter, but he obviously just knocked the man unconscious to give us time to get away." Shaken by the realization, Melissande swallowed a wave of fervent regret he had not ended the assassin's life. Perhaps deep within her she possessed a bit of warrior's spirit, as well. "Unfortunately, he protected me, but did not bother to protect himself."

Roarke tucked the arrow into the leather band that encircled his waist and stood. "I will ask one more time, Melissande. Please return home with me." He extended a beseeching hand to her, embodying all her girlhood fancies with his fairy-tale handsomeness and gallant manner.

But he lacked the rugged appeal of the man who had captured her heart. Nor did he possess the endearing scholarly disposition her warrior knight kept hidden beneath his fearsome facade.

He was not Lucian.

"I cannot. I owe him this."

Roarke studied her in the flickering candlelight, as if seeking some hidden truth. "Have you fallen in love with my brother?"

The question unnerved her, echoing the recent musings of her own mind. She could not meet his eyes, for fear he would read her indecision.

She didn't love Lucian, did she? He had pushed her away, betrayed her at the most cruel level when he'd handed her over to Roarke. How could she love a man who would so dishonor her?

"Nay."

Satisfied, Roarke nodded. "Then there is no excuse for not wedding me. I will see you as my bride, Melissande."

They were back at this again? She thought to argue, but 'twas too much for one day. She was glad to see him go, glad to be left in peace to pray for Lucian's recovery.

Not that she loved him.

Roarke had stepped just beyond the hut's threshold when a thought occurred to her.

A sudden flare of hope sparked within her breast. If Lucian had not really slain the man who trailed them in France, perhaps he had exaggerated the circumstances of Osbern Fitzhugh's death, as well.

And Roarke had witnessed the whole thing.

"Roarke?" She raised her voice, unwilling to leave Lucian's side or to release the continual pressure she had applied to his wound for hours.

"Aye?" He ducked his massive frame into the shelter once again.

"Lucian said you were present when he fought with Lord Fitzhugh."

She could see Roarke's jaw working even in the dim light. His words came through gritted teeth.

"Aye."

"Did he truly, that is, do you think he really…killed him?" Perhaps Lucian had overstated his role in the man's death.

"He may have thought to raise his sword in self-defense, but I saw into his eyes, Melissande." Roarke fixed her with the vacant stare of a man lost in memories. "I've never seen Lucian more furious than on that day. He killed Osbern Fitzhugh as surely as an assassin's arrow struck him down this morn."

Shaking his head, mayhap shaking off a ghost of the past, Roarke stalked off into the night.

For days Melissande watched over Lucian in the tiny shelter. Each night, Roarke returned, offering her escort home, but she steadfastly refused. He provided her with a horse so she might leave whenever she chose. He supplied her with food and moved or lifted Lucian whenever she asked him to.

Melissande was extremely grateful, yet their relationship grew even more strained. Roarke hounded her for a wedding date, despite her insistence that he return her to the abbey. His accusation that Lucian meant to kill Osbern Fitzhugh had created a barrier between them.

As Melissande washed Lucian's forehead five days after he had been shot, she wondered how he could be shot just inches from his heart and still cling to life nearly a sennight later. Yet Lord Fitzhugh had been wounded in his arm and he'd died within one day.

Had Lucian's attack really been so vicious? The picture Roarke painted of Lucian in his fury matched Melissande's lifelong mental image of a warrior—ruthless and lethal.

She dipped her linen cloth to clean it, then ran it along Lucian's face and neck, wondering if he could possess such a violent nature.

With wistful fingers, she brushed a stray strand of hair from his face. She knew she should not devote so much of herself to untangling the complex mysteries of this man who was determined not to have her anyway.

Yet she could not stop herself from unearthing every piece of information she could about him. Could she still blame her desire to make sense of his past on her notorious curiosity? Or did her need to know more about him go far beyond that, into regions Melissande was not yet ready to face herself?

All of this ruminating would be for naught if he died. The fear dominated her thoughts. While her musing frequently went far afield, they always came back to that one frightening truth.

Aside from the slow, steady thrum of his heart and the shallow rise and fall of his chest, there was no sign of life in Lucian. He did not seem to dream. He did not call out in his sleep. Nor did he have a fever.

He just lay there, so still that Melissande frequently lay her ear to his chest to assure herself he lived.

She often whispered prayers over him, but began to fear her unconfessed recent sins had rendered her supplications less effective. It had been months since her last confession, and heaven knew, she had strayed from her convent teachings lately.

Over the past few hours another idea had begun to niggle the back of her mind. Prayer was not helping, her healing skills didn't seem to have much effect on him, but there was one other, outrageous approach she thought of trying.

What if she kissed him?

Could the touch of her lips to his breathe life—even a will to live—back into his motionless form?

No doubt she would be disappointed. If kissing worked for

physicians, surely she would have read about it in one of the medical texts she translated. Certainly Abbess Helen would say the very idea was ludicrous.

But Abbess Helen wasn't here.

The idea had taken root, and no matter how much Melissande tried to rationalize herself out of such an impulsive gesture, some contrary force within her refused to forget it.

Truth be told, she also could not bear the thought of never kissing him again. Whether he felt anything for her or not, Melissande could not deny that Lucian had aroused something within her too potent to be categorized as mere friendship.

A brief brush of her lips certainly could not harm him.

Gently she lifted his head to offer him a drink. More wine spilled to the floor than went into his throat, but she was satisfied with the effort. With trembling fingers, she wiped his cheek and chin.

Nerves harassing her, she picked up the wineskin and helped herself to a long swallow. She braced herself for courage and leaned over him.

Closing her eyes, she drifted nearer. She settled one hand on his shoulder at the same time she eased her lips to his. Just a taste, she told herself. It struck her as unseemly to kiss a man on the verge of death.

But this was Lucian, not just any man.

Once she had pressed her mouth against him, a sigh shuddered through her. Something about being next to Lucian felt utterly right—not unseemly or foolish in the least.

Growing more brazen, she flicked her tongue tentatively between his lips. It felt as heavenly as she remembered, but her rational mind taunted her. Was she such a love-starved nun that she had to extract pleasure from kissing a senseless man?

Curse rationality. She could have sworn she felt a hitch in Lucian's breathing.

Throwing off all vestiges of logic and reason, she dipped her hand into his tunic to run idle fingers through the silken hair of his chest.

He groaned.

Melissande was so startled she stopped to look at him. He made no further movement, but she was sure she had heard him.

Desperate to succeed, she pulled his head into her lap and stroked his hair, whispering heartfelt pleas for his recovery.

When he still made no move, she lowered her lips to his once again. She forsook the more tender kisses to partake of his mouth. Hungrily, she demanded some response from him, unwilling to think she could have imagined his signs of life.

For a long moment he did not move. Then his breathing seemed to deepen.

Giddy with the kiss and the thought of Lucian alive and well, Melissande pressed the vibrant warmth of her body to his cool one, being careful not to touch the wound at the center of his chest.

Then suddenly his arm wrapped itself around her. His lips came alive under hers and he kissed her as though he thought to make her as senseless as he had been just moments before.

The drumming of her heart pounded in her ears. In the far recesses of her mind, she thought she heard a noise outside the shelter, but nothing seemed as important as Lucian's health, his touch, his mouth upon hers.

She couldn't have stopped him if she tried, although she was desperate to look into his eyes and to assure herself he was no ghost. But the warmth of his mouth, the insistence of his tongue, held her captive.

"What the hell is going on here?" The fury of an intruder's voice yanked Melissande and Lucian apart.

They turned as one, still breathless and clinging to each other, to confront a red-faced and furious Roarke Barret.

Chapter Seventeen

"You're still the back-stabbing bastard you were two years ago, I see." Roarke leveled Lucian with flashing green eyes.

Melissande jumped up, shaky and off balance. "It's not what it looks like. I—"

"I'll just bet it's not." He stood frozen in the doorway, his anger filling the room. "You've gotten just what you wanted, Mel." Roarke swung his gaze to her. "Our betrothal is obviously nullified."

She didn't bother to remind him they were never betrothed. He looked enraged enough to strangle her. "I am sorry."

"Not half as sorry as I'll be when Lucian comes swaggering back to take his earldom with his new bride at his side." He shook his head in disgust. "That'll teach me to lend a hand next time my big brother needs help."

Purposefully he spit on the floor before he spun on his heel and left.

As the sound of the hooves of his horse faded into the distance, Lucian and Melissande stared at one another. She noted his pale complexion and hurried to his side.

"You are not well enough for this." She struggled to help

him lie back down on his pallet, but he remained propped up on one elbow, staring at her as if she had lost her mind. "You must rest, Lucian, or you will no doubt collapse again and—"

"Why on earth would we have been kissing just now?" He looked both confused and annoyed.

Melissande flushed, embarrassment heating her cheeks and neck. "I'm not really sure."

"Recall you do not lie well, Melissande."

How could he be cornering her, his voice as vital and strong as if he just woke from a short nap, when not half an hour ago he seemed on the verge of death?

She folded her arms across her chest. "I will answer you if you lay down, please."

Glaring at her the whole way, he did as she bid.

"I thought a kiss might call you from unconsciousness. You have been lying there as if dead for five days now."

A moment of shocked silence greeted her words until Lucian absently rubbed a hand over his chest.

"I had been shot, Mel. A man needs time to recover." His voice scratched with lack of use.

Her fingers flexed in an effort to remain calm. She breathed deeply. "Yes, well, your 'recovery' looked ten paces from death."

"And so you kissed me?" He sounded horrified.

She lifted her chin, though she thought the deep blush in her cheeks probably counteracted any pretense of defiance. "Yes."

Wiping a frustrated hand through his hair, he cursed.

Melissande stiffened.

"Well, it seems I am recovered now." He tried to prop himself up and failed. "Perhaps you could ride to Barret Keep for one of the grooms to play valet for me. I should appreciate a man's help getting out of here."

The invincible warrior had spoken. Pale as a wraith, weak as a babe, he would give orders and assert his command. Memories of the way her father had treated her mother ran through her mind.

He was dismissing her. The ingrate.

If she thought he was in any danger, she would not allow him to scare her off. But he would be fine until she could send someone to fetch him.

"Very well, sir. I leave you to your rest." She gave him a curt nod and strode from the room, swallowing back the tears that threatened. He had her so confused she didn't know what to think or how to feel, but she knew his treatment stung.

She realized what she needed to do, however. When life turned this turbulent, this confusing, there was only one place to go to find a sense of peace. Although she no longer had Abbess Helen to turn to, Melissande could seek comfort in the chapel at Barret Keep.

She was already mounted on the white palfrey Roarke had provided for her when she recalled she had forgotten her book.

Lucian listened to the pounding of her horses' hooves as she thundered away, hoping like hell she wouldn't come back to witness more of his weakness. Frustrated and aching, he thumbed through the pristine pages of the *Odyssey,* trying to sort out the latest debacle of his life. Like the words in the text, his next move was inscrutable.

Only Melissande would try to cure a man by kissing him. Where the hell had she come up with that harebrained idea?

Lucian realized he loved her all the more for it. After everything that had transpired between them, he didn't think he could stop himself from adoring her if he tried.

Heaven knew, she was not to blame for the passionate turn her healing method had taken. Lucian had floated up from the depths of a dark dream to the exquisite feel of her pressed against him. Her scent, her taste, her touch had given his senses something to latch onto in the hazy shadows that had claimed him for days.

He came alive in her arms, filled with the sense that his body could be whole and strong again. Her gift of life convinced him he was not ready to die.

The time for wallowing in guilt had passed. No longer would Lucian accept that half-death he had been walking through for the past two years.

If he ever wanted to deserve a woman as pure and innocent as Melissande, he needed to stop wearing his guilt as a battle shield and to start slaying the demons that haunted him.

Our Father, who art in Heaven...

More eloquent words eluding her, Melissande took comfort from the most simple of prayers as she knelt before a statue of Mary in the Barret family chapel four days later.

The sainted mother of Christ had been a living, mortal woman once. She had known the love of a family, the heart-wrenching joy and pain of motherhood, the contrasting demands of her heart and the holy path.

It made her seem approachable today, when Melissande's heart was torn. No priest presided here. The chapel existed as more of a spiritual sanctuary for the keep's residents and a place for visiting clergymen to preach.

Melissande felt at home immediately. Stripped of the pomp and ceremony that accompanied many of the masses at St. Ursula's, the church resonated with a quiet, personal spirituality that filled her with reverence.

"I do not know how to proceed," she confided to Mary, her voice echoing over the stone walls. "Pray, send me guidance that I may know what to do."

"Melissande."

The feminine voice, full of maternal authority, made Melissande jump. As her heart pounded a furious rhythm against her chest, she realized the voice did not issue from Mary.

A petite woman with laughing blue eyes called to her from across the chapel. Cloaked from head to foot in coarse black wool despite the heat of the day, her well-wrinkled face attested to her wholehearted embrace of life.

Melissande thanked heaven for the speedy answer to her prayer. Relief washed over her. "Abbess Helen."

Melissande's mentor from St. Ursula's entered the nave, flanked by one of her men-at-arms to the left and by Roarke to her right. The abbess emanated as much authority as either of the men.

"You found me." Melissande rose shakily to her feet, drinking in the comforting sight of a woman who had been the only mother she'd known the past ten years.

She looked wonderful, cheeks still wind-burned from a brisk ride, her normally perfect habit and wimple a little bit askew.

"Although snow in the mountains detained our riding party nearly a fortnight and frustrated me to no end, it seems God has ensured that I would arrive just in time." The abbess hurried forward to greet her. "You seem most agitated, Melissande." Turning to the men, she nodded. "I shall be fine now, gentlemen. Thank you."

Roarke did not even spare a glance for Melissande before spinning on his heel along with the other man. She wondered if he would ever forgive her.

Abbess Helen squeezed her shoulders, bestowing a warm

smile upon her. "I can fairly feel the tension flow from this keep, child. Do you care to tell me what is afoot here?"

Melissande warmed to the woman's rare touch. The convent did not encourage demonstrativeness, but Melissande thrived on the attention the abbess gave her now. "Of course. Won't you have a seat?" Melissande steered the nun toward a pew. "I must confess I am surprised you came all this way."

Abbess Helen chuckled as she took her seat. "You know I never do anything in half measures, Melissande. I could not give up until I found you."

"You got my letter?"

"A few weeks after you sent it, I believe. Would that we could have caught up with you and saved both of us the travel, but we lost much time due to the mountain snow."

Melissande felt the blush steal over her cheeks as she thought of several times along the way when she would have been mortified to have been discovered unawares by the abbess and her troop. "We had to change paths midway when an assassin stalked us."

Abbess Helen crossed herself. "I had no idea you were in such serious danger."

Thinking of the man who guarded her, Melissande smiled. "I was well protected."

Briefly, Melissande recounted her tale, omitting the more intimate details of her relationship with Lucian. Oddly, those details stood out foremost in her mind as she thought back on the journey.

She had no choice but to admit her recent mishap with Roarke, however. Her new status as his unwanted bride meant she could leave Barret Keep right away.

"I brought nothing with me, except for my—the convent's—book," Melissande explained. "Since I have nothing to pack, I am ready to depart anytime."

The abbess regarded her skeptically. "You say this Roarke Barret no longer wishes to marry you because of the devotion you demonstrated toward his wounded brother?"

"Actually, I—" Would Abbess Helen reinstate her as the primary guardian of Emilia, Andre and Rafael if Melissande admitted what she had done? She had no choice but to tell the truth, of course, yet the words did not trip easily from her tongue. "I kissed his brother."

"Ah-hh." The abbess frowned. "This is most serious, Melissande."

"It was all a mistake." Had it been? "I didn't mean to—" She could not complete the thought for it would have been an outright untruth. She had meant to kiss Lucian.

"We have much to sort out, Melissande. I can see why I felt called to journey all this way for you, child." She smiled at Melissande and tucked an errant red curl behind her ear. "I had no idea your hair had grown so long again. You look lovely."

Melissande smiled at the abbess's praise. It was not so much the compliment that pleased her as the gentle touch of the woman's hand. Losing her mother at a tender age had made Melissande more needy for such simple kindnesses. "Thank you."

The abbess stood. "I will need to interview all parties involved to determine the best course of action."

"Excuse me?"

"Obviously we need to make sense of this tangle before we do anything rash. I will speak to both of the Barret men and get everything sorted out in no time. All will be well, my dear."

If the abbess learned the full extent of Melissande's sins, she could never go back to St. Ursula's. "But—"

"Do not trouble yourself. I will not disturb your patient until he has rested a few more days." She stretched her arms by her sides. "I am afraid I could use a few days' rest myself before I face the journey back. But when everyone settles down a bit, I'm sure I'll discover just what needs to be done here."

Nervous and at a loss for words, Melissande watched her depart. Her life rested in Abbess Helen's hands, as it had for a decade. The thought both disturbed and comforted Melissande as she toured the small chapel.

There was some sense of relief to have difficult decisions lifted from her shoulders, but could Melissande be happy with what someone else decided for her?

She had to make sure the abbess did not wheedle the truth of what transpired between she and Lucian on the journey home. If the pious woman knew Melissande had lost her innocence to him, Abbess Helen would not allow Melissande to care for the abbey orphans anymore.

She would just have to get to Lucian before the abbess did. Certainly he would be happy to do whatever he could to ensure Melissande left England forever.

Although she should have taken reassurance from the notion, Melissande couldn't suppress the urge to cry.

Lucian had been situated in his chamber at Barret Keep for nearly a week when a timid knock broke his concentration on the Greek letters late one afternoon.

Roarke's serving wench was the most humble little mouse Lucian had ever met. "Come in, Isabel!" he shouted, even though he knew his recent habit of growling at whoever ventured into his space probably didn't make the girl feel any more at ease.

He felt her presence the moment the door swung open.

Not the timid mouse, but the woman who haunted his dreams. Heaven only knew how, but he could feel the woman even across the room. She sang along his nerves and warmed his blood at twenty paces.

"Melissande." He longed to hide the book. It embarrassed him to be caught with it—as if he were missing her and fondling the one part of her he possessed.

He cleared his throat. "I am teaching myself Greek," he announced. It was partly true, anyway. She didn't need to know he'd missed her.

Melissande closed the door behind her.

The intimacy of that act caught him off guard. He shoved aside the book, wincing at the burning in his shoulder as he moved too quickly. "You wanted to…talk?"

He hoped she wanted to refresh her memory on how incredible he could make her body feel. He wanted to see that peculiar flush in her cheeks, the wonder in her brown eyes.

"Do you really think you can learn Greek on your own?" There was wonder in her voice, but not exactly the kind his lust-hazed brain had envisioned.

"I have deciphered several of the letters from memory. I recalled the first few lines of the story best, though not perfectly, and I've translated some of the words accordingly."

She looked so impressed he had no choice but to pull out the volume and show her. She sat beside him on the bed.

"The opening words were 'Sing in me, Muse,' so I know for sure all of these letters." He pointed to his roughly scratched list, along with the letters that still puzzled him.

"You could have just asked me." She chastised him with her eyes. "I would have been happy to translate the first page for you."

She smelled so good—a little like the kitchens, a little like the chapel. He could discern both the scent of baking bread and sweet frankincense about her.

What a beautiful contradiction she was.

"I thought it best we did not spend any more time together." He closed the book again and slid it to the far side of the bed. Without the Greek tome to focus their attentions on, they suddenly seemed much too close together.

"That is why I am here, as a matter of fact." She plucked at her surcoat, a rich burgundy garment that accurately conveyed the boldness of her spirit.

He lifted a curious brow, but said nothing; instead he wondered where she had obtained new attire.

"I don't know if you have heard that Abbess Helen arrived here some days ago."

He hadn't heard, thanks to Isabel for never opening her meek little mouth. "She is here to drag you back to the Alps?"

"I want to go, Lucian."

"To catch your death this winter? Or to work yourself to exhaustion in the scriptorium so you might scrounge a few moments to play with the orphans you love?"

She tossed him a disdainful glare. "You and I both know the abbey is the best place for me. I have no desire to wed a warrior knight who kills for a living, and neither you nor Roarke want me here. Therefore, it will suit all of us if we can convince Abbess Helen to take me back in my capacity overseeing the children."

"You think I kill for a living?" Lucian remembered a time when she believed in him. Had she changed her mind?

"You freely admit that you do, much as you despise it." Her eyes softened to liquid honey as she gazed at him. "Although you have taught me that there are redeeming aspects of a warrior, I can also see that you will be entrenched in bloody warfare all your life as a permanent penance."

Lucian didn't quite know how to respond to this new Melissande. She was a combination of the cool reserve she had learned at the abbey and the bold girl of his youth who was not afraid to speak her mind.

"Anyway, remaining here is out of the question, so I've come to beg a favor from you."

Even more interesting. Maybe now she wanted him to refresh her memory on how incredible he could make her body feel. "And what favor might that be, Angel?"

Her breath caught at the endearment. Lucian could see the flutter of nervousness that trembled through her.

"I need you to omit a few things when Abbess Helen comes to interview you about our relationship."

"You want me to lie to a holy woman?"

"Nay!" She caught her bottom lip between her teeth. "I would just ask you to skip over some of the more—" she blushed, hesitating with her answer "—intimate parts."

"'The honest obtains God's favor, the schemer incurs His condemnation,'" Lucian quoted, allowing some perverse demon within himself to needle her. No doubt he had been convalescing for too long that he deliberately quarreled with Melissande to keep her in his chamber a bit longer.

"'The trustworthy keeps things hidden,'" she returned, crossing her arms over her chest in smug triumph.

Lucian couldn't suppress his grin. How had he ever thought it a burden to listen to Melissande talk? His heart had thirsted for a hint of her musical voice over the past few days. "In exchange for my silence, Lady Melissande, you must be willing to give me something."

She went still, staring at him with wide eyes. Lucian longed to wrest a kiss from her, but settled for something almost as satisfying.

"You will finish the *Odyssey.*" He thrust the book in her hands, gratified by the brief flash of disappointment in her gaze. Had she hoped he would ask her for a kiss? Did she think about the time they shared by the creek half as much as he did?

"I've told you the tale is rather…romantic at the end." She took the heavy volume from his hands.

Perhaps he was ready to admit there could be happy endings for a warrior hero. Although Lucian could never hang his battle sword above the hearth in retirement, he understood the desire to escape to a more peaceful existence.

Hadn't he sought to ensure Roarke would never have to know the torment of killing by making him the next earl? Lucian would not wish the guilt and nightmares on anyone. "I want to hear it anyway."

Melissande settled in a chair beside his bed and read for hours, providing Lucian with time to study her.

She did not wish to wed a warrior, yet Lucian knew he could never let her return to St. Ursula's and an early death to lung fever. Melissande deserved to know the joys of motherhood, the love of a family.

Roarke would understand once Lucian spoke to him.

Or so he hoped.

Lucian had sent missives to his brother three times in the past few days, none of which were answered except for a terse note informing Lucian of a few more details surrounding their mother's death.

Although saddened to learn of her passing, Lucian knew she had been in failing health ever since their father returned from an earlier crusade. His formerly open, spirited mother, had become a woman full of secrets after her husband's return. What disturbed him most, oddly enough, was the fact that she had died before he ever revealed the truth of Osbern Fitzhugh's death to her.

Maybe he never would have, but now he'd never know. The chance to be honest had passed him by and he would carry yet another sin to his grave.

He couldn't lie to Abbess Helen, no matter what Melissande asked. For that matter, he didn't think he could equivocate to Roarke, either.

Lucian did not deserve her. Yet, watching her eyes fly over the lines of Greek, her mouth quickly spouting the words while her clever mind translated them all, Lucian knew he desired her above all things.

He might never be worthy of her, but he would lay down his life for her. And, in light of the years she suffered in the Alps, he would make damn sure she was never cold again for so much as a moment.

"Are you quite sure you're listening, Lucian?" Melissande asked suddenly. "You don't want to miss Penelope's clever trick."

Indeed he didn't. His mind resolved about his course of action with the Abbess, Lucian turned his full attention back to the story. Penelope was about to test the identity of the man who claimed to be Odysseus, returned to her after their twenty-year separation. Testing the man's reaction, Penelope told her maid to make up the old bed her husband had built and to move it outside the bedchamber.

In a fit of anger, the stranger raged at Penelope and Melissande stood to mimic the impassioned diatribe. "No mortal in his best days could budge that bed with a crowbar. There is our pact and pledge, our secret sign, built into that bed— my handiwork and no one else's!"

It seemed Odysseus had constructed his home around an olive tree and, after cutting it down, had carved the standing stump into an elaborate marriage bed.

She finished the tale then, which thankfully had one more battle scene before the end, redeeming the story in Lucian's eyes.

When she completed the tale, however, it was not the battle that Melissande spoke of.

She sighed, gazing up at Lucian with wistful eyes. "The bed was the centerpiece for their home, its roots extending into the earth to provide the whole foundation for their family."

"Thus she knew the man to be Odysseus," Lucian observed.

"He was the only one who knew about their bed."

"Does it not strike you as odd that she did not recognize him sooner?" Lucian was not certain that he liked the brief romantic turn the tale had taken. A warrior ought to have a more welcoming homecoming than to be put to the test by his own wife.

"I did not recognize you at first, either, and it had been only ten years since we'd seen one another," Melissande countered.

Night had fallen as they'd talked and read. The keep had grown quiet since the evening meal, which neither of them had missed. Tapers flickered in their sconces, no doubt lit by the silent maid who often waited upon him.

Lucian realized they had not spent such time alone since their journey. He had missed the intimacy of talking to Melissande, a closeness as potent as their kisses.

"I deliberately concealed my face from you."

"But people change, and in far more significant ways than their appearance." Melissande's glance seemed to probe the depths of his soul.

How could a woman be so wise and yet so innocent?

"You changed, too." Lucian recalled how he had spied on

her through the convent enclosure, waiting for confirmation of her identity. "I didn't know it was you until after you finished reading to the children."

Melissande grinned, the happy memory chasing shadows from her dark eyes.

"When your young charges wrestled you to the ground, I heard your laughter and glimpsed a lock of your hair. Then, there could be no mistaking the girl I remembered." Lucian reached to tug at an errant curl that had worked its way loose from her silver circlet.

Melissande blushed. The urge to pull her into his arms battled with his need to explain his plans for her future.

He hated to upset her, but he would not allow her to return to the Alps under any circumstances.

A sharp rap at his door halted his confession.

"Yes?" Lucian called, his gaze locked on Melissande.

"'Tis Abbess Helen, my lord," an efficient feminine voice returned. "May I have a word with you?"

"St. Ursula's sainted brow," Melissande whispered as she leaped from her perch on his bed. "Hide me!"

Chapter Eighteen

"Come in, Sister."

Melissande could not believe her ears when Lucian blithely invited the abbess into his chamber. What was he thinking?

The door swung wide and the nun bustled in, a rather sheepish Roarke close at her heels. The abbess's gaze landed squarely upon Melissande. "Ah! Melissande. I hoped to find you here."

Melissande fidgeted with the sleeve of her gown. "I thought to help Luc—that is, Sir Barret—pass his convalescence with a story." She held up the *Odyssey* in self-defense, hoping the flickering candlelight did not illuminate the heated color of her embarrassment.

Abbess Helen cast her an indulgent smile while Roarke glared at his brother.

Lucian gestured to the wooden bench some feet from his bed. "Please have a seat, my Lady Abbess."

Although Abbess Helen took her seat with grace, Melissande and Roarke were left standing awkwardly on the fringes of the narrow chamber.

"Lord Barret," she addressed Lucian, although everyone

else in the room knew the title belonged to Roarke. No one dared to correct Abbess Helen. "It seems I have stumbled into a most troublesome situation here at Barret Keep."

"I'm sure my brother, the earl, will find a way to make your stay more pleasant, Sister." Lucian bowed his head in courteous deference to Roarke.

Melissande fumed inwardly, still disturbed that Roarke would steal away Lucian's inherited right.

"Unfortunately, he and I have talked at length and cannot rectify the unhappy problem to which I refer." She looked pointedly at Melissande. "That is, what to do with my young charge, Melissande Deverell."

Melissande bristled at the notion that she needed to be taken care of. For years she had been taught to accept the teachings of the elder nuns, to do as they commanded without question or complaint.

But just now, the urge to argue on her own behalf tempted her sorely.

"She will be well cared for, I assure you," Lucian remarked.

It took a long moment for his words to penetrate Melissande's brain. When they did, his betrayal hit her with the force of a blow. She stepped forward.

"I do not wish to remain here," she asserted, striving to be civil for Abbess Helen's sake, but seething with anger at Lucian. How could he force her to remain here and wed Roarke?

"Well cared for by whom, my lord?" Abbess Helen ignored Melissande's interjection and lifted a skeptical brow in Lucian's direction. "Your brother has told me he cannot marry her. And given the fact that it is *you* who ruined her reputation, I cannot in good conscience force him to wed her."

Heat flooded Melissande's cheeks. She hastened to interrupt again. "But I wish to return to the convent, Abbess Helen."

The powerful nun and the warrior knight did not acknowledge her. They stared at one another in a silent battle of wills.

Melissande wanted to rage at them both, but with her whole life hanging in the balance, she feared alienating the abbess.

"What are you suggesting, Lady Abbess?" Lucian's question hissed through the chamber.

Melissande leaned forward.

"You ruined her reputation, even if your kiss was most innocent. Because of your rash act, your brother will no longer accept her, and I certainly cannot bring her back to an abbey where three impressionable young children are in her charge. I deem it your responsibility to determine an agreeable fate for her. You're the one who abducted her and spent months on the road alone with her."

"Nay!" Melissande stamped her foot, glaring a warning look at Lucian before she pleaded with the abbess. "Do not separate me from the children. They need me so much and—"

Lucian clamped warm fingers about her wrist. "I will wed her," he announced.

Melissande swung on him, livid. "You will do no such thing!" Who was he to decide her fate for her?

"Be reasonable, Melissande," the abbess coaxed, laying a comforting hand on Melissande's shoulder. "There is really no choice—"

"There is most certainly a choice!" Melissande raged, raising her voice in Abbess Helen's presence for the first time in her life. To no avail, she attempted to withdraw her wrist from Lucian's grip. "Take me home to St. Ursula's where I belong."

The abbess eyed her long and hard. "And are you prepared

to swear, despite the proof of your affection for Lord Barret
and the weeks the two of you spent alone together, that you
have never been…intimate with him?"

Oh, Lord.

Melissande's rage dissipated as guilt stole through her.

Vivid memories of the day by the creek with Lucian assailed her. She had eagerly given him her innocence, had sac-
rificed her future at the abbey for a few stolen moments in
his arms.

They all waited, staring at her.

She could not tell an outright lie to Abbess Helen. Besides,
the time had arrived for Melissande to grow up. No matter
how much easier it was to blame Lucian or the abbess for her
predicament, Melissande knew her own passion and curiosity had led her to this.

*Are you prepared to swear…you have never been intimate
with him?*

This was one bit of mischief-making Melissande could
not deny. And heaven knew she didn't lie well.

"I cannot," Melissande responded finally, knowing her
flushed cheeks answered more tellingly than any words she
might devise.

The abbess drew a sharp breath.

Lucian's gaze remained on Abbess Helen. "We will wed
at once." After a final squeeze of Melissande's hand, he released his grip on her fingers.

Set in grim lines of determination, his bleak visage conveyed to even the most innocent of human observers that Lucian's heart was not in a wedding.

Tears begged for release from beneath her downswept
lashes, but Melissande would not grant herself the luxury of
crying.

"Then it is settled," Abbess Helen noted, drawing Melissande to her side. "I would like to witness the nuptials before I depart so that I might leave with a peaceful heart. Would that be admissible, my lord?"

"I am not the lord here, my Lady Abbess, but I welcome your presence."

Abbess Helen stood, nodding her approval. "I will take care of the banns to promote a hasty marriage. Would tomorrow be too soon? Shall we say noon?"

Melissande nodded, too overwhelmed to speak.

She would never see her children again. And it would not be, as she had once foolishly hoped, because Lucian had fallen in love with her and wanted her to be his wife.

No. She would be separated from the orphans because she had acted on impulse one too many times and now paid the price in marriage to a hardened warrior who lacked a heart.

Roarke approached his brother as the abbess readied herself to leave. "If I might have a word with you, brother."

Melissande saw Lucian nod, but all their movements seemed disassociated from herself, as if she were far removed from this time and place.

The foundation on which she had built her life seemed to have dropped out from under her.

"Come, Melissande." The abbess called to her from where she stood beside the door. "We have much to prepare for tomorrow."

The abbess's words jolted Melissande from her musings. Resolutely, she followed her longtime mentor.

Although Melissande could not stop her marriage, she vowed she would never allow Lucian to rule her as she had been ruled all her life—first by her father, then by the abbey.

Starting now, she would reclaim her life as her own.

* * *

Lucian watched Melissande walk away, her spine stiff and unrelenting. Apparently his offer of marriage came too late. While he hadn't expected her eternal gratitude, he had hoped she would be a little less angry about his proposal.

His gaze fell upon Roarke as his younger brother approached. At least Roarke could be counted on to support Lucian's decision.

Roarke cleared his throat. "I am leaving Barret Keep, Lucian," he announced. "Forever."

Lucian shook his head, hoping he hadn't heard his younger brother correctly. "What?"

"I cannot be happy here any longer." Roarke met his gaze evenly, as if he somehow stood taller than he had in a long time.

Lucian could not give his younger brother's latest flare of temper any more attention than absolutely necessary. He combed his fingers through hair that had grown too long over the past months. "I am sorry about Melissande, Roarke, but I will take her away from here so you will not be vexed by our presence. You will find a woman you are happy with a bit closer to home."

Roarke shook his head. "Nay. I will not. I spoke at length with the abbess over supper, and I realize I am not happy with what I have made of my life."

Good God, what had the meddling holy woman wrought now? "Do not let a busybody nun talk you out of a—"

"That is unfair to Abbess Helen." Roarke reproached him with his glance. "I feel fortunate to have recognized why I am not happy while I am young enough to change it. I have been disturbed by a few things mother said before she died, disjointed ramblings I need to research before I settle down. I will leave a few days after your wedding to make my way in the world as a landless second son."

Lucian threw off the bed linens and stood to face his brother. This was not like Roarke at all. Hadn't the younger Barret coveted the earldom and all the benefits of the firstborn from the time he was a child? "You have lands! I promised them to you, Roarke. Do you think I would ever go back on my word? If you want to grant me something, I can be your vassal at the old Deverell Keep."

Roarke folded his arms across his chest. Lucian realized for the first time his brother had grown every bit as broad of chest as he.

"I know you are far too honorable to request your rights back, Lucian. But this is not about you, it is about me. And the ravings of our mother on her deathbed." He cast Lucian a look. "I did not want to believe it at the time, but the more I piece together her whispers, the more I fear…we may not share the same father, Lucian."

Lucian shook his head, determined to dislodge the thought. "What is this madness? We were raised together. Fostered together. I can think of no woman more honorable, more noble, than our mother."

How dare Roarke suggest such a thing?

"It is only a thought, I dismissed it as well at the time, but since it preys upon me still after six months, I have no choice but to try and disprove it so I may rest easy at night. I will have the satisfaction of making a name for myself outside of Northumbria, perhaps in the Holy Lands."

"So you can die before you make a name or find a home for yourself?" Lucian could feel the blood of his anger pound against the place in his chest where the arrow had pierced him.

"My battle prowess may not be so lacking as that, brother." He turned toward the door, but paused when he reached it. "No matter what you think of my plans, I dispatched a letter to the king yesterday, telling him of your return and my departure. You are already the earl, Lucian, as you have always truly been."

What was Roarke thinking? How could he blithely throw away his future? "Roarke, wait—"

"You must admit," Roarke interrupted, grinning, "Melissande was destined to be countess here."

Before Lucian could protest any further, Roarke slipped out the door. Lucian sank to his bed as the door shut behind the sibling he had loved and struggled with since childhood. Dear God, what if there were some truth to Roarke's words?

Impossible. Roarke was worse off now than if Lucian had never given him the title. Struck by some noble urge to seek his own fortune in the world, Roarke might be gone for years…might never return.

And Lucian now possessed everything he had always dreamed of having. His earldom restored, his lands prospered, his beautiful bride awaited him on the morrow, and surely a family could not be far behind.

Yet a bitter ache robbed him of all joy the rewards should have bestowed. His brother harbored details that would set any man's world on its ear.

Worse, a killer still stalked him to mete out justice for Lucian's past sins. With so many people depending on him for protection, he stood to lose much more than just his life to Osbern Fitzhugh's avenger.

Although in all likelihood, the man who shot him was Peter Chadsworth, the larger threat still loomed. One day, Damon Fitzhugh would return from war and demand satisfaction for his father's death.

Lucian had to make sure the woman he loved was protected when that day came. No matter what Melissande thought of his proposal to marry her, Lucian knew he would take his vows very seriously.

To keep her safe, he would have to live his life as the warrior knight Melissande reviled.

As much as Melissande loved to talk, she grew weary of the endless niceties she was forced to exchange with the hundreds of well-wishers who attended her wedding feast.

More days had passed since the abbess's decree that Melissande and Lucian should wed. Yet, somehow the inhabitants of Barret lands had assembled an elaborate feast. Lucian seemed to grow stronger by the moment, his health improved by walks about the keep and—much to Melissande's dismay—trips to the practice yard where he swung slow arcs with his sword.

Ever the warrior.

Now their lives were joined after a few simple words intoned by the local priest. She'd barely absorbed the fact that her wedding day had arrived when she was whisked off to the celebration amid much song and strewing of flowers. Still, no amount of frivolity could take away the fact that she'd wed a man of dark, brooding passions. A man who had scarcely acknowledged her despite her lovely blue gown, a simple beaded surcoat that had belonged to Lucian's mother.

Now she sipped the last of her wine while the villagers danced, her gaze tripping over the festivities in search of her husband.

For reasons she did not fathom, Lucian had been reinstated as earl, making their wedding an even more significant event. While all the outlying tenants paid their respects to the new Lord and Lady Barret, Melissande puzzled over the sudden turnabout between Roarke and Lucian. She had tried to query Roarke about the matter, but he had turned as closedmouthed as her husband.

Strange things were afoot.

She raised her cup in the direction of the server, perhaps indulging in more wine today than she ought. But as new mistress of her own destiny, Melissande had made a pact with herself to answer only to her conscience and God from now on, despite the vows she took to obey her husband.

Sipping from her refilled horn, Melissande sought Lucian, never a difficult task since he and Roarke towered over the other men present.

She stabbed a bit of wedding cake onto her knife, musing over her bizarre new circumstances.

Never had she expected Lucian to offer for her. After he'd given her to Roarke, Melissande knew he did not return the feelings she had developed for him.

Why had he offered for her now? The abbess had maneuvered him, to a certain extent. But Lucian could have easily demanded she return to the convent.

His reasons for marrying her were too obscure for her to understand, especially after she downed her third glass of wine. Or was it her fourth?

Gazing at Lucian while he spoke to one of his tenants, Melissande sought reassurance that he was still the same man who loved to read and could speak Sanskrit.

Such a man would be gentle with her on their wedding night, would he not?

She knew better than to expect the tender treatment he had lavished upon her by the creek's edge. Lucian would be too annoyed with her for cornering him into a marriage he did not want to treat her to such exquisite passion.

Just recalling the incredible wealth of sensation the man could arouse in her made her cheeks flush.

Or maybe it was the wine.

Melissande set down her cup, hoping to cool the nervous anticipation that skittered through her no matter how many times she told herself not to expect any tenderness from Lucian on their wedding night.

Hadn't he been cool to her all day?

Lost in conflicting thoughts of her husband, she jumped when Abbess Helen took her by the arm.

"Dreaming of your groom, my dear?"

Melissande spluttered an incoherent reply and the nun laughed heartily. Melissande wondered if the good sister had not indulged in a few too many cups of wine herself.

"Do not be abashed, child! 'Tis only natural." She tugged Melissande forward through the crowd. "I will help you prepare yourself for him."

Melissande gulped. "Is it that time already?"

"Aye! Well past it, judging by the looks you two have been exchanging. Come with me." Abbess Helen drew her up the stairs, forcing Melissande to pause at the gallery overlooking the hall to wave to her guests one last time.

A cheer went up in response, and then all eyes turned to Lucian.

Like the dutiful, practical man he was, he lifted his cup to her in salute, earning more cheers and shouts throughout the hall.

Melissande knew his good humor to be an act, however. She had spent enough time alone with Lucian Barret to recognize the degrees of his brooding moods.

"Do not look so glum, my dear," the abbess clucked as she drew Melissande into the master chamber Roarke had already vacated. "I hear a wedding night is great fun at the hands of a man who cares for his wife."

"He does not care for me," Melissande muttered, allowing the abbess to unlace the simple beaded surcoat that served as her wedding garment.

"Of course he does, child, or he would not have been kissing you when Roarke discovered the two of you." The nun hung the tunic and retrieved a lightweight night rail from within the small wardrobe.

Melissande gasped at the sight of it, never having possessed such a fine and impractical piece of clothing. It surprised her a bit that Abbess Helen, of all people, would own a blatantly seductive garment. "Where did you get it?" She fingered the gossamer-thin material, tracing the intricate pattern scrolled over the bodice.

"Many of the sisters arrive at the convent with some of the finest clothes in Christendom." She winked. "We are just not allowed to wear them."

"You brought this all the way from St. Ursula's?"

The abbess helped Melissande slide the garment over her head, then smoothed the wrinkles with gentle fingers. "When I received your note, I did not know what to expect when I finally caught up with you. It seems to me that when a woman is abducted by a man, a wedding is always a possibility, and you know I don't take any chances when I pack."

"Whose was it?" A contrary part of Melissande longed to know which sister had brought such an uncompromisingly romantic piece of froth with her to the abbey.

The abbess sobered. "Sister Adelaide, a sweet young woman who was dismissed from St. Ursula's before I arrived, apparently."

Melissande remembered too well. "She was forced to leave

because a boy was enamored with her and would not cease throwing notes and trinkets over the enclosure wall. Her family could not afford to take her back."

"I heard later that his family could and did, however, so give her no more thought." Abbess Helen fussed with the ribbons at Melissande's waist and neck. "She has been happily married for almost nine years."

Melissande clapped in delight, relieved the young woman's story had a happy end. "You checked up on her when you arrived."

"The rumors of how the sisters tossed her out did not sit well with me, so I made sure she was happily settled. Adelaide gave me this gown as a token of her appreciation." Abbess Helen gave Melissande a sheepish grin. "I am a bit of a romantic myself, so I was very tempted by this garment. But I never once donned the gown."

On impulse, Melissande hugged the woman who had been both mother and inspiration to her. "I will try hard to do well here."

"Try hard to be happy, Melissande. Your joyousness has the power to infect all those around you." Abbess Helen stroked Melissande's cheek with maternal affection.

"Nay. My husband will never know joyousness, my Lady Abbess. He does not truly care for me," she confided, unable to halt the confession her pride told her she should have kept hidden.

"He has not learned to love and forgive himself, Melissande. He cannot possibly offer love to another until he first heals the unhappiness he wears like a shield." The abbess guided Melissande to the huge master bed and tucked her into the rose-scented linens. "You might help him do that, Melissande. 'Twould be a good place to start."

Melissande pressed a kiss to the abbess's hand, her heart lighter than it had been for weeks. "I will."

She would have done anything the abbess asked of her, but this quest appealed particularly to Melissande. The wise woman who reigned supreme over a hundred diverse, gossip-prone women had not gained her position by accident. A shrewd eye for human nature and a tender heart had won the nun an abbey full of staunch supporters.

Melissande would heed her advice well.

"Now enjoy your wedding night, child." Abbess Helen backed toward the door, smiling as she left. "I wish to see the happy flush of love upon your face before I leave, Melissande, so I will still be here on the morrow."

As the door closed behind her, Melissande wondered how long her mentor would be willing to stay to see that sign of love. It seemed Melissande was destined to live without it.

Although she promised herself she would find a way to help Lucian overcome his guilt to triumph over the past, she intended to guard her heart until that time.

Her convent home was already lost to her, and she no longer had a home or family to return to in England. She had also lost the love of her children and the joy of watching them grow to adulthood.

She had no intention of losing her heart to a hardened warrior who could never share his in return.

Chapter Nineteen

Lucian stared into his drinking horn and fought to concentrate on his conversation with Roarke. His brother deserved his full attention. Too bad the only thing on Lucian's mind at this moment was his wedding night.

Ever since the abbess had led Melissande from the hall to retire, Lucian's thoughts focused solely on the bedchamber where his wife lay.

His wife.

He could scarcely believe fate had granted him Melissande for a bride. For as many years as he could remember, Melissande had been the secret dream of his heart. Now she belonged to him.

How long must he wait to tread those steps to the master suite and claim the prize he thought he'd never obtain?

"...when Damon Fitzhugh arrives."

Roarke's mention of Lucian's mortal enemy jarred him from his daydreams.

"What did you say?" Lucian studied his brother, wondering if he knew something Lucian did not.

"I am trying my best to warn you despite your obvious lack

of attention." Roarke clapped a hand on Lucian's shoulder. "It is whispered that Osbern Fitzhugh's son is on his way home from the Holy Lands at last. You would do well to watch your back, brother."

The precariousness of Lucian's newfound happiness hit him with the force of a Saracen blade. Damon Fitzhugh would soon seek revenge for his father's death.

Normally, Lucian had every confidence in his ability to defend himself. But this would be a battle in which he was morally wrong. Surely God would contend on Damon's side when Lucian's enemy came to call. Where would that leave Melissande?

Lucian could trust only one man with her fate. "You will come back for Melissande if anything should happen to me."

"You will not be defeated, brother."

"Nay?" Lucian quirked a brow at the confidence in Roarke's tone.

"You have overcome even death to take your rightful place here." Roarke slid his hand from Lucian's shoulder and straightened. "You were fated to rule the Barret lands."

"Nevertheless, I would have your word that Melissande will be protected if I should die." Her safety was too important to be left in the hands of fickle fate. No matter what doubts plagued Roarke about his place in the family, they would always be linked by brotherhood in spirit.

"I pledge my life to her service." Roarke met his gaze and, for the first time, Lucian saw a hint of the regard his brother still bore for his wife.

Lucian nodded, acknowledging the vow at the same time he prayed he would never need to call upon it. He could not abide the thought of leaving Melissande in anyone's care but his own.

"You have waited long enough, by the way," Roarke added.

Lucian's gaze swung from the door of the master chamber to his companion. "What?"

Roarke laughed. "I am sure she is ready by now."

Lucian could not restrain his own grin. "Then I shall not idle with the likes of you any longer." Slamming his horn onto the nearest server's tray, Lucian bid Roarke farewell and bolted for the stairs.

Shouts and whoops of goodwill drowned out his thoughts as he launched onto the gallery. Roarke led the wedding guests in a noisy toast to his brother's fertility.

After a quick bow to their generosity, Lucian backed toward the door where Melissande awaited him. Anticipation and love for his wife made him slow his pace. This would be her first time, after all, though his naive bride thought she had already experienced lovemaking. He had no doubt she had been well satisfied the day they'd kissed by the creek's edge. If he were to maintain the passion he had kindled in her that day, he would need to initiate her into the rites of marriage most tenderly.

As his hand hovered over the door handle, he considered that this might be one way to win a bit of his wife's affection.

Not for the world would he miss out on such a chance.

He stepped into his future and, for tonight at least, shut the door behind him.

"Lucian?" Melissande's heart picked up speed as the huge, shadowy form of her husband entered the chamber.

She had not waited in the bed for him long, but the few moments alone in the massive chamber had given her plenty of time to grow nervous.

Of course, she knew what to expect from the marriage bed

after their encounter by the creek. But knowing what was expected of her made the butterflies in her belly flutter more furiously.

Intimacy between a man and wife meant disrobing. Melissande had bared almost her whole body to Lucian the day they made love.

Now that Lucian would be sleeping with her, would he remove all his clothing, as well?

The thought both intrigued and worried her.

She had never seen a naked man before.

Melissande watched him as he slid off his boots and padded across the floor to the bed. The scar on his temple caught the firelight, a white streak of lightning in the dark sky of his bronze face.

Yet the scarred visage and rock-wall chest of her warrior husband did not frighten her tonight. His strength beckoned her, begged her to touch and to test the hard muscle of his powerful body.

Eagerness to be close to him sent a pleasant shiver of expectation down her spine.

"You are cold?" Lucian reached the bed and sank beside her.

Melissande shifted against the pillows to see him better. He gazed down at her with gentle concern.

"Nay—" she began, then wondered what he might do to warm her. "Maybe a little."

Lucian dropped a finger to her exposed neck and drew a languorous line down to the ribbons of her gown. "'Tis no wonder when you are garbed in naught but an airy bit of silk."

He deliberately wound the silk ribbon about his finger, and another chill tingled through her nerves.

"The abbess gave it to me for tonight."

Lucian raised a brow in amused surprise, then pushed the

linens down to bare a bit more of the garment. Cool air fanned over her body, no match for the heat of his gaze.

"She has my utmost gratitude."

Leaning over her as if to study the intricate pattern of embroidery at her bodice, Lucian traced the swirls in the complicated weave with his thumb.

Mesmerized by the circuitous dance of the touch, Melissande's eyes drifted shut.

"Very beautiful," he commented, his mouth mere inches from her breasts. The caress of his breath drew the crests beneath to tight peaks against the fabric.

She sighed languorously as he began the trek with his thumb again, then cried out when he ceased his progress where one of the woven decorations curved around her nipple. "What, Angel?"

Melissande dragged open an eyelid to see him gazing at her as if she were a sweet confection to be devoured. She was willing to bet the man knew all too well what she wanted.

For now, she craved his touch.

Deep inside, she also yearned for his heart.

Willing to settle for a thorough sensual exploration tonight, Melissande threaded her fingers through the dark hair that touched his collar and tugged him nearer to her straining bodice.

His mouth settled upon her, heating her tender flesh right through the filmy barrier of gossamer fabric.

Molten pleasure sizzled in her womb. Her body arched toward his mouth and the source of her delight. Hungry to experience his kiss without impediment, Melissande wriggled her hands free to brush away the moist silk.

Lucian paused long enough to peer up at her with a mixture of lust and…humor, mayhap?

"My bride is more eager than I could have hoped."

She was not sure if he teased her. Ineffectual as it seemed when she was already half naked, she lifted her chin in proud defense. "You have taught me a kind of pleasure that I am impatient to experience again."

He dropped a kiss on the curve of her neck, breathing his warmth into her hair. "Tonight I will teach you the rewards of patience." Another kiss circled her ear.

A sensual thrill shuddered through Melissande. "If ten years in the convent cannot make me patient, my lord, I do not think you will accomplish the feat in the course of a night."

Lucian skimmed his fingers down the inside of her arm, barely brushing the underside of her breast with his hand. "When the prize is wondrous enough, Melissande, even you will wait for it."

"But I have sampled the wonder of the prize, Lucian—" she felt the blush creep over her cheeks as she admitted it "—and it is because the reward is so good I find I cannot wait."

He cradled her face in his palm and stroked her cheek with one broad thumb. "Angel, you don't know the half of it."

How could that be? If there were more to the intimacy between a man and a woman, Lucian had plenty of opportunity to tell her before now. "But when we were by the creek—"

Lucian toyed with a lock of her hair, idly teasing the strand over her neck and breasts. "When we were by the creek, we committed only the precursors to lovemaking. There is much more to the wedding night than that."

The bout of butterflies returned, and with it, overwhelming inquisitiveness. "More?"

"Much more."

"But what if—"

Lucian raised his fingers to her mouth. "Melissande, I have made a vow to cherish your sweet voice and your incessant chatter, but I do not think I can uphold it tonight."

She might have been incensed had he not chosen to quiet her offending lips with his own.

Questions faded from her mind as Lucian savored her mouth in a thought-stealing kiss. Her blood heated by slow degrees as his body moved against hers, molding her softness to the hard muscle that covered every inch of him.

The knot in her belly began to tighten, reminding her of the miraculous rapture Lucian could ultimately bring her… only now she knew it wasn't the ultimate pleasure. What more could there be to intimacy than what she'd already experienced?

Excited to find out, Melissande pressed herself still closer to him, sealing their bodies in a passionate tangle. Calling on her limited knowledge of lovemaking, she inched her leg up the length of his leather braies until she could wrap it about his waist.

His leg fell between hers, brushing deliciously near the center of her growing need. He groaned at her brazen act, but obligingly increased the pressure of his thigh against her.

Something else moved against her as he did so…something rigid that pressed into her belly with as much force as his thigh pushed into her feminine softness.

Curiosity mingled with passion, driving her to more desperate measures.

She whimpered her impatience, needing more from him than the slow torment he seemed insistent on wreaking.

She reached for the tie at his waist to undo the leather encasing the lower half of his body, ready to unveil what mysteries of the male form it kept hidden.

Just as her finger slipped between supple leather and warm flesh, Lucian manacled her wrist in one strong hand.

"You might not be ready for that, Angel." He raised his head to whisper hoarsely across the sultry space that separated them.

"For what?" she whispered back, hearing as much anxiety in her voice as interest.

Gently he changed his grip upon her wrist, no longer imprisoning her but guiding her toward the mystery she hoped to unveil.

As her hand fell upon the unyielding object in the front of his braies, it moved.

Melissande yelped, her hand leaping away from whatever it was that seemed to have a life of its own. Her gaze flew to Lucian's face.

Lucian's chuckle dissolved into a groan.

"What is it?" She sensed her cheeks flushing, felt horribly ignorant. Never had she been more intensely aware of the disadvantages of being raised in a convent.

She watched Lucian make a valiant effort to suppress the grin still twitching his lips.

"'Tis me, Angel." He reached for her hand again and she allowed him to settle her fingers around the hard length of him.

This time, Melissande did not pull away when he moved, but allowed her fingers to curve around him as much as the leather separating them would allow.

"'Tis how I will consummate our marriage this night."

Still amazed Lucian could possess a part so incredibly foreign, Melissande tested and measured him with her palm, already putting together a new mental image of lovemaking.

"You mean you will…" She could not quite articulate the picture that entered her mind. Although she had seen animals engaged in such crude behaviors, she would have never, in her wildest imaginings, thought that man and woman would join in such a manner.

She looked helplessly to Lucian. "And I will—"

"Receive me."

"St. Ursula's slipper." The vision coalesced in her mind's eye. Now she knew what happened. Abruptly she let go and shook her head. "I cannot."

Lucian wiped his hand over his forehead, massaging the scar at his temple. "We are not truly married until the deed is accomplished. 'Tis the ultimate sealing of the wedding vow."

She considered it for a moment more, tempted to indulge in more kisses but not at all tempted by this coarse new version of marital relations. "Perhaps we could just continue as we did the day at the creek."

Lucian eyed her for a long moment, finally pulling her close. "Aye, we will. But I am no longer content to stop there, Melissande. What we did before is merely a pleasurable prelude. It does not fulfill the promise of the marriage bed."

His words did little to persuade her. "But—"

He tightened his grip upon her, his eyes lit with new determination. "We cannot make a baby unless we approach this my way."

Her heart expanded and softened at the idea. "A baby?"

"Aye!" The half grin reappeared to tease at his lips. "There can be no babes without the completion of the marriage act."

A vision of herself filled with Lucian's child eased her fears. What would it feel like to carry a babe in her belly, a new life nestled beneath her heart for nine moons?

She steeled herself. For a child, she could undergo most anything.

Perhaps, too, this consummation of wedding vows might be a way for her to give something to Lucian. Her heart had grown so irreversibly attached to him. If only he would commit himself to his family rather than a life of battle, Melissande could finally allow herself to love him.

Maybe tonight she could show him a measure of the love that awaited him if he would only reconsider his warrior ways—his sense of responsibility for the whole world that weighed upon him as tangibly as chain mail.

Willing herself to relax, she snuggled closer to her husband, confident he would handle this troublesome ordeal of baby-making. "All right."

Relief poured through Lucian a he released a breath he had not realized he'd been holding.

Thank God.

He would never have proceeded without her acquiescence, but it would have tortured him to wait for her.

As she burrowed into the shelter of his arms, he reminded himself how much he coveted her affections. He would not risk her tender feelings to satisfy his long-suppressed desires.

Thankfully, she was as passionate as her hair was red. It shouldn't take too much effort to draw out her innate curiosity and to entice her irrepressible fingers back to his body.

Ruthlessly he bit back the primal urge that surged through him as he took in her slender thighs, her bared breasts. Instead, he tipped her chin up to gaze upon her, focusing his attention on her wide brown eyes and delicately quivering lips.

"Come kiss me, Angel."

Her siren's body teased his to painful proportions as the length of her sweet self rubbed over his chest in the slow journey to his lips.

Yet he did no more than kiss her, calling forth the banked hunger he knew still lay within her.

And, dear God, but she warmed to him in no time. Her restless hands soon wandered his chest and shoulders—always careful not to press upon his wound—her impatient body wriggled against his.

Yanking the forgotten night rail down her shoulders, Lucian dispensed with her scant garb to bare her completely. His eyes feasted on the sight, especially the delightful balance between her rosy nipples and the shield of red hair at the juncture of her thighs.

Gritting his teeth against the temptation to sink himself between those fair legs, Lucian laved one generous breast and then the other with his tongue.

When he trailed kisses down her navel and to her thigh, Melissande's breathy whimpers turned to little moans, half eager, half fearful.

He debated pausing, taking more time to arouse her, when Melissande rolled her hips in an invitation she probably hadn't consciously meant to deliver.

Lucian blessed his wife's impatience.

Gladly he parted those silky red curls to kiss the heated jewel of her womanhood.

He barely had a moment to savor her when she came apart in a broken cry that inflamed him almost as much as the honeyed response that signaled her readiness for him.

With infinite care he tasted his way back up her body, reveling in the flush of heat that covered her skin, the erratic heartbeat that pounded through her.

Pulling off his tunic with his uninjured arm, he poised himself above her, wishing desperately he did not have to hurt her.

Her eyelids remained closed, her face still relaxed into the lines of joyous rapture she had only just experienced.

Taking advantage of her momentary lack of awareness, he

unlaced his braies, thinking it might be better if she didn't grow fearful all over again. She was ready now.

He kissed her cheek, her neck, the shell of her ear, all the while shifting her legs apart to minimize the pain she would feel. His heart pounded as though it would erupt with wanting her, his manhood strained past the point of torment.

"Melissande," he whispered in her ear.

"Mmm?"

"Lovemaking hurts the first time." He cursed himself when her eyes flew open, but he thought it only fair to warn her. "After that, it is only pleasurable, like what we just did."

She fidgeted beneath him, trying to move her legs together again, but she was impeded by the stalwart barrier of his body.

"Can you trust me, Angel? That it only hurts this first time?"

She relaxed a little, then nodded.

"Good girl." He brushed his lips over her, encouraged for their future together. She trusted him. Perhaps one day, she would learn to care about him, battle sword and all. "Now put your arms around me."

Dutifully, she wrapped both arms about his neck and gazed up at him warily.

The taste of her still lingering on his lips, Lucian could not wait a moment more.

He slid one finger inside her to test the breadth of her sheath. Although gratified at the joyous sigh Melissande emitted at his touch, he couldn't help but worry at the implications of her snug grip around him.

His feat would not be easy, but he couldn't deny he also looked forward to it.

"'Tis for a babe," he whispered as he removed his finger and eased himself within her.

Melissande's eyes widened in surprise as he hit the obstacle of her innocence. Sweat beaded his brow from the constraints he had put on his body.

In this instance, however, he knew the deed would hurt less if done quickly. Looking down into those trusting eyes, he willed her to understand, then drove himself the rest of the way inside.

He captured her cry with his mouth, wishing he could absorb her pain so easily. He fought to stay still within her, hoping to accustom her to his presence before he moved again.

When he could stand no more, he withdrew carefully and rocked into her again and again, too delirious with his own pleasure now to hold back anymore.

"Lucian!"

He heard his wife cry out, and he wanted to stop, but heaven help him, he could not.

"Lucian…" Melissande called his name again as he hurtled over the edge of desire, spending himself between her thighs in the ultimate sealing of their sacred vows.

He yanked his eyes open to peer down at her—to beg for forgiveness if necessary—and saw her face frozen in ecstatic pleasure.

Only then did he realize her own body quivered in the aftermath of passion.

The urge to laugh bubbled in his throat. He had worried so much about her and all the while his lusty, convent-bred bride had been lost in the throes of fulfilled desire.

She sighed his name once more before her breathing slowed into the even cadence of asleep. Warmth curled through him, as potent and gratifying as the passion he had just spent.

He withdrew from her slowly, then pulled her head to his chest, cradling her as if she were a child. He covered her cheek with his palm, allowing his fingers to stray into the damp curls at her temple.

Now he knew why Odysseus fought so long and hard to return to his wife.

Lucian would battle any odds to protect the precious gift Abbess Helen had entrusted him with. He could not allow Damon Fitzhugh to rob him of a lifetime in Melissande's arms.

Not now when he sensed he might be able to one day win her love.

Not now that after two years of penance and pain, guilt and remorse, Lucian had, at long last, come home.

Chapter Twenty

$\infty\!\!\!\sim\!\!\!\infty\!\!\!\sim\!\!\!\infty$

Melissande pried one eyelid open in spite of the relentless sunlight that penetrated the master bedchamber. Her first thought was of her husband.

Languid pleasure flowed through her veins. The man had introduced her to delights she had never imagined, then cradled her against him as if she were more precious than gold.

All night she'd dreamed of him. Between dreams, Lucian had held her and kissed her hair, whispered endearments and promises of forever.

She couldn't wait to see him, to be sure she hadn't really dreamed the heaven she'd found in his arms last night.

But where was Lucian?

Raising up on an elbow, Melissande scanned the room for signs of him. His clothes and sword were gone, though his side of the bed still held the huge rumpled imprint of his warrior's body.

The other side of the bed also held a tiny scroll tied in white ribbon.

Melissande reached for the small piece of parchment opened it. A bold, masculine scrawl covered the missive.

"The rose dawn might have found them together still had not gray-eyed Athena slowed the night when night was most profound, and held the dawn under the ocean of the east."

It was from the *Odyssey*. The passage was a loose translation of the moment when Penelope and Odysseus were at last reunited.

That Lucian would even recall the passage surprised her. The fact that he would convey the same message to her, as if he loved her as deeply as Odysseus loved Penelope, made her want to weep with joy.

Love and hope blossomed in Melissande's heart at his sentimental act. Her world-weary warrior had penned her a poem on their first morning together.

Although her husband wasn't there to witness the monumental occasion, for the first time ever, Melissande was speechless.

Obviously, Lucian sought to please her. Perhaps now that he was the earl, he would consider retiring his sword and remaining on his lands. Was there a chance he could forsake his trade of killing now that he possessed a wife and had obligations to land and family? Would he consider making their marriage a true partnership in which she could have a voice in how they raised their children?

She pressed the parchment to her heart. Recalling Abbess Helen's advice, Melissande wondered if there was a way to help Lucian heal his past and to allow him to face his future. What could she do to help him overcome the guilt that had haunted him for two years?

An inspired idea rousted her out of bed and sent her scurrying about the chamber for fresh garments. Her body protested the activity after the love play with Lucian the previous night. But she could not afford to laze about in bed when there was a chance she could help her husband forgive himself.

Bubbling with anticipation—of running into Lucian, of implementing her clever scheme to benefit him—Melissande dragged a comb through her hair and covered it with a sheer veil and circlet. She could braid it later, after she set her plan in motion.

For nostalgia's sake, she pulled the forest-green kirtle from Linette's mother out of the wardrobe and over her white tunic. The gown brought back so many happy memories. She could almost smell the campfires from her nights on the road with Lucian.

She raced out the door and down the stairs to the great hall, hoping to find the man who could help her execute her new stratagem. She found him seated at the dais table, her husband lounging to his right.

"Good morning," she called to the Barret brothers, blushing a little to see Lucian after the night they had shared.

Roarke managed a pleasant greeting, but Lucian looked nearly as tongue-twisted as she felt. Did he regret leaving her the poem?

"I have come to seek a favor of you, Roarke, if you have a moment." She did not want to speak to him with Lucian present. He would never agree to her plan.

Lucian stood hastily, as if glad for an excuse to leave her. Melissande bit her lip, worried things were not as well between them as she thought.

Her husband walked around the table to where she stood. Melissande grew both nervous and hopeful as he neared.

He clasped her shoulders in his broad palms and a jolt of

awareness surged through her. Memories of their wedding night assailed her, making her long for dusk to fall again so they might be together.

"You're beautiful," he whispered huskily, his lips hovering over hers. Somewhere in the back of her mind, she heard Roarke begin to hum loudly.

Lucian noticed the dress. Pleasure simmered through her at his blatant attention, although the look in his eyes made her distinctly aware that he itched to relieve her of the garment.

She would have thanked him for the poem, but he kissed her before she could reply.

When he released her, she swayed on her feet.

"Until tonight." With a half smile, he turned and stalked from the hall, leaving her to recover her senses on her own.

"You look...well-rested this morning, Lady Barret," Roarke observed.

Melissande shook off the sensual fog that clouded her brain to shoot her new brother-in-law a withering look. "I am, thank you."

Roarke laughed, then shoved aside Lucian's breakfast plate. "I do not mean to tease you so early in the day, Mel. Come sit down."

After plucking some fresh quinces and a slab of bread, Melissande joined him. She hoped his good humor indicated there were no hard feelings about her wedding Lucian.

"I am sorry to hear you are leaving—" she began, wanting to make peace before she asked favors.

"Do not be." He patted her hand. "It is past time I grew up and sought my fortune. I honestly look forward to it."

"Truly?"

"Aye. In a way, I have you to thank for giving me the impetus to go."

That did not make her feel much better. "Because you saw me kissing Lucian."

"Because you made me realize I have nothing of real value to offer any woman, nothing I can be truly proud of." His eyes darkened at the words, revealing an emptiness she had not suspected lurked inside him.

She offered him a bite of quince. "Perhaps, if you are indebted to me, you will not begrudge me a small favor."

"Name it."

"I need to locate the midwife who cared for Osbern Fitzhugh before he died."

"Melissande, I don't think—"

"There's no way Lucian's blow to Fitzhugh could have killed him so fast." She latched onto Roarke's arm, willing him to see the sense of her argument. "You saw how Lucian clung to life for days after being shot in the chest, right near his heart. If Lucian could hold on so long with such a serious wound, why would Osbern die so soon after a glancing blow?"

"Infection?" Roarke looked a little less sure of himself.

She shook her head. "Not likely. Lucian told me the midwife gave him something to ward off infection."

Roarke studied her, his eyes searching hers for answers she couldn't give.

"I just need to talk to her, Roarke. Please."

Although Roarke remained quiet, Melissande knew she'd won by the slump of his broad shoulders. "I don't know what you can possibly hope to accomplish."

Impulsively she kissed his cheek. "Your brother's salvation."

He touched the place where her lips had been. Melissande hoped she had not offended him.

"It is a good day's ride from here," he warned. "And I hear she does not practice healing anymore."

Melissande stood, satisfied the first leg of her plan was under way. "That doesn't matter."

"I don't know that I'll be able to convince her to come here with me," he called as she moved to the door.

She paused and glanced over her shoulder, eyeing Roarke with an objective gaze. He was an incredibly handsome man, though that came as no surprise since he was Lucian's brother. Melissande had forgotten how appealing she had found him when they were children. "I'd be surprised if you've heard many a feminine refusal in your day, brother."

With a wink, she hurried off to her next errand, but not before she heard Roarke mutter, "Only one."

Lucian struggled to ward off thoughts of Melissande all day long. From the moment he had extracted himself from her arms to pen a hasty love note, he had daydreamed of his wife nonstop.

Now, as the sun set low on his first full day as a married man, he couldn't wait to get back to her. He handed his horse to a groom and cut the quickest path to the keep, anxious to find Melissande.

After consulting with his brother that morning, Lucian had ridden out to seek Damon Fitzhugh. Not one to wait docilely for his fate to come to him, Lucian was prepared to greet it straight-on.

Pausing to wash his face and hands at a small well, Lucian ruminated over the dismal outcome of his day's wanderings. Rumors abounded that Damon Fitzhugh was within a night's ride of his home. Lucian had also learned Peter Chadsworth was in Northumbria as a guest at Fitzhugh Keep.

Much as he desired to put this business between he and Damon behind him, Lucian was not ready for hand-to-hand combat. The wound in his chest had healed nicely, but the days abed had left his sword arm slower than usual. Now was not a fortuitous time for facing his former friend in battle.

Lucian knew he could not delay the meeting, however. His love for Melissande would not allow him to go about life trapped in guilt and remorse any longer.

Before he could fully realize the joys of marriage and reveal the extent of his feelings for Melissande, he needed to know their future together would last.

Their marriage would give her absolute security and financial independence, even if Lucian died tomorrow. But confiding his love for her would only hurt her if he were to meet an untimely end at Fitzhugh's blade.

Lucian longed to secure Melissande's love, but she would never grant it as long as he continued to wield a sword. And he had no choice but to wield it for at least as long as Damon hunted for him.

No. Melissande must not know the depth of his feelings for her yet, not until the threat of Damon could be eliminated.

Maybe then he would consider exchanging his chain mail for the refinements his new position afforded him.

Maybe.

Much as he wanted Melissande to love him, Lucian didn't relish the thought of forsaking his whole life's training. How could she condemn knighthood in such a broad sweep?

When he reached the hall, Melissande was nowhere in sight. Nor was his brother, for that matter.

After signaling to a server, Lucian wove through the trestles to the men-at-arms' table. He approached the biggest man, Roarke's closest friend. "Collin, where's my brother this eve?"

The man wiped his mouth on his sleeve before responding, carefully juggling the two ladies seated on his lap. He spoke over the blonde's curly head. "He left the keep on an errand for your lady, my lord."

Lucian wondered what Melissande could possibly need outside the keep. "And do you know the whereabouts of my lady?"

Collin shook his head and returned to his evening's entertainment while the server Lucian had called stepped forward.

"Lady Barret asked to dine in the master's chamber, my lord," the boy offered. "She is abovestairs."

Perfect. Now they would not have to sit through the lengthy protocol and niceties of supping in the hall. Lucian could seduce her all the sooner.

After ordering a second plate to be brought up to him, Lucian climbed the steps to the gallery, more eager than ever to see his wife.

He ignored the pessimistic voice that kept wondering if this would be their last night together.

His hand started for the door handle, then paused. He knocked instead.

"Lucian?" Her voice chimed through the heavy oak.

Was it his imagination or did she sound hopeful? He pushed the door open, surprised at the wave of heat that assailed him as he did.

In spite of the mild temperature out of doors, a merry fire crackled in the hearth. Melissande sat near to the blaze, her feet much too close to the hot cinders for his comfort. Why would she risk burning her toes, unless…

Panic seized him. Could she have suffered a relapse from the lung fever? "You are ill, wife?"

She turned to smile at him, her grin more full of warmth and cheer than the leaping flames. "Nay…just decadent, I suppose."

Understanding soothed his racing heart. She was well. Lucian promised himself he would whisper countless prayers of thanksgiving when he went to chapel the next morning.

He trusted Melissande could get along in life without him, but not for the world would he want to suffer being left without her.

Lucian strode closer, then pulled her to her feet to stand before him. She was vibrant, full of life and vigorous health. "You are reliving youthful days of good cheer in front of a fire." He recalled her sadness at being deprived such pleasures in the abbey. "I am glad. You never have to deny yourself comfort in our home."

Melissande caught his hand in one of her own and pressed her cheek to his palm. His words soothed her soul, eased her spirit.

How blessed she was to marry a man who understood her so well. Lucian seemed to have more insight to her mind than she did herself at times.

She considered broaching the topic of the children. Emilia, Andre and Rafael were never far from her thoughts. Yet, spying the grave seriousness in Lucian's eyes as she stood to face him, she thought her request might keep another day. After witnessing Lucian's considerate treatment of her, she had reason to hope he would consider a partnership where their children were concerned.

"I have missed you," she told him finally, at a loss for any other words to convey the complex feelings of her heart. This much, at least, was true.

Although she could have told him she feared she had fallen deeply in love with him, Melissande could not risk her heart until he confirmed his intentions. She had been abandoned before by a man she loved, her father, the man who had prom-

ised her to a convent even though she had begged him not to
send her away.

Even after ten years, she had not recovered enough to risk
such rejection again. If her father could reject her, a gentle
man who had promised to adore her no matter what, how
could she trust a warrior knight who had not uttered one word
of love?

He tipped her chin to peer down into her eyes. "As I have
missed you, Angel." With one hand he pulled the circlet from
her head and threaded his fingers through the hair she had
never gotten around to braiding.

"Will you go away again soon?" She had not meant to ask
so bluntly, but her lips seemed to have a will of their own since
she'd left St. Ursula's.

His brow furrowed. "As lord of a sizable holding, I will
spend much time visiting my vassal knights and overseeing
the use of our lands."

"That is not quite what I mean." Melissande could be more
than content with that sort of life. She could be ecstatic. She
took a deep breath, stealing herself for the inevitable disappointment her next question would unearth. "From your note
this morn, I gathered you would not return to battle again."

Tension quivered through her, steeling her for his response.

"I am a knight, Melissande." He gripped her shoulders as
if willing her to understand. "Not a miller or a priest, but a
warrior. Battle is the obligation and reality of my life."

A violent death would also be his reality, Melissande
thought, eyes burning with unshed tears. She wanted a family, and a man who would return to his children day after day.
Lucian, it seemed, wanted something else.

She searched her mind for some semblance of cool logic
that would appeal to her practical husband. "Yet you didn't

slay the man who shot at us in the Alps. You set him free and gave him the chance to nearly kill you in England. Surely that proves you possess a merciful nature."

Something flashed in his eyes, a passionate emotion at odds with the reserved man she knew. His hands fell away from her shoulders. "My merciful nature killed my foster father, Melissande. No matter that I prided myself on being able to control my temper with one of the most unpredictable men in northern England. I lost it that day."

"But maybe—"

"Maybe I wanted him dead." He looked at her levelly, his eyes cold and flat. "For one moment, as I recalled the way he'd humiliated all of his foster sons at one time or another during a drunken rant, I think I might have willed his death."

She struggled for the right words to console him. "Everyone thinks a horrible thought sometimes. That doesn't mean you acted upon it."

"Didn't I?"

She shook her head, refusing to believe he was right, trusting her instincts that he wasn't. "No matter how hard you try, you will never recreate that moment in your mind exactly as it happened. Perhaps your sense of guilt is embellishing what happened so that you may lay the blame fully upon yourself, but it must have all happened so fast. You can't spend your life punishing yourself for this, Lucian."

He quirked a brow, a humorless smile crossing his face. "In that you are right, Angel. Sooner or later, Damon Fitzhugh will shoulder the burden of meting out justice."

Fear knotted in her belly. Despite the heat of the blaze in the hearth, the chamber seemed to have lost all its warmth. "Damon." She'd forgotten about Osbern's son. "But he is in the Holy Lands, is he not?"

"He will return."

He left unspoken the rest of the thought—that only one man would walk away from that confrontation. When Lucian next greeted his childhood friend, he would be forced to draw his sword against him.

"You will be faced with a difficult choice when he returns, my lord." An impossible choice.

Her throat grew tight, imagining the horror of that moment. Would she be left a widow after that fateful day? Or would she be left with a warrior husband whose battle victory would ensure the defeat of her marriage?

Her only hope rested on the shoulders on a runaway healer. She prayed Roarke would find the midwife before it was too late.

Lucian closed the distance between them. His intent gaze heated her flesh, stirred her blood, despite her fears.

"We cannot live in fear of the future." His hands found her waist, then shifted lower to curl around her hips.

Her heart kicked up a notch, her body attuned to his slightest touch. "Neither can we hide from it."

He pulled her against him, allowing her to feel every muscled nuance of his body. The leather of his braies slid against the thin silk of her night rail, igniting a deep hunger for him.

"We shall not hide." He teased her lips with his, chasing her fears to the corners of her mind, calling forth her desire in its place. "We shall await it together." He nipped her lower lip gently with his teeth, then soothed that place with his tongue.

Warmth pooled in her belly, then flooded her limbs. She prayed time would work on their side, couldn't stand to think about the consequences if it didn't. "In the meantime, we will discover one another and strengthen one another," she assured him between kisses, giving her fingers free rein over his shoulders, his arms.

Melissande absorbed the feel of him, drank in the taste of him, wishing just this once they could make time stand still. If only Athena could hold the dawn under the ocean, the way she had for Penelope and Odysseus.

But she would take this one night to hold Lucian in her arms. And she would greedily take every night hereafter until Damon came and their dreams of a future came to an end.

"I will give you a babe before then," he promised her, running one splayed hand over her belly.

Tears burned her eyes, but she refused to let them fall. She framed Lucian's face with her hands, trailing one finger down the imperfection of his scar. "I would like that. I would like *all* of my children here with me."

He rained kisses over her throat, but she felt his nod in the curve of her shoulder. "I will see what can be done, Melissande."

Hope curled through her at the thought of seeing the abbey's orphans again. Would Lucian truly retrieve her children? Perhaps he meant to fill her life with a family, knowing he might face death before he could give her all the sons and daughters she craved.

As much as the notion tore at her heart, she couldn't resist his primal invitation, his slow seduction of her senses. Lucian was with her, here and now.

His hands grew restless at her bodice. He tugged the silken ties open and plundered deep into her neckline to cradle her breast. The rough heat of his palm sent a shudder coursing through her.

He rubbed his cheek against her hair. The day's growth of beard prickled her scalp. "How do you feel today?" he whispered.

She leaned back to peer up at him. "Frightened of what lies ahead, but I am quite content to be in your arms tonight."

A grin tugged at his lips. "'Tis not what I meant." He allowed one hand to trail down the inside of her thigh. "How do you feel in the aftermath of your wedding night?"

"Oh." Heat climbed her cheeks. "I feel very well."

He stroked one broad palm over her hair, skimming the length of it to rest on the small of her back. "I did not hurt you?"

She found it difficult to meet his gaze, but she didn't falter from speaking her mind. "You brought me only pleasure."

The low growl that emanated from him vibrated through her and thrilled her to her toes. He hoisted her into his arms and carried her to their bed, depositing her in a nest of warm linens.

The hearth fire leaped and crackled, casting a heated glow around them. Melissande held her arms out to her husband, eager to pull him into bed beside her.

"It is too soon for you, wife," Lucian mumbled as he trailed kisses down her neck.

"It is not nearly soon enough for me, my lord." She edged her fingers into the collar of his tunic, tugging the ties apart as she went, reveling in the breadth of his chest.

She could feel Lucian's smile against the column of her throat.

"You are dangerous, woman."

"You have no one but yourself to blame." Was she too brazen to raise the hem of his tunic, to splay hungry fingers over the muscles of his chest? She prayed not, because her husband was too tempting to resist.

"And how do you arrive at that conclusion?" He assisted her by pulling the tunic over his head, then turned his attention to kissing the straps of her night rail off of her shoulders.

"You are the one who went searching for the bold and brazen Melissande." She shimmied out of the night rail, only too happy to press her bared body to Lucian's. "And I believe you have found her."

She interpreted his throaty groan as acquiescence. The low growl reverberated right through her, inspiring a wave of shivery tingles all over her exposed skin.

"I want that woman." Lucian's hands sought her belly, her hips, her thighs. And lingered. "In fact, I want all the sides of you. Every part of you."

The words soothed her spirit while inciting her body. His fingers worked minor miracles, causing tingles to course down her spine and flash fires to sizzle up her legs. Her back arched, seeking the solid strength of him. She couldn't possibly be close enough to this man that turned her inside out.

The blaze from the hearth cast him in shadows above her. Golden light danced over his skin, highlighting taut sinews sprinkled with dark hair. Her fingers followed the flickering light, skimming all the places that warm glow touched. Heat radiated from him as if the fire originated within, his whole body simmering with need.

"I have thought about this often today," she admitted, hunger swirling through her as liquid desire coursed through her veins. "I had no idea marriage could be so…fulfilling."

He grazed kisses over her breasts, his tongue lavishing her with the kind of attention she'd been dreaming about all day. "I vow to fulfill you as often as you like, wife."

Pleasure hummed through her as his kisses slowed, strengthened. He palmed her thigh, spreading her legs with warm, calloused hands. She gripped his shoulders, willing him to touch her *there* where she needed him so desperately. Bending to whisper in his ear, she confided her wish.

"I think I would like it right now."

His groan rumbled through them both, the sound vibrating

against his lips as he kissed her. Still, he seemed to agree to her request as his hand dipped between her thighs. Cradled her.

Her whole body melted against that broad palm.

He found her innermost core with his finger and gently teased her with gentle strokes.

"Yes," she agreed mindlessly, ready to give this man all that she had, all that she was capable of. She shifted her legs to give him further access, trusting him to give her everything she wanted in return.

Heat gathered in her belly and between her thighs. Desire tightened into a spiral, ready to spring at any moment. Her breathing quickened, her heart hammered.

She was so close to that glorious release that when Lucian lowered his head to grant her that most intimate of kisses, she flew apart in a million directions, the sensations rocking her body with more force than ever before.

He entered her before the glorious sensations subsided, and the thrust of his body only added to the magic of the exquisite feeling.

She dug her fingers into his back, her ankles locking around his waist, holding him deeply inside her until he refused to be held any longer.

"I will take you there again," he promised, his words a ragged whisper in her ear. "Do not fear."

She loosened her grip upon him to run her fingers over his naked chest. "If I don't take you there first, my lord."

In answer to her wriggling beneath him, he allowed her to sit on top of him, rolling their bodies so they might exchange positions.

Melissande marveled at the new opportunities this granted her. She tested his reaction to her every move, delighting in the power she seemed to hold over the mighty warrior knight.

When she had decided he'd waited long enough, Melissande used her new knowledge to bring him to the brink of fulfillment.

"Too dangerous," he announced hoarsely. He flipped her underneath him once again to fully claim her body in the moments before he spilled his seed inside her, bathed her in the life-giving force she craved almost as much as his love.

He made love to her all through the night, sometimes with the fierceness of a warrior and other times with the thoroughness of a scholar. Still, their time together was tinged with the knowledge that it wasn't forever, that their time together was borrowed.

Just before she fell asleep, she considered how perfect life would be if the threat of Damon Fitzhugh did not hover between them. But until Lucian faced his past, there could be no future for their marriage and no hope for love to grow between them.

Chapter Twenty-One

"My Lord Roarke wishes to see you, my lady," the maid Isabel whispered over Melissande's still bleary-eyed form the next morning.

Melissande chastised herself for sleeping late yet again. The sun shone into the narrow slits in the wall above the bed despite the occasional ominous rumble of thunder.

"Thank you, Isabel." Melissande struggled to sit up as the maid scurried out the door. If Roarke wanted to see her, it could mean only one thing. He'd found the midwife.

Eager to converse with the healer, Melissande bounded out of bed and promptly winced. Her night with her husband left an ache in her body, though not nearly so keen as the one in her heart.

She tugged on a dark yellow surcoat from the small chest of items Abbess Helen had brought for her and made quick work of her hair by wrapping a single braid around her head to hold the rest of the strands from her face.

Melissande shoved open the door and headed down the stairs, praying the healer held a key to Lucian's past—a key to their future together. If she could somehow prove he did not bear full responsibility for his foster father's death, perhaps Damon Fitzhugh would listen to reason.

Moreover, perhaps Lucian would be ready to give and to receive love. After the last two heaven-sent nights she and Lucian had shared together, Melissande desperately wanted to capture forever with her husband.

With any luck, the midwife could help Melissande to do just that.

Entering the great hall, Melissande stopped short to see the woman Roarke had brought to Barret Keep. Small and fair, with snowy curls peeking out from a modest linen cap, the healer would have been exceedingly pretty if not for the mulish frown creasing her lips and the heavy rope girding her waist and arms.

Melissande hurried over to them, prepared to take the younger Barret to task. "By St. Ursula's wimple, Roarke, why is she bound?"

"She turned six shades of pale and ran when she saw me coming, my lady." Roarke turned narrowed eyes on the midwife. "My guess is she stole something before she left Barret Keep and is afraid I've found her out."

A surge of excitement shot through Melissande. She had a much better idea why the midwife ran. But unless Roarke halted his intimidation tactics, Melissande doubted they would uncover the truth.

As thunder rumbled outside, the great hall was cast in abrupt shadows. The sudden darkness provided a baleful backdrop to Melissande's hopeful mood.

"Regardless, she is my guest now." Melissande adopted an authoritative manner that would make Abbess Helen proud. "Would you untie her please, so she might join me to break our fast?"

Roarke studied Melissande for a long moment, perhaps attempting to discern her motive, but finally began to loosen the bonds.

"When you finish there, would you be so kind as to dispatch a maid to the abbess? I am sure she would like to join us." Melissande smiled brilliantly, hoping Roarke would not balk. She wanted to give the recalcitrant midwife the impression that Melissande was in charge.

Melissande had to discover the truth of the elder Fitzhugh's death so that Lucian could forgive himself for the past. She needed to discover what the midwife knew.

Now.

Roarke cocked a curious brow in her direction, but only bowed politely. "Anything else, my lady?"

"Would you mind checking on the whereabouts of my husband, please?" Melissande hoped he was close at hand in case she was able to extract new information regarding Lord Fitzhugh's death.

Roarke stepped closer, as if he would deny her high-handed commands. He flashed a wicked grin intended for her eyes alone. "I am, as always, your humble servant."

He strode from the room, clearing his throat in a gurgle that sounded suspiciously close to laughter, but Melissande's guest did not seem to notice. The woman stared out a narrow window at a summer rainstorm whipping through the courtyard.

Melissande gauged her opponent now that they were alone. Although the young woman made a show of lifting her chin and maintaining a reserved demeanor, Melissande could see the flicker of fear in her sky-blue eyes.

After a lifetime spent getting into one mischievous mess after another, Melissande could well read the mantle of guilt when worn by another.

If Melissande could adapt the tactics Abbess Helen used when questioning a wayward novitiate, maybe she could convince the young woman to share her secrets.

"You know," Melissande began, mentally flipping through the Book of Proverbs as she filled two cups of watered-down wine from the sideboard in an effort to loosen the woman's tongue. "I just happened to read a lovely passage." Smiling, she handed one of the cups to the former midwife. "Perhaps you are familiar with it? 'The truthful witness saves lives, whoever utters lies is a deceiver.'"

The healer's hands trembled as she accepted the wine. "I never meant to be deceptive, my lady." Her soft voice hinted at an inner strength her delicate form lacked.

Melissande froze. "Then you and I must talk at length. I am Lady Melissande of Barret Keep. How shall I call you?"

"I am Alisoun of the Woods." Her blue eyes pinned Melissande with a gaze at once suspicious and proud. "I may have sinned by keeping my secrets, but I swear to you I never meant to hurt anyone."

Melissande's heart thrummed so noisily she feared she would miss the young woman's words. "You speak of Lord Fitzhugh?"

Alisoun responded with a tight nod, her body rigid.

Relinquishing her wine to the sideboard, Melissande knelt beside the woman and covered Alisoun's hand with her own. "You will come to no harm if you confide in me."

Alisoun shook her head and cast a pleading look toward Melissande. "I do not care for myself, my lady. But I have children who depend upon me."

Melissande's heart softened in sympathy. "I will not allow them to come to harm, either, Alisoun."

"I would never have run in the first place if I didn't fear

for them," Alisoun whispered, her voice hoarse with unshed tears. "But after Osbern…rather, after Lord Fitzhugh died, I could not be certain that the children would be safe."

Melissande tried to imagine what lengths she would go to if her own children were in danger. Perhaps more accurately, she tried to imagine what she *wouldn't* do. She could not think of a thing.

"Too many lives depend upon the truth now, Alisoun. I can help you keep your children safe." Or Lucian would. Her warrior husband could protect anyone.

But it was up to Melissande to safeguard him.

Alisoun nodded. "You are right. I know in my heart you are right." She squeezed Melissande's hand, the action spurring the tears to stream down the woman's cheeks. "It seems I have kept my secrets long enough."

Lucian had been tempted to stay abed with his wife this morning and forego the quest to meet his destiny with Damon Fitzhugh.

Had he listened to his selfish heart, he would still be languishing next to Melissande instead of fighting his way through the sudden storm that drained buckets of rain upon him.

He had been on his way to the Fitzhugh holding when the storm hit and foiled his plans to meet Damon. Much as Lucian wanted to settle the differences between them, whether by word or sword, he refused to enter his enemy's home dripping like a wet rat.

'Twould hardly further Lucian's fierce reputation to ask his host for a dry linen before meeting him in combat.

Damon might not arrive home until tomorrow. Even if he did appear earlier, he certainly would not seek out Lucian in this wet wrath of Poseidon.

Now, Lucian had won yet another day's reprieve to enjoy his wife. Another day to plant his seed in her belly and to give himself the satisfaction of knowing that, if he died at Fitzhugh's hand, Melissande would at least carry the babe she'd always craved.

Between his heir and the surprise he had asked Roarke to acquire for her, Melissande would be secure without him.

Of course, Lucian had no intention of going down without a fight. Although Damon was reputed to be one of the best swordsmen in England, Lucian's new intense will to live would no doubt render him a credible opponent.

More than anything he wanted the peace of mind that he could have a future with Melissande, despite his warrior livelihood. Couldn't she see the need for men who were willing to die for their beliefs? Their land? Their families?

He longed to reveal his love for her, whether she returned it or not. He would spend a lifetime winning that love in slow degrees.

His thoughts inflamed with images of his sweetly sensuous wife, Lucian hastened his mare into the Barret stables and wiped the excess rainwater from his face.

Lucian cared for the horse himself, there being no groom in sight due to the weather. He dried and hung the tack on the stable wall.

Engrossed in his task and lulled by the steady din of thunder, Lucian heard no warning of a stranger's approach.

"Barret." A man's voice penetrated the tumult.

From the deep bass of the sound, coupled with the edge of cool hatred, Lucian knew who he would face when he turned around.

"Fitzhugh." Lucian exhaled the name along with two years' worth of pent-up guilt. Instead of repentant, Lucian felt oddly relieved as he swung about to greet his former friend.

Feral eyes gleamed back at Lucian. Lean and hard, Damon Fitzhugh looked every inch the brutal warrior. The squared jaw and thin line of his lips did nothing to relieve the impression. Rainwater sluiced from his hauberk to pool on the dirt floor.

Lucian saw for the first time how Melissande might have arrived at her impression that all knights were a bloodthirsty, intimidating lot. If Lucian Barret felt a small taste of apprehension, he could only imagine how his convent-bred wife must feel in the presence of such thinly disguised violence.

"I have been looking for you." Damon reached across his body to rest his hand on the hilt of his sword.

Lucian simmered with the heat of the coming battle. He knew Damon would not walk away until he slid his blade deep into Lucian's chest.

"For the wrong reasons," Lucian returned.

All of Melissande's insistence that Lucian was innocent of murder had fallen on deaf ears, until now. As he confronted the man who most desperately needed to hear the truth about his father, Lucian realized he had not purposely killed Osbern Fitzhugh. He'd acted in self-defense. He was only a man—subject to human error.

"For the best reason of all, Barret," Damon corrected him, drawing his sword. "You murdered my father."

Lucian's mind recalled another day when he faced a violently angry Fitzhugh holding a sword. Only this day would not have the same brutal end. He could not allow it.

"I raised my sword to ward off one of his fits of temper, Damon." Lucian's natural instinct when facing a furious man with a sword was to draw his own weapon. His hand itched to do just that. But some faint hope in his heart refused to let him. "He plowed right into my blade trying to come at me."

Damon's fingers clenched, white-knuckled, on the hilt.

Lightning flashed behind him, illuminating his hulking silhouette in the open door. "Such a glancing blow would not have been mortal, Barret. You are not so inexperienced a fighter as to expect me to accept that."

"Wounds can be fickle, Fitzhugh. I did not deal your father a fatal blow. 'Twas some infection or illness that set in afterward."

"He died that same night, Barret." Damon's nostrils flared with his rising fury.

With a sinking heart, Lucian knew Damon would not believe him—did not want to believe him. And who could blame him? Lucian had refused to believe it for two years.

They would be forced to fight and Lucian would either kill or be killed.

Melissande would either hate him for engaging in mortal combat or mourn him for losing.

Damon stepped closer. "My father was strong as a bull and we both know it. He could have fought off a petty wound with a few stitches and some attention from that sweet little midwife." Damon took a deep breath. He seemed to grow even larger as he stood there. "Now draw."

Good God, Lucian did not want to. Damon had once been his close friend. Besides, Lucian's injury from the arrow was too fresh. His body was not yet ready to combat one of the best knights Christendom had to offer. "Damon—"

"Draw!" Fitzhugh barked the word, his tension and anger radiating through his drenched garments.

If Lucian had thought it might help his cause to stall, he could have chastened Damon with the news that Peter Chadsworth had tried to kill him. Damon was a good knight and an honorable man, and he would not want to fight a man who was not at full capacity to defend himself.

It would also gall Damon to know simpleminded Peter had been corrupted with his lord's mission for revenge.

But ultimately Damon would not be robbed of his revenge. And Lucian's sense of honor demanded he fight.

He drew.

Hands steady, heart hardened against his former friend, Lucian raised his blade. He hoped God and Melissande would forgive him.

With a vicious clash of steel against steel, the battle of Lucian's life commenced.

Melissande's feet flew toward the stable before she made a conscious decision to go there.

There is a battle going on out in the stables, my lady, we think it's…

Melissande hadn't needed to hear the rest of the server's words. She knew exactly who fought out there and why. Who else but Lucian would be wielding a sword a mere fortnight after getting shot in the chest?

Rain soaked through her tunic and kirtle before she realized she should have grabbed a cloak. Mud spattered her skirt as she tore through the soaked grass to the planked home of the keep's horseflesh.

A thousand thoughts plagued her as she ran. Vaguely she marveled that her mind could sort through so much information in such a short span of time.

She berated herself for not dragging Alisoun, the midwife, out into the storm. The young woman possessed the answers that could halt the fighting.

Another corner of her brain feared she would be too late, that Lucian would be dead by the time she arrived. He did not have the benefit of fighting full-strength because of his recent injury. Her heart wrenched at the thought, spurring her feet to such long strides she fell in the mud.

Barely registering the cold layer of dirt caked on her gown, she hauled herself up. She had almost reached the stable when a man came tumbling out of the building and sprawled on the ground at her feet.

Melissande screamed, even after she realized the fallen knight was not Lucian.

Stunned, she turned to see her husband edge his way out of the planked building, his eyes never leaving his opponent.

She couldn't believe her husband, still healing from his bout with death, could knock down a man the size of the giant at her feet.

A jolt of pride took her by surprise.

She had spent all her convent years disdaining the vain-glorious Crusaders who frequented St. Ursula's table. She had been sickened by their obvious bloodlust, offended by their boastful tales.

But Lucian had shown her a new side to a warrior.

Never prideful or eager to kill, he was a protector because of his God-given strength and an innate sense of justice.

For the first time Melissande appreciated exactly who her husband was and what made him that way. Warrior protector or scholarly speaker of Sanskrit, Lucian Barret embodied all that was fine and noble about a man.

"Get back, Mel," Lucian shouted, his eyes still trained on his quarry.

The other knight, who Melissande recognized as Damon Fitzhugh grown to manhood, scrambled to his feet.

As their swords crashed together, Melissande realized she had lost her chance of intervening. Mayhap she had even stolen Lucian's moment of advantage over his hulking opponent.

"Wait!" she screamed, her cry of no avail. She saw the intense concentration on their faces as they circled each other in the pouring rain. These men would not halt their battle for her.

She turned to call for Roarke, prepared to shriek her throat hoarse, when she spied him striding through the rain, tugging Alisoun along behind him. The abbess hurried two steps behind them, one cloak about her shoulders, another draped over her head.

To Melissande, the mismatched threesome looked like avenging angels come to her rescue. Between them, they could put a stop to this insanity.

They had to.

"Hurry!" she cried, wondering why Roarke walked as if he had all the time in the world.

She flinched as the swords rang in a discordant crash, wondering how much longer Lucian could fend off his huge—and healthy—opponent.

Roarke arrived at her side and squeezed her shoulders as she watched the men struggle. "He can hold his own ground," he confided.

"We cannot just let them battle it out!" she called back, striving to be heard over the clamor of the storm. "He could be killed."

"If Lucian would not stop for your sake, Mel, he sure as hell won't throw down his sword for me."

As they debated their options, Abbess Helen marched past Roarke and jumped straight into the fray, unarmed but for the silver cross about her neck. This she held proudly before her, as if to ward off any evil spirits that dared to tread near her.

"Cease in the name of God and our Sainted Ursula, gentlemen, or prepare your souls for His wrath," she shouted effortlessly, as if she were accustomed to laying men low with the power of her voice.

Both men halted, their swords frozen in midair.

Warrior knights were no match for the abbess.

"I know your quarrel is deep and well-founded, my lords." She nodded respectfully to both of them. "But I have news that may alter your dispute."

Long accustomed to following Abbess Helen's lead, Melissande knew her cue. She strode forward, arm-in-arm with a trembling Alisoun.

"All will be well," Melissande whispered, squeezing the girl's hand.

"You found the midwife," Lucian noted, his gaze jumping from Melissande to Alisoun. "She knows something?"

Damon made an impatient gesture, his fingers flexing on the hilt of his sword. "I am sorry, Sister, but I cannot—"

Abbess Helen gave him a scathing look. "There is enough time for killing, sir. You might give a few moments to hear the girl."

The rain continued to beat down on all of them. Melissande felt her dress adhere to her skin with the persistence of a leech. She wished they could settle this indoors, warm and dry, but Damon Fitzhugh did not look as though he would be amenable to any more manipulation.

"I killed him," Alisoun blurted, her poor body shaking convulsively.

"Not deliberately," Melissande amended, wrapping her arm about the woman's slender shoulders.

Damon's gaze darkened, settling on the former midwife. "How so, woman? Do you mean to tell me you wielded the sword that bore my father's deathblow?" He glared at Lucian.

"I was not meant to be a midwife. I had so little experience," she cried. "I—I tried to staunch his bleeding with what I thought was woundwart." She looked helplessly at the abbess, blue eyes full of tears that were obvious even through the driving rain. "After I applied it, I realized it was wormwood. The labels looked the same and I was so frightened by all the blood."

Alisoun collapsed in a sobbing heap against Melissande's shoulder, whispering apologies no one else could hear.

"What the hell does that mean?" Damon asked, frustration radiating from his body along with the steam of his recent exertions.

"Wormwood can be deadly," Melissande explained, "especially in concentrated amounts. She applied the herb quite liberally, thinking it was something else."

"Jesus!" Damon ignored the abbess's flinch. "My father was not struck down in combat with a man, but rather—" he looked scathingly at the pitiful mass of coarse clothing and blond hair that now streamed haphazardly over the midwife's shoulders "—by this mite of a woman?"

He stepped toward Melissande and Alisoun.

The menace in his gaze terrified Melissande. She knew too well how brutal a warrior knight could be.

Lucian edged in front of her, planting himself between danger and the women. "I still struck the blow."

Melissande wanted to bury her head in the crook of his arm, to revel in the sense of protection her husband had always imparted.

How had she ever viewed Lucian as a cold-hearted killer?

"But she killed him with her vile treatments." Damon's big hand shook with rage when he pointed a finger at Alisoun.

Melissande froze as Damon raised his sword high over his

head, his face a mask of fury. For a moment, it seemed he meant to cleave Alisoun in two.

Swearing an ungodly curse, Damon turned and smashed the blade deep into the trunk of a sturdy maple tree. The air echoed with his oath while the sword seemed to reverberate with the awful power of the swing.

Although Melissande breathed a shaky sigh of relief, a nervous tremble shuddered through her in the aftermath of such violence.

"She was barely more than a girl," Lucian remarked quietly.

"Then maybe you shouldn't have called her to aid my father." Damon yanked his blade from the tree trunk, his words slightly more calm than they had been a moment ago.

"I am still ready to defend myself," Lucian assured him, stepping forward.

"I called Alisoun," Roarke interjected. "I knew your father enjoyed her…company."

Damon squeezed his eyes shut, lifting his hand to rub over the sockets.

"Perhaps we had best sort this out inside," Abbess Helen suggested, laying her fingers on Damon's arm.

"Nay." Damon stepped away from her, his gaze falling swiftly on Lucian. "Not yet."

The huge knight hefted his blade once again.

Melissande's heart sank. How could he still want to kill Lucian after all this?

Lucian straightened, his sword in its scabbard at his side, but seemingly unafraid.

In a ritual Melissande had not witnessed since childhood, Damon Fitzhugh lowered his massive body to one knee and turned his sword around so he might hold the blade.

"Lucian Barret, I swear my fealty to you this day, before these witnesses, and claim you as my sovereign lord."

Curiously, a smile crooked the corner of Melissande's lips even as a tear formed in her eye.

Her sire had humbled himself before Lucian's father in this way year after year to show his allegiance to the earl. But the sight of her slight father, with his scholar's demeanor and cleric's righteousness, bowed before another man had not made such an impression.

To see a knight as magnificent as Damon Fitzhugh kneel in deference to her husband sent a shiver through her.

At last Lucian was restored to the glory of his birthright, hailed as lord by a man who'd called him enemy the day before.

Melissande had not felt so much pride since she watched little Andre learn to read.

Lucian Barret, soaked to the skin and more regal than she'd ever seen him, gripped the hilt of Damon's sword with both hands. "I accept your pledge, Fitzhugh, with glad heart."

A sense of peace washed through Melissande, more cleansing than the pouring rain. Happiness could prevail in her household now, if only Lucian would allow it.

As Abbess Helen crossed herself and Roarke awkwardly patted Alisoun on the back, Melissande thanked God she had arrived in time to safeguard her husband's life.

Lucian pulled Damon to his feet. They exchanged quiet words for a moment before Lucian clapped him about the shoulders in the fashion of an old friend. "To the keep!" he shouted.

Later that night in the privacy of the master bedchamber, Melissande smiled to herself as she recalled that moment.

"Damon is an honorable man," she observed, combing

through her damp hair while her husband stripped off his garments.

Good heavens, but Lucian did curious things to her heart. And her pulse. And her knees.

Melissande sat on the bed to disguise the tremor that shook her every time she looked at all that raw male power unveiled. Tonight, she would tell him the words that had echoed in her mind all day.

Now that she had seen Lucian at his most warrior-lethal, Melissande knew she would no longer revile his power to kill. She respected his judgment and restraint to use his might only where needed. His warrior spirit was superbly controlled by a brilliant mind.

Moreover, Melissande had realized that his strength, his battle prowess, were part of what made her sleep so soundly at his side. With a man like Lucian Barret to depend on, she need never be afraid again.

Lucian would protect her, now and always.

And she loved him for it.

"I will be sad to see the abbess leave," she remarked absently, though her mind already envisioned various ways and times to tell Lucian she loved him. "And your brother, too."

Naked but for the leather braies that encased his legs, Lucian plucked the silver comb from her hand and laid it on a small chest. "We will see Roarke again soon enough."

Melissande blinked. "I thought he itched to wander the world?" Lucian had confided Roarke's conversations with their mother before her death, along with his reasons to suspect his parentage. The news greatly upset Lucian, but didn't really surprise Melissande. The men bore little resemblance to one another, their characters as different as their countenances. Still, she hoped Roarke would find peace in his travels along with the answers he sought.

Lucian enjoyed this moment—had looked forward to it ever since his fight with Damon Fitzhugh had ended peaceably. He wanted it to be perfect.

Settling himself beside her, he pulled her body against his. "Roarke *will* wander…as soon as he does a small favor for me."

He could almost feel the curiosity zinging through her. Melissande sat up to look at him.

"What favor?"

"He is picking up my wedding gift to you."

"A gift for me?" Her brown eyes shone with pleasure. Her red hair seemed to dance in the soft candlelight.

"Oh, Lucian!" She clapped her hands like an eager child. "What is it?"

Lucian relished every moment of her excitement, wanted to spin out the joy of the news, but found his own enthusiasm wouldn't let him dangle the surprise before her much longer.

"If I tell you, it won't be a surprise," he warned.

Her hands flew to his shoulders, hands clenching his flesh. "Don't you dare keep me in suspense, Lucian Barret."

"He rides to St. Ursula's with the abbess," Lucian admitted, savoring her puzzlement as her brow furrowed.

"Abbess Helen does not need his escort…" she started, then her breath caught. Her gaze narrowed. "He is retrieving something for me?" she asked.

Lucian could see the pulse flutter at her throat. Her hope was palpable.

"My gift is your children, my lady."

She smothered him with a bear hug that knocked him flat on his back. She squeezed him so tightly it took him a moment to catch his breath.

"Rather our children, Mel," he corrected himself, smiling as he wiped a strand of her hair off his face. "That is, if you agree to share them with me."

For a long moment she did not speak. She remained burrowed into his shoulder, her arms still squeezing his neck.

"Angel?" Then he felt the shudders that racked her slender body. "Melissande?" He pushed her off of him so he could see her face, lifting them both upright again.

Tears streamed down her cheeks. Her brown eyes were ringed in bright red.

"Oh, Lucian, I love you so." She sniffled, wiping a hand over one drenched cheek. "Even before you told me about the children, I loved you. I can't believe you would do that for me, for them."

Lucian's mouth went dry as he staggered with the weight of her gift, so tender and unexpected. He had longed to share words of love with her this night, but he hadn't dreamed of hearing them back from her. At least not yet.

He took a deep breath and handed her his heart. "Angel, I've loved you since you were in braids."

Her eyes widened.

"Since you were old enough to start pining over my brother."

She grinned sheepishly.

"More precisely, since the day I taught you to fish."

Lucian smiled to see he had rendered her speechless. He decided, much as he had grown to adore her sweet voice, he liked this new power of quieting her, too.

"Truly?" she finally squeaked, her cheeks tinted with pink.

He slid his arms around her, more complete than he had ever been his life.

"Truly." He kissed her tears away one by one, brushed her

0805/04a V2

MILLS & BOON®

Live the emotion

Historical
romance™

BETRAYED AND BETROTHED
by Anne Ashley

Poor Miss Abbie Graham had never felt so betrayed! She
had found her betrothed in a compromising position
with another woman! Refusing to marry
Mr Bartholomew Cavanagh has resulted in six years of
family quarrel, and now Abbie's been packed off
to Bath. Can things get any worse? They can, and
they do – when Bart joins their party...

MARRYING MISS HEMINGFORD
by Mary Nichols

Miss Anne Hemingford acts upon her grandfather's
final wish that she should go out into Society and
make a life for herself. In Brighton, Anne is frustrated
by the lack of purpose in those around her. The
exception is Dr Justin Tremayne – he is a man she
can truly admire. But then his sister-in-law arrives.
There is some mystery surrounding her – and it
intimately involves Justin...

On sale 2nd September 2005

*Available at most branches of WHSmith, Tesco, ASDA,
Borders, Eason, Sainsbury's and most bookshops*

Visit www.millsandboon.co.uk

0805/04b V2

MILLS & BOON®

Live the emotion

*H*istorical
romance™

THE ABDUCTED HEIRESS
by Claire Thornton

City of Flames

Lady Desire Godwin's gentle existence is shattered
when a handsome brigand crosses the parapet into
her rooftop garden. She watches, dismayed, as the
impudent stranger is carried off to gaol. But as fire
rages across London Jakob Balston uses the confusion
to escape. He expects that Desire will have fled town
– only she's still there, alone…

TEMPTING A TEXAN
by Carolyn Davidson

Fatherhood hits wealthy banker Nicholas Garvey
from completely out of the blue. He's the legal
guardian of a niece he never knew he had! And then
he's rewarded with an even bigger surprise – the
child's beguiling nanny, Carlinda Donnelly, a woman
who makes his blood race and his passions soar…

On sale 2nd September 2005

*Available at most branches of WHSmith, Tesco, ASDA,
Borders, Eason, Sainsbury's and most bookshops*

Visit www.millsandboon.co.uk

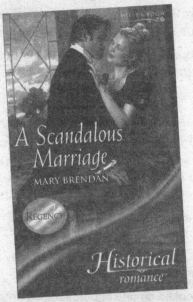